There is a River

To Jed —
Blessings in Jesus!
Ron Shafer
Col 3:23

Ron Shafer

ISBN 978-1-0980-8937-5 (paperback)
ISBN 978-1-0980-8938-2 (digital)

Christian Faith Publishing, Inc.
832 Park Avenue
Meadville, PA 16335
www.christianfaithpublishing.com

This is a work of fiction. Names, characters, businesses, places, events, locales, and incidents are either the products of the author's imagination or used in a fictitious manner. Any resemblance to actual persons, living or dead, or actual events and locations are purely coincidental, though current events of the late 1980s are occasionally evoked to enhance realism and heighten the historical sense of time and place.

Printed in the United States of America

Acknowledgments

A special thanks to Hannah Bowser and Ashton McGinnis for posing as "Jude" and "Cory" on the covers.

I also extend a special thank you to Mike, Lisa, and Brandon Beale for the loan of their horses, Blaze and Coltrane, in the cover photos.

Finally, I express my gratitude to photographer/graphic design artist Cassie Clouse for photographs and for assistance in layout of front and back covers.

Chapter 1

Jude Hepler's journal

C ory gave me a verse plaque many years ago. A favorite scripture—"There is a river whose streams make glad the city of God"—has often inspired me, but at this panicky moment, it is her written statement on the back that offers fleeting solace. Years ago, I memorized its every lyrical syllable:

> Around the hills and through the vales, the
> river winds and curls its jeweled journey to the
> sea. The river forges forward, finds a way, never
> stops. Our love is a river, just like the massive
> Allegheny. Though it narrows to gurgling trickles
> around the mighty rocks, it never loses heart. It
> keeps the faith, knowing a better day will come
> when its surging mass will triumphantly parade
> to the sea. Our love is that shimmering river of
> glistening gold. It will endure. It will not fail.
> We'll always keep it centered in the deep channel
> so that it will never run awry on the rocky shoals.
> I believe in the river of life as I believe in the river
> of our love and as I believe in you, Jude Hepler.
> This is our verse. Forever this will be my song.
> Always remember, Jude—there is a river!

Adapting that image from Psalm 46, Cory had always likened our love to a shimmering river, but after the debacle of *The*

Pittsburgh Hamlet and still floundering amid mushroom mine chaos, she said that "corridors of ghastly gloom" had become a more fitting metaphor.

As I surveyed the damage of the massive mushroom mine cave-in, I kept thinking, *How accurate your phrase, "Corridors of ghastly gloom!"* I tightly held her. *My love, you prophesied that one perfectly!* Though the whole room was now strewn with limestone rocks, we had at least survived the horrific blast and were, as far as I could tell, unhurt. *Thank You, God, for saving us! I'm still holding my beautiful dreamer. Starlight and dewdrops await her, await us all, but apparently not yet. Please, God, not yet!* Clutching her firmly, I felt her shaking. "Cory, you're trembling!"

"I can't stop! I'm probably in shock!"

As a result of the explosion, the center section of the floor had fallen through to a vast room below where the limestone had been extracted years before. Standing on a recessed shelf of limestone which projected outward from the wall and tilted slightly upward, we were now separated from the spot where Abe had stood by a very deep ten-foot-wide seam which ran through the center of the floor.

My eyes feasted on Cory. *I can't believe she's standing here!* "Beautiful dreamer, you're alive. We're in the land of the living!"

"How did we ever survive?" Weeping hysterically, we hugged each other tightly.

After checking to make certain we were all right and hadn't been struck by the blasting rocks, I shined my light down the crevasse but, owing to the thick cloud of dust, could barely see anything let alone the bottom. "I have no idea how deep that abyss is."

I learned later that during the mining operation which commenced in 1896, the limestone in two lower-level rooms had been experimentally quarried from a randomly selected vein but rejected due to its inferior quality. As a result, the mining shifted to the higher-grade limestone in the seam above, eventually producing the labyrinth of corridors of the current mushroom farm. But in this one rogue area, the limestone operation had errantly extended over the two lower rooms, which had been experimentally quarried earlier, thereby producing the dangerous tiered-room phenomenon.

Because great caution had been taken in the early years, all traffic had been forbidden in the perilous upper cavern, separated from the lower one by a mere band of earth, but in the intervening years, that critical information was somehow lost, the peril of the weakened floor forgotten, and the top rooms irresponsibly fitted for use. The explosion created the deep rift in front of us which, though narrow, sprawled like the Little Colorado River Gorge.

After the rocks stopped falling, the dust began to settle amid the deathlike stillness. We continued to hold each other tightly. *Never have I more enjoyed holding your beautiful body next to me! What an exquisite luscious moment, and never have I loved you more! Beautiful dreamer, I praise God you're alive!*

My mind raced wildly. *I remember that split second right before the explosion when, pulling her tightly against me, I tenderly cupped her forbidden fleshy fullness. How divine!*

We were safe for the time being, but in the dusty gloom, I couldn't see Zoe. Was he still there? Or had he fallen into the abyss? I didn't mention him to Cory in case he perished! I tried to take stock of our desperate situation. We were safely crouched against each other on our tilted island of stone, but the roof above us was severely cracked in this little anteroom. The support pole, which Cory had earlier twirled, had miraculously been blown onto our raised stone ledge. Standing it upright, I managed to wedge it against the cracked limestone roof to prevent it from buckling further into our little cubicle.

I hope and pray that we are protected, but as the dust continues to settle, I see a second seam running down the sidewall of our small room. As I've often been told, cave-ins come from the sides as well as the top! Cory, don't look in that direction! I turned her toward me.

As the dust cleared, I saw our surroundings more distinctly. *What about my dad?*

Then, all of a sudden, I saw Zoe beside us. "Where have you been? I felt you standing against us, but you disappeared right before the blast." *Have you been here all the time?* I thought of his heroism in leaning against us to offer protection during the blast. "Thanks, Zoe.

You're a ministering spirit who saved our lives!" We petted him and took turns hugging him.

"Are you sure you're all right, darling?" I held her close to me and stole a quick glance at her front. *I'll never forget that blissful hug!*

"Yes, I'm all right. I can't believe we survived." She peered into the ravine below and instinctively pulled back in fear. "Look how deep it is!"

"I was just getting ready to tell him when he threw the dynamite. In fact, I think I said the word *son*, but it never registered."

"Yes, you did tell him. I heard it distinctly. He sarcastically said that if you were the son, then he was Jeremiah! Or Ezekiel. Yes, he said both names."

"You're right." I squeezed her body against me. "Do you think we could have convinced him?"

"I think so since we have incontestable proof. He's super smart and would accept the facts if he heard them."

Zoe began to growl.

"Settle, Zoe. It's all right."

Across the ravine, Abe Badoane stepped out from the corner and walked toward us! "Cats with nine lives, accept what facts?" he cockily smirked.

Cory screamed and wrapped her arm around me. Through the dust, Abe's miner's light temporarily blinded us.

I shined my flashlight across the abyss. Like a venomous serpent, Abe Badoane slithered toward the ravine!

Chapter 2

Jude's journal (continued)

As Abe moved slowly toward us through the rubble, bags of explosives dangled from each of his hands. In Robert Frost's "Mending Wall," the poet describes the neighbor who, each spring, helped him—technically, helped the speaker in the poem—repair the stone wall fence between their properties.

> I see him there
> Bringing a stone grasped firmly by the top
> In each hand, like an old-stone savage armed.
> He moves in darkness as it seems to me.

Even in that hellhole, my associative mind could not stop dredging up those lines of poetry which paralleled our dire situation so aptly as Frost describes a stone-age neighbor. *That's exactly what I behold across the ravine, but instead of rocks, this heartless savage, moving in draconian darkness, carries lethal explosives!*

I tried to interrupt him, "Abe, listen to me. I have something important you need to hear."

He cut me off, "No, you listen to me. This is my time to talk!" He spewed these words loudly but then softened his voice. "I see you survived my little fireworks party. Happy Fourth of July! Well, what do you think your chances are of surviving this?" He held up the explosives in his hands. "That was the opening salvo, the first little shot of our private Gettysburg, if you, English professor, can pardon my mixed metaphor. Now it's time for Pickett's Charge, but I hold the Union high ground, and you are a Confederate clay pigeon on a cursed and open plain!"

"Abe, Dad, please listen to me! Do you hear what I'm calling you?" In total panic, I jumbled my words all over the place. "I'm calling you dad because you really are!"

He's not listening and probably doesn't even hear me! Though I tried several more times, he continued his mad chatter. "What do you think your chances are of surviving these? That little puppy was a mere stick of dynamite, a firecracker compared to these monsters." He nonchalantly held up the explosives as if they were bags of merchandise purchased at the local mall. "This is a perfect blend of nitroglycerin, diatomaceous earth, and sodium carbonate antacid. I'm proud of this mix since I followed the directions meticulously!"

"Dad!"

Again, he cut me off, "The first blast was a little pop in the night, a mere stick of dynamite." He held up the bags of nitroglycerin concoction in front of him. "This will be your Hiroshima!"

"Dad!"

"You see, by the way, that I'm fine. My assessment is that the cataclysmic devastation will be confined to your little quadrant over there. After I ignite these, do you think you'll be safe in your cozy room, your little prayer closet? My getaway vehicle is over there around the corner, but yours, alas, is nowhere to be found!"

I tried to interrupt him as he talked, but he blabbed through every single interruption. Finally, I screamed in desperation, "Dad, you're my dad! I am *not* your enemy! You're my dad, and I'm your son! *We have proof!*"

"Yes, and I'm Ben Franklin. Or Bill Mazeroski. Or Jeremiah, the prophet. Or maybe Abaddon the Destroyer. Your attempts at impersonation won't work, though your performance is Oscar-winning, my thespian son."

"Abe, listen to me. You are my dad. We spoke with Old Mary, and she told us what happened in the OB unit at the hospital the day I was born."

Screaming hysterically, Abe shook the explosives in his hand. "Don't you dare mention that awful day!" Issuing from deep in his throat, his words were gutturally inhuman. "I died that day, as did my dreams of everything I ever wanted. Stop talking nonsense!" He took a step forward. "You're merely trying to delay the inevitable."

Cory drew her head toward mine and whispered, "Make him stop shaking those bags! They're going to explode!"

"Please listen, Dad!"

"Don't you dare disgrace the memory of little JJ who lives on in my illusory son, Martin! You already contaminated the sanctity of his room and tried to destroy the only fiction that made this hellish life bearable. You will not do that again because I absolutely forbid it!"

"But we have proof!"

The savage appearance of his face—the flared nostrils, the slit eyes, the engorged jugular veins, the spraying venom saliva—is inhuman. Words shoot from his mouth like a cannon blast. Abe screamed so loud his voice broke, "I will not allow you to do it again!"

"Dad, I beg you to listen. Please put down the explosives and just listen. Here's what happened. Your wife, my biological mother, Freda, was sick and dying at the time she birthed me. Old Mary told me that the doctor knew she was sicker than even you realized and was surprised she had survived the birth."

"This is nonsense."

I didn't allow him to break in again and madly gushed on since, at last, he was quiet enough for me to talk. "Old Mary knew that Mom wouldn't live to raise me." I took a step toward him. "Mom feared that you wouldn't make a good father because of your incessant rage."

"None of this makes an iota of sense!" Though he yelled, the fury had drained from his speech. "You're just stalling."

"Dad, look in your heart. You know what I'm saying is true. Here's what happened." Abe lowered the explosives to his sides. "Another woman—she was one of Mom's good friends—gave birth in the bed beside mom. The day after I was born, that woman's baby died in the middle of the night. I was the healthy infant."

I stopped talking for a moment and eyeballed Dad. *The next line is the really tough one.* I paused to calculate my chances. *Will this set him off again? I have to risk it.* "When Mom saw how heartbroken the woman was because her baby had died, she allowed the babies to be switched." *Dad's face is expressionless.* "It was Mom's idea." *Cory, I can't read him. I'm going crazy!*

Finally, he gathered sufficient strength to speak, "You expect me to believe this improbable fiction, this tale of madness?"

Should I stop while I'm ahead or lay the whole matter before him? I have no choice but to gamble! "Yes, believe every word. Mom feared for my life if you raised me. She thought you'd subject me to the same abusive fury she endured day in and day out." My voice choked as Mom's agonizing life flashed before me. "She couldn't bear the thought of such a dreaded existence for me." I couldn't help it, but I started to weep. "Mom figured I'd have a more loving home with her friend than with you."

"It's a pity there's no proof for any of this."

"There is proof!" I paused to give Dad time to digest my words, but he said nothing. *Am I getting through to him? I have no idea, but since I temporarily hold the high ground, I'm going on offense.* "Why all the vitriol? Why were you filled with so much hate that my mother wanted me to be raised by another woman? Such monstrous hate that she was forced to give away her own baby?"

"You exaggerate! You distort the facts!"

"I do not!" Cory told me later that, though I remained oblivious, so much anger arose in me that I screamed that response. "Why did you hate Mom? Why do you hate Cory and me? Everything I say is true. You hate everything, and you know I speak true!" *I may never get a second chance, so I'm going to vent completely!* "Are you going to willfully slay your son?" *And now for the kill shot between the eyes.* "Your anger separated us the first time." For the sake of drama, I paused. "Will your hate do it this time?"

Abe staggered backward a step and nearly lost his balance. "I don't believe any of this!" His voice was subdued, his shoulders slouched, his fury diminished. *He's speaking so softly I can barely hear him across the ravine.* "My little JJ died of SIDS, and you're not JJ."

"That was the excuse Mom gave at the time she cradled the other woman's dead baby and said it was hers. According to Old Mary's explanation, you were crying so much in the obstetrics unit that you weren't seeing clearly. In your hysteria, you couldn't see well enough to realize that the baby you were holding wasn't yours!"

"Why do you expect me to believe this desperate fantasy?"

"Because it's true, and you know it is. Dad, I'm your son! How could Mom do this?" *He looks devastated!* "How could she give away her own baby? Because they feared she'd die in childbirth, the doctor gave her an abnormal amount of medication. Old Mary explained that Mom was very heavily medicated."

"I remember that vividly. At least you say one true thing."

"She probably went through with the crazy baby-swapping scheme because the pills clouded her judgment. Surely you remember how mixed-up Mom was. Old Mary says that half of what she babbled was pure nonsense."

"For the sake of argument, let's say I accept this fantastic, changed-babes tale. What's the proof?"

Suddenly, I heard a rumbling sound coming from the seam in the sidewall of our little niche. *That's the grating sound of rock against rock!*

"Oh, no!" Cory screamed. She grabbed me tightly. "There's going to be another cave-in!"

Chapter 3

Jude's journal (continued)

Hearing the sound, Zoe jerked his head in that direction and barked frantically. Glancing around, I saw some building materials that had been used by the roof-bolters and picked up an eight-foot two-by-far. By suspending my weight, chin-up style, I wedged it tightly between the walls of our antechamber and behind the upright beam.

I blathered on as I worked, "I do have incontestable proof. Old Mary was in the OB unit on the day of my birth. She stood around the corner from the two mothers when they concocted their mad plan. Old Mary had started into the room, but upon hearing the scheme, she ducked out of sight so as not to be seen. Completely concealed, she heard every word." *The look on his face is pathetic!* "Her decision of a lifetime was what to do with the information: go along with the baby-swap ruse or expose it on the spot. Agonizing horrifically in that brief moment, she chose silence and has been tortured by that wrong decision ever since."

Continuing to soften, Dad looked pitiful. *He wants to believe but is scared to do so. His shoulders slump, his head droops, his eyes are lusterless.* "Dad, why do you think she loves you? Old Mary has taken your part all these years because she made you suffer through your entire life. To this day, she's mentally tortured because she treated you unfairly."

As Dad weighed these distressing revelations, I continued to fill in the background. "In those frantic moments, Old Mary reasoned that a loving woman would make a much better caregiver than an angry man. That woman—I think her name was Ilene—was Mom's very dear friend, and Mom's heart was ripped apart when her baby died. Even in her drugged state, she was happy to see the joy the swapping of the babies gave that hurting woman."

"This is unbelievable!"

Though Dad again hung his head, I watched the tears trickle down his cheek. *His face is drenched!*

"Dad, I'm sorry all of that happened, and I regret that we've been separated all these years, but the past is ancient history, and we can have a new life together. I love you! Believe this incredibly good news." I drew Cory closer to me and put my arm around her. "Your son didn't die in the OB ward. He lives, and I am that son!"

Struggling to make sense of this barrage of information that assaulted his brain, Abe wept profusely by this point. "Jude, are you my beloved Judah?" As he stumbled toward us, he neared the edge of the ravine. "You're telling me that you're my sweet little JJ, the adorable infant I held in my hands those precious minutes?"

"Dad, watch that crevasse!" *Through the dust, his tear-blinded eyes prevent him from seeing clearly.* "You're only inches from the edge!"

"Judah, I believe you. I think I believe you because I want to so much. Are you my son, my adorable little JJ?"

"Yes, Dad, I am your son, and here's further proof. Remember the photo of you and Mom holding your newborn infant?"

"Yes, I do."

"The nurse in the photo is Old Mary!"

"Yes, I knew she was the attending nurse in the nursery, but I had no idea that she was part of a sinister plan, the accomplice at the center of the whole mad scheme. What else? You said you had another proof."

"You've been told my middle name is Jonathan." *This point will finally convince him!* "It isn't. It's Jedidiah. Why that name? According to Old Mary, Mom insisted on it. My mother, your wife, Freda, said she'd agree to exchange the babies but that she wanted the woman to use the middle name she had picked out. The woman readily agreed but asked why Mom demanded that unusual name so vigorously. Mom said it was the name her husband—what *you*—wanted! She urged that her husband be honored in this way!" *He's absolutely overwhelmed!* "Dad, I am Judah Jedidiah!"

"My son, I believe you! This is surely true! Anybody fabricating a tale wouldn't know that obscure detail. You have to be telling the truth. I believe you. I want to believe you! We can do the DNA test to prove to the world that you're my son! My son was dead and is alive again, was lost, and now is found!"

"Yes, it's wonderfully true!"

As we spoke, the dust continued to settle, and I saw Dad more clearly. "Old Mary begs your forgiveness. She knows she made a dreadful mistake and prays you'll forgive her. She thinks God has kept her alive all these years just so the two of you can be reconciled. Please don't let her die before you've forgiven her completely."

"My son, my JJ, lives! I wanted so much to have a son to ease the pain of my losses that I invented an imaginary boy. I couldn't bear to call him JJ, so I called him Martin." Abe smiled and stretched his hands toward me. "Jude, forgive me for what I've done to you and Cory across these many years!" Raising his arms and looking heavenward, he gasped a kind of prayer, "I tried to kill my son, but God has thwarted my intent. Praise God that He kept you alive!"

He stopped speaking and looked around. *His brilliant mind is shifting gears. Don't lapse into disbelief again!* "Please don't resume your cynical doubting!"

"Not even close. I'm wondering how I can get the two of you out, for between us, there is a great gulf fixed." He gaped at Cory. A huge smile on his lips. "You'll be my daughter-in-law? My daughter, can you forgive an old sinner like me? And is there room at that cross for me?"

Cory pinched my arm in excitement. "The level ground at the cross welcomes all sinners. If it accepted us, it certainly will you!"

He pointed. "I mean that cross!"

Cory looked perplexed. Out the side of her mouth, she whispered, "What's he talking about?"

"Put yourself in his shoes. From where he stands, he's seeing a cross—this upright battered post and the horizontal beam which I just positioned. Though there's a small gap between the boards, they form a cross from his vantage point."

"Of course, it does!"

We have to come up with a plan! "Let's put our heads together since all things work together for good. If we accomplished the difficult reconciliation feat in minutes, surely we can devise an exit strategy!"

"Say again that you're my beloved son, those utterly sweet words!"

"I am!"

Abe set his brilliant mind to work. "We have to get you out of here immediately." Frantically, he looked around. "Getting back across this cavern is the only way. I'll go back to the shop to get a few twelve-foot two-by-ten planks and lay them across the ravine to form a makeshift bridge since the seam is no more than ten feet. On my way out, I'll call mine emergency for a stretcher. We can carry Cory across the makeshift bridge and drive to the exit in my cart."

Abe stopped jabbering and gawked at us with that ear to ear smile. "Judah, I love you. Cory, I love you, my daughter-to-be." In his excitement, Abe, tears blinding his eyes, edged closer to the ravine. "You're sure there's room at that cross to forgive me? Dearer to me by far, is there room in your hearts to accept me?"

I screamed hysterically, "Dad! Watch the ledge! You're standing right at the edge!"

He extended his hand toward me or maybe reached toward the cross, just as the limestone slab under his feet slowly gave way. As he stumbled forward and started to fall into the ravine, he instantly pivoted around and caught himself on the jagged ledge with his elbows.

The two bags of lethal explosives slid down the wall of the huge crevasse!

Chapter 4

Jude's journal (continued)

The scene of Abe's fall and flailing arms instantly brought to my mind the memory of another man who had also reached into the void, caught thin air, and plummeted to his death in a barn. In that microsecond, a lightning thought flashed in my mind as I saw Grandpa, as he always does, reach for me. *Will I lose this man, my father, at the moment of reconciliation? After all those torturous years of separation? Will the other important male in my life also fall to his death? Welcome, Judah, to Stephen Foster's "rude world!"*

Dad carefully eased himself up from the side of the crevasse onto the mine floor and then shined his light down the ravine. One of the bags of explosives lying on a narrow ledge at the side of the ravine some fifty feet below didn't appear to be a threat. At least for the time being! *For some miraculous reason, it didn't explode!* Dad again scanned the pit with his miner's lamp. "There it is!" He spotted the other bag which was tucked into a niche in the wall and temporarily snagged on a protruding chard. "See it there, partially hidden, but it's starting to slip downward!"

Turning to face us, Dad shouted, "Crouch down! It's going to let go, and then there'll be a horrific explosion. My son, I'm so sorry I've mangled this!"

Though he was shouting to make himself heard, the look of panic was completely gone as he calmly raised both his hands in a goodbye gesture. He then blew us a kiss. Looking at Dad in that sad moment, I saw, for the first time, the upside-side cross tattoo on his raised arm—"tattoo cross explodes the game"—and then I noted his moist eyes filled with compassion, just as the explosives slid into the crevasse.

That was the last thing I saw before the deafening explosion, that huge ball of fire that shot up the chasm and sent massive limestone rocks flying in every direction. The exploding flames were like the images of the horrible fire in Yellowstone Park which we'd been seeing daily in the news. Cory and I crouched in our little cubbyhole under the safety of the cross. *Will it protect us this time? What of Abe, my father? What will happen to him?*

After the initial explosion, a deafening avalanche of rock cascaded into the pit as though the tectonic plates had shifted and caused a massive earthquake. Then we heard a booming sound of heavy metal grating against metal far above us. Large rocks, caroming in every direction, bounced off the walls and smashed into the upright beam against which we cowered. The noise was so loud that I feared deafness! Both of us held our hands over our ears.

As the rock and debris continued to fall, the rocky ledge on which we stood shook violently. "This is like standing beside an earthquake!" I yelled to Cory. We huddled more tightly into the cross for protection.

"Look!" Cory screamed through the din. "The floor in front of us is completely gone!"

As we instinctively cuddled into the cross, I clutched Cory tightly. Both of us were unscathed by the explosion of ricocheting rocks, though the upright beam had been struck several times. Deep gouges were present in the two beams which were now battered and splintered. "We survived!"

After a while, Cory took her hands from her ears. "Yes, praise God! This complete silence is beautiful!"

I ran my fingers along the jagged edge of the upright beam. "The old rugged cross did its work!"

"Again!"

Though the horrific noises subsided, we still had to keep our eyes closed and mouths and noses covered because of the thick clouds of dust. *The dust swirls like volcanic ash at Mt. Vesuvius, but for the time being, we've averted disaster. Zoe had hovered over us during the first small explosion, but where is he now?* When I peeked through my fingers and shined my flashlight, I saw only billowing thunderheads of ash. "Are you all right?"

"Yes!"

With one hand, I shielded my eyes, and with the other, I held Cory tightly to my breast. "Cory, are you absolutely positive that you are all right?" *But what about Dad? Did he survive?*

"None of the flying rocks hit us, but talk about projectile missiles!"

I tried to lighten the atmosphere, "In 'Beautiful Dreamer,' Foster speaks of the sounds of the rude world heard in the day. Those sounds were a bit over the top!"

"You'd find humor in anything!"

Once the deafening noise of the avalanche ceased, I felt Zoe licking my hands. *Like the dove returning to Noah's Ark, I see in this simple act a sign that it's time to survey the damage and assess our situation.* "Zoe's right here!"

"Thank goodness!"

The ravine which had run down the center part of the floor in front of us was now vast. Whereas the former dynamite explosion had created a seam, now the entire room where we had stood, except for our niche, had collapsed into the monstrous chasm below. Our small platform of limestone was a mere ledge that overlooked an immense sprawling cavern. *We stand on a lone promontory high above a sheer drop-off!*

To take precaution, we crouched against the cross for a long time. With one hand still covering my face to keep the dust out of my eyes, I yelled for Dad. "He doesn't answer!" Eventually, I gathered enough courage to creep to the edge of the precipice and shined my light into the immense cavern below. *This is like looking down the side of the cliff of Grand Canyon at Mather's Point!* There was no sign of Abe.

"I don't see him anywhere!" *My poor dad!*

Chapter 5

Jude knew that surviving both the cave-in and explosion was so unlikely that, to preserve it, he wrote up a narrative account of it, later published in the prestigious *International Journal of Speleology*. He used the first-person point of view throughout his narrative. The following excerpt from that article picks up after the initial explosion.

*Excerpt from Jude's article in The International
Journal of Speleology*

"What do we do, Jude? How will we ever get out of here?" Cory's foot throbbed with pain as she hobbled around our cubicle to test its strength.

"Pray. What else?"

"I am, but I'm also interested in the what-else!"

We were quite certain that we had no other injuries and that, for the time being at least, the threat of additional cave-ins had passed. Slowly rousing myself from paralysis, I feverishly tried to come up with a plan. *It's best to divert Cory's thinking from our peril. Come on, dummy, think!* "Have you ever seen anything more amazing in your life? That has to be the Guinness record for the shortest duration of a newly reconciled relationship!"

"Absolutely!" Cory hugged me tightly. "Do you know what else was strange?"

"What?"

"The scent. That aroma. I smelled something very sweet right before the blast. Did you?"

"Yes. I caught the scent immediately before the explosion, a fragrance like that frankincense I smelled in a bazaar in Salalah, Oman."

"I remember your talking about that."

"This aroma was exactly the same. I picked it up just a bit at the time of the first small explosion, but it didn't saturate the air then as it did before the second colossal explosion."

"I didn't know it was frankincense. I felt warmth too. Did you notice that?"

"Very much so."

"As though our niche was heated for that moment by a coal-burning stove!"

"I've never experienced anything remotely close to this."

Cory started to speak, then stopped, and eventually mustered the courage. "Jude, what about your dad?" She paused again, fearing to voice what was in her heart, but our desperate situation impelled her to blurt out the words which social decorum often restrains and occasionally forbids altogether. "Do you think he made it?"

There was a quality of bravery to her emotional honesty, a typical Cory trait, but in this instance, it rattled me. Severely. "I have no idea. I can't see Abe down there. Unless his angel showed up, he didn't make it."

"He stood there like Stonewall Jackson at Bull Run."

"You're right—iron-willed, imperturbable, and monolithic. Right before the blast, he lifted his hands as though bestowing a blessing or maybe praying. It was so strange!"

"It really was."

"When the explosives detonated, the flash illuminated the entire cavern as though it was high noon." I paused for a moment to see the event in my mind's eye. "Immediately before the blast, I saw a huge smile on his face, yet there were tears in his eyes. How very strange!"

"He was looking directly at us, arms outstretched."

"Not a trace of panic on his face."

"I've never seen anything like it!"

Again, I loudly yelled, "Dad, can you hear me? Where are you?" *Nothing!*

We sat for a while in stony silence. Despite our own peril, I could think only of Abe. Why do I say "Abe?" He was my dad, and much of his tragic life owed to his separation from me. Tears ran down my bloody dust-caked face.

Cory, ever the realist, steered the ship of my mind from the calmer waters of reflection to the churning waters of action. "We have to get out of this pit. Please switch that brain of yours from past-tense contemplation to present-tense escape!"

"I'm working on it!"

"You sound like Indiana Jones, but this isn't a movie. Our situation is ghastly."

As we sat there in bewilderment, the gravity of the situation became more and more apparent to me. Cory's ankle was badly bruised. *Of course, I have no way of being certain, but I actually wonder if it's crushed, even though I see she moves it slightly.* I also chose silence regarding my head injury, for it seemed my tourniquet wrap was seeping more blood. Because my head throbbed, clear thinking eluded me. Normally, my male brain attempts to devise a point-by-point plan, what good friend Chuck one day called "your linear logicality." *That's not the case now. My brain is bereft of intelligent thought—linear, circular, or geometric!*

We stood on a small ledge from which there was no exit. Our little cave niche had protected us, and for that, we were most grateful, but the walls of our cubicle were solid stone. *There's no escape!* Even worse, the chasm below us was massive. Getting to the bottom of that ravine would be the next thing to impossible. Even if I managed to lower myself into it, I'd be in a large room without an exit since the entrance to this lower room had been completely blocked by a huge pile of limestone which had avalanched at the end of the room. I faced the terrible truth. *We're sealed in our coffin of death! If Providence doesn't show up in some demonstrable, miraculous way, we won't get out of here!*

That's when I felt Zoe licking madly at my hand. Once he had my attention, I noted that he assumed his bird dog-pointing stance and faced upward toward the ceiling of the cavern. I sarcastically crowed, "Nice job, Zoe, but get your head out of the clouds. Our focus just happens to be here, not there, and no little bluebirds dart about this prison of death!"

Then I smugly gazed above to prove to him that, for just once, he was wrong, and that's when I first saw it. "Can you see it?" In utter amazement, I cried, "Look at that!"

"What? What is it?"

"I can see something but can't make out what it is. It looks like some huge contraption hanging from the roof."

"What in the world could it be?"

We trained our flashlights on the large object. "It looks like it's made of metal."

"Is it a conveyor belt? See the gears at the bottom and treads up the center."

"What in the world is it doing in the roof of a limestone quarry?"

"I have no idea, nor do I know what it was used for."

"Well, if that thing wasn't so far away, we might be able to use it. But what good if we'd reach it since we'd still be a half mile underground?"

An idea came to my mind, and I hastily took off my backpack, opened it, and withdrew the mine map.

"What are you looking for so frantically?"

"I just happened to think of something."

"What?"

"I want to look at this map of the mine."

"Why?"

"Your dad said that the old abandoned coal mine operation at Winfield lay directly over this section of the mushroom mine."

"I also heard him say something about that. What are you thinking?"

"I once talked to the geologist about this. He said that the Winfield coal mine had been abandoned years ago because the seam from which they extracted the coal was perilously close to the limestone quarry immediately beneath it. Only a dangerously thin strip of earth separates the coal seam from the limestone quarry below."

"You're right. Now I remember Dad saying that!"

"The coal mine had been hastily abandoned in this particular section through fear that the miners might break through to the limestone tunnels and fall to their death." I looked at the map and then the metal object overhead. "Do you see what happened?"

"No."

"I think that's the coal mine above. If so, then the blast blew out the small strata of earth that separated the coal and limestone seams."

"That must have been what happened!"

"The sustained roaring sound during the cave-in was the limestone, earth, and coal crashing into the cavern below. That last horrific metallic sound was the conveyor belt falling through the roof and the avalanching coal bouncing off it. That must be the conveyor belt which carried the mined coal up to the coal cars."

"How amazing!"

I continued to look up at the conveyor belt in dumbfounded amazement. The slow wheels of my gray matter train started to chug a bit. "You see what this means? If we could get to that conveyor belt, we could climb it to the mine floor above and then follow the old rail tracks to the mine exit!"

"There's a thought divine!"

"That's not to say we'd make it."

"Why?"

"Those abandoned mines are often saturated with methane gas. Speaking of which, I hope the deadly gas doesn't filter down here!"

"Now I see why our hands and faces are black. This isn't limestone dust. It's coal dust!"

"Yes, and that's why the cavern down there seems so dark."

"We're looking at coal instead of limestone!"

I peered into the abyss below. "Well, one thing is sure: Martyrs don't select the place of their martyrdom, nor do trapped victims select the kind of rock on which they die!"

"You're such a pessimist!"

Chapter 6

*Excerpt from Jude's article in The International
Journal of Speleology (continued)*

"Watch as I shine my light around," I jabbered to Cory. "Look over there at that large limestone boulder."

"Why? What about it? It's hundreds of feet away!"

"The front which faced the blast is black with coal dust, but the backside still has its original limestone color."

"I see what you mean."

"The explosion sprayed coal and dust like cannister from a Civil War cannon." I continued to survey the canyon. "So this massive cavern is layered with limestone on the bottom and coal on top."

Cory again peered toward the ceiling. "You're saying that if we'd have been blown up there, we could have ridden the railway to heaven."

"Now who's trying to lighten things up?" The whole time we spoke, Zoe maintained his pointing, bird dog stance in the direction of the conveyor belt. "Yes, Zoe, we see this strange contraption from Mars!" I tussled his fur. "Why do you keep gazing at it as though it's our railway escape to heaven?"

We slumped down against the wall in depression. *Our situation is awful. Loss of blood from my head injury makes me light-headed and weak. That is really bad since I'll need full strength if we're to escape this deathtrap.*

I must have been a fright to behold. Blood, coal, and limestone dust caked my face, my hair was matted in blood, and Cory's scarf, to stop the bleeding, was turbaned on my head like a moor from

Alhambra. Limestone and coal dust had also fallen on Cory, but because it wasn't smeared with blood, she wiped most of it away. *Her eyes look like Elizabeth Taylor's Cleopatra eyes with their kohl-blackened, feathered crowfeet!*

Our desperate need for water worsened the situation considerably. Because we had ingested huge quantities of dust, our mouths were so dry that we could barely talk. We could not produce an adequate amount of saliva and therefore choked and hacked incessantly. Alas, we had only one small bottle of water in my survival gear backpack and took turns sipping the precious liquid.

Cory broke the silence, "I'm trying to be positive here and think how applicable a verse in Psalms is to our mad plight."

"Go for it, Bible baroness!"

"'The dark places of the earth are full of the haunts of cruelty' (Psalm 74:20). I call that relevant!"

"That's excellent. Maybe you'll get me thinking. Got any others?" Huddled against me, Cory reflected for a moment.

We were both cold, Cory especially, so I gave her my sweatshirt. Very chivalric, knight in shining armor, but that means I merely wear a t-shirt and shiver like crazy in this fifty-six-degree temperature! Though I know little about hypothermia, I have the feeling I'm a prime candidate!

"I thought of another verse. Maybe it's in Psalm 147. David bemoaned this to God when his spirit failed: 'Don't hide your face from me'—catch this part—'lest I be like those who go down into the pit' (Psalm 143:7). That too is pretty suitable, even if David's pit is Hades."

As the dust continued to settle, we had a clearer view of the cavern below. *Ah, no! This canyon's as deep as Hades!*

While Cory was citing these verses, Zoe used his snout to lift up the front of my backpack, which leaned against the upright support beam. Rummaging in the backpack, he soon dug out the rope and laid it at my feet.

"So you want to play a game, Zoe? On this narrow ledge?" I rubbed the back of his ears and thought again of how he had tried to rouse me when I was unconscious. "What a good doggie!"

"You're right. This is like looking into the Grand Canyon—at night!"

You make me think of Matthew Arnold's "Dover Beach:"

> *And we are here as on a darkling plain*
> *Swept with confused alarms of struggle and flight,*
> *Where ignorant armies clash by night.*

But the ignorant we fight are satanic forces! Good luck with that, Jude and Cory!

I ran my hand along Zoe's fur. "Since there's no Colorado River in that canyon, there'll be no floating merrily downstream!"

"I thought of another verse. Something about God's opening up 'rivers in desolate heights and fountains in the midst of the valleys' (Isaiah 41:18)."

"We could use a river here!" I stopped talking, figuring I had pushed my sarcasm far enough. I drew Zoe's snout to my head. *The soot on my cheek smudged his snout!*

Zoe took an end of the rope and walked around the beam and then did so again. He sat down and looked at me as if to say, "Your move, boss!"

He then took the other end of the rope, put it in my hand, and resumed his bird dog stance in the direction of the metal contraption above. "Sorry, Zoebud, but we're not on the same wavelength. You want me to do something, but what?"

Cory was the first to catch on. "Jude, I got it! He wants us to tie one end of the rope to this upright support post and then fasten the other end to the conveyor belt up there. If we could shimmy along the line to the conveyor belt, we could climb the belt to the top. Then we'd be in the coal mine tunnel above! Voila!"

"Once there, maybe, just maybe, we could find a way out. What a brilliant and lovely fantasy."

"Couldn't we try it?"

We trained our flashlights on the large object. "That would be impossible."

"But it's a lifeline to try!"

"What are the chances of succeeding? I don't mean to rain on your parade." I looked at Zoe. His eyes were bright, and he started to prance excitedly. *So this is the "game" you want to play?* "You want me to tie one end of the rope to the cross and attach the other end to that metal contraption in the heavens?" Zoe spiritedly barked. "I can tie the rope to the upright beam—that isn't a problem—but how could I ever secure the other end to the conveyor belt way up there?"

"On the plus side, you have an excellent throwing arm. Whatever we ask in prayer, believing, we will receive—Matthew 21:22. This is a good time to bank on that favorite verse."

"I love that one."

"Tie the end of the rope around a chunk of limestone rock, and then throw the rock at the belt. Eventually, it might loop and form a good bite."

"Too bad I'm not Pirates pitcher Bob Walk or Doug Drabek!" I shrugged my shoulders and despairingly hung my head.

"It's worth a try!" As she muttered, she wrapped her arms around me, clenched me tight, and looked directly into my eyes. "What other chance do we have?" She gestured toward the cavern. "There's no river of escape through that canyon!"

"And no Isaiah fountain in the midst of that valley. I just wish I had the throwing arm I used to have!"

"You can do it, but aim for the middle of the conveyor belt so that if it catches, you'll have a place to plant your feet on the treads."

"Good idea."

I tied one end of the rope to the beam and then uncoiled the rope so it lay free. Rocks were everywhere, so it was easy to find a fist-sized rock around which I tightly tied the rope. "Here goes nothing!" I gave the rock a good throw. It fell considerably short. "It's a lot further than it looks."

"You just didn't throw hard enough, Alice. Now use some muscle!"

"I'm doing my best, queen of sarcasm!" Though I threw repeatedly, I missed the belt altogether. A few times, I caught it square, but the rope didn't loop around the belt. "Getting it to wrap the conveyor is tricky. If this plan is to work, it has to bind tightly."

"I'm betting on you!" Cory continued to cheer me on. "Imagine you're Bob Kipper coming in from the Pirates bullpen. You're the ace reliever, and I'm the Pirates parrot. Throw strikes, baby, down the middle, ace!"

"You're ridiculous!"

Time after time, I threw the rope-tied rock, but I could never get it to loop the conveyor belt. Once the rope wrapped around it, but when I tugged on the rope to secure it, the rock came loose from the rope and fell into the cavern below. *It took a long time for that rock to hit bottom!* "It's a fur piece down 'ere!" I guffawed, mimicking an old western drawl.

"Try again, sweetheart. You're getting closer!"

Back to work I went, throw after throw. I felt like Doug Drabek, one of the starting Pirates pitchers. "Wearing down, parrot cheerleader, failing fast!"

"No, you're not. You're just getting warmed up. You don't want the backup relief pitcher to show you up, do you?"

Finally, the miraculous happened! The rock encircled the conveyor belt, and then the rope repeatedly twirled around itself like a hangman's noose, forming a good bite.

"Cory, we did it!"

"Hallelujah!"

Chapter 7

Excerpt from Jude's article in The International
Journal of Speleology (continued)

I loosened the end of the rope from the base of the support beam,
drew it taut, and retied it as tightly as possible near the top of the
post. "How much rope do we have here?"

"Why do you want to know?"

"I'm calculating distance. I know the rope is one hundred feet
long." I measured some five arm-width stretches of rope, each about
three feet. "We have about fifteen feet here. Guess I'll enjoy the priv-
ilege of shimmying some eighty-five feet across a deep canyon."

"With me on your back!"

"Grooms carry brides across thresholds, but don't you think
shimmying across that chasm is ridiculous?"

"No time for joking, Jude! How can you do it?"

Afraid of additional cave-ins, Cory, by this time, was not in the
mood for silliness. _Her foot must be paining her a lot though she doesn't_
complain. On top of that, I'm scared to death at the prospect of shimmy-
ing across a deep canyon carrying 120-pounds!

I looked at my hands and contemplated the rope burns and
beating to which they would be subjected. _Cory once told me about_
Albrecht Durer's painting of the hands, often viewed as Christ's praying
hands. She explained to me that Durer had sketched the tortured hands
of his would-be artist brother, Albert, who had devastated them through
torturous work in the mines so that Albrecht could become an artist.
What will my hands look like after this grueling test? Gnarled like Albert
Durer's praying hands? I can't tell Cory what I'm thinking!

"I've been pumping iron all summer. See these bulging biceps, dazzling delts, and this hard-as-phallus pectoralis?"

"Stop it!"

"How about this one? Nothing to fear, get your rear in gear with no leer or jeer, come here darling dear."

"You're ridiculous! Sorry, I'm in no mood for joking, and look at your flashlight. Is that beam fading? Or is it my imagination? I know what it's like to be in the mine without light!"

I'll make no comment about the flashlight beam, but I think she's right. It doesn't seem as bright! I chose to lighten the atmosphere. "Mark Twain once said, 'Hilarity hideth a heavy heart!' Or something like that." *That perfectly describes me!*

I checked the top of the support beam in our little niche, which had lodged so tightly against the uneven limestone ceiling that I knew it would support the extraordinary weight of our two bodies. The thick rope, industrial-grade, was made for heavy use. My fear, in short, was not the support post or rope. I was the fragile variable, the proverbial weak link in the escape-plan chain.

How can I shimmy across that rope with Cory on my back? Even if I make it to the conveyor belt, how can I carry her up the treads to the coal tunnel above? Flashing back to my grandpa's death when I climbed the barn beam as a little boy, I broke out in a cold sweat and started to shake. I turned away in horror from the conveyor belt. *Just what I need—a full-blown anxiety attack!*

"Jude, what's going on? You're shaking all over!" Cory vigorously massaged my arms. "Are you hyperventilating or having an attack of hypothermia?"

No use holding back. She might as well know! "Don't you see what's going on? What happened the last time I climbed a ladder with something slung across my back? When I look up at that conveyor belt, I see Grandpa falling! Look at these hands. I'm trembling like crazy!"

"You can do it, Jude."

"Remember when I climbed the beam in Grandpa's barn with a stool dangling across my back?"

"Far too vividly."

"I made it to the top of the platform and carefully slid the stool off my back. I even opened it and gingerly positioned it on the hayloft platform. Grandpa kept saying, 'You're doing a good job, little Jude. Just be careful!' The whole time, his arms were trembling terribly from suspending his entire weight by that rope—this rope! When I looked at him and saw what danger he was in, I lost my concentration just as he was lowering himself onto the stool. I bumped against it and watched it fall to the barn floor while I fell off the other side. I'm seeing the whole tragedy as if in slow motion."

When Cory drew near and wrapped her arms around me, I paused to let my words sink in. "Do you understand what I'm saying? Grandpa let go of the rope and reached for me to keep me from falling to my death instead of clutching the support beam. He could have saved himself but reached for me instead. His hand caught my outstretched hand and gripped it tightly, but he couldn't hang on. I harmlessly fell on the large hay mow, but he fell on the hard barn floor that crushed the life out of him." I stopped my gushing monologue to catch my breath. "When I look up this rope, I see Grandpa at the other end." I was shaking violently by this point. "If I fail this time, I'll kill both of us!"

"You're forgetting that I saw it all—every sordid detail. We have to pray the peace of Christ upon you. I know you are inadequate for this extraordinary challenge, but that doesn't prevent you from tapping into the peace and power of Christ in you. Get your strength from Him. You're doing this in the energy of the flesh and, in the process, negating divine empowerment. Sorry to sound like a preacher, but you know I speak truth."

The next thing I knew, Cory had closed her eyes and started praying. "Lord, I pray that Jude will be anchored on Your bedrock strength as solidly as we're grounded on limestone." She paused. "Help him defeat his fear." Another pause. "Give him strength to trust You. I pray this in the name of Jesus Christ. Amen."

I suspended myself from the line, bent my legs, and hung in the air over our rock ledge. Then I shimmied out beyond the ledge and was hanging in empty space. All of a sudden, when I realized that I was actually suspended over a horrible abyss, a flood of nausea overwhelmed me. *How can I do this?* I bounced on the rope slightly to test it. *The rope is secure. At least I don't have to worry about that, and I know this old tree post can bear the weight.*

"I just thought of something," Cory said as I shimmied back to our rock ledge. "You always associate this rope with your grandpa's death."

"Have I ever!" I drew close to Cory and stuffed my hands in my pocket so she couldn't see them shake.

"Today, that's going to change. This rope will be our salvation."

"How sweet that would be!" When we took turns hugging Zoe, he whimpered loudly. I spoke to him as if to a human. "I'll take Cory up the rope and, it's our hope, out of the mine. Then I'll come back to get you." I hugged him again. "Zoe, I won't leave you down here alone!"

I put on the gloves which I had taken from my backpack. *Do your work, lads!* I perused my poor hands and thought of the extraordinary task they were called on to perform. *Cory, do you know how impossible this task is which we're about to attempt?* "Get on me piggyback-style and wrap your arms around me. Ready for the ride of your life?"

Cory gingerly climbed on my back, partly to be gentle but partly to keep from bumping her throbbing foot. "I can't hold my arms under your legs to support you, so hold on really tight. I think you'd prefer that I shimmy with two hands!"

"I guess I prefer that!"

With Cory on my back, I lumbered to the edge of the ravine above the valley of death, thinking of Tennyson's famous poem. "Remember Alfred, Lord Tennyson's 'The Charge of the Light Brigade?'

Theirs not to reason why,
Theirs but to do or die.
Into the valley of Death
Rode the six hundred.

"Good parallel. But in our case, *above* the valley of death rode Jude and Cory."

"Go for it, Galahad! I'm ready when you are!"

"I've drawn the rope as tight as I could, but when I step off the ledge, our combined weight will make us fall a lot. When the rope draws taut, we'll bounce really hard. Hang on as tightly as you can for that initial jolt. That will be the first tough test. Don't worry about squeezing the tar out of me!"

The do-or-die moment is here! I stepped off the safety of the ledge into the vast void.

Chapter 8

***

Jude's journal

The number of things that could have happened at that moment was multitudinous. The line could break, the support beam could kick free, or the metal conveyor belt could pull loose from its moorings and fall into the abyss. Then there was the real chance that I wouldn't be able to support our combined weight during the long upward climb.

And what of dear Cory? Could she support the entire weight of her body with her arms around my shoulders and one leg hanging helplessly? *No doubt about it—this is the toughest physical test of our lives!*

The initial jar was worse than I anticipated for one main reason. Just as I was stepping outward, it dawned on me that my initial reach on the rope would have to be a very long one so that Cory, when coming off the ledge, wouldn't scrape her back against the wall. I had to allow for the combined and considerable width of our two bodies. I reached as far as I could out the line, yelled, "Hang on!" and hurtled into black space.

We fell several more feet than I anticipated simply because of the combined weight of our bodies. The rope withstood the initial impact, and I managed to hang on though I felt my hands slip on the rope. What shook both of us a moment later was the loud sound coming from the metal contraption above. *Ah, no!* We heard a grating noise, metal on metal, and felt the belt slide downward an additional foot.

"What was that?" Cory screamed.

Is the belt about to dislodge from its moorings? And will the whole massive structure plummet into the pit below? Afraid to look for fear of what I might see, I settled for a fast sideways glance at the conveyor belt. *It hangs farther down into the cavern, but at least it stopped moving!*

Once we stopped our swinging on the rope, I slid my hand, inch by inch, along it. At the beginning of the torturous climb in the dark, I kept seeing Grandpa at the top of the conveyor belt, hands outstretched toward me. *You can do it, little Jude. Take your time! No need to hurry!*

Cory was deathly quiet as I climbed. We both knew it was imperative to conserve our energies, but when she sensed me straining and slowing down, probably fearing that I was again reliving my childhood trauma, she tried to distract me. "Don't you have a relevant quotation in that encyclopedic head of yours?" She paused to complete her thought.

She's probably wondering if speech will help or hinder my herculean task.

"Something about gaining freedom inch by inch as we're trying to do?"

If distraction was Cory's intent, it worked. I felt less tense as I climbed along in the dark, though I was still shaken by the length of rope I had to traverse, for every time Cory shone my flashlight upward toward the conveyor belt, I saw a giant white umbilical cord, our sole lifeline stretching across the vast womb of night. *Will the baby—our escape—be successfully birthed? Lord, deliver this child of faith!*

To minimize the horror of the moment, I thought of Cory's question about gaining freedom inch by inch. "Funny you...should ask." The best I could do was speak in monosyllabic grunts, especially at the outset. "Was thinking...about... Jefferson's letter... to a friend...after...his return...from France." Realizing the pressing need of conserving my energy, I temporarily stopped talking. *The name of Jefferson's correspondent comes to my mind.* "Reverend... Charles... Clay." Another pause as I inched upward. "Jefferson wrote,

'The ground…of liberty…is to be…gained by…inches.'" *As our liberty is gained by inches!*

During a longer pause, Cory softly whispered. "That's excellent, but don't talk."

She was, I guessed, having second thoughts about using speech as a distraction. *She speaks quietly, even hesitantly, probably thinking that even simple speech exacerbates this horror.* I stopped talking to fight for a breath of air to finish the thought. *Now that I've started Jefferson's quote, I want to finish.* "We must…press forward…for what is yet…to get.'"

"'The ground of liberty is to be gained by inches.' How fitting that quote! We'll gain it inch by inch." She was again whispering, "For now, I stop talking except to say I love you!"

I remained silent and shimmied upward, one agonizing death grip after another. "Ten feet…down. Just seventy-five…to go!"

As I climbed upward on the rope, the weight of Cory digging into my back, I feared my tortured hands would not be able bear the horrific weight of our combined bodies. Frantically diverting my mind, I forced myself to remember something Gabe had once said. *If you don't feel the punishing weight of the cross on your back, then it's likely because you haven't yet picked it up. If you are not excruciatingly burdened by your heavy cross, then you'll never understand Christ's suffering.*

Amid the sounds of my groans and grunts, I recollected more of Gabe's sermon. *"One amazing thing about cross-bearing is that Christ always fits the back to the burden. When you carry your cross, it will actually feel good, because it's tailor-made for your body. Though hacked and harsh, allow that cross to nestle into the contours of your body, lovingly and caringly fitted for its heavy load. Remember: the ghastlier the cross here, the more golden the crown there!"*

As I inched upward in the dark, I felt the sweat roll down my face, mixed with blood and dust. I reflected on Gabe's notion that the cross will, strangely, feel good because it is "your specially-designed, perfectly-suited, Christ-exalting cross." I thought again of Cory on my back. *What's my attitude here? Is my beloved a horrible weight which*

I fear losing as I had Grandpa? And does that fear worsen this test? Or is she a snuggly presence curled warmly and comfortably against me?

Reframing my perspective entirely, I softly whispered, "I like... that you're snuggled...against me."

"I love it too!" She tenderly kissed the back of my neck.

Chapter 9

⁓

Jude's original intent was to offer a succinct but accurate journal description of their dramatic escape from the mine, the foregoing culminating that intent; but when he reflected later on how miraculous and impossible the odds of escape, he composed a longer, more descriptive narrative. The following excerpt picks up where his journal entry stops.

Excerpt from Jude's account of their miraculous escape

As Cory and I inch-wormed our way along the rope, I began to have second thoughts about whether or not I could make it. We had progressed about a third of the distance, but because the ascent became increasingly steeper, it was getting harder to climb. Since the whole thing was excruciatingly slow, a thought relentlessly hammered my brain. *Will my arms be able to withstand this interminable journey across the galactic void?*

The thought that Cory was a snuggly buddy which had seeped into my brain from a Gabe sermon worked temporarily, but reality soon returned and, with it, the crushingly hard truth that my muscles had been tested to their absolute max. My arms started to spasm violently, the physiological consequence of the colossal demand put on them. *These spasms are so intense that they're making my muscles convulse. Even with our combined weight, the entire line shakes!*

Cory remained absolutely silent when she saw the quivering line, but I'm sure that occasioned some very intense prayer! After a while, she quoted a verse which gave me enormous encouragement. With the gentleness of a summer zephyr caressing the soft petals of a gardenia blossom, she whispered, "I have fought the good fight, I have finished the race, and I have kept the faith," adding a moment later, "as you too will finish the race. My love, you're already near the halfway point!"

Mindful of my intense concentration while shimmying upward, Cory spoke only one other time. "I can only imagine the punishment to your poor hands!"

By then, the spasms halted, for whatever reason, and the line stopped quivering. "It's a good thing"—another pause while I struggled for breath—"that I...put my...gloves on!"

Realizing that those handful of words took their toll on my energy level, Cory spoke no more, but what I had said was certainly true—the gloves were indeed my salvation. *My hands would be cut to shreds if I didn't have these, but their loose fit, with every grip, makes me fear slipping out of them!*

The other major worry was the conveyor belt itself. The explosion had ripped the top half of the metal plate away from the mine wall. Bent over on itself, the rusty metal plate was now fastened to the wall by only one row of corroded bolts at the bottom. *How shocking that this huge contraption is suspended by a couple of very old bolts! Across the decades, the moisture and rust have probably weakened the once strong metal of this conveyor belt. Now it hangs in space like an abandoned flying saucer! Beam me up, Scotty!*

We were probably close to two-thirds of the way up the rope, when our weight caused the conveyor belt to slip. It started to move slowly, almost imperceptibly, but then jerked downward a fast foot or so. I thought it was coming loose completely, but it suddenly jerked to a fast stop. Though the enormous bottom bolts pulled loose from the wall, the massive weight bent them in half, causing them to bind temporarily! *How long can those rusty bolts bent at a ninety-degree angle hold this massive tonnage?*

When the belt jolted to a sudden stop, it bounced Cory so hard that she lost her grip and fell completely away from my shoulders! Sliding down my torso, she completely separated from my body for an instant and, free-falling in midair, she reached outward and desperately clutched at my pants. Her right hand caught hold of my belt which pulled my jeans and underwear halfway down my rear end! For that split second, her entire body, flailing outward perpendicularly, dangled in space, attached by only her right hand! Her left hand frantically clawed but couldn't hook the snugly tightened belt on my left side!

I was totally frantic! *Her right hand holds the entire weight of her body over this immense cavern. For that one second, she was parallel to the floor! Lord, please keep her holding tight! I can imagine what she's thinking: God, don't let his pants fall off, and please help me get back to his shoulders!*

Repositioned again on my back, she bear-hugged me so tightly that I could barely breathe. "Never...been so...scared!" Virtually hysterical and gasping for air, she spoke no other words.

I think she's in shock! "Praise God...you caught...my belt!"

Cory whimpered into the back of my neck. *Her breath feels as warm as the wood burner at Cory's cabin!* Secure again, she tightly pressed against my body. *Her entire body trembles fiercely!* "Hang...on tight! You...can do...this!"

"Can't believe... I caught...your belt!"

I tried to console her. "We're almost...there!"

During the next moments, I heard only primordial grunts, but a short while later, I could distinguish a couple words. "Was flying... in space! Thank... You... Jesus!"

That of course was our single scariest moment. She had been prepared for our first step off the ledge and clung to me extra tightly for that initial plunge, but this jolt when the conveyor belt unexpectedly slipped caught her unprepared. Fortunately, I wore the wide leather belt which I had purchased from the Amish during our jaunt up to Smicksburg earlier in the summer. *That heavy leather belt supported her entire weight and saved her life! What a close call!* "You...all right?"

Though she didn't answer, I felt her quivering body cling to me more tightly than ever. Then she tenderly pillowed her head against my neck.

That feels so good!

"Can't...stop shaking!"

"Almost...there!"

She remained silent as she calmed herself, and I continued to creep my way, like a snail, along the rope. Occasionally, an utterance escaped her lips. *A whisper of prayer, a sliver of Holy Writ?* I couldn't make out the sounds above my groans and labored breathing. Focused so intently on my life-and-death climb, I was, for the moment, oblivious to everything else!

At one point, I looked down when Cory flashed the light into the cavernous abyss. That was a big mistake. The dust had settled by then, and the flashlight shone clear to the bottom. *We're so much higher above the canyon floor than I imagined!* I again began to lose heart. *I can't do this, but I have to! We're almost there, yet my arms and hands are numb except for an occasional pain that stabs my arm like a lightning bolt!* I bit my lip so hard it bled!

Sensing my fear and calm enough to speak again, Cory softly whispered a line from one of the psalms to encourage me and keep me going. "'For you have...delivered my soul from death. Have you not kept...my feet from falling'—listen to...this next part—'that I may walk before God...in the light of the living?'"

Because that verse, Psalm 56:13, powerfully spoke to me in that moment, I looked it up so I could include it in this account. I couldn't believe that Cory, shortly after her near-death fall, came up with that astonishingly relevant verse. "What a...godsend!" *God, please keep my feet from falling so that we will again walk in the light of the living!* "Have another... Scripture? That was...great!"

"Only the verse... I often use to describe you. 'The lips of knowledge...are a precious jewel'" (Proverbs 20:15).

"Your words...of knowledge are...rubies!"

"Job says, 'How forceful...are right words!'" (Job 6:25).

"Your words...are...pearls and...diamonds!"

To keep our minds diverted, Cory then cited Psalm 94:18, "'If I say, 'my foot...slips,' Your mercy... O Lord, will...hold me up.'"

Much later, when I commended Cory's propitious citations to Pastor Gabe, he too was impressed that she had come up with those perfectly applicable verses in that moment of crisis. I asked him, "What other verses applied to our life-and-death struggle in that hellhole?" He suggested Psalm 141:10, "Let the wicked fall into their own nets, while *I escape safely*." I told him that verse was also excellent, for it perfectly described our horrible experience. Then he said, "Psalm 37:23–24 is equally relevant: 'The steps of a good man are ordered by the Lord, and He delights in his way. Though he fall, he shall not be utterly cast down; for the Lord upholds him with his hand.' As He upheld you!"

He shall not be utterly cast down. I said to Gabe, "How true, for the Lord upheld us with His right hand." I found that to be even more true once I neared the very end of the rope. My muscles ached so much by that point, and my energy was so spent that I could barely move my hands. *What if my hands freeze-lock on the rope! What would I do then? I can barely move these cramped fingers!*

At last, the miraculous happened, and I daintily tiptoed onto the conveyor belt! I leaned against that cold hard metal and wept. "We...did...it!"

"*You* did it! Thank You, Jesus! You were amazing, Jude!"

Oh, God, you have delivered our souls from death. You have helped us win this race and You have kept us from falling. Without You, Father God, we would never have done this! Tears gushed from my eyes as I embraced the cold metal like a long-lost friend. "We made it!"

"You made it, my love. You really did!"

We wildly rejoiced that our feet had landed on terra firma, those beautifully solid metal treads of the conveyor belt, for at last I had something firm under my feet. In fact, Cory shed tears of joy that we had escaped this death trap. Shimmying across that ravine was an incredible feat, and I rejoiced that my cramped fingers no longer supported three-hundred pounds of weight. Obviously, our gratitude was pronounced, which is why we both wept tears of joy, yet for me, an equally difficult part of the escape lay before us.

There's a simple explanation for that. While shimmying across the deep abyss, I kept telling myself that I was in military boot camp. That mental sleight of hand had enabled me, more or less, to suppress the memory of Grandpa and concentrate on the brutal physical challenge of shinning myself along the rope.

But once I started climbing up the conveyor belt with Cory on my back, I could no longer dodge the bullet. Every step up the belt treads recreated my fateful climb in a barn when I was a little boy. Instead of the barn beam, it was the mine conveyor belt. Instead of a stool on my back, it was my beloved Cory. Instead of living Grandpa at the summit of my climb, it was his ghost. I kept seeing him up there—always reaching, always missing, always plummeting to his death! *I watch him fall, tumble, writhe, thrash, helplessly flail in space, and land with a deafening, sickening thud!*

I was living in the past so completely—was again little Jude on that barn ladder—that I actually lost my footing on the conveyor belt at one point when it slipped completely off the tread! I thought for sure we were goners, but my foot, though in midair, felt as though it landed on solid rock. I completely missed the step and fell down several inches—I have no doubt about that—yet my foot was anchored in space and seemingly guided back onto the belt. It all happened so fast that I have no explanation, but that bizarre incident was my scariest moment as Cory's slipping down my body was hers.

Beside the emotional stress of the tough climb on the conveyor belt, there was the physical one too. The ladder climb on the belt was more difficult than I anticipated since there was only enough room for the balls of my feet on the narrow treads. Also, a couple of the rusty ones broke when I lowered our combined weight on them. That made me fear that the rickety steps might give way completely. *These treads were designed to hold chunks of coal, not the massive weight of two mangled bodies!*

As I climbed the conveyor belt, my mind went into overdrive. *Be positive! The worst is behind us. After another twenty feet, we'll be at the top of the belt and in the main tunnel where we can walk upright to the exit. Exiting the coalmine will likely pose its own problem, but that dilemma will be nothing compared to this. Yet climbing these conveyor treads with Cory on my back is becoming increasingly more difficult. Why? The flashbacks of Grandpa's death intensify with every step I take!*

As if those challenges weren't enough, the conveyor belt again slid downward a couple inches. Near the top, I had a good view of the long bolts. *They have been pried loose from the metal plate so far that several inches of the bolts are exposed. Only two bolts hold the entire weight of the massive conveyor belt!* I placed my toes on the remaining steps with the ease of a mother slipping out of the nursery after gently lying her colicky baby in the crib. Easy does it!

On the final steps of the belt, when I thought we'd make it after all, Cory broke the silence. "I've thought of the most applicable verse of all—Psalm 17:3—'Uphold my steps in Your paths, that my footsteps may not slip.' That describes you perfectly because your footsteps will not slip!"

Moments later, we stepped off the belt and stood on firm ground again. We hugged each other wildly and danced an awkward bad-foot-challenged caper. "Praise God!" Cory shouted again and again. Right there on the spot, we knelt—well, I knelt, but Cory couldn't—and prayed and cried like babies. I was so spent that my arms and legs began to quiver violently. *I can't believe we're on terra firma! Thank You, God, for helping me shimmy up that umbilical cord!* I knelt down and kissed the solid ground.

I shined my flashlight down at Zoe. He looked pitiful on that little ledge of rock above the huge cavern. *He's resting his head on my backpack, either to make it a pillow or to safeguard his only tangible link to us. The recessed ledge with the crossed beams is much narrower than I realized, and the drop-off into the cavern is straight down! How close to death we were!* The pit was so deep that I could not, from this elevation, see the bottom, though the beam that shined on Zoe also illuminated part of the electric cart jutting out from the limestone and coal. *Ninety percent of our getaway cart is buried!*

But where is Dad? I wanted to pan my light across the entire face of the abyss but was afraid I'd see an arm or a leg sticking out of the debris. *I must do this, even if it upsets Cory!* At last, I got up the courage and shined the light back and forth across the whole area.

No Dad!

Did he, like Grandpa, perish in the fall? Has the other important man in my life been cruelly snatched from me?

Chapter 10

Jude's account of their escape (continued)

Holding Cory tightly to me, I sobbed for joy. We couldn't believe we accomplished the impossible. I shook all over and couldn't determine if the violent shaking owed to my body's reaction to the grueling physical challenge or to shock, likely compounded by hypothermia. *This shaking is like the involuntary spasms which I experienced while shimmying across the rope!*

Eventually, I calmed down and collapsed to the mine floor in exhaustion. Though with difficulty, Cory struggled to lie down beside me and more or less succeeded in keeping the weight off her leg. For padding, she placed her injured leg across mine. *Never has a damp, brutally hard coal floor felt so very delectable!* "This is like a comfy bed in Buckingham Palace!"

"I couldn't agree more!" Cory laughed. She struggled to get to her side, hugged me, and then pecked me on the cheek. When I shined my flashlight to the side of her head, I saw traces of coal dust and blood on her lips. *I can only imagine what I look like!*

After celebrating our victory over death and luxuriating in our hellhole escape, I slowly rose to my knees. *There's work to do, and we have miles to go before we sleep.* I yelled down to Zoe. "I'm taking Cory outside. I'll come back and get you soon." Zoe barked and lay down, his head resting on his outstretched paws as if contentedly lying by a Christmas Eve fireplace. "What an angel you are!"

Cory and I began to hobble down the mine tunnel. In the main line, we were able, fortunately, to walk upright instead of crawl. Because we had several hundred yards to get to the exit, my next concern was losing our way since numerous side spurs branched from the main tunnel. While the sign posts assured me that we were sticking to the best exit route, I was nevertheless afraid that I wouldn't be able to track back in the dark to this particular section. Realizing this, Cory dropped torn bits of tissue every fifty feet or so.

As we neared the end, Cory again recited the biblical text that became our mantra—"Shall Your wonders be known in the dark?" Coincidentally, she was reciting that very verse when we came around the last turn in the tunnel and flashed our lights on the mine entrance door! She shouted for joy. "There, at last, is our escape! God has indeed shown His wonders in the dark!"

The next challenge will be getting the bolted door open. It's probably barred with a couple locks to keep out curiosity-seekers. Happily, only one lock barred the door. When I gave the door a savage kick, the rusty lock gave way, and the door flung open. "We're free! We made it to the land of the living!"

When the glorious summer evening light flooded into that dark underground hell, we shielded our eyes from the bright sun. As our eyes gradually adjusted to the brightness, we surveyed the beautiful fields below, radiant in their summer glory. Never did green, green grass look more inviting, lush, and luxuriant! I looked with the poet's sanctified imagination. *Ah, the velvet verdure of the emerald vale!*

"Have you ever seen such a lovely sight?" Cory cried. "Remember the verse Gabe used in his sermon last Sunday? 'Truly the light is sweet, and it is pleasant for the eyes to behold the sun'" (Ecclesiastes 11:7).

"How sweet this light! How pleasant this sun!" I greedily scanned the horizon. "Look at those cattle. Talk about being reminded of 'the cattle on a thousand hills.'"

"David's phrase in the psalms."

"Where does he say that?" I asked the question rhetorically, merely indulging in post-trauma conversation rather than desiring yet another fact for my data-thirsty brain.

"Psalm 50:10."

I shouted, "Fifty ten! That's it!"

"That's what?"

"It's 50:10! That's the location of Grandpa's novel! He said it was buried in a mine corridor called 50/10. His dying gasp was 50/10!" I hugged Cory so hard that we nearly fell over.

"Jude, your carotid arteries are pulsating wildly and your eyes blaze like fireworks! How amazing that you recall the hidden location!"

"It might also be called 'Deep 50.' I vaguely remember that too. Now maybe I can find the lost novel and redeem myself at last! Thank you, thank you, Cory, and your massively 'inscripturated' brain!" I gave her another giant hug and passionately kissed her.

It took me only a moment to find a grassy spot and help her recline under a tree where she had a commanding view of the Allegheny River. "Sweetheart, there *is* a river!"

That's the good news. But the bad news is that we are in the middle of nowhere. The old southwestern Pennsylvania mining town that used to be here was abandoned decades ago. Sadly, we are miles from civilization, and even the road which led to the mine has been thickly reforested.

We rejoiced that Cory could move her foot, so we assumed that her earlier prognosis, a very bad sprain, was most likely correct and that it had not been crushed by the large limestone slab. Nevertheless, because of the jostling of her leg on the rope and conveyor belt, her pain had intensified significantly. When I gingerly took off her shoe and sock, I noted that the swelling had increased considerably. *Cory has a very high pain threshold, but she yelped a lot when I removed her boot. That's not good!* "Sorry to add to your misery."

"Not to worry."

I gathered together some branches and sticks to create a makeshift hassock to keep her leg elevated. "That really helps. The throbbing has subsided a lot." The lacerations to her face were minimal as was the cut to her hand. *Since I removed the backpack before starting our escape, the necessary first-aid items—wound dressings, ointments, and water—are with Zoe in the valley of death. How we desperately need water!*

My appearance most likely equaled my actual condition. Because my head wound had bled a lot, my t-shirt was saturated in blood as was the sweatshirt which I gave to Cory earlier. Under normal circumstances, I would have worried a great deal about considerable blood loss and blunt head trauma. *Forced into survival mode as we are, we have no time to dwell on pain and even our substantial injuries. Circumstances compel us to press on.*

Since Cory no longer needed my sweatshirt now that we were outside in the evening warmth, we ripped the sweatshirt into cloths and wrapped our wounds. It was a relief to wrap my head wound tightly since additional loss of blood was a real possibility. *I need to worry more about loss of blood than cool temps when I return to the mine!* I lost my balance and nearly fell while leaning over when tending to Cory. *Do I have a concussion? How severe is my head injury? How much blood have I lost?*

My plan was to get immediate assistance for Cory and come back to get Zoe later. I had even started planning our strategy to get home, but she would have no part of such a plan. "Over my dead body! Get Zoe first since that won't take long. Together, the three of us will return to the land of the living."

"I should tend to you first. Zoe will be fine. Trust me, wonder dog won't wander off!"

"It won't take you long to walk back to retrieve our good buddy. Hop to it, Professor! You're wasting time!"

At first, I wouldn't even consider her plan. "That's foolish given the severity of these maimed bodies!"

But then she made a point that won me over. "We'll need Zoe's navigational instincts to get home. Are you forgetting who spotted the conveyor belt as our ingenious escape route?"

"You're right, and Zoe also gave us the idea to use the rope as the lifeline."

"Perhaps you failed to notice that you've been checkmated!" Then she gave her hearty laugh. "Go! I'll be fine."

I was forced to contemplate the stark truth. *What she says is true. We're a great distance from home, and without Zoe's navigational resourcefulness, we might not make it.* Reluctantly acquiescing, I agreed to quickly retrieve Zoe and then, together, commence the final leg of our miraculous journey back to life. *It's our best and only shot!*

"Goodbye, beautiful dreamer. I'll be back soon!"

But how to get Zoe out of the mine? As I departed Cory and shuffled toward the entrance, I thought about my quandary. I had learned that one needs emergency survival gear when working in the mine. In the early weeks of my employment, I laughed it off and chuckled at the numerous first-aid stations positioned throughout the mine. *Excessive precautions*, I used to think. Later, I realized the wisdom of keeping a few things in my backpack because of the miles and miles of subterranean labyrinth which Cory and I roamed while cave-exploring. What if an accident were to occur when we were gallivanting far from civilization? Mainstay items in my backpack included rope, water, first-aid kit, flashlight, map, and even a small tarpaulin on which one could lay a body during treatment.

Then inspiration struck. *I can fashion the small tarpaulin into a makeshift bag, put Zoe inside, and strap it to my back. Zoe is less than a third of Cory's weight, so shimmying along the rope to the conveyor belt won't be a problem. That suits me just fine since these arms still throb with pain, and my hands*—again I looked at them—*are virtually clenched balls and sickly white from lack of circulation. Despite incessant massaging, I can barely move my fingers. The good news is that retrieving Zoe won't take long. Suck it up, Professor! This is your only intelligent option.*

At the mine entrance, I looked back at my beloved beautiful dreamer. *How hard to leave you there!* I nearly changed my mind, thinking it would be better to go to the ER first to have our wounds treated. Watching me hesitate, she knew what I was thinking.

"Get Zoe first, and then we'll go to the ER!" I continued to hesitate. "Compared to lugging this divinely gorgeous body"—another laugh—"getting Zoe will be a cakewalk!"

"All right, mind-reader!" I laughed, blew her a kiss, and entered the mine. *Divinely gorgeous body is right and then some! I know what I saw at Beatty's Mill!*

Her tissue markers worked perfectly and led me to the conveyor belt in a matter of minutes. When I was at the top of the belt and peered down at Zoe, he barked frantically. "I'm coming to get you! Just be patient, my angel of light." *How much easier the second time around! Zoe and I will rejoin Cory very soon. Hate to say it, but maybe she was right after all.*

The only real variable was Zoe. *Will he allow himself to be placed in a sack and inelegantly strewn across my shoulders? Alpha dogs exert control, and this one, for good measure, concocts brilliant escape strategies! How will he handle this ignominious role reversal?*

By this time, I had stepped onto the conveyor belt. I kept the flashlight on but placed it in my shirt pocket and put Cory's flashlight in my back pocket since I'd have no free hand to hold a flashlight when shimmying the rope. I gingerly placed my toes sideways on the treads as I faced the belt and climbed down backward. Each time I clasped the sides of the metal conveyor, I felt shooting pains in my hands and arms. *Maybe I have torn muscles or tendons. I hadn't considered that real possibility!*

In a matter of seconds, I had descended the treads of the conveyor belt. *This was definitely easier!* When I completed the downward climb and eased myself as gingerly as I could onto the rope, the transfer of my weight produced an inevitably hard jolt. The bolts of the conveyor belt pulled loose from the wall, and the massive contraption plunged downward into the cavern!

All of a sudden, I hurtled through black space like a trapeze artist!

Chapter 11

Jude's account of their escape (continued)

The rope, which I had looped around the conveyor belt, remained securely tied both to the upright support brace in our niche and to the conveyor itself. The rope guided the conveyor belt into the ravine wall where it slammed with a thunderous crash and then grated back and forth along the jagged cliff edge. As it swung like a pendulum, flying sparks made the limestone cliff eerily flicker in the dark. *It sparks like a welder's arc!* Fortunately, the rope snapped where I had looped it around the conveyor belt instead of where it lipped the jagged edge above me—another instance when my good angel protected me! Down crashed the conveyor belt into the dark abyss as I desperately clung to the rope!

Cory told me later that she had heard the distant sound of two crashes, the first the smashing of the enormous conveyor belt into the wall, the second the delayed and even louder crash when it hit the limestone floor at the bottom of the cavern. She was immediately thrown into wrenching despair as her journal entry attests.

Cory's journal

(Note: Cory had always kept a journal, but enjoying the greater detail and inclusion of increased description in my journal, she started composing more voluminous entries during her week of convalescence. The following entry exemplifies the shift in her journaling technique.)

A sublime calm came over me as I waited
for Jude. The pain in my leg considerably less-

ened once I propped it on my leafy footrest. The evening was lovely, and I knew that in a short while, Jude and Zoe would be joining me. Feeling halfway comfortable, I even started to enjoy the beauty of the evening after our harrowing experience. The view down the Allegheny River valley from this high elevation was sublimely peaceful. As often happens, a line from one of Gabe's sermons darted in my brain, this one from Isaiah 48:18. *Something about your peace will "be like a river." What an accurate description as the peaceful river slowly glides along this lovely summer eve!*

With an artist's imaginative eye, I allowed myself the luxury of looking at the domed hills which line the river banks. *They look like giant scoops of lime ice cream cozily stacked in a fairyland row. Thank You, God, for preserving us and allowing me to see Your beautiful handiwork,* and *now please bring my beloved Jude again to me!*
Lying there on the soft grass, I reflected again on my scariest moment when I slid down Jude's back and saved myself by that frantic and thankfully successful grasp of his belt. After opening my eyes, the first thing I saw was the right half of his exposed rear end, his jeans and underwear angled diagonally across it. *Kidding aside, that's what saved me. Mr. Jude, you have the most beautiful derriere in the world!* Were he the same as many older men, like Dad, for instance, with their less defined gluts—"Most weak hams," as Hamlet says to Polonius—I would have pulled his pants completely off and plummeted to an instant death in the canyon below! Thank goodness for his "sweet cheeks" as Duke had once wittily jested!

To further calm me as I reclined on my leafy bed, I reflected on landscape paintings like the scene before me—paintings like Turner's *Ivy Bridge* and *Chicester Canal*, Constable's *The Hay Swain* and *The Cornfield*. Then I thought of Asher Durand's famous *Kindred Spirits*. I was especially happy when that painting came to mind because it depicts two men, Thomas Cole and William Cullen Bryant, standing at the edge of a rock atop a large river valley, just as Jude and I often stood at The Narrows above the Allegheny River at Brady's Bend.

I once showed the Durand painting to Jude, and he immediately alluded to Bryant, a favorite early-American poet. Citing lines from Bryant's "To a Waterfowl," he referred to the bird as "lone wandering but not lost." Then he elucidated, "That was us during our years of separation— wandering in darkness but never completely lost!"

While resting there, I reflected on something Pastor Gabe had said in last Sunday's sermon. He told us to take note of how Jesus had stooped down to the level of the woman taken in adultery and how He had descended smack dab into the middle of her wretched world. "Jesus compassionately identified with her amid the jeering men who haughtily towered over her. How loving of Him to stoop to her and then, as if that wasn't enough, tenderly touch her, a totally forbidden gesture in that patriarchal culture!"

Is that not exactly how God aided us in our rescue? Stooped to our little world and, through Zoe, gave us the escape plan? How I marveled at His love! Cast your cares on Him, for He cares for you. *How true!*

That's where things stood—the picture of the stooping Christ in my mind—when I heard the crash of the conveyor belt. There were two of them: a single loud banging crash and then a more sustained one when the conveyor belt hit the floor and bounced to its rest. I screamed in horror, and though my leg throbbed in pain, I impulsively crawled toward the mine entrance. Overcome with light-headedness, I collapsed to the ground, screamed for Jude, and wept like a baby!

The longer I waited, the more certain I was that Jude had been killed. *The conveyor belt crashed since nothing else could have made such a horrific sound!* I realized as well that even if Jude had miraculously escaped that fall, his only exit had been shut off. *But he could not have survived that crash. Face the truth, utterly lonely woman: he fell to his death in the canyon below!* I prayed, screamed, and wept. *How alone I am! Now I've lost everything!*

Through my tears, I again peered at the Allegheny River gleaming in the evening sunlight. *That was to have been our escape route, our river of life! How fast it's become the Styx, the hideous river of death!*

Sprawled face downward, I buried my head in the grass and cried for my love. *Again, I've lost him, but this time, he's gone for good! Jude! Jude!* Totally despairing, I fell asleep in the grass.

Jude's account of their escape (continued)

I had managed to hold on to the rope when I slammed into the wall. That was a very tricky part of my survival since I had to make certain as I crashed into it that I stayed above and clear of the huge conveyor belt. As the belt and I hurtled through space on parallel trajectories, I thought for a moment that I was on the trapeze like one of the famous Flying Wallendas! The conveyor crashed into the wall with tremendous force.

Another fear instinctively came to mind in that split second when I rocketed through space. *When the belt hits the wall, the rope, my fingers wrapped around it, will grate back and forth against the sharp limestone. My fingers will be smashed, shredded to bits, and probably severed!*

The impact of the massive conveyor belt against the wall snapped the rope at the point where it fastened to the conveyor belt. Miraculously, I held the rope at a place in the wall that was concave instead of convex—that is, the section of the wall where my hands gripped the rope dipped in rather substantially. That recess in the wall protected my hands and fingers which never even touched the jagged rocks! *Thank You, God!*

Those two blessings were offset by a real loss. My flashlight flew out of my shirt pocket when I smashed into the limestone face. When my body stopped swinging along the wall, I clung desperately to the rope. For that moment, everything was deathly silent. Then I heard the faraway tinkle of the flashlight hitting the floor below. *I can't believe how deep it is!*

High above the canyon, I hung against the cliff of the wall!

Chapter 12

Jude's account of their escape (continued)

Shimmying up the rope, I saw Zoe silhouetted against the dim corridor backlight and distinctly heard him whimper far above me. *You watch over me, Zoe. I can picture your paws dangling over the sides!*

Once on the floor of our raised plateau, I took Cory's light out of my back pocket and crawled to the base of the cross where I embraced Zoe and collapsed in a nervous heap. Near shock and trembling all over, I was nevertheless levelheaded enough to know that the cross had literally saved me a second time. But this deliverance in a limestone mine, unlike my spiritual salvation, was temporary, for I couldn't escape the very shocking truth: our only exit has been destroyed. I now inhabit my tomb! As if that wasn't crushing enough news, my arm bled badly from a nasty abrasion that occurred when I smacked the wall. *Be positive, Jude! At least Cory survived and is in decent shape, and Zoe's here with me!*

I panicked at first. I have to be honest about that because it felt like checkmate. *Cory joked earlier about checkmating me, but now I really am!* It was a huge distance from the original floor of the coal-mine where Cory had rapturously encircled the support beam earlier in the evening to the bottom of the canyon. Though I couldn't determine the distance, I knew it was much longer than the rope. *If I lowered myself to the end of the line and then dropped the remaining distance, I'd break a leg if not my back or neck!* Even so, that was an option, but if I survived the drop to the floor, I couldn't be certain that there was an escape route from that lower level. *What if I end up in a huge cavern with no way out? I'm forced to rule out that grim option!*

Hypocritically, I prayed only after I realized the severity of my situation, and while the prayer alleviated my panic, I still didn't come up with an escape plan. When I later described that feeling to Gabe, he cited a perfectly suitable verse (as he always does), Isaiah 9:9b–10: "We look for light, but there is darkness! For brightness but we walk in blackness! We grope for the wall like the blind, and we grope as if we had no eyes." I told him that indeed described my feeling when I was in that dismal place, "madly wanting light but fearful in the dark and groping like the blind!"

I casually remarked that he always quoted an appropriate verse. Without hesitation, he fired Isaiah 50:4 at me, "The Lord has given me the tongue of the learned that I should know how to speak a word in season to him who is weary."

"Sir, how you speak to this weary wanderer! You remind me of Proverbs 10:20, 'The tongue of the righteous is choice silver!' Your words are always silver!"

Back to my account: The platform Zoe and I stood on jutted out a few feet from the limestone wall, but a slight ledge lipped its front, a thin strip some nine inches in width which went in the direction opposite the conveyor belt and back toward the room's original entrance. After strapping on my survival gear backpack, I tiptoed along this thin ledge a short distance but was soon dismayed to see that it narrowed to a couple inches! Because the wall leaned inward, I was able to scrape my body tightly against it as I inched along, but that didn't keep me from breaking into a nervous sweat. *This is like treading a narrow mule trail above the Grand Canyon!*

When I made it to the end of this narrow strip around a slight bend, I was elated to see that I was standing on the original mine floor, the lone section which had not caved into the canyon below. I was near the entrance of the room which we had merrily waltzed through, carefree as bluebirds earlier in the evening. I was elated, but my joy was short-lived. The cave-in had blocked the original entrance and filled the entire area with fallen limestone. *There's no way out of here as I face a Mount McKinley of fallen limestone!*

I continued my reverie, *Is it better for Zoe to stay back in our niche or be here beside me? The ledge is so narrow that I'm afraid he'll resist coming to me, for I've witnessed his fear of heights in the past.* Just as I was ready to turn and yell for him, I felt Zoe against my leg. Despite his acrophobia, he had followed me across the narrow ledge. "Zoe, what a relief to have you here! You're a good doggie!"

I continued babbling, "We have to get out of this Hades, Zoe. Find us a path!" To my left, as I faced forward, was the immense chasm into which the conveyor belt had fallen, and in front of me was the original entrance into the room, now blocked by a gigantic pile of rocks which extended from the floor of the cavern to the ceiling both before me and to the right. To my rear was the narrow ledge which we had just traversed. "There's no way out of here, and we have little time." *These flashlight batteries won't last forever. Worst of all, my energy is spent!*

In addition to my entrapment and the beating of my tortured body, I subconsciously processed two hurtful realities—Cory's well-being and the other colossal one, the fate of my dad. *Yes, my dad! I have a father. Abe Badoane is my father! But, Dad, did you survive the explosion and the cave-in? Are you alive? And are you truly my father? Will I see part of his buried body?* I flashed my light into the abyss. *No dad!*

Panicking out of my mind by this entrapment in hell, I nevertheless could not stop thinking about Abe. *Of course, Abe Badoane is my father! I believe it all, but the whole thing continues to be so unreal to me. One minute, I learn that this man, though hating and desperately trying to destroy me, is my father who is eager to reconcile, and the very next minute, he's taken from me. Will my faith be strong enough to fend off the encroaching bitterness? Why be tantalized with a good father/son relationship only to have it instantly snatched away? How cruel!*

Retreating deeper into my brain to deny the grim reality of my entrapment, I thought of the famous lines from *The Rubayyat of Omar Khayyam*:

> *Ah Love! Could thou and I with Fate conspire*
> *To grasp this sorry Scheme of Things entire,*

Would not we shatter it to bits—and then
Re-mold it nearer to the heart's desire.

How nice to remold life closer to the heart's desire! It will take a mighty effort on my part to check this torrent of negative thinking. The love of my life, my heart's desire, lies sprawled on the grass with a foot injury above ground while I, a mangled mess, blindly stumble in a cavernous world of darkness below ground!

But what of Khayyam's talk of fate? As if blind chance rules the universe! That flies in the face of my Christian belief in a sovereignly-governed universe. If this whole cave-in and botched escape happened, then God's permissive will allowed it. My challenge is to react properly, to somehow benefit from it, and like little mushrooms in their compost beds of lonely darkness, to grow because of this crisis. To properly mature, those miniature mushroom spores have to enter their scary world of dark soil.

Gabe spoke of this phenomenon in one of his sermons. "'Unless a grain of wheat falls into the ground and dies, it remains alone, but if it dies, it produces much grain' (John 12:24). The seed must enter the black darkness to grow, for it is utterly useless if it remains on the barn floor. To reach fruition, it enters the darkness, completely cut off from all other seeds. We arrive at a shocking truth, dear friends. Aloneness in that underground world constitutes isolation at its worse, but if growth is to occur, such isolation is absolutely necessary."

I remember asking Gabe about the resulting fruit and identity, and instantly, he countered, "'God gives it a body as He pleases, and to each seed its own body' (1 Corinthians 15:38). One discovers his true identity when he dies in that womb of darkness. Once birthed to new life, he's inhabited by the Christ, no matter his form. Concerning identity, remember this: God 'fashions their hearts individually' (Psalm 33:15).

All right, back to the business at hand. Zoe and I have to get out of here fast, so I'd better direct my mind toward an escape plan instead of poetic jewels and philosophic rumination. The possibility of another cave-in is very real, and this flashlight won't shine forever! "Zoe, we've got to get out of here!"

With the ledge which we had just traversed behind us, Zoe started to scale the pile of rocks which towered in front of us like a medieval fortress. *What good is ascending a pile of rocks which goes clear to the roof?* But trying to stave off panic, I knew we had to try something. I followed Zoe, torturous step after torturous step.

Climbing the mountain of limestone was difficult since the rocks shifted under my feet with every step. *What a long delay from the time they slide from the pile and hit the limestone floor below!* One of the limestone rocks crashed into the electric cart and reverberated like a shot in an echo chamber. *That was supposed to be our getaway! To think that cart once zipped along lovely green fairways. Laughing carefree golfers sat in your padded seats! Wormwood!*

As Zoe climbed upward, his paws slid on the jagged rocks. *His paws are not compatible to this terrain.* Nevertheless, we trudged up the mountain of rock. As I neared the top, I encountered a most pleasant surprise. From the narrow ledge below, it looked as though the gigantic pile of rocks extended to the ceiling, and indeed, some of the large rocks at the front of the pile were tightly wedged against the mine roof, but between these large boulders, there was a very narrow crawl space. We burrowed through that skinny opening, Zoe leading the way.

Wriggling through the narrow gap equated to creeping in a cramped crawl space underneath a building. In places, I had to kick rocks away to make a pass large enough to squirm through. *As I scuttle along on knees and elbows, the jagged rocks cut into the abrasions on my arms like knives!*

At one point, where the ceiling was exceptionally low, I took off my backpack and dragged it behind me to make room to squeeze through. In several particularly tight places, I miscalculated the height of the ceiling above me and smacked my head against it. Waves of nausea swept over me as my head pounded furiously. *What if the ole noggin starts bleeding again?* Several times, I retched. *I'm going to throw up! How much further? How much can I take?*

Normally, I'm not a claustrophobic person, but I panic every time I wedge myself tightly against the ceiling. When that happens, I have to squirm and wiggle my way loose like a butterfly escaping its cocoon. Just like Eliot's Prufrock, "sprawling on a pin…pinned and wriggling on the wall." *That's me—sprawling, ingloriously pinned, madly wriggling…* *like a bug!*

After one such extrication, I broke into an area with a nearly three-foot high ceiling and, reveling in the space, shone my flashlight on my forearms. The left arm had been scraped and steadily bled. I scooted my legs to the side to shine my light back across the path we had just traversed. I was sickened to see a trail of bloodstained rocks. I looked again at my arms. *Surely, the blood from my abrasions wouldn't account for that gory trail. That's a lot of blood!*

That's when I brushed my hand across my face and noted that my head wound had started to bleed again. In addition to the agony of finding my way out of this hellhole, loss of blood worried me very much. I lay on my cold stone bed and cradled my head on my folded arms.

I couldn't stop the racing thoughts. *Cory, will I ever see you again? There's no river of life down at the bottom of this abyss. The encircling gloom is black as Hades, and I am very far from home!*

Filled with exhaustion and despair, I remembered what the Gospel writer Luke said of Jesus in Gethsemane when, returning to His disciples after a private prayer, He looked upon the sleeping triad and "found them sleeping from sorrow." *I completely understand! Who can withstand this awful sorrow?*

I nodded off to sleep.

Chapter 13

Jude's account of their escape (continued)

Soon I heard a whimper which awakened me. Zoe was ahead of me some thirty feet. I looked at my watch and determined that I must have fallen asleep for several minutes. Though I had dozed off briefly, I felt refreshed and emboldened to continue our death-crawl. I flashed my light on Zoe who seemed to be hobbling forward with more energy. *Wonder why?*

My hopes were quickly dashed. I shined the flashlight on the path Zoe had just trod and was appalled to see that it was blood-strewn. *I get it! Most of the blood I've been seeing on the rocks issues from Zoe, not me! His rear paw's really bleeding!* "You too sport a red badge of courage in our battle against the Grim Reaper!" *He favors his one hind leg and tries to keep it in the air. To this point, I've been relying heavily on his natural canine instincts. What if Zoe can't continue our death trek?*

Drawing closer to Zoe to see what, despite his injury, occasioned his current excitement, I shined my light on him. "Hold still, Zoe. I want to look at your paw." While beside him, I noted that he was either shivering from the cold or trembling from exertion. *Is the fur on his back moving as if blown by a breeze?* As usual, Zoe understood my command perfectly and froze in place. *If he isn't trembling, and it appears he isn't, then a gentle breeze must be blowing across him. That means an opening must lie ahead somewhere! Might it provide an escape?* For the first time, I felt a twinge of hope.

But that hope was quickly incinerated. When I checked Zoe's wounds, I noted that he had sustained cuts in two of his paws. *The one on the front paw appears to be a surface cut since I see just a small amount of blood, but his rear paw has a deep laceration.* Again, I fought panic. I reached for the lower part of my t-shirt and with my pocket knife cut off a strip of my shirt which I fashioned into a bandage for his leg. He licked my face as I tended to his wound. "That's the best Doc can do in these circumstances, but this bandage will stanch the flow of blood and give you padding too. Now let's find the source of this breeze!"

Together, we crawled in the direction of the airflow and soon came to a place where two large rocks were jammed together. A strong current of air blew through the crack between them. "Zoe," I screamed, "there's an opening here!" I lay on my back, put my feet against the smaller of the two boulders, and eventually felt it move slightly when I pushed. *That wasn't much, but I definitely dislodged it.* The gap between the two rocks was now larger, the current of air stronger. I shone my flashlight into the darkness but saw absolutely nothing.

I wiggled myself into position, found a good place to lodge my hands, and with all my strength began to push the boulder with my foot. To my surprise, it slid downward about a foot. I again placed my feet against the boulder and heaved with all my might. This time, the boulder gave way completely and crashed below. I waited for it to hit, trying to judge the distance to the limestone floor below. *It only took a moment to crash to the bottom, so I'm guessing it fell only eight to ten feet. It hit with a thud, so that means it landed on a solid surface instead of a pile of rocks.* "Have we found a mine corridor? And will it lead to freedom?"

Slowly, I crawled head-first to the edge from which the rock had fallen. Dust was still in the air, but once it cleared, I could see that I was in a corridor of some sort. It was too narrow to be a main mine corridor, and certainly, the mine mules could never navigate its narrow width, but still we had made it to some sort of abandoned hallway. The side of the wall down which I climbed was not steep, so I managed to carry Zoe to the corridor with no problem.

What a relief to have terra firma under me again! I lay Zoe gently on the floor and looked again at his paws. As much as my search for an escape route, he was a real priority. *I need to comfort the one who has sacrificed so much for us.* I tore off another piece of my tee shirt to add more padding to his makeshift boot. "The more insulation for you, Scout, the better!"

Having tended to Zoe, I next focused on my location. My initial gut instinct was that we had stumbled into a remote corridor. The sections of the limestone quarry that had been converted to the mushroom farm were well-marked, but not all of the one hundred-fifty miles of tunnels had been appropriated for the mushroom operation. *I have no choice but to walk until I find signage which I'll use as coordinates to ascertain my location.*

Zoe's limp remained severe, even though we now walked on a smoother surface instead of the ragged moonscape terrain. *What should I do about Zoe? Abandon him a second time? Try to carry him? My own physical endurance has been tested to the limit. Our grueling escape reminds me of my high school buddies' accounts of their Marine boot camp at Parris Island!*

Cory, of course, was never out of mind for a single second. *How is my beloved? She would have heard the horrific crash of the conveyor belt crashing to the floor. Is she in total panic by now? How much agony can she endure?*

Nor do I for a second forget Abe Badoane—I mean Dad. Did he make it? Is he alive or buried beneath tons of limestone and coal? When the rocks started falling, he could have run for safety, but he didn't. He stayed in a bowed position by the side of the ravine, blessing us, bidding farewell, or maybe praying. Dad, where are you? As I ambled along in the dark, I adapted Kent's reference to old King Lear in Shakespeare's moving tragedy. *Has the wrack of this tough world stretched him out longer? Or is Dad at last free of its agonizing torture?*

Mindful that Zoe could only hobble, I had no choice but to commence a fairly brisk walk down the corridor. *Zoe, I have to move quickly since my energies dwindle as fast as the flashlight in my hand!* Orientation was impossible to determine at this point, but my gut indicated that our way out lay in the direction in which I had arbitrarily started walking. We had gone a short distance when, thankfully, I saw one of the most welcome sights of my entire life, a sign on the mine wall, 48/8, which indicated that we were at marker 8 in corridor 48. I instantly sat down and dug out my map to determine our location. *We are miles from any part of the mine we've ever explored and probably a half mile from the closest exit.*

I deduced that this remote exit lay in a rural area of the county away from any roadways. Still, in a life-or-death situation, an exit is an exit and the beginning of our happy return to civilization. I started off in one direction—it turned out to be the wrong way—but pursuing that course was nevertheless a real blessing. We had gone a few hundred yards when I saw a narrow side-cut that joined corridor 48 with the parallel corridor 49. So intent was I to find a way to the nearest exit that I initially missed the significance of this fact. I trod through the side-cut, Zoe hobbling by my side.

We had walked a short distance when I recalled Cory's citing Psalm 50:10 with its reference to the cattle on a thousand hills. That chapter and verse enabled me to recollect, at long last, that Grandpa's novel was buried in Deep 50/10. Traversing the side-cut between corridors 48 and 49, I stopped to check the map and found that corridor 50 ran parallel to corridors 48 and 49. *Might I possibly be in the vicinity where Grandpa had buried his masterpiece?* I was wild with excitement!

Presumably, corridor 50 is fairly close, but I have no way of knowing where marker 10 is since these corridors often stretch for a mile or more. If I'm at marker 8, then marker 10 in the parallel corridor shouldn't be so far away. I spoke to Zoe. "Grandpa's novel might be only a few hundred yards from here. We can find it, Zoe. God is giving me a chance to redeem myself!"

The jubilation no sooner poured from my lips than I thought of Cory. *Should I return to her first, though I have no idea at this point how I'll get back to her or try to find the buried manuscript?* My anguish was intense. *Cory was fine when I departed her, but not trained medics, we couldn't determine the extent of her injuries. Her emotional duress after the collapse of the conveyor belt would have been intolerable, and on top of that, she probably thinks I'm dead, just as we both think Dad didn't make it.* My head again began to throb. *Much as I hate to admit it, I can't underestimate my own injury and loss of blood.*

The reversal in Cory's and my situations amazed me. During my concussion-induced reverie, I had vividly imagined Cory's death and my sad life after her demise. How real it all had seemed to me, owing to my rich imagination! *Now our situations are opposite. She's alive and most likely imagines me dead! What horrors does she experience at this very moment?*

Since corridor 49 lay in the direction of the nearest exit, I continued on my path. Crossing to corridor 49, we walked a short distance in it before I saw an unmarked side-cut to corridor 50 which we took. *I'm presumably in the corridor where Grandpa buried the novel all those years ago! I can picture him somewhere here, a man possessed, frantically digging to bury his beloved manuscript.*

Before I started off for marker 10, I tried to coolly assess my situation. *What's my closest exit? Is it the same as the one I had noted when back in corridor 48?* I was surprised to see that it was not. According to the map, corridor 50 terminated at its own separate exit. Like the one at 48, however, it was in a remote part of the county. The mining roads of the previous century, crude-cut to extract the limestone, had been abandoned after the termination of the quarrying operation and were now densely reforested.

My only way of getting back to Cory is a stream that eventually flows into the Allegheny River. If I follow it, I'll be within a half mile of Cory. Once I reach that spot, I'll merely have to climb the riverbank and traverse the fields to the old abandoned coal mine entrance where I left her.

Since corridor 50 lay in the direction of my exit route, I would be traversing it to get to the exit. Now it was decision time. *Should I exit the mine immediately and head for Cory or stop en route long enough to dig for the manuscript? No matter what I do, I have to act quickly since the exigencies of the moment—Cory's plight, Zoe's injury, my waning energy, and a fading flashlight—loom in front of me like the vast canyon into which Cory and I peered from our ledge.*

In those harrowing moments, I reduced survival mode thinking to bare essentials. *I have to get to Cory as soon as possible, but possibly I might get lucky. How? If Zoe can pick up Grandpa's scent as we make our way for the exit, I might be able to retrieve the manuscript in minutes! Will my cup run over with blessings per Gabe's preaching?*

I quickly fumbled for the rope and Grandpa's hat which, along with the survival gear, I always carried with me because they were my sole remaining links to the great man.

"Zoe, get this scent. We have to find where Grandpa dug! Maybe it was here somewhere!"

Could I actually be in the immediate area of Grandpa's manuscript?

Chapter 14

Jude's account of their escape (continued)

I was certain that Zoe, being Zoe, understood my command perfectly, but instead of starting off, he sat down and whimpered. "Zoe, what's with you?" Initially, I thought he was nursing his paw injuries. *Searching for the manuscript, even briefly, would intensify your pain and delay our escape. I understand, Zoebud!* I walked a few steps ahead without him.

Soon I came upon marker 10 in corridor 50 and trembled with excitement. "This is it!" I cried to Zoe who by then had reluctantly hobbled to my side. "This must be the place where Grandpa's novel is hidden. We have to try to find it!" *I can't believe that after myriad brushes with death, I'm on the verge of unearthing his novel. Talk about patience being rewarded! To do this while en route to my beloved Cory fills me with unspeakable joy, yet my emotions are all over the place: ecstasy that I just might find the long-lost manuscript, anxiety that I left Cory alone, sadness that Dad is buried under a mountain of rock, and further down the scale, fear that my dwindling energies won't sustain me on the torturous last stretch.*

Zoe again plopped down and whimpered. *It's pretty obvious that his excruciating pain is taking its toll!* When I observed his upward gaze at the mine roof, I too peered at the ceiling and realized in an instant why he had halted so abruptly. Corridor 50 was so dangerous that walking any farther into it was utterly foolish. Numerous piles of limestone littered the corridor, and visible roof cracks indicated the real possibility of an impending cave-in. *Ever intelligent Zoe sensed all of this upon entering this corridor whereas I blithely blustered in here! How true—fools rush in where angels fear to tread!*

Aware of our peril in a way I wasn't earlier, I fought to stay calm and think rationally. *How clear the choice is to me: to search for the missing manuscript or not to search.* "I know this is dangerous, Zoe, but I believe God led us here and will protect us." I indulged myself a favorite Christian platitude: The will of God will never take you where the grace of God will not protect you. *I claim that promise!*

I ruminated again on the sequence of events that led us to this spot. *Will I respond in fear or faith to this chance of a lifetime? I simply can't believe that God, through this incredible sequence of providentially orchestrated phenomena, has brought me 95 percent of the distance only to abandon me on the final stretch. As if that isn't enough, I'm simultaneously moving toward the exit and the love of my life!*

"It's here! It has to be here!" I again shouted. "I'm feet away from it and must see the tragedy of the missing manuscript culminate in an eleventh-hour victory!" *That consummation devoutly to be wished!*

Sensing my fierce desire, Zoe sniffed Grandpa's Pirates baseball cap and limped into the corridor. *I think he registers the scent of the hat but will he be able to pick it up at the site where Grandpa had dug all those years ago? Aye, there's the rub!*

As he limped along, Zoe occasionally peeked up at ceiling cracks. At one point, when I followed his gaze upward, I saw a security camera. I watched it for a moment and was greatly relieved to see that it blinked, indicating active use. Because corridor 50 was a main ventilation line into the mine, it probably posed a major security risk. Huge fans at the end of the corridor sucked in desperately needed fresh air from the outside and blew out the stale air. If saboteurs wrecked these fans, the air quality would quickly deteriorate and in short order become lethal. *The placement of that security camera gives me enormous comfort, for if I don't make it, officials might find my corpse by using the camera footage. I have of late lost all my mirth! Wonder why!*

A few overhead lights also lined the corridor. While most of them were burned out, enough were lit to allow security camera technicians to make periodic inspections. A closer look at this particular camera revealed that it was a different model from those Morley showed me. *Maybe the corridor was monitored more closely in the past than now. Something has to account for this old-style camera, the extinguished overhead lights, the deteriorated ceiling, and the rock-strewn corridor.*

I stopped my ruminations and turned to Zoe. "Track this scent." I held the hat to his nose again. As we started down the corridor, he sniffed along the floor like crazy, though he often cast a wary eye at the ceiling. Every once in a while, I heard a noise but, preoccupied as I was, could not determine if it was the sound of crunching stones under foot or shifting rock overhead. I grew more uneasy as we proceeded into the corridor since we had entered an area where more fallen rocks littered the floor and multiple fissures were clearly visible in the ceiling.

When I rounded a slight bend in the corner, I immediately saw a shovel leaning against the wall. *Is this the shovel Grandpa had used all those years ago? I bet it is!* With adrenaline pumping in me as it did for Franco during his Immaculate Reception, I ran a couple hundred feet ahead of Zoe to pick up the shovel and dig in that area. *The floor is smooth and undisturbed here with no traces of digging!*

As I continued my exploration in the area near the shovel, Zoe all of a sudden barked softly, a muted noise just loud enough to get my attention. Did he know that loud resonating sound waves increase the danger in precarious places? I had learned to stop questioning Zoe's intelligence long ago!

Hurriedly running back to him, I watched as he sniffed at a specific spot at the base of an old oak frame where there was a lot of loose stone. To secure the roof, the original limestone quarriers had spaced sturdy oak frames at regular intervals, which antedated the perfected roof-bolting techniques of later years. *Did Grandpa bury the manuscript in this loosened jack-hammered rock, knowing it made for easier digging than the hard limestone floor?*

As I looked more closely, I could see that the area immediately beneath the support beam had been trampled. Possibly to disguise the buried treasure? *Very clever, Grandpa!* I grew more excited by the minute as I realized that I might be digging in the spot where Grandpa had buried his manuscript so many years ago!

As I continued shoveling out rock and dirt near the support post, Zoe stepped back a short distance to a large puddle of water on the opposite side of the corridor. Typically, runoff and wall condensation collected in these shallow puddles throughout the mine, though in some instances they were actual pools of water that were part of the underground network of rivulets within the limestone seams. According to the mine geologist, the miles and miles of underground corridors "intersect numerous underground streams and springs."

I paused a quick moment from shoveling to rest my weary arms, took a couple paces toward the pool, and tossed a stone into it. A column of water spouted upward indicating considerable depth. "Be careful you don't fall in, Zoe. There is a river there!"

Back at the hole, I dug deeply in the loosened rock but still didn't unearth the buried manuscript, and then a horrible thought hit me. *What if it isn't here after all? Surely, I should have found it by now since I've extracted a considerable quantity of rock and dirt. Zoe obviously picked up Grandpa's scent in this location, but that doesn't necessarily mean that the novel itself is here.*

I dug at the edge of the hole to unearth another hefty shovelful. That was the mistake I could not undo, for when I speared the wall side of the hole, the earth above it jiggled loose and caused the dilapidated oak frame, both vertical post and the attached top crossbeam, to slip nearly a foot down into the hole. Two large overhead slabs of limestone, previously held in place by the crossbeam, were now dangerously exposed. I was staring at a sickening gap between the horizontal beam and two enormous rocks which, though now unsupported, stayed in place only because they were temporarily wedged together. *They hang perilously in that space of death above the crossbeam!* At first prancing nervously and then hobbling toward the exit, Zoe tried to get me to leave, but again, his barking was muted.

"I can't leave, Zoe. It's here! I know it is!" When I dug again in the center of the hole away from the wall, I heard a muffled sound as my shovel struck something solid. *Is that it?* This time, my voice was not stifled. The shovel hit the object again and again!

As I dug around the sides of the object to unearth it, the entire frame slipped further down into the hole. Knowing full well of the extreme danger, Zoe began to bark frantically. Even though the gap between the crossbeam and ceiling was now much greater, the two immense limestone rocks remained wedged together. *How long until they crash down? The falling chunks of limestone around me indicate extreme danger!*

Seeing that the ceiling slabs were stuck for the time being, I figured that I had been given a moment of grace to dislodge the manuscript, so on my knees I frantically dug. The miracle complete, I soon unearthed a metal filing box. I hurriedly opened it and pulled out a satchel, under the flap of which was another carefully-sealed package. *I can't take time in this unsafe place to unwrap the inner parcel, but this has to be Grandpa's manuscript!*

I cast the metal box aside and was in the process of standing up, my hand firmly grasping the strap of the satchel when Zoe lunged into the center of my back, striking me right under the shoulder blades. As I awkwardly stumbled forward, the satchel flew out of my hand and slipped back into the hole where the vertical post crashed down directly onto the center of it!

Zoe must have seen the two large rocks start to fall, so he lunged at me with such force that I shot forward some ten feet in an awkward stumbling run. *It's a wonder he didn't snap my spine or whiplash me into paralysis!* I slammed to the ground, rapidly jumped to my feet, and started running all in one fluid motion, the entire time hearing the sickening sound of overhead rocks grating and grinding against each other.

Knowing I had to evacuate the area instantly, I sprinted as fast as I could some fifty feet, speaking to Zoe as I ran, "Good job, angel dog! You saved my life!" I glanced down at my sides to give him a running pat, but he was not there. As I continued to sprint, I looked further down the corridor, thinking he had, despite his injured paw, somehow managed a burst of speed and sped past me. But when I carefully scanned the corridor, I saw that he wasn't there either.

I stopped in my tracks, turned around, and spotted Zoe trapped behind the two giant boulders that completely blocked the corridor! *The boulders must have crashed down when Zoe was in his midair lunge.* At the side of the left rock, I could see him through a small crack which was too narrow to allow him to pass. Even through the dust, I saw lots of blood, possibly from his side and definitely on his front paws. *I wonder if the rock or the crossbeam gashed his ribs. There's blood everywhere!*

I saw all of this in a moment and had just broken into a sprint to go back and hoist Zoe over the rock when the ceiling directly overhead started to shake and rumble. Behind and partially to the side of the boulder, Zoe slowly raised himself to his haunches and then lifted his broken front leg.

Even though his mangled paw dangles lifelessly, he bids me farewell!
"Zoe!"

Chapter 15

—— ⟨⟩ ——

Jude's account of their escape (continued)

Zoe jerked himself down from his sitting position and scuttled along on his damaged paw when an avalanche of stone crashed down. The massive cave-in extended outward into the area to which I had just fled. I heard a huge rock plop into the pool beyond the hole, indicating that the ceiling gave way in that direction too. Tons of limestone rock filled the corridor and buried everything under it...including Zoe!

I bowed my head and hastily shuffled away from the cave-in. Despite all the things that had happened in those turbulent moments, I could not think of anything but Zoe. *Instead of running away when he saw the rocks starting to jiggle loose, he lunged at me to get me out of harm's way. He chose to save me instead of himself! No greater love can a man show than that he lay down his life for his fellow man. An hour ago, I lost my dad, and now in a single minute, I've lost the manuscript and the greatest dog a person could ever know. He treated me like a best friend or brother instead of a master.* I staggered forward, collapsed on the floor, and wept bitterly. *How much can I endure? Call me Job. I suffer and then suffer some more! As the Austrian-German poet Rainer Rilke said, "Wie viel ist aufzuleiden!" (How much suffering there is to get through!)*

As my senses returned, I realized that, though some distance removed from the cave-in, I was still in a very dangerous area. I struggled to my feet and stumbled down the corridor a hundred yards or so to get to a safer place. Having cleared the cave-in area, I squatted along the mine wall, buried my head in my hands, and eventually got up the nerve to look back. Floor to ceiling, the cave-in filled the corridor with rocks which extended in my direction some fifty feet from the original spot where I had been digging. *Zoe and the manuscript are buried under tons of limestone!*

Completely overcome with emotion, I crumpled into a ball and wept. *My dad is dead. Zoe's been taken from me, the manuscript is forever gone, beautiful dreamer whom I abandoned to save a dog is miles away, and I'm physically exhausted and injured too!* I had turned off the flashlight to conserve the battery and was essentially sitting in the dark, only the slightest halo of light filtering through the dust from a faraway ceiling light.

That was my low point. The novel was lost all those years because of me. I had never shirked from assuming full responsibility for its fate because with his dying breath, Grandpa had given me a clear direction concerning its whereabouts. *I came so close to rescuing it and regaining my dignity, but again, I failed—miserably, completely, unforgivably! Jude, you are the ultimate loser!*

Because the roof above appeared to be secure and no stray rocks lay on the floor in this particular area, I felt free of immediate danger but still knew I was at the crossroads of my life. Physically spent and dying of thirst, I clutched a flashlight that was fading. A completely broken man, I crouched against the mine wall and prayed as never before.

No sooner did I finish my prayer than I realized that my fixation on these negative circumstances had defined my current emotional state and, worse, plummeted me deeper into a swirling whirlpool of self-pity.

It's time to reframe the entire situation! The events have been awful—no denying that—but they are not the only realities of my life. Cory's alive, we managed a miraculous post-explosion escape, a glorious future lies before us, we're surrounded by wonderful people, and the best part by far, the arm of the Lord has not grown short!

As I ruminated in that dark place, I realized that even in such desperate circumstances, I still was able to control my thoughts, decide as I wished, and act as I chose. In *Man's Search for Meaning*, Viktor Frankl makes the point that when people lose their spiritual grip, they are subject to mental decay. *If I remain spiritually positive, I'll halt this downward emotional spiral.*

Trying to fixate on positive spirituality, I recalled the Gabe sermon when he memorably cited Dwight L. Moody's renowned axiom, "Character is what you are in the dark." Gabe made the point that people don't know what they're made of until tested in "the fiery furnace of affliction." Fortunately, Gabe's sermon started coming back to me.

The real character crucible is that very low moment when, at your nadir, you can go no lower. How will you respond in that dark hour when the Lord allows you to be tested to the absolute limit? Wise Solomon makes this point metaphorically: "The refining pot is for silver and the furnace for gold, but the Lord tests the hearts" (Proverbs 17:3).

Children of God, do you understand this momentous truth? Just as the fire purifies gold, God's righteous adversity purifies the human heart. "The Lord will not allow the righteous soul to famish" (Proverbs 10:3). He will care for you. Therefore, don't shrink in that awesome day from the God who lovingly and carefully singles you out for that exquisite moment when you're at the apex of your ultimate test. God meticulously crafts that character crucible just for you. Instead of running from it, learn from it, delight in it, even snuggle into it. If you don't flee from the test like a sulking child, you'll eventually learn to love this place of torment because you'll realize God is present in it. You'll feel so close to Him that you can imagine reaching out and touching the very face of God! This is David's astounding truth in Psalm 41:13, "You (God) set me before Your face forever."

Crouched in that dimly lit corridor, I felt the soothing words lather my parched soul like the comforting balm of Gilead. Chastised in my spirit, I racked my brain for uplifting psalms as Cory often did during stressful moments. *Why didn't I memorize more of them?* Finally, I was able to think of a verse Pastor Gabe had encouraged us to memorize. *"I would have lost heart unless I believed that I would see the goodness of the Lord in the land of the living. Wait on the Lord; be of good courage, and He shall strengthen your heart; Wait on the Lord"* (Psalm 27:13-14a). I kept repeating this marvelous verse over and over. *Yes, I will live to see the goodness of the Lord in the land of the living. The goodness of the Lord in the land of the living. The goodness of the Lord in the land of the living. Cory, we will one day stroll by our river of gold in that beautiful land! Wait for me, beautiful dreamer! I'll be there very soon!*

I tried to think of other psalms, and after a moment, another verse came to mind. *"Because he has set his love on Me, therefore I will deliver him; I will set him on high because he has known My name."* Only later did I learn that I had quoted Psalm 91:14. *God will deliver me and set me on high since I have chosen to love and worship Him. He will deliver me and set me on high. Out of this pit. Out of this hell.* The words soaked into my withered soul like a gentle rain on a dried waterbed of south Israel's Negev Desert.

Able to focus again, at least partially, I began to think of an escape plan. I struggled to my feet and trudged back toward the place where I had been digging. *The rubble extends further into the corridor than I first surmised. The spot where Zoe rose to his hind legs is some seventy-five feet away. Was he bidding farewell? It surely looked like it, but now that entire corridor is filled with rocks. You were the smartest, most loving dog imaginable, Zoe, but not even a thinking human could escape that death trap.* I bowed my head in silence. *This is your burial service, and I commend you to the grave. Goodbye to you, my trusted friend. You sacrificed your life for me!*

I rechecked the map to determine my best exit route, put on my backpack, and trudged toward the exit. The distance was fairly short, and as I neared the exit, I was relieved to see the setting sun shoot its golden rays through the cracks in the door, pinpricks of life-giving light that pierced this black dungeon of death. I recalled the verse, Ecclesiastes 11:7, which Cory and I quoted when we escaped out of the coal mine: "Truly the light is sweet, and it is pleasant for the eyes to behold the sun." *How beautiful this magnificent sunlight!* The door was secured with a single dilapidated lock. One firm kick, and it burst open. Blinding light crashed into the darkness, and more importantly, into my soul.

Outside again, I held my hands over my eyes until I gradually adjusted to the bright sunlight and surveyed the scene before me. Atop a hillside slope, I gazed across a carpet of emerald undulating hills which frolicked and rolled along to the stream. Lush hay swayed to the cadence of the evening breeze. Backlit by the setting sun, the dancing leaves of the trees refracted a lime-green diaphanous glow. *Wordsworth, I imagine your ecstatic outpourings! "Across the vale, the rustling leaves warble a lyrical lay like the mellifluous lilt of an Aeolian lyre. Wild summer flowers waft their scent through winding glen and wandering glade!"*

Standing there in that moment of gratitude, I felt as though I had risen from the grave. *I am Lazarus, come from the dead, Come back to tell you all. I am back in the land of the living! Thank You, Jesus—You Rose of Sharon, Lily of the Valley!*

But Zoe and Dad have not come back from the dead!

I couldn't stop the literary allusions from firing in my brain, even during these moments when my emotions bounced around like popcorn in a kettle. I first thought of a verse Pastor Gabe had recently cited in Deuteronomy, "For the Lord your God is bringing you into a good land, a land of brooks of water, of fountains and springs, that flow out of valleys and hills" (Deuteronomy 8:7). *Like the good land I see before me!*

Then I recalled an Edna St. Vincent Millay poem, "God's World," which I had memorized as a high school kid. *"O, world, I cannot hold thee close enough."* At first, I had trouble remembering it, and only a phrase flashed in my mind—the woods "all but cry with color." Then the lines started coming back to me:

> *Long have I known a glory in it all,*
> *But never knew I this;*
> *Here such a passion is*
> *As stretcheth me apart. Lord, I do fear*
> *Thou'st made the world too beautiful this year.*
> *My soul is all but out of me.*

There on the sun-blanched hilltop, my soul experienced ecstasy, yet my emotions oscillated wildly. In one moment, I was enraptured with the world around me, but in the next, my soul was excruciatingly dragged through the valley of the shadow of death. *How can one mind process so many contrary emotions simultaneously? I feel elation that I've been spared and that Cory and I will, in time, cozily snuggle and entwine in our love-nest dream, yet I despair that I've lost so much in a single cursed hour. How sad to come so close and then to lose it all—life and death, agony and ecstasy, hell and heaven, earth's lush vitality and the subterranean world of diabolical darkness!*

Sitting in the lush grass, I examined the topographical map of Armstrong County to get my bearings. *This exit from the limestone quarry, like the one where Cory lay at the abandoned coal mine, lies in open, uninhabited land with no road nearby, not even one of the country lanes, which are still prevalent in the remote areas of the county. My best alternative is to go down the hill to Buffalo Creek and follow it as it winds through meadows and woods to the vicinity of the coal mine, not far from which Cory lies on her leafy bed. Dearest Cory, what hell, what infernal unimaginable hell do you endure at this very moment?*

I estimated my journey to be about a mile or so by stream. My only concern was identifying the right spot on Buffalo Creek where I would cut up over the hill and walk cross-country to Cory. *What I can't do in my weakened state is miss that turnoff and clomp needlessly out of my way downstream!*

To keep my thoughts from being sucked again into that cyclonic vortex of despair in my head, I tried to think of Solomon's proverbs. Finally, a couple came to mind. "Keep your heart with all diligence, for out of it springs the issues of life" (Proverbs 4:23). *That's right! The springs of life, including all my hopes and aspirations and motives, are rooted in the heart, but the gravitational pull in mine is toward the dark and not the light!*

"The spirit of a man will sustain him in sickness, but who can bear a broken spirit" (Proverbs 18:14)? *My broken spirit wouldn't sustain me let alone Cory, so I have to bank on faith to get me through this!*

I was about to descend the hill to commence my downstream journey when, impulsively, I took a few steps in the opposite direction along the top of this hill just to luxuriate in my return to life. As I walked along the slope, reveling in the sheer beauty of the summer evening, I made the most amazing discovery. I remembered the canoe ride I had taken back in May just after I arrived in Armstrong County when I found myself in a waterless creek—exhausted, thirsty, hemmed in with thick foliage, and frustrated out of my mind. The event had been very annoying to me since I had anticipated a leisurely ride down the fast-flowing stream of yesteryear but instead had run aground in a dense thicket surrounded by swarming mosquitoes and was thirstier than a Roman galley slave rowing at ramming speed.

A thought had occurred to me as I sat in the canoe that May evening. *This is a microcosm of my life: stuck in the mud, shackled to the past, exasperated beyond words, and immobilized in despair.* When I spoke to Pastor Gabe about my perpetual thirstiness, he turned to a verse in Isaiah. "Jude, you must remember this truth: 'I will pour water on him who is thirsty, and floods on the dry ground' (44:3). Only God 'satisfies the longing soul' (Psalm 107:9). Only He will quench your thirst." *Sir, my soul really needs quenched!*

I paced laterally some hundred yards. *There below me is the exact spot in the stream where I had run aground last May! At the time of that canoe ride, I thought that Buffalo Creek, normally deep enough for swimming, had dried up over the intervening years. Little did I know that I canoed in a shallow tributary that spurred from the creek!* Run aground that day, I was a mere hundred yards from the fast-flowing creek! There were "rivers of water in that dry place" (Isaiah 32:2), but I didn't realize it.

I continued my reflection. *What a distance I've journeyed to get to this life-giving water! It was there the whole time, a mere hundred yards away, but in the dark labyrinth of my mind, I completely missed it!* As I neared the bottom of the hill, I broke into a run until I reached the swiftly running stream.

There is a river here, and how glorious it is!

When Gabe spoke me with me later about this matter, he directed me to two verses that perfectly described the contrast between the dried-up tributary and the fast-flowing stream. "These verses also apply to your plight: God 'turns a wilderness into pools of water, And dry land into water springs'" (Psalm 107:35). Aim for that day, Jude, when the wellspring of your wisdom is a flowing brook (Proverbs 18:4). In time, you'll become that instead of a brackish stream."

What an amazing contrast—from dried-up stream to a gushing water spring!

Chapter 16

Jude's account of their escape (continued)

I again checked the topographical map of the county and calculated that I'd rejoin Cory in some thirty minutes depending on the riverbank terrain along the stream. The trek was refreshing, and the evening sun and breeze strengthened me physically and emotionally. By that time, the aching in my arms had eased, and the stabbing pains diminished. I ambled along paths which fishermen, swimmers, and nature lovers had trodden for decades, though at times, I was forced to circumnavigate dense thickets along the stream. In shallow places overhung with dense foliage, I stepped into the shallow water and walked under the boughs. Occasionally, I wandered into areas so thick that I thought I was in the Amazonian jungle instead of southwestern Pennsylvania.

At one point, the stream snaked through a forest of huge glacier-deposited rocks. Larger than big buildings, the lichen-covered boulders radiated a misty green hue in the evening sun. One of these towering rocks, I had once been told by locals, was named Indian Head. *In some of these places, the evening sunlight filters through the dense trees onto rocks, tree trunks, and fallen timbers with such intensity that it looks like green flash-burn!*

After quite a distance of meandering, I left the stream at a sharp bend and headed up over a steep and long hill to walk across country in the direction of the coal mine entrance. It was an educated estimate but, as it turned out, a good one. *I merely have to tack east the final quarter of a mile to the coalmine entrance. What will I say to her?*

About a hundred yards away, I could see Cory lying against the tree where I had left her a couple hours earlier. *How much has transpired in that time!* I yelled when I drew close to her and ran the rest of the way. Never have I been so happy in my life! Nothing approximated the sheer bliss I felt in those moments when I rejoined her. *I'm with my love at last!*

"Cory, my love, I never thought I'd see you again!"

"Love of my life, I thought for sure you were dead! How did you get out of there alive?"

We hugged and madly kissed and cried, and when I stopped holding her tightly and backed slightly away, she popped the dreaded question, "Where's Zoe?"

Breaking into an uncontrollable sob, I gushed with the torrent of emotion which I had bottled up since the trauma of the cave-in, our perilously close call, Zoe's death, and Dad's disappearance. For several minutes, I shook violently as Cory held me close to her. *Surely, she surmises the worst since I can't talk. Say it, Cory! Don't make me tell you that Zoe was killed! You say it for me!*

Finally, I gained control enough to tell her the whole sad story start to finish—the collapse of the conveyor belt, our search for an escape route, the discovery of Papa's novel in 50/10, Zoe's desperate attempt to save me from the cave-in, the avalanche of stone that killed him and buried the novel, and my harrowing escape out a remote exit.

Then it was Cory's turn to weep in despair. Never in my life have I witnessed a woman cry like that! Most of it was sadness over all the losses: Abe's fate and her fear that he had entered a Christless eternity, Zoe's death, the loss of the novel, our escape trauma, and, far and away the worst, fear that she had lost me forever. But I soon realized that it wasn't just the immediate circumstances of the last hours that ripped her apart, awful as they were. She was at the same moment flashing back to her mom's death, her dad's hard life, and her decade-long struggle, all of it compounding together in a volcanic explosion of emotional release. We sobbed in each other's arms.

"My Jude, my Jude! You're alive! You made it! Our good God spared you! You're here!"

Then it hit me. *Cory's torrent of emotion is partly joyful. Some of these are tears of joy! The possibility of our surviving the explosion was very slim, a fact we could not deny, and the chances of my dodging the bullet of the last cave-in even slimmer.* As we joyfully lay in each other's arms, our tears of sadness morphed to tears of joy.

Totally spent, we could not deny our physical state, but we had one good thing in our favor. The entrance to the coal mine was situated at the top of a high hill overlooking the Allegheny River. *It will be a difficult descent down the mountainside since our elevation is hundreds of feet above the valley floor, but I'll take this over an uphill climb! We have no choice but to limp our way to the bottom. Cory, we're not out of this mess yet!* "The struggles just don't stop, but hang on, kid. We didn't come this far to give up!"

"This leafy bed is far superior to the high wire act over the canyon and the torturous climb up the conveyor belt!"

"And in the sun no less!"

"Right you are!" Cory thought for a moment and scratched her head. "While I was lying here, I thought of this relevant verse from the Psalms which Gabe had told me to memorize after mom died. 'He also brought me up out of a horrible pit, out of the miry clay, and set my feet upon a rock, and established my steps' (Psalm 40:2)—another applicable verse!"

"The best of all. I'm amazed at how much Scripture you've crammed into your head!"

Silent for a moment, she looked down the mountainside. "But given the trouble you'll face going down that steep hill, I give you Job: 'Man who is born of a woman is few of days and full of trouble' (Job 14:1). I emphasize the trouble part. To quote you, 'It's a fur piece down 'ere!'"

"It is that!"

Her faint smile indicates increased hope and a firm resolve to carry on, even though this next leg of our journey won't be easy. Keep smiling, beautiful dreamer, keep smiling! I carefully looked at Cory as she lay there. *The swelling on her foot has ballooned considerably. I fear a break despite the fact that she can move it slightly. Nor do the spasms of pain which periodically shoot up and down my arms, legs, and head allow me to forget my own beleaguered state. What a pair we are, but back to civilization we go—without Zoe, without Dad, without the manuscript!*

Because the distance from our perch atop the high hill to the valley floor below was so far, I knew it would be impossible for Cory to hobble to the bottom, so I devised the idea of tying together a bunch of small logs and thick tree branches to fabricate a makeshift sled. To bind together the small logs and branches, I used Grandpa's rope, previously an agent in his death but latently the agent of our salvation. Once finished, I placed a stack of leafy limbs and ferns on it to cushion the inevitably bumpy ride.

Cory gently eased herself onto the sled. "It's not a chariot of gold or a palanquin for Caesar, but nun's fret not at their convent's narrow walls. Nor do I complain!"

"At least we're alive!"

"But I pity you as you have to lug me the whole way down the mountain."

"No problem."

"First you carry me across a rope, then up a ladder, now down a hill. It's about time I carry my own weight!"

"Nothing but a light and joyful burden, Princess!"

"Ever chivalrous, Jude!"

"I won't rest until the last carriage."

"Explain."

"The carriage across the threshold of our honeymoon suite!"

"That most delectable of all fantasies!"

Down the side of the mountain, I began to drag her, foot by treacherous foot. Doing my best not to stumble on the uneven terrain, I tried to think of something that would distract the two of us from our injuries and despondency. Zoe's death had hit us with the force of a Pennsylvania summer thunderstorm when a towering thunderhead, with absolutely no warning, deluges tons of water on an unsuspecting community below. Though we didn't speak of it, little else was on our minds as we began our painful descent.

We have to distract ourselves. "Wish you'd come up with an applicable verse as you did after the cave-in," I remarked after several minutes of weary sled-dragging.

"That's exactly what I've been trying to do as I cruise along in my Cadillac limousine."

All of a sudden, she winced in pain as the sled jolted into a hole hidden by a fern alley. I stumbled but quickly regained my balance. Poor Cory was nearly thrown from her couch of luxury. "Sorry! That monster hole was completely hidden!"

"Not to worry. I'm all right." She resumed her thought about a verse. "I know there's a verse in Jeremiah. I can't quote it exactly, but I can paraphrase it: 'I will lead them. I will cause them to walk by the rivers of waters'—catch this next part—'in a straight way in which they shall not stumble'" (later, she learned that she had paraphrased Jeremiah 31:9).

I was astounded that in the middle of our desperate plight, she had come up with that verse at the very time I was trying to get to the rivers of water and not stumble. "Cory, you're amazing! If that verse correlates...to our situation the way the rose vision does, then I guess it means...we won't stumble, so just hang on for dear life!" I laughed in spite of myself. "We'll eventually get there...even if this path isn't the smoothest in the world."

"Right you are!"

Keep talking to occupy our minds. "The last time I traversed ground this bumpy...is when I took the shortcut trail at Beatty's Mill."

"So glad you drove like a maniac that evening!"

We trudged along, step by agonizing step. I rested for a moment, and when I asked her how her foot was, she said, "*C'est foule* (It's sprained)."

She spoke French. That's good because it makes her use her mental faculties.

We finally made it down the hillside to the river. The worst part had been the wear and tear on my gnarled hands because as when shimmying across the canyon, I tightly clutched the rope which again balled them into tight fists. At the bottom, I had to massage my fingers to get them to move again. *May I never have to do that again!*

Fortunately, I had to walk only a short distance before I found a canoe lying on the bank. Canoes and kayaks are frequently tied along the river bank at various places on the Allegheny River, even though the owners' camps or summer homes aren't in the immediate vicinity. I quickly carried a small canoe back to Cory. *This is a great break for us since we'll likely have to travel a short distance till we come to civilization. I can return the canoe later!* "We're going to make it, sweetheart!"

With less difficulty than I anticipated, I managed to get Cory into the canoe and then paddled down the broad river. As the current was fast after the summer rains, I could not help but contrast our impressive river speed to the agonizingly slow climb in the mine where I had struggled to inch my hands along the rope and then climbed, toehold by toehold, up the conveyor belt. I lay the paddle down to rest my tortured arms.

"Remember what the sign says in Little Gidding." Cory cupped her chin in her hand. "'If it's of man, it's forced; if it's of God, it flows.' This is what I call flowing!" She then recalled Isaiah 43:16, "The Lord 'makes a path through the mighty waters.'"

"Like this glorious path!"

Eventually, we came to a place on the river where there were several houses. *Remnants of a village, I surmise.* Soon we saw a man running toward his dock. What a welcome sight—big man, smiling face, very cheerful, and extremely helpful. He told me his name was Aaron and that he had been at the top of the ridge spotting eagles through his binoculars.

"The eagles frequently glide along this part of the Allegheny River." He pointed to the top of the hill. "The vantage from up there in that power line right-of-way gives a good view of the entire valley." He turned to Cory. "When I spotted you, I could see that your leg was propped up on the side of the canoe."

"The pain's less when I elevate it."

He looked at me. "The turban bandage on your head was the other dead giveaway that you were in big trouble and needed a first-responder immediately."

"What a bright man you are!" I laughed.

"So I jumped on my four-wheeler and raced down the trail. I call that perfect timing!"

"Yes," I agreed. "We arrived at the same time!"

Aaron knew we needed immediate help, but the problem was getting Cory up the long flight of riverbank stairs to the flat lawn above. Clever man that he is, he retrieved a narrow door he had recently removed from his pool-side shed along with a glider cushion. "We'll use this improvised gurney to carry you up the stairs."

The man was a saint and his idea clever. With Aaron on the lower end of the makeshift gurney and me on the upper, we managed to get Cory up the long flight of metal stairs with a minimum of difficulty. On the flat lawn above, we gently slid her into the back of his Suburban which he backed across his lawn to the riverbank. During our ride to the emergency room of the Armstrong County Memorial Hospital, we filled him in on the recent harrowing events.

At the ER, the doctor immediately tended to our wounds and x-rayed Cory's foot. In a short while, he informed us that it was "sprained badly but not broken." He put a boot on her foot and treated our various abrasions and cuts, especially my head wound. As it turned out, the doctor was quite concerned about my injuries. "Your loss of blood and possible head trauma are more of a problem than Cory's foot."

"I knew I lost some blood."

"We gave you two units. That's a lot of blood. Drink lots of liquid today."

He turned his attention to Cory. She showed her rising spirits in the ER by translating the doctor's statement into French: "*Je vais vous donner analgesique* (I'll give you a painkiller)."

*****

It was not until later while in the ER that we learned of the many events that simultaneously occurred that climactic Friday evening. As we fought for our lives in the mine, Tina and Duke attended a revival meeting at the Center Hill Church of the Brethren and decided, during that service, to forsake their lives of self-sabotaging madness. Their decision to walk to the front during the concluding altar call was a life-changing victory for them.

"Hell, I knew it was high time to give my life to God!" Duke later told me. I laughed when he said that and thought of a witty comment Old Mary had made at the Fourth of July picnic: "Mr. Rogers didn't actually prepare me for all the people in my neighborhood!" *Duke, some of the neighbors aren't prepared for you!*

That same evening, Charles beat his long-standing cardiac fear and climbed the whole way to the top of Mt. Washington in an epic if exhausting endeavor. That too was an exciting chapter of his life which he subsequently described for us.

Joey's coming of age and confronting a derelict football coach at the Friday football game turned out to be the joyous equivalent of our disastrous mine exploration and, without a doubt, our favorite aspect of that monumental day. Once she had learned of all these concurrent happenings, Cory succinctly wrote in her journal: "It appears to us that God ingeniously coordinated a lot of events this evening. What a beautiful tapestry He wove!" How true her statement!

But as Aaron drove us to the ER that Friday evening, we knew about none of those concurrent events. That's why I delay their narration, except to point out the irony of Cory's passing comment as we arrived at the ER: "I wonder how Joey made out at the football game this evening. This was the first big game." What a story that is!

Chapter 17

Always zealous to develop his strong, muscular physique, Joey Mohney is a remarkable young man who demonstrates exceptional maturation. Through the summer during which the events of this story occurred, Joey had been working out and running daily, creating a body by summer's end that was a perfectly shaped, superbly tuned machine. As Jude quipped one day, "You could appear on the front cover of *Men's Health* or *Men's Fitness*!" In short, Joey had done his part to be in shape for football training camp at the end of the summer and was ready for the big Friday evening football games. In western Pennsylvania, these fall games garner excitement second only to that of the Pittsburgh Steelers. Little wonder the area had produced so many legendary athletes.

The problem of previous seasons, however, continued to plague Joey. The coaches, for whatever reason, did not give him his chance. Week after week, he scrimmaged with the second team at practice and rode the bench during the preseason exhibition games. No matter how hard he tried to impress the coach, he was resolute in his decision to start other players. "It infuriates me, Jude. I run laps more doggedly than my teammates and sprint faster than the starting backs and defensive secondary." His athletic prowess was evident in the way he threw and caught the ball, blocked for running backs, and tackled the speedsters on the team. "But none of this makes a difference. The head coach plays his favorites and benches me!"

This unjust treatment on the football squad, the one that most touches the Jude/Cory narrative, was not Joey's only problem. Hailing from a family that was, to put it euphemistically, challenged economically, Joey wore jeans that showed wear, out-of-style shirts and sweatshirts, and dated shoes. But Joey Mohney was not bothered by any of this. Confident in himself and his abilities, he was a young man whose self-esteem was not tied to either appearance or peer acceptance.

That very self-confidence, however, miffed the formidable clique of football players who established the norms and crafted the unwritten rules of conduct for the students' power structure. The elites did not like it that Joey not only survived their rejection but also prospered without a fawning parasitic attachment to their powerful host organism. His levelheaded poise and the pronounced singularity of his character piqued them, especially the insecure ones whose sense of self-worth derived from their symbiotic allegiance to the jock hierarchy. As a result, Joey was often the butt of their jokes and horseplay.

This was the state of affairs for Joey Mohney on the epic Friday evening when so many events, including Jude and Cory's escape, transpired. The athletes continued to shun Joey, the proverbial underdog never given a chance, despite his prowess, superior build, and excellent performance. Because Joey rejected and even on occasion ridiculed the clique members for their libertinism and endless bluster of unrestrained exploits, they blacklisted him and slowly tightened the social stigma noose that surrounded him.

Inwardly, Joey scoffed at their acting out. "They're preppie junior-high kids in adult bodies—period!" He could never determine how much of the talk was real and how much windbaggery, but either way, he rejected all of it. "Their antics don't impress me, nor do I care what they think of me." Christ's command to be in the world but not part of it had become his credo throughout his high school years. His favorite verse, which his sister Cory had given him when he started high school, was Psalm 119:9, "How can a young man cleanse his way? By taking heed according to Your word." The more steadfastly he tried to follow that "high calling in Christ," as Pastor Gabriel called it, the more they tightened the noose.

That he could withstand the withering ridicule of the jocks who suavely fraternized their way up the power structure ladder was a fascinating dynamic in and of itself. Professor Charles had discussed this topic with Joey at different times. At the peach festival in the Center Hill Fellowship Hall a couple weeks prior to the epic Friday evening of Jude and Cory's escape, Charles specifically asked Joey how he "survived their debauched antics."

"I never thought much about it," Joey quickly responded. Seated by Laura, they were enjoying delicious peach sundaes at a back table. "Probably it comes from living from the inside out." He wiped his mouth with a napkin. "Here's what I mean. A handful of these guys are masters of reconnaissance. That's Jude's fancy phrase, by the way. I don't have to tell you that I don't talk like that!"

Both Joey and Laura laughed.

"What do you mean?" Charles asked. "Rather, what does Jude intend by that phrase?"

"That they're always checking out how other people act, talk, and dress. They see themselves as successful when they mimic the standards the 'cool' guys set."

In an effort to fully understand Joey's plight, Charles delved more deeply, "You're saying that the elites have created a kind of blueprint, and the members of the clique see themselves as successful if they stuff, contort, and wrench themselves to fit that insanely lauded template. Is that it?"

"Bingo!" Joey finished a bite of his sundae. "You use more 'Jude words' than Jude! You professors and your big words! I suggest you speak in English!"

A college professor who spent his adult life working with young people, Charles enjoyed and was intrigued by the dynamic which Joey described and decided to push still further. "So how does one develop strength to resist the formidable influence of these influential power elites?"

"That's where Pastor Gabe helps a lot," Joey replied, devouring another scrumptious bite. "He said that God is not mocked and that a man reaps what he has sown. He also quoted Proverbs 11:18, 'He who sows in righteousness will have a sure reward.'"

"How do you apply Gabe's explanation?"

"I understand it this way. The crops we reap in life correlate to the seed we plant. Plant bad seed—like doing evil things, spreading lies, living a carnal life, and abusing our bodies—and in time, we reap a bad harvest. But if we do good things, we eventually reap a crop of blessings. That truth makes me try—I emphasize *try*—to align conduct with inner convictions. That last phrase, by the way, is a direct quote from Gabe's sermon. Now you know what I mean by living from the inside out. I consult my heart, what Pastor Gabe calls the inner compass, and try to act accordingly."

Seated beside Joey, Laura broke in, "We think that many of the guys at school do the exact opposite. They live from the outside in, as Joey said earlier. They're like little kids sitting around a table in nursery school who first check to see what the other little kiddies think, do, and say. Then they pattern their own behavior to fit that prevailing norm. It's pretty sick, really!"

Joey looked up at the basketball hoop as he formulated his thought. "Because they don't consult their hearts, they eventually become strangers to themselves and don't know who and what they are. For me, that approach to life is messed up." He took another bite. "But this peach sundae isn't! It's the best ever!"

As Charles, Joey, and Laura conversed on this subject, Pastor Gabe, making the rounds in the Fellowship Hall, stopped by their table. They brought him onboard and explained that Joey had just been synopsizing one of his sermons. "Care to add a couple words to our discussion?" Joey asked.

"Asking a pastor to share a couple words," Gabriel began, "is a dangerous thing, but since brevity is the soul of wit, I'll be brief. I see it this way. Sin and the carnal indulgences are horrible weights which drag them down and keep them from hitting the lofty heights God intends. As I noted in that sermon, such people are 'caught in the cords of their own sin'" (Proverbs 5:22).

"You just offered a perfect description of the guys on the team!"

"Because sin blocks the free-flow of the Holy Spirit in their lives, such dissolute people eventually run amok. Here's my point: what they hang on to for their enjoyment—I'm talking about their kicks, reprobate thrills, and shameless indulgence of the flesh—undermines the work of the Spirit."

"Thanks, Gabe," Joey commented. "You always have a way of making things so clear."

"Jude told me that's what happened to him over at IUP before he came back here and got together again with Cory." Pastor Gabe stopped when he noted Joey's confused look. "Surely you know about those tormented days. Jude said he was derailed and didn't even know it."

"Jude derailed?" Joey speared the ice cream with his spoon. "Do you know what a successful prof he is? One of my friends from Kittanning had him for class. He said the students love him."

"I'm sure of that," Charles agreed.

"Yet, I know what you mean." Joey spooned a peach on top of the ice cream. "He was a heartbroken man after he lost sis." Joey stopped monkeying with the peach sundae and smiled at Laura. "I'd feel the same if I lost a certain girlfriend." Joey put his arm around the blushing Laura.

"On the outside," Charles opined, "Jude was, in those days, the manicured picture of perfection. My guess is that the other grad students were jealous of his mind and his intellect and maybe his teaching ability too. Yet, through it all, there was a sadness in his eyes during those years."

"Why do you say that?" Pastor Gabriel asked.

"Here's why. I attended a conference of the Pennsylvania College English Association in Gettysburg shortly before Jude came back to Armstrong County. There's a 1912 statue of Lincoln in Gettysburg's National Cemetery by Henry Bush-Brown, which I saw one morning when I took a break from the conference. Perhaps you don't know that bust of Lincoln. It's the one that shows those eyes of inexpressible sadness. The same was true of Jude. I sat across from him in one of the sessions and observed how his sad eyes contradicted the huge smile. Lips can lie. Eyes can't. Gabe, you'll recognize that I just filched one of your favorite axioms!"

The four of them—Pastor Gabe, Charles Claypoole, Joey, and Laura—glanced over to where Jude and Cory stood by the kitchen serving-window. "Look at him now." Pastor Gabe nodded in his direction. "Jude has found his lifelong mate and is as much in love as any man I've ever met. He's regained his spiritual moorings and is right with God, Cory, and the world. What more could a man want?"

"Not much!" Admiring her sweetheart, Laura slipped her arm through Joey's and gently pulled him close to her, the lovely high school girl totally enthralled with her guy.

"Except a fair break. I just want my chance on the gridiron!"

"You'll get it," Laura cheered. "This is your year!"

Charles smiled broadly at Jude. "The big game with Freeport is coming soon. We hope Laura is right."

Excusing themselves, Joey and Laura went over to join Jude and Cory. Once they were out of earshot, Pastor Gabe stared at his clasped hands. "I must pray more fervently about this football business. Joey's clearly distraught."

"Yes, we need to do that now that the season's upon us. I just hope Laura's right when she says this will be Joey's year."

Chapter 18

The last days of August usually feature warm days in western Pennsylvania, but the atypically cool Friday evening of Jude's escape and the Center Hill service carried with it the feel of autumn. The stands at the football field were full of cheering fans who were excited about the prospect of a winning season for their beloved football team. Having sung the National Anthem, the crowd then moved into a rousing rendition of the Kittanning High School alma mater, the joint effort in bygone years of teachers Mildred Montgomery (the lyrics) and James Colonna (the music):

> By the winding Allegheny
> There's a spot that we adore;
> We pledge our faith to Alma Mater
> And our love forever more

Bouncing with youthful zest, the cheerleaders roused the fans with enthusiastic cheers as Kittanning battled a tough competitor from down the river, Freeport High School. Freeport's teams were notoriously tough, and this year was no exception, but Kittanning was a good match for them because of their high number of returning lettermen and superb talent. Though the teams had struggled vigorously through most of the first two-quarters of the season opener, the score remained 0–0 in a hard-fought, defensive struggle. The two teams continued to battle it out, but near the end of the first half, Freeport scored on a huge play when one of their receivers slipped past the Kittanning safety and caught a long pass which he ran for a touchdown. Freeport went into the locker room at halftime with a 7–0 lead.

Joey was not only a gifted athlete, but endowed with a coach's analytical mind, he also saw what did and did not work on the playing field. *The coaches aren't making the necessary offensive and defensive adjustments!* He squirmed in his seat as the minutes of the third quarter ticked by. *The same players are still on the field, and yet Coach runs the same failed plays again and again! It bugs me that some fine athletes ride the bench!* Sitting on the sideline, Joey dug a trench in the dirt with his spikes, the cleats of which, swinging pendulums, nervously arced back and forth.

Now we're in the fourth quarter and no change! His increased nervousness was not due to the team's inability to score or even worry over his performance if he were put into the game in such a high-pressure situation. Reserves who went into the games in the final minutes and seconds dreadfully feared making the catastrophic mistake that would lose a game and brand them losers, but on this particular evening, Joey's nervousness was rooted in his fear of confronting his coach about not getting in the game. He longed to vent but, lacking courage to confront him, sat timidly. The longer he delayed, the greater his exasperation and the deeper the divots in the grass. *The fullback was stacked up again at the line of scrimmage!* He dug his thumbnail into the wood bench.

Midway through the fourth quarter, his mind wandered to the Heinz History Center and the exhibits of Pittsburgh's athletic teams. Images of the immortal plays, the great heroes, and their legendary exploits when the teams won against impossible odds pounded his brain. Highlights of the Steelers' great seasons in the 1970s blazed before him. *No wonder the slogan, "Steelers nation," is more reality than myth in recent years!*

Nervously fiddling with his kneepads, he heard the blaring announcer from the press box, "Another three-and-out for Kittanning."

Joey hung his head. *Only six minutes to go! No wonder the crowd is restless and the team as lifeless as a sick cow! This is the long-awaited season opener which the fans expect us to win. Yet nothing's working, and we're staring at a 7–0 loss!* Joey could not resist the comparison between the fiery Pittsburgh athletes of yesteryear and his own pathetic timidity as he warmed the bench doing absolutely nothing. *Compared to them, I'm such a loser!*

Four minutes left in the game. In his mind's eye, he saw Bradshaw complete those dazzling passes to Swann and Stallworth and then Franco and Rocky run like gazelles into the end zone. Somehow, the image that stuck in his mind the most was that of Jack Lambert who was the middle linebacker and nerve center of the powerful seventies defense.

Lambert stood up against the toughest opponents and even fired up the legendary Steel Curtain! In the Heinz History Center, I was transfixed when I saw the famous poster of him at the end of a grueling game— teeth missing, blood seeping, totally spent, warrior-scarred. Lambert giving all, me giving nothing. Lambert putting everything on the line, me warming the bench. I just want one good chance! He glanced up at the clock. *Three minutes! Just to have a shot at getting out there and trying! Lambert did it. Mazeroski did it. Clemente did it. The Pirates, the Steelers, and the Penguins routinely do it. Why can't I?*

Bowing his head right there amid the din of the jubilant crowd, he prayed not to win but to overcome his fear. *"Whatever is not of faith is sin." I know that verse and I know it's true. Then why can't I beat my fear? Sis did it in Pittsburgh during the* Hamlet *play. Why can't I do it here? If I perish, I perish. She said it, so I say it too!*

Then the image of Martin Luther confronting the corrupt church of his day rose before his eyes. Luther had the courage to stand against the mob. "Here I stand." Joey recollected his memorable exchange with Pastor Gabe: *"When you come to a crossroad in your life, you'll face a monumental, defining moment, just as Martin Luther did. You'll feel overwhelmed and scared to death, but that's the normal response of a person who waits on God and seeks His will. Joey, God is prepared to bless. Are you positioned to receive? God is activated only at the point of deep faith. The greater your trust in Him, the more demonstrable and miraculous His intervention in your life. Whereas fear undercuts the operation of His Spirit, faith animates it. Remember what your sister did in Pittsburgh during the production of* Hamlet. *Even with hundreds in the audience, she stopped the entire play cold, and you know the wonderful good that came out of her act of heroism. Faith on occasion requires fortitude like Luther's and bravery like Cory's!"*

God is activated only at the point of deep faith. God is activated only at the point of deep faith. Sitting on the sidelines, Joey repeated this to himself over and over again. Imagery of Pittsburgh's sports heroes and Luther's legendary stand, like a hospital patient's fast-drip IV, unleashed a rush of adrenaline in Joey's veins. He looked up at the scoreboard. *Less than two minutes left in this 7–0 game!* The officials had just called a timeout while the trainer examined a Freeport player.

If I perish, I perish! Joey stomped over to the head coach and looked him in the face. "Sir, I intend no disrespect, but it's obvious that our game plan's failing. Why not try something different in these last minutes?" Joey moved closer to the coach. "You have some decent talent riding that bench. Yes, I include myself!" He was inches from the coach's face. "Shouldn't those guys be given a chance?" *I can't believe I feel so calm and am actually doing this!*

Here he was, talking to the head coach, this macho man who, across his life, was notorious for his honed skills of controlling others through intimidation and well-timed outbursts. The coach backed up a step as Joey's verbal barrage continued, "What we're doing isn't working, so why not try something else and give other players a chance?" Dumbfounded, the speechless coach stared at him. "Miss Painter says that doing the same thing over and over again and expecting change defines insanity." Starting for his place on the bench, he glanced back at the coach. *I inhabit a mental institution with a bunch of insane residents!*

The other coaches stared in amazement. Here was Joey dressing down the head coach, and while considerate and courteous, he nevertheless dominated the conversation and stood toe to toe with him.

Some days later, Charles bumped into one of the assistant coaches at the McConnell Waterson store on Market Street in Kittanning. "I've never seen anyone get in the coach's face like Joey did Friday night! The teachers have talked of little else for days! The coaches were completely astounded at Joey's gutsiness!"

Looking at the player still down on the field, Joey retraced his steps. "One more thing, sir. Western Pennsylvania has produced a lot of great NFL quarterbacks—Unitas, Marino, Montana, Kelly, Blanda, Namath, and others. These guys didn't start out as superstars, and I bet they were backed by coaches who encouraged them and gave them a chance!" Joey took a step and again put his face close to the coach. His eyes flamed with passion. "If those superstars had been coached the way we are, they'd have never made it. I intend no disrespect, sir, I really don't, but you'll never convince me I'm wrong!"

Joey stomped back to the bench, the players and coaches around him deathly silent. Joey's teammates stared at the ground and nervously fidgeted with their helmet straps and anxiously chewed their mouthpieces. Who was this wallflower kid who had come out of nowhere and talked to the coach in such a fashion? Further down the bench, Morgan whispered to Bauer, "Mohney must have the balls of a bull!"

"I'd say coconuts!"

"The kid will run Death Valley for weeks!"

The coaches conferred among themselves. After the injured player had hobbled off the field, the head coach strode over to Joey. "Get in there as quarterback and do something to win this game! Go! Now!" As Joey sprinted out on the field, the coach put his hands to his mouth and bellowed, "And be the tiger you were here on the sideline!"

Chapter 19

The astounded Joey sped out to the huddle of the Kittanning High School Wildcats. Although the team had already called their play, Joey told the quarterback that he was out of the game. The quarterback, Todd Cravener, shoved Joey. "I'm not going anywhere! Back to the bench where you belong, a-hole!"

Joey pushed him hard and nearly knocked him off his feet. "You're delaying the game. The coach put me in! Go!"

The astonished quarterback looked at the coach who frantically motioned for him to run to the sideline immediately. "Get off the field! We can't have a delay of game!"

After Joey called a pass play, the team lined up in formation, and Joey dropped back to pass near the end zone. His line blocked poorly, and the opposing defenders swarmed past the front linemen who stood as lifeless as the mannequins in the Montgomery Ward front window. Almost called for a safety, Joey managed to struggle out of the end zone before going down in a disgraceful sack on the two-yard line. Loud boos ascended from the packed bleachers.

Though the adrenaline surged, the jitters evaporated in an instant, and he calmly took control. "Come on, guys, block. We can win this game! The defense ran right through you like melted butter. Block someone!"

He called a pass play, shouted out the signals, and not able to hang on to the faulty snap, fumbled the ball on the one-yard line. He momentarily lost the ball but recovered it at the last second. As the fans booed, the players sluggishly shuffled back to the huddle. Buzz Moorhead, one of the cocky running backs, spoke to Joey as they huddled, "If Todd can't beat this team, I'm sure a hick loser like you can't!"

Grabbing Buzz by the shoulder pads, Joey shoved into another player so hard that both of them were knocked off their feet. Joey leered over Moorhead as he lay on the turf. "You play hard for these ten seconds or you'll answer to me. Do you understand?" With one arm, Joey yanked him to his feet and screamed in his face, "We'll find out who's the man here!" Their helmet guards touched each other. The running back was white in the face.

Some of the crowd booed when they saw this display of temper but most cheered, inspired by Joey's fiery courage which breathed new life into the players. Because of this altercation, the clock ticked down to seconds before a delay-of-game call. Joey was forced to call the last timeout. Ten seconds remained on the official game clock.

On the sideline, Joey chatted with the coach. "They didn't block on the first play, and then the center gave me a bad snap on the second. Moorhead hassled me about being quarterback instead of Todd. Sorry, Coach, I had to put him in his place. That's what the fuss was all about. We can win if we play as a team!"

The coach was greatly heartened by Joey's leadership. "Guys, listen up. We have time for one play, maybe two. We're going to call two pass plays. You linemen block as never before, and you receivers do something to get open. Joey's got the arm, and he'll hit you deep. Now get out there and win this game!"

Back on the field, Joey called the signals. The line blocked well except for the right guard. His opponent came through with ease, but Joey sidestepped him, set up, and fired a forty-yard strike to his wide-open receiver. The ball hit him on the letters, but the receiver dropped the ball. A loud groan went up from the crowd. The clock ticked down to two seconds.

Back in the huddle, Joey calmed the receiver. "Shake it off. Anybody can drop a pass." *Time for one last play!*

"Hit me again, Joey. I can outrun their safety and get wide open!"

Lord, help me. Give me Your wisdom for this play. May Your will be done and may glory come to You. The prayer was fast but sincere.

"No, we're going to fake them out. Everybody in the stadium's looking for a Hail Mary pass, and they know I have the arm." Joey looked downfield between two of his linemen. "Look at the secondary. Those backs are way deep in a prevent defense. I'm calling a quarterback draw. I'll drop back as if to pass, look down field, and fake the long throw, and then run a draw. We can make this work. You linemen need to give me a whole, and the rest of you block downfield!"

The right tackle interrupted, "Lamison missed his block on purpose. He wanted you to be creamed!"

"I did not, a-hole!"

Joey glared at Bart Lamison, the right guard who had missed his block. "I'm running up your tail, pretty boy. If this play fails and we lose this game, it will be because you missed key blocks in the last plays. What will the coach say tomorrow when he sees your two flubbed blocks at this very key point in the game? Get off your rear end, pretty boy, and block your man!"

"The coach said to run pass plays."

"But I have a better vantage here than he does there!"

The two safeties were at midfield, the defensive corners had even dropped off the line some thirty yards, and the four linebackers were also laying back, waiting for the inevitable Hail Mary. Because only three down linemen rushed, Joey at the last minute set the play up in such a way that Freeport's left guard and tackle were double-teamed. "You guys make a hole I can drive a Mack truck through. This play and the game depends on *you!*"

All the fans were on their feet and shouting loudly. They had grown quiet in the fourth quarter, sensing the impending defeat, but Joey's leadership energized them. Heartened as they hadn't been since the start of the game, they were heard the whole way down Wilson Avenue.

Breaking the huddle, Joey dropped back to pass as planned and slyly cocked his arm for a fake pass. Seeing the play develop, the entire team, except for the three down linemen, hastily backpedaled in their prevent defense. Joey looked over the field as though searching for a receiver, cocked his arm, and then zipped through the hole in a mad sprint.

Two linebackers converged on him. While the first one tangled him up and slowed his speed, the second linebacker gave Joey a crushing hit to the side, wedged his hand around the ball, and nearly yanked it out of Joey's grip. Joey managed to hold the ball tightly and delivered a vicious elbow to the linebacker's shoulder pad all in one fluid motion which knocked both linebackers to the ground. Free of the line and linebackers, he streaked down the right sideline, the corners and safeties descending on him as a huge roar went up from the crowd. Approaching the fifty-yard line, he sidestepped the first corner and straight-armed the second. *Only two safeties stand between me and paydirt!*

That's when he heard it. "Run, Joey, run!" Rising above the deafening din, a booming voice issued from the right sideline near the end zone. "Run, Joey!" Joey shook off the first safety and slipped by the second one who, by now a few steps behind him, tripped and fell to the ground.

"Run, Joey, run! Run!" The yell was so loud that Joey, out in the open and running freely along the sideline, looked downfield. Cheering and yelling like crazy, Pete Mohney stood on the sideline. He waved his curled fist madly, and the jugular veins in his neck were engorged as he yelled again and again, "You can do it! Run, Joey, run!"

Though winded, Joey, upon seeing his dad, increased his speed and broke into a huge smile as he sprinted into the end zone near where his father stood. The photo of the smiling Joey was the one that graced the front page of the Saturday *Leader Times*. Joey dropped to his knee, bowed his head for a quick but meaningful prayer, and rose to his feet just as his jubilant teammates pounced on him. The crowd cheered in ecstasy.

"Great job, Joey!" his dad thundered above the din. "You did it!"

As the team gathered back in the huddle to call a play, Pete Mohney ran toward the coaches and from the sideline yelled, "Call a run around the left end! Their right end and corner are completely winded!"

Conferring among themselves, the coaches looked at these two defensive players. Rich Boggs, one of the assistant coaches, said to the head coach, "The guy's right. They're dragging their butts!" He turned to look at Pete. *Who is this guy?* The coach sent in a play.

In the huddle, Joey took charge. "We're going to run a quarterback keeper around left end. I'll drop back to pass and then run. If you block your man, we win the game! It's that simple!" The team clapped in snappy unison, broke the huddle, and lined up. Dropping back to pass, he scanned the flooded right end zone for his receivers, waited while the linebackers drifted back to defend the pass, and then blasted around the left end. The tight end's block on the defensive end was good, but as Joey neared the end zone, the linemen and linebackers swarmed on him like a pack of wolves.

This won't be easy!

Chapter 20

Joey Mohney gouged his feet in the turf, one plodding gash after another. Digging and trudging, his muscles strained, his heart heaved, and adrenaline exploded in his veins as he slowly bulldozed the mountain of flesh forward. A mass of players atop him, he trudged his way to the goal line, stretched his arm full length across it, and collapsed to the turf. He had scored the two-point conversion!

But when his arm was outstretched across the goal line, a foot from one of the defenders slammed down on his hand which encircled the ball. As the defensive player twisted sideways in the surging pile, his spikes dug into Joey's hand. Once the players untangled themselves, Joey tucked his hand behind his back to keep the cavorting players from banging into it.

"We won!"

"You did it, Mohn!"

"You were great! We won!"

"That was fantastic!"

Unaware of his hand injury, the players exuberantly pressed against Joey to congratulate him.

The noise issuing from the stands was deafening as the fans ecstatically cheered. The happiest person in the stadium, Pete Mohney stood along the fence hoping to see his son. Joey glimpsed at his father as he trotted toward the bench.

"You did it, Joey! You did it!"

Back on the sidelines, Joey approached the head coach. "I apologize, Coach. I intended no disrespect." He looked into the eyes of the man he had earlier flummoxed. "Sorry for running a quarterback keeper when you called a pass play."

"You don't have to apologize for anything. I apologize for keeping you on the bench through the exhibition games. You were amazing. I heartily congratulate you for a superior effort."

An assistant coach beamed with joy at the star athlete. "The guys played as a team, but you were the spirited leader."

"Thank you, Coach!"

Before going into the locker room, Joey went over to see his dad. It was a sweet meeting on the sideline as a wet-eyed father hugged his son. "God blessed you real good, Joey! I'm so proud of you!"

"Thanks, Dad."

"To think I almost didn't come to the game. What an answer to prayer!" He looked admiringly at his son. "You did it, Joey! I love you so much!" Pete hugged him again and bowed his head in gratitude. "I just wish your mom was here to see this great day."

"I wish so too, but you're here, and that's a big miracle!"

The whole time they talked, Joey kept his injured hand behind his back, but now he showed his dad. "Dad, I have to get this taken care of." Oozing blood where the cleats dug into the flesh, the thumb had already started to swell.

"How bad is it hurting?"

"A little. Not so much. The joy in my heart is greater than the pain." Joey looked admiringly at his father. "Thanks for coming, Dad. The coach said they'll take me to the hospital to have it x-rayed. I could see you at the hospital if you want to go there."

"Yea, I will."

Joey gave his dad a hug and joined the cheering team and coaches on the sideline. The celebration was frenzied, and the people in the stands chanted in unison, "Go, Joey! Go, Joey!" When Joey lifted his helmet to acknowledge the enthusiastic fans, they yelled and cheered all the more.

Once in the locker room, the trainer examined Joey's hand and temporarily taped it. "You might have a break there or maybe it's just swollen badly. We'll have to take you for x-rays to be sure."

Joey hurriedly showered and dressed. Once out of the locker room, he and the trainer stopped by the after-game party in the gym to briefly join the celebration and acknowledge the team's accolades. He was clearly the center of attention amid the cavorting players.

"Thanks, guys," Joey said when they urged him to comment. "No need cheering me."

"Joey Jazz! Joey Jazz!"

"Come on, guys! Don't praise me! It was a team effort, and the defense played hard the entire game."

"Joey Jazz! Joey Jazz!"

"They gave up one score only. Nobody does that against Freeport. Good work, guys. You won an important game." He held up his bandaged hand. "But right now, we're going for an x-ray."

The *Leader Times* sports writer cornered Joey as he fought his way toward the door. "Can you give me a minute for a fast interview?"

"Sir, talk to the other players instead. They'll give you what you need."

Though the trainer was waiting to take him to the hospital for an x-ray, Joey's immediate intent was to see Laura who waited in the front lobby. Like palace courtiers creating an aisle through which their monarch might pass, the crowd parted as Joey made his way to the lobby, but he was strangely oblivious to the celebration.

I just want to see Laura!

Out in the lobby, Laura stood by the trophy case as planned.

How I love her! "Hi, Laura!"

"Joey, you were fantastic! I'm so proud of you!" Even in the presence of the trainer and many fans who had wondered into the lobby, he kissed her on the cheek.

"I was there with the guys in the gym," he whispered, "and obviously enjoyed the victory, but I wasn't there in my head if that makes sense. I just wanted to be with you and the family."

With the assistant coach waiting at the door, Joey and Laura decided that she would drive Joey's car to the hospital and meet him in the ER. They said their goodbyes, and Joey, abiding by school policy, rode with the trainer.

Out on the field, meanwhile, Pete Mohney ambled along the sidelines in a joyous daze. *Earlier, I lay on the couch in despair, but now a mere few hours later, I'm more joyful than I've been since Ruby was alive. Over these past weeks, I couldn't find a hole deep enough to die in, and now I'm king of the hill!*

A couple friends spoke as he ambled along the sideline. "Congratulations, Pete. Your son was great!" "He won the game—no doubt about it!"

A feeling of utter joy overwhelmed Pete as he made his way to the south end of the field where the band rapturously played after the stunning come-from-behind victory. The cheerleaders cheered as the band played one rousing song after another. Relishing the sweet victory, the fans continued to shout, dance, and high-five each other.

During a break in their cheering, one of the cheerleaders—her name was Molly, Joey and Laura's good friend from the Center Hill church—approached Pete as he stood by the fence. "Hi, Mr. Mohney. You must be so happy. Joey was fantastic!" She drew closer. "Now you come over here and dance with me!" Molly locked her arm in his and pulled him onto the field. "Don't be shy. We dance to honor Joey!"

Before he knew what was happening, always-vivacious Molly led Pete through the gate and toward the end zone. "Come on, get those feet moving. Just like this."

Swept up by the emotion of the moment, Pete Mohney danced and gyrated and whirled in utter bliss to Chuck Berry's 1957 hit, "Rock and Roll Music." It maybe was not dancing, but as he twirled in ecstasy, the tears gushed from his eyes. "What a victory!" He hastily wiped the tears from his eyes. *Molly, you couldn't know my joy nor the hell I've lived through these last months!*

"Yeah, sweet victory, just like the name of this street," Molly shouted as she glanced toward the street.

"What are you talking about?"

Molly pointed to the street sign behind the band stand. "Look there. This *is* Victory Street!"

"Nice coincidence! Well, it was an amazing victory." *In more ways than one! I want to live!* Tears streamed down his face. *Lord, I want to live!*

"I'd say someone's prayers were answered." She gave him a big hug. "Goodbye, Mr. Mohney. Hope you're in church on Sunday.

It's been a while since we've seen your smiling face." She gave him a wink. "We miss you!"

"I'll definitely be there." *It's good to be back in the land of the living. Pastor Gabe, you were so right!*

By himself for a minute, Pete walked over to the spot in the end zone where Joey had sprinted for the winning touchdown. *He crossed the goal line right here. And what a run it was!* He then went over to the other side where Joey had struggled for the extra two-point conversion. He found the spot and dropped to his knee to examine the divots where Joey's spikes had repeatedly dug into the earth. *I can see his cleat gouges. How he struggled to leverage the ball forward!*

He bowed his head in prayer. *Jesus, I thank You for this day. Thank You for standing by me and helping my children even though I turned my back on You. Thank You for this glorious evening*—he turned mid-prayer and peered across the field—*and for what happened here. From now on, I'll be like Joey and Cory and worship You as I should have right along. Please forgive a terrible sinner!*

Outside of the football field, Pete Mohney looked up at the street sign. *Victory Street. What an appropriate name!* Bowing his head in gratitude, he was reminded of the pastor's statement in the sermon he had listened to during the week: "Faith is the ultimate victory." *Never were truer words spoken! Faith is the final, sweet victory, and I want to be victorious again!* He wiped away the tears with the back of his hand.

After walking to his car, Pete drove down North McKean Street, cut over to North Water, crossed the bridge, and went up the hill through the Highlands to the Armstrong County Memorial Hospital.

As he was soon to learn, the ER was a busy place that evening for the Mohney family.

Chapter 21

This Friday evening in late August was a great climax in Jude and Cory's "golden summer of love," a term Cory used in her journal since many spokes converged at this center point, what T. S. Eliot in *Burnt Norton* calls the "still point of the turning world." On that historic night, various principals in the story—Jude and Cory, Professor Charles Claypoole, Tina Reynolds, Duke Manningham, Pete Mohney, Joey, and even Zoe—struggled to inch their way forward against odds that were, for each, personally formidable and life-defining.

The evening was significant not only because so many of these people simultaneously experienced their "marvelous maturation moments"—another Cory journal phrase—but also because numerous instances of divinely orchestrated phenomena were amply evident. One of these occurred at the hospital where three people, Jude and Cory and Joey, simultaneously converged for treatment, Pete and Laura anxiously standing by.

Directly across from the ER station, Jude and Cory's wounds were treated in the center bay after their cave-in disaster at the mushroom mine. The door to their room closed when Joey entered the ER with his trainer, Jude and Cory did not realize that Joey had proceeded to a side bay.

When Pete Mohney entered the ER a short while later, however, to inquire at the station about his son's whereabouts, Jude heard him. Shocked to see Cory's dad out of the house, let alone the hospital, Jude dashed out to the desk. "Mr. Mohney, what in the world brings you to the ER?"

Even before x-rays and treatment, the tending nurses allowed Joey to go over to Cory's bay. Because their respective stories were complicated and lengthy, they could not talk through the details, but each gave a sigh of relief that their injuries, obviously evident, were not serious. Cory minimized the injury to her foot—"It's only a sprain"—and saved the catastrophic cave-in details for later, just as Jude dismissively noted that the cut in his head, despite the large dressing, was "not a big deal." His precise words, for Cory's benefit, were, "A scratch, a scratch. 'Tis not so deep as a well nor so wide as a church door, but 'tis enough, 'twill serve."

Cory smiled and quipped, "*Romeo and Juliet!*" She turned to Joey. "Jude can't sleep at night if he hasn't quoted Shakespeare at least ten times through the day!"

Joey then offered a couple-sentence summary of his exploits on the football field. Jude and Cory delighted in seeing the effervescent Pete enthralled with Joey's exploits. Cory watched with fascination. *Our tale of woe can wait since Joey is rightfully center stage!* Pete beamed with joy as Joey summarized the victorious game.

Forced to settle for this hasty ER greeting, they had no choice but to delay their detailed account of the day's momentous events. Like an outside observer, Jude philosophically ruminated as he watched the proceedings. *We'll talk about these events when we recon-vene at the house later. For now, I won't mention that in the space of a couple hours, I found and lost my dad, found and lost the manuscript, and found and lost Zoe. I haven't seen Cory's dad animated like this in months. He stands with his shoulders back, faced locked in a full smile, and fingers repeatedly creasing the brim of his hat. I simply do not have the nerve to tell them that their beloved dog is gone forever. Why do I have to be the one to spoil this bliss?*

Back at the farmhouse a short while later, the evening of gut-wrenching mood swings began. Elvis Presley's "When My Blue Moon Turns" played in the background:

> Well, when my blue moon turns to gold again,
> When my rainbow turns the clouds away,
> Well, when my blue moon turns to gold again,
> You'll be back within my arms to stay

Over Cory's homemade apple dumplings, drizzled with cara-mel sauce, the family discussion journeyed through a blow-by-blow description of the day's events. The item that launched the conver-sation was the answer to Joey and Pete's painful and inevitable ques-tion, "Where's Zoe?"

Since only Jude and Cory could answer that query, they jointly shared their account first.

"We'd rather hear the details of your exciting victory," Cory began as she looked at Joey, "and Dad's emotional turnaround that landed him at the game, but you'll want to hear this first since it involves our beloved Zoe." She laid her hand on Jude's arm. "You were with him the entire time, so you go first."

With that, Jude related the sad account in the mine—Zoe's bravery, their near-death experiences, the cave-ins, the strange rev-elation of Abe Badoane, and Grandpa's lost manuscript. Cory took over at this juncture and described their escape through the coalmine tunnel, their torturous journey down the hill, the easy glide on the river, and the help of the gracious man who met them at the dock and took them to the hospital. Putting his arm around Cory, Jude concluded the narrative, "It's a tale of loss, and that loss is great, so I won't minimize it, but our relief and gratitude that we survived these calamities is obviously greater."

Laura beheld Jude and Cory with wonderment. "What did it feel like when you saw light streaming in the coalmine door?"

Cory immediately responded, "A verse in Ecclesiastes perfectly describes it—'Truly the light is sweet, and it is pleasant for the eyes to behold; But if a man lives many years and rejoices in them all, yet let him remember the days of his darkness' (Ecclesiastes 11:7–8). The dark hours were truly awful, and we'll never forget them, but the light was sweet beyond description!"

Jude picked up the thought, "How could we ever forget those hours of darkness in the mine when the Lord delivered us so miracu-lously?" *I still can't believe we got out of that trap alive!*

"Listen to the lyrics of that Elvis song," Laura interjected. "Your blue moon has turned to gold, at least a large part of it!"

Eating their dumplings, they listened to the Elvis song in the background:

> When the memories that linger into my heart
> Memories that make my heart go cold
> However some day they gonna live again sweetheart
> And my blue moon again will turn to gold

"Good job, Laura!" Joey swallowed a big bite. "That song is really relevant!"

While all five of them reflected again on the various losses, it was Jude's comment that sobered the proceedings. "Through all the joy, the loss of my dad pains me a lot. He was a man of such potential, but his life tragically derailed decades ago." Still working the kinks out of his arm, Jude slid his hand back and forth along the top slat of the chairback. "That man's blue moon did not turn to gold!"

Of the Mohney family members, it was Pete who was most shocked to learn that Jude was Abe's natural son. "I just can't believe it, but it makes sense when you think about it."

"In what way?" Joey inquired.

"They're both brainy types, and Jude even has some of Abe's mannerisms." Pete reflected for a moment. "How sad to learn he's your dad one minute and lose him the next!"

That Jude lost his dad was heartbreaking, but Jude had lived his life without a father, so his loss was not like that of the child whose life had been intimately intertwined with the parent on a daily basis. Because the novel, similarly, was never in hand, its existence in Jude's mind had only ever been insubstantial and tenuous, its discovery a very long shot, so that loss, while poignant, was not egregious.

Zoe was a different matter altogether. Over the last couple months, he had become their constant companion, "our best bud" or "Zoebud," as Joey often called him. It was Zoe's sacrificial attempt to save Jude and Cory that brought tears to their eyes.

"Such a selfless sacrifice!" Jude said over and over.

"He literally laid down his life for us," Cory added.

"This will sound crazy," Jude continued, "but I actually feel some guilt that I made it and he didn't!" *He died in my place!* "Not to end on a down note, I feel, quoting the Elvis song, that those memories of Zoe make my heart go cold."

As Jude and Cory finished their tale, Laura turned to Cory. "What was it like to lie there alone all that time? I can't imagine what you went through, especially after you heard the crash in the mines and assumed Jude was dead."

"I was out of my mind berserk! Period!"

"I couldn't have waited in agony like you."

Tears formed in Cory's eyes as she relived the trauma. *Where do I start?* "Cerebrally, I knew I should be strong, look to God, and put my trust in Him. I know the maxims, the comforting truths of our faith, but I didn't bank on them as much as I should have." She took a sip of tea. Sitting beside her, Jude massaged his deltoids and biceps and then squeezed Cory's shoulder.

How to best describe my experience? I might as well say it! "Truth is, I've never been more scared, not even close. I wept terribly and collapsed emotionally. I had hobbled toward the mine entrance, even made it halfway, but then it hit me that I didn't have a light since I'd given mine to Jude. I'd have seen nothing. I crawled back to the tree and collapsed in a heap because I was too unsteady to limp on my foot. I tried to pray, and words gushed forth, but they were little more than the frantic screams of a desperate woman. Like Claudius in *Hamlet*, "My words fly up, my thoughts remain below. Words without thoughts never to heaven go."

"Good connection to *Hamlet!*" Jude interrupted.

"Well, that was me. You can imagine what it was like. The longer I dwelled on it, the more certain I was that Jude and Abe had been killed and Zoe too. How does one handle that kind of sorrow?"

"I know I couldn't!" Laura exclaimed.

"I was totally frantic and thought I'd go insane with grief. Like Job, I had lost so much! 'Jude, Jude!' I kept crying."

Cory paused again and ran her finger down her foot boot to massage her lower leg. "I was up in my room getting ready a while ago and thought of how I should have reacted. I know one can't stockpile the faith, the strength, the wisdom, and the grace that are needed when hardship hits us broadside as it hit me this evening. God gives us those traits only in the moment of need, but in my case, I wasn't a giant of faith. To be honest, my cries were borderline hysterical." She stopped her account and looked blankly out the kitchen window, tears forming in her eyes. "I just knew Jude was killed. How does one handle grief like that?"

Laura squeezed Joey's hand. "I know I couldn't!"

Cory wiped the tears from her eyes, got up from her chair, and sat on Jude's lap. "Did I have faith when I needed it? Not to the extent I should have, but a verse came to me—'The angel of the Lord encamps round about thee'—which calmed me some and at least tempered my hysteria. I suppose my cry was probably that of all people in such a hideous place. I wanted to believe and remain stoic and calm, but I lacked adequate faith to actually feel that."

"You were incredibly brave!" Laura remarked.

"Here's how I see it. I settled down after a bit, but the larger truth is that God answered my prayer despite my lack of faith." A smile came to her face. "The answer to that prayer is right here!" Cory craned her head sideways and kissed Jude.

After Jude and Cory finished their narrative, Pete filled in some gaps about the history and operation of the coal mine that lay atop the limestone quarry.

"You've answered the question I've incessantly pondered," Jude remarked.

"Which is?"

"How could a coal conveyor belt drop through a limestone ceiling like magic?"

Pete expanded his explanation, "Because my dad had worked in the coal mine when I was a little boy, I visited it various times and learned quite a bit in those years."

"I had no idea," Joey interjected, "that Grandpa was a coal miner."

"Yes, he was, a very long time ago. That mine's been closed for decades."

Cory looked admiringly at her father. "Now it's your turn. How did you end up at the football game?"

"It begins with Gabe's sermon which you gave me to listen to. It made me take heart in a way I hadn't for many months. I'd been under deep conviction and even embarrassed to tell the truth for being such a poor father." He pointed to Joey and Cory and warmly clasped Joey's shoulder. "The sermon helped me see that I had to shake depression and my addiction to pain meds too. I'd become a kind of addict because I was afraid of what would happen if I quit taking my pills." A lump formed in Pete's throat. "I was in an awful hole, but the thing is, I didn't know it. Nobody had more self-pity than me."

Joey rubbed his bandaged hand. "Don't be so hard on yourself!"

"I knew I had to resume normal living. Listening to the radio broadcast of the football game on WTYM was the final straw. Maybe I should let it go at that."

Cory spoke for the group, "Are you kidding? You haven't talked like this for years. We've been praying for such a happy day, so keep going!"

Pete gazed at the smiling faces of his family. *I guess the others want that too!* "The radio broadcast roused me a lot. 'What am I doing?' I admonished myself. 'My son's trying his best to get on the football field while I sit here missing his first game. Maybe this will be his big day.' I quickly dressed and drove to the football field. I haven't moved that fast in ages! Well, I arrived halfway through the third quarter and saw all of the fourth quarter including Joey's touchdown and two-point conversion. I was on the south end of the field when Joey streaked into the end zone. I was right there and saw it all. I yelled at him during his touchdown run. Joey, did you hear me?"

"Are you kidding? You roared like a T-rex! That spurred me to run faster than ever!"

"What a moment!" Pete stared for a while out the kitchen window. "I've never seen him run like that. And to think I nearly missed it!" He again clasped Joey's shoulder. "Your mom would have been so proud of you!"

"Thanks, Dad."

Pete drew the back of his hand across his cheek to wipe a tear. "But I couldn't figure out what was happening during those first two plays after you went in the game. Something with that other player."

"His name is Blake Moorhead, but the players call him Buzz. He wanted Todd to quarterback instead of me. He's a mouthy kid, and like his family, always in trouble. I wasn't about to take anything from him."

As Pete ended his account, he remembered a final detail. "One last thing. Remember Molly at our church, the cheerleader?" The group nodded. "She came up to me after the game and danced with me in the end zone!"

Cory's mouth dropped open. "You were dancing?"

"I kid you not. Before I knew what was going on, she had me dancing right there at the end of the football field. Your old man went from dozing on the couch to dancing on the field! People must think Pete Mohney is looney. I was ready for the little men in white coats to take me off in a straitjacket!" The group heartily laughed at one of the few comic statements Pete Mohney had uttered in a long time.

Cory, who had suffered the most, sat in bliss, a smile on her lips as she beheld her father. *Dad hasn't been this joyful for years!*

As the evening wound down and each had completed their narratives, Pete acted as family patriarch for the first time in ages. He motioned for everyone to get quiet and tilted his coffee cup to savor the last drop. "There's one remaining thing before we call it quits for the day. We should have a brief memorial service or something to thank God for Zoe and these wonderful victories."

Joey spoke for the group, "You're right, Dad. That is a great idea!"

Chapter 22

P ete nodded at Cory to indicate that she, rightly or wrongly, was the family's spiritual head who should take charge.

Knowing his body language, Cory reached for the Bible which lay on top of the Monopoly game. "What should I read?" *What Scriptures can buoy up hurting hearts like ours?*

"You're the Bible expert," Jude casually remarked, "and nobody will disagree!" Though solemn, they all chuckled.

Cory rose to the occasion. *I can do this.* "When we think of Zoe, we think how mysterious his presence was among us and how he always had two natures—the canine and the human. His thinking, actions, and even emotions were more human than doglike, so how do you wrap your head around something so mysterious? Also, he was a gift from God, and like most spiritual matters, his life was one big mystery." Cory located a specific text. "This verse addresses the notion that many aspects of spirituality remain a difficult secret. Deuteronomy 29:29 says, 'The secret things belong to the Lord our God.' Other verses make a similar point."

Jude nodded in agreement. "I completely agree. There are many things about God which one never figures out, just as Zoe's two natures baffled us."

We need to pay tribute to our amazing pet. That's what this is all about. "Zoe was such a gift to all of us," Cory continued, "so that's why James 1:17 also applies. 'Every good and perfect gift is from above and comes down from the Father of lights with whom there is no variation or shadow of turning.' Isn't that so true? Zoe was a

God-given gift to all of us. Anybody else have a verse or something else to say?"

Jude reflected as he massaged his temple. "Here's another strange thing. Remember when I said that I didn't see Zoe during the explosion? That still puzzles me. I honestly don't think he was there, though I admit that the explosion and blasting rocks distracted me just a bit!"

"Was it that bad?" Joey asked.

"The explosion was a huge bomb blast that sprayed rocks, limestone, and coal in every direction."

"Tell them about the gouge in the cross."

"Good idea. We forget to tell you guys that the front of the upright beam has a really large and deep gouge in it. If we hadn't been standing behind that cross, we'd have been goners. But let me return to the mysterious business of Zoe. He wasn't there, but after the explosion, he was there by our sides again. Absent one minute, present the next!"

Pete leaned forward so far that he nearly tipped over his bowl. "Where had he gone?"

"I have no idea, but here's another strange thing that happened when I lost my step on the conveyor belt. When my foot slipped, we should have plummeted to our deaths, but it was as though my foot landed on something solid in midair. I'll never been able to explain that. My foot had literally come off the skinny belt tread. It was all so crazy at that time, and I certainly wasn't thinking properly, but I'm still sure that happened."

"What's your foot slipping got to do with mystery dog Zoebud?" Joey asked.

"Just when I regained my footing on the belt and breathed a huge sigh of relief, I looked down. I don't know why—maybe to see if Zoe had seen my near disaster. I scanned the area for him, but I'm positive he wasn't there. At the time, I couldn't dwell on it because I had a few things on my mind...and a lovely lass on my back! Still, I'm certain he had moved from the spot where he'd been."

Cory broke in, "Did you hear Jude say that it was Zoe who had looped the rope around the cross and then pointed like a bird dog at the conveyor belt? It sounds crazy, but the escape plan was Zoe's and not ours. Right, Jude?"

"Absolutely. Zoe was our savior."

Overcome with emotion, all of them grew quiet. Pete fingered a picture of Zoe which he brought from the den and occasionally brushed a tear from his eye. *I can't believe he's gone! What if this makes me lapse back into depression? When Cory was at work and Joey at school, I spent hours and hours with that dog. I loved him!*

Laura reached for the Bible. "I keep thinking of what I was reading recently in the psalms. When the Jews had been transported to Babylon, they were so sad. The writer speaks of that in Psalm 137 when he says the deported Jews sat down by the rivers of Babylon and wept when they remembered the destruction of Jerusalem. May I read this verse?"

Cory nodded vigorously. "Please! It sounds very relevant."

After finding Psalm 137, Laura perused the verses. "Here it is. 'We hung our harps upon the willows in the midst of it.' Then when their captors asked them to sing a song, the psalm writer says, 'How shall we sing the Lord's song in a foreign land?' That's exactly how I feel tonight. We're trying to put a happy face on this, but we're all as sad as exiles in a foreign land." She paused and looked in at the den. "That's how it feels without beautiful Zoe in there on the couch. Sorry to put it so bluntly, but there's no song in me."

Pete stood up and stretched. *I should be the family leader. It's time for me to be a man again!* "Yes, but we must press onward, just as Cory and Joey pressed forward after their mom died, and I took a shameful vacation from life." He turned to Cory and Joey. "You moved on when I didn't. All of us have to do that now. I'm not about to relapse, even though our Zoe's gone." Pete looked at Jude. "I'm sorry too about Abe, but Cory and Jude made it, and we have to really praise God for that."

"That's what the Apostle Paul says about struggling against defeat," Jude responded. "That's in 2 Corinthians, isn't it?" Laura handed him the Bible and Jude turned to the passage in 2 Corinthians. "Yes, here it is in chapter 2, verses 8 and 9. 'We are hard-pressed on every side, yet not crushed; we are perplexed, but not in despair;

persecuted but not forsaken; struck down but not destroyed.' Sad though we are, we are not destroyed."

They held hands in a circle around the table as Cory offered a prayer of thanksgiving for Zoe and their safe escape. "Increase our understanding, we pray, to comprehend the deep things of life which people can't grasp, like Abe's tortured life. We pray for the healing of our distraught emotions as we work through this painful adversity, especially Jude's loss of his dad and the coveted manuscript. And, Lord, how we do thank You for our marvelous pet, Zoe!"

When she was done, Pete prayed as he hadn't in years. "I'm not one who prays often, especially in public, but the circumstances are very different this evening." He bowed his head. "Thank You, Lord God, for the way my children took over headship of my poor family and the farm too. And how they handled themselves. I mean, after their mother's death and my awful depression."

Because prayer is something that is very private and difficult for Pete Mohney, he spoke haltingly at first, especially since his emotions were rocking like a raft during a storm on Lake Erie. Growing more confident as he proceeded, he then prayed for forgiveness. "And, God, I pray that you'll forgive me for forsaking my duties as a dad through all these years. I've been awful. Thank You for loving me and standing by me and my dear family when I didn't deserve it. I guess you could say for giving me another chance. Forgive me for…hating You when You allowed my dear Ruby to die. She was a beautiful jewel!"

Completely overcome with emotion, Pete temporarily stopped altogether. The others patiently waited. "I especially thank You that Cory and Jude are alive. And that You gave Joey the chance he wanted and deserved for so long. We love You, God. I just want to say all this, even though I don't know how to pray. I don't even know what prayer is. It's just my way because I'm the lost little lamb alone in the dark!"

Tears of weeping and tears of joy streamed down every face. After a round of heartfelt hugs, the epic Friday evening ended.

*****

Trying to make sense of it all, Charles attempted across many long months to piece together the components of the Jude/Cory saga, a mission that led to his reflecting by the hour on the various people and events of their love. He rode along the back roads of Armstrong County, sat in the Center Hill church cemetery, spent evenings in Little Gidding, dined at The Mariner on the Allegheny River, and immersed himself in other key environments—Vinlindeer, Heinz Chapel, Jude, and Cory's trail on the ridge in Reesedale—to deepen his insight into their precious love, "more hauntingly beautiful," he wrote in his journal, "than a Grecian tale of triumphant love."

Of the hundreds of events, this late Friday evening gathering at the Mohney farmhouse was the one Charles relished the most. "It's always been my favorite chapter of their love story," he explained to Pastor Gabriel one evening in his library study. "I tell you, Gabe, I luxuriate in its loveliness the way a connoisseur repeatedly rolls a gourmet wine in the mouth to prolong the savory joy. Well, you don't know that joy, but we sometime winebibbers do! The image of this loving family sitting around the table and telling stories, laughing, sharing, hugging, and embracing the way they did that Friday night warms this old heart every time I think on it."

"It was a lovely evening."

Charles closed his volume of Shakespeare's play which he had been reading. "I'm sure you know why, Gabe. They have what I never had—loving family members. But it's not just that."

"What else?"

"They relish life in a way I envy, and don't get me started on Cory and Joey's faith. Pete and I have always been part of the 'I want to believe but don't seem to quite get it' crowd. You know about the world's doubting Thomases!"

"The heart can doubt, but don't let it become hard, for 'he who hardens his heart will fall into calamity'" (Proverbs 28:14).

"In the academic world of skepticism and cynicism, the emotive lust for life, so amply evident in the Mohney household that evening, died a slow and painful death, decades ago, on the altar of modernity. I assure you, however, that Grove City College, like Hillsdale College, remains and island of sanity in a raging sea."

In the end, it was Cory and Jude's journals that afforded Charles the best window into the Friday evening post-game gathering in the Mohney kitchen. Capturing so graphically many of the details, Cory at Charles's request shared several pages of her journal, which enabled him to become a participant in that evening. Reading her account, he vicariously smelled "the aroma of the freshly baked apple dumplings, drizzled with caramel sauce and the cinnamon spice sticks that filled the air." When people commented on the tastiness of her apple dumplings, Cory invariably replied, "I always use Old Mary's recipe."

Her journal entry was filled with an artist's visual details: "The vanilla ice cream melting down the sides of the piping hot apple dumplings, the flickering flame of the Pumpkin Harvest Candle, the moon playing hide n' seek with the clouds through the kitchen window, Dad's fingering the bone which Zoe chewed by the hour, and Joey reenacting the fake he put on the linebackers when he adroitly avoided their tackles."

Charles was also drawn to the details which Jude included in his journal: "Pete's standing by the sink with his arm proudly around his son, Joey's holding his arm up much of the time so his hand didn't throb in pain, and Laura's washing dishes at the sink so Cory didn't have to stand on her injured foot." Cory noted as well that Jude "often ran his fingers along his bandaged head, massaged his temples (he still had a mild headache from the accident), and rubbed hand lotion into his rope-burned fingers."

The thing that struck Charles the most was the way in which the Mohney family handled the turbulent events and devastating losses of the day. Joey's victory, Pete's sloughing off depression, and Jude and Cory's escape were triumphs—"history-making moments in a family's life," Charles opined to Pastor Gabe. "But those happy successes were undercut by some pretty heavy events of the day. Of course, I refer to Abe's death, the loss of Jeremiah's precious manuscript—I really do believe it was a masterpiece—and the death of their beloved pet. Those are big hits, Gabe, very big hits!"

"I completely agree, but they fainted not. They remembered wise Solomon's aphoristic gem: 'If you faint in the day of adversity, your strength is small.' They fainted not, professor, because their strength is great indeed. By the way, for your benefit, I quoted Proverbs 24:10."

"Maybe that's why they could withstand all that loss and adversity and still brim with buoyant life as they sat around the kitchen table that momentous evening. I once talked about this very thing with Jude. I've never forgotten his response. 'You, Professor Chuck, merely witnessed the spontaneous outpouring of the family's deep and abiding spirituality.' Spontaneous outpouring! I find that extremely profound."

"Of course, it's profound—just like Jude."

"Well, then Jude winked at me and, smiling, quipped, 'Maybe it's time you take an inventory of your spirituality.'"

"How did you respond?"

"I wisecracked, 'My spirituality is code blue. It needs a shock with the spiritual paddles!' I put a huge smile on my professorial face, but comic disguises don't mask the anguish of a desperate heart. You men of the cloth know a bit about such duplicity."

"A great deal, in fact!"

Chapter 23

S tartled awake by a strange dream that same night, Joey resolved to share it with Cory and his dad the next morning, even though the family was still a bundle of emotions. Jude and Cory were alive, and the gratitude for that was endless, but the house, in Pete's words, is "unbelievably empty without Zoe!"

Joey greeted Cory and Pete at the breakfast table. "How's your foot, sis?"

"Not so bad, thanks. I have to hobble a bit, but it's nothing to what it could have been. How's your hand? That's a nasty injury."

"Just a hairline fracture. It's more like a bad bruise."

Cory turned to Pete. "And how did you sleep, Dad?"

"The best I've slept in months, even though Zoe's gone, and I miss him terribly!"

It's time to tell them, even if they think I'm crazy. I want them to know about this strange dream. "In my dream, I kept hearing swashing sounds, sort of like splashing water. It was so real as if the sounds were right beside me. I listened more carefully—I'm talking about in my dream—and after a short while, I thought I heard someone swimming. At first, I couldn't identify it but felt I should be able to since I've heard that exact sound before. I got more frustrated by the minute that I couldn't identify it. After listening some more, I made out the noise of hard breathing as someone does during vigorous exertion. Or maybe swimming. I've heard that exact sound but can't remember where or when."

Cory tried to be empathetic but couldn't grasp the significance of the dream. "I know this is important to you, but why be startled awake by swimming sounds?"

"It's hard to explain."

"What's so significant about a dream of swimming or water sounds? Sorry, but I'm missing the significance."

"Here's the really strange part. I listened very carefully to the panting, grunting sounds of the swimmer. I couldn't make them out for the longest time, but then it hit me. It actually startled me awake in the middle of the night. The sound was exactly like the one Zoe made when I swam with him at Bella Lou on the Allegheny."

"Really?"

"That's it! I dreamed of Zoe swimming!"

Between bites of bacon and egg, Cory contemplated Joey's dream. "You dreamed of a time when you swam with Zoe? How does that differ from the dreams all of us have had of Zoe? I don't mean to be difficult, but I'm not seeing the importance."

"That's the part that's tough to explain."

"Now that he's dead, we'll all be thinking about him and probably dreaming too. I did last night, in fact."

"Keep going."

"In my dream, Zoe was lying between Jude and me up on Vinlindeer, and then he took off after a chipmunk. Wonder what Freud would make of that little nothing incident! I simply dreamed of a typical Zoe incident, and maybe that's what you did too."

How can I make her understand? "Here's what I'm saying." Joey hesitated. *She's going to think this is really strange, but I have to say this.* "I think Zoe's alive, and I believe I was hearing him swim during the night. I don't think it was a dream."

"I wish you were right. How sweet that would be!" Cory excused herself to go upstairs to retrieve a sketchpad in her bedroom.

Joey wiped his mouth with a napkin and stood up to depart. "Got to go too, Dad. I want to call Pastor Gabe and get his opinion on this before Laura picks me up pretty soon. She's taking me into school so I can view the films of last night's game. Had I told you that? Guess what part I want to see most?"

"Your touchdown!"

"No. When I knocked Moorhead off his feet!"

"Before you go, I want to ask you something." Out of respect for his father, Joey sat down again. "Do you really think Zoe's alive? You're serious about your dream?"

Giving the question honest thought, Joey reflected. "I don't know what to say. I know it's just a feeling, but it was so very real. Sorry, Dad, but I have to go."

"I know you do."

"We'll pick this up later."

On the way into school, Joey and Laura chatted about Kittanning's victory.

"I just can't say it often enough, Joey. The game was great, and you were super!"

"Thanks, but right now, it's this dream of Zoe that excites me."

"No wonder!"

As they continued their conversation in the lobby, a number of the players approached Joey to congratulate him for Kittanning's big win. No doubt about it, Joey Mohney was the hero of the hour.

After several others acknowledged his prowess, Joey and Laura, strolling to the lobby corner, tried to piece together Zoe's final moments: his exploits in the mine, his heroism in trying to save Jude, his death, and Joey's dream. It was the latter point they hadn't yet discussed.

"Maybe Cory's being overly skeptical," Laura suggested. "Just because we don't understand dreams doesn't mean they're not important."

Todd the quarterback, Buzz Moorhead, Bart (Lamy) Lamison, and a couple other players sauntered over to Joey and Laura as they chatted about Joey's dream of the swimming sounds. Still licking their wounds from the humiliation of the night before, the three players were especially agitated at seeing Joey the recipient of so much praise. In front of the whole town, Todd, the rising star expected to be sought after by college scouts far and wide, had been ingloriously upstaged, and Moorhead and Lamison publicly humiliated. Their hatred of Joey, fueled by his new acclaim, eclipsed their joy of the come-from-behind victory. Though several feet removed from Joey and Laura, the three football players eavesdropped.

After listening to Joey and Laura a bit more, the trio interrupted. "Excuse me for listening in"—Todd took the lead—"but I want to know if I have my facts right. I couldn't help but hear your intelligent conversation. You say wonder dog was buried under tons of limestone out at the mushroom mine but now lives and swims at night? Just resurrected his sweet little ass right up through that mountain of stone!"

"*No hay problema* for Super Dog," Moorhead sarcastically taunted. "Just like Jesus, eh? Sounds perfectly logical!"

Strident and belligerent, Todd squared himself to look directly into Joey's face and then snickered sarcastically. "Bart, what do you think? I mean, who could doubt such a sensible story?"

"The thing about you religious fanatics," Bart Lamison joined in, "is that you can't accept cold hard facts. You're not living in the real world. Our sociology teacher told us about a book he's reading that says you Christian freakfaces have lost your critical thinking skills. That's what's happened to you. Your freaking dog died!"

"Use some reason!" Moorhead jeered. "Put your big boy pants on and get over your damn loss!"

Todd drew closer to the couple. "Maybe Super Dog will be at your house when you get home this evening. Maybe, like Hercules, he cleaned all the rubble and filth out of the mine stables."

"Or maybe he helped you win the game last night," Lamison taunted.

"No," Todd cut in, "that's impossible."

"How so?"

"Because I saw on TV that Super Mutt swam the English Channel and is now being interviewed on the Eiffel Tower!"

The relentless ridicule was little different from what Joey endured much of the time from this small clique, but today, there was a notable exception. Apart from Todd, Moorhead, and Lamison, the other football players, for a change, avoided the mockery fest. Genuinely impressed by Joey's athletic feat, they were not eager to dethrone the obvious star.

Secretly wanting to befriend Joey and even publicly compliment him for his outstanding performance, they wanted to acknowledge him as the team leader, but in keeping with the typical actions of the weak, they were peer-pressured into silence by the dominants. Choosing allegiance to the group over respect for self, the tribally defined minions stood in shameful silence and witnessed the verbal mugging of an excellent athlete. As Jude explained to Joey, "Wiping off the slime of self-betrayal at day's end has become a commonplace ritual for these pathetic weaklings!"

Chapter 24

W hen Charles stopped by the farmhouse that afternoon for a short visit, Pete told him about Joey's dream. "I'm not sure if I believe it or not—I refer to the part of Zoe living—but I sort of do because I want that so much. When I told Joey that, Cory said I was most likely confusing 'emotion, what I wanted, and reason, what was possible.' She said people do that a lot. She's probably right, as usual, so I kept quiet." Temporarily dropping the subject, Pete kicked a stone on the lane.

As the two of them strolled along, they hit briefly on highlights in the news—the earthquake in Armenia that killed 60,000 and the launching of the Hubble Space Telescope—and then Pete again brought the conversation around to Joey's dream. "The longer I listened to Joey and Cory this morning, the more I thought about the crazy events of the last twenty-four hours. I'm not an overly religious person, Chuck. I don't have to tell you that because you and I share some pretty heavy doubts." He smiled indicating that he meant to say nothing offensive.

"No offense taken. Keep going."

"Well, even thick-headed me can see the miracles that happened right before our eyes. Joey came out of nowhere to be the hero of the football game, and Jude and Cory escaped that death trap. I know the mines and have often visited the ones in the county, including Cadogan, Sagamore, Numine, Brady's Bend, Brick Church, and many others. No one gets out of a situation like that, Chuck. I mean nobody. Both of these events defied all odds."

"They were astounding."

Pete rested his foot on the fence rail as he looked across the meadow. "Here's what I'm trying to say. If both of those events were miracles, and who could say they weren't, why couldn't Zoe be alive too?" Pete stole a fast glance at Chuck and noted his obvious skepticism. "You don't believe it, you doubting Thomas!"

"I just don't know what to think."

"I'm saying that the Mohneys may experience yet another miracle."

"Anything's possible."

"Joey even wants to go up to Reesedale to look at the river where they used to swim. By the Tarzan rope. I think he has it in his head that he might find Zoe swimming there! I know that sounds crazy, but Joey's convinced he's alive."

More expansive in his speech than he had been in months, Pete continued talking to Charles as they delighted in the beautiful Saturday afternoon. Charles was elated at the fast turnaround in the family's fortune. Having spent many lonely evenings with the Mohneys across the years, he had desperately hoped for this type of change. The truth is Cory's sorrow, her near-rape, and Abe Badoane's death have been deeply traumatic. *I won't tell Pete, but these events have pushed me even closer to unbelief. If my friend here only knew how I struggle with my faith these days!* "Go on, Pete."

"After Joey went out the door, I called Pastor Gabe. Joey didn't get a chance to tell me what pastor said to him during their conversation. Guess I just couldn't wait any longer."

"What did the wise one say?"

"He was sympathetic and thought the idea that Zoe might be alive wasn't all that far-fetched. I can't get his words exactly right— something about faith not looking through 'rational eyes.'"

"Sounds like Gabe."

"When I asked him to explain, he said faith doesn't 'rely on logic and is never based on it.' I wrote that statement down since half the time that guy's over my head." Pete reached for an envelope in his shirt pocket. "Where is it? It was in one of these pockets. Got it. Welcome to Gabe's world. 'Logic is the death knell for people who live by faith.'"

"That's Gabe, our exemplar and chief practitioner of faith!"

Pete ran his hand along the fence rail that had been painted earlier in the summer and stepped back to appreciate its beauty. Lifting his eyes to the barn and buildings, he also marveled at their pristine condition. "These young folks have sure made this place beautiful. It was a mess before they restored some order."

Charles surveyed the buildings. "I completely agree. They've worked hard." *It's obvious that Pete wants to continue the topic of Joey's dream and Gabe's tantalizing comments on faith. Time to track back to that favorite subject!* "What else did Gabe say?"

"Before he hung up, he asked me what the chances were that Daniel could escape the lions' den or Shadrach, Meshach, and Abednego survive Nebuchadnezzar's fiery furnace. In both cases, the miraculous occurred because—this is vintage Gabe talk—faith 'specializes in the impossible.' That's another of his phrases. Pastor told Joey that God didn't stop doing miracles in Bible days. So I ask you again, Professor, just what do you make of this? You're a deeper thinker than me by a long shot."

Charles thought for a long moment before responding. "Truth is, I don't know what to say. It was a miracle that Jude and Cory escaped. I'm not at all uncomfortable in saying that, and Joey's exploits on the football field were wonderful and long overdue, I might add. But Joey's dream is qualitatively different. If you don't mind, I prefer to reserve comment on that for the time being. That's a bit more implausible, but to be perfectly honest, my skepticism is coming apart at the seams these days. Reading Stephen Hawking's *A Brief History of Time* has complicated my thinking on this enigmatic topic."

"I hadn't heard of that book."

"It's a *New York Times* best seller that just came out this year." Charles stroked his mustache and then his beard. "Frankly, I don't know quite what to think anymore, but I will confide this to you, Pete. It isn't just my ongoing reason-versus-faith battle that worries me right now."

"I've sensed that since I detect a preoccupation."

"It isn't just the faith thing." Charles placed his hand on the top rail and grasped it so hard his fingertips turned white. "It's something else that's been eating away at me." *How much should I say to Pete in the wake of the jubilant happenings of these last joyous hours? I don't want to rain on his happy parade, but as we've been good friends for many long years, I feel the need to come clean.*

"Go ahead and say it, Chuck. I want to hear what's on your mind."

"It's Abe Badoane. I can't stop thinking about that brilliant man who was always so misunderstood. What a wretched life!"

"Misunderstood and then some!"

"Jude told me that he felt some guilt that he made it out of the mine but Zoe, and especially Abe, didn't."

"He's mentioned that several times."

"I've always felt profound guilt that I got the teaching job over Abe and had the easy life while he didn't. Talk about guilt!" Charles wiped the dust from his shoe. "I caused Abe to go belly-up. Charles Claypoole is the reason his life is one never-ending dejection ode."

"Whatever that means!" *Charles just looked at his watch.* "I know you have to go—you said that earlier—but I suggest that you swing by early in the evening to personally commend Joey on his victory. That would mean a lot to him."

"I'd enjoy that, and I wouldn't mind hearing a few more details on Jude and Cory's miraculous escape too. Note the word I'm using, Pete. Their escape was a modern *miracle*."

"I agree!"

"So there's hope for me. Ha! Good day then."

Chapter 25

━━━━━━━━━━━━ ⟨℘⟩ ━━━━━━━━━━━━

After the football team meeting and the completion of farm chores, Joey picked up Laura and brought her to the house. Since a clever idea had come to Joey—namely interrogating the implant chip in Zoe's collar—they decided to delay their trip up the river to the Tarzan rope at Reesedale until Sunday. Zoe's behavior had been so unnatural in those first weeks after he mysteriously showed up that Jude mentioned his behavior during lunch one day to a group of men.

During that conversation, Morley Spencer, the security technician at the mine, commented to Jude, "You ought to do what's been done with the bears in Cook Forest and Clear Creek State Parks."

"What's that?"

"Each of the bears has been tagged so the forest rangers can monitor their behavior. It's called bilateral cochlear implantation. It's helped them learn a ton about black bears."

"Same with the elk up in Elk County," Glassy interjected. "They put implants in their ears so that they can track and study the elk."

"You ought to do that with your dog," Morley suggested. "You're always talking about the crazy human things he does."

"Maybe I ought to."

"If I were you, I'd put the chip on the collar and not bother with the actual implant. You'll save a nickel by doing it that way."

"That's a great idea."

"I can do it if you're interested."

The upshot of the whole discussion was the implantation of the device in Zoe's collar a few days later. Once it was there, Jude and

Cory checked it for a few days but, as it revealed nothing of particular interest, they forgot about it.

At Joey's suggestion, Jude decided to telephone Morley as soon as Joey returned from morning football films. "Brilliant idea, Joey. I'll call Morley right now."

"I'm not doing a thing, Jude," Morley responded a moment later. "Why don't you and Cory come to my office this afternoon? Does 2:30 work for you?"

"Yeah, the time's perfect, but Cory's giving her injured foot a rest this weekend. I'd love for her to see it, but as much as she dislikes this immobility, she's following doctor's orders!"

"Too bad, but no problem. She can check it out later."

"Cory did suggest I bring along someone else."

"Who?"

"Her brother, Joey."

"You mean *the* Joey Mohney."

"There's only one!"

"The hero of last night's game! It will be great to have the star of the game sitting in my office. Wait till I tell my little boys that I was with Joey Mohney today! We were at the game, and my boys went crazy when he scored that touchdown. Do you remember Paul and Henry?"

"Sorry. Not very well."

"You had met them at last summer's plant day at Kennywood."

"Oh, by the Jack Rabbit, right?"

"Yes."

"Great guys!"

That afternoon, Morley uploaded the chip so they could track Zoe's movements. Because the chip log was inscribed with the date and time, they could trace Zoe's precise day-to-day movements. "This is fascinating," Jude exclaimed, "until we get to last evening."

They fast-forwarded to the previous evening and closely monitored Zoe's movements. How strange it was to relive Zoe's final hours in this fashion. Jude and Joey were especially interested to get to the escape scene after Jude and Cory had climbed to safety. Long interested in the labyrinth of entangled limestone corridors, Morley, on the other hand, was curious to see how Zoe and Jude had gotten from the area of the newly developed rooms over to 50/10. "That amazes me since according to the map, there are no connecting corridors."

"Here you can see that Zoe and I are in 50/10," Jude explained a while later. The device appeared as a moving dot on a radar screen. "Can you blow it up?"

"Yes, I can, but what good would that do?"

"I want to see if Zoe's hobbling will be visible in a close-up."

"I see."

When Morley greatly enlarged the image, they carefully noted Zoe's movements down the corridor. "There seems to be a slight jig-gling movement in the dot. I'm guessing that jerky motion is Zoe's limp!"

"Probably so."

When they came to the part of Zoe's lunge, the dot was momen-tarily still. "This is when Zoe watched me shovel dirt. He was per-fectly still as he beheld me digging. Watch this fast movement com-ing up. Right there! That's when Zoe bolted forward and knocked me down. Look how fast he moved, even with a hurt foot. Now he's not moving. See that? He's perfectly still, not even the slightest wiggle!"

"Unbelievable!" Joey expostulated. "Zoe looked on in perfect stillness though he knew you were in a deathtrap!"

"Exactly," Jude agreed, his eyes fixed on the screen. "This is when he was trapped behind the big boulders that blocked his path and couldn't get to me." Closely watching the screen, Jude soon clutched his throat in anguish. "Can you put it on pause for a sec-ond? I'd like to run out in the hall and get a drink from the cooler. Do you mind?"

"Go ahead."

"Can you grab one for me too, Jude?" Joey stifled his tears. "Looking at all that dust is giving me a dry mouth!"

Returning with two paper cups of water, Jude rejoined the oth-ers. "If you have tears, prepare to shed them now. I know what's coming!" Morley hit play, and the film rolled again.

After a moment, Jude yelled, "Did you see that very slight movement? Please rewind and play that again. Right there! That's when Zoe struggled to his hind legs and bade me farewell. I can't believe we're seeing his final moments of life!"

"Maybe we should examine this part later," Morley ventured. "I bet you want to see the next section. Does the chip continue to move or does it stop? That's going to tell the tale about Zoe's fate."

Joey slid his chair backward and folded his arms on his chest. *Uh-oh!*

Morley fast-forwarded the chip log, but the dot remained deathly still.

Jude drooped his head to his chest. "It stops right there. The dot's completely gone. There's no additional movement, and the screen is completely blank because the chip, along with Zoe, is buried under tons of limestone."

Joey tried to stifled a sob. "I see."

Jude paused and put his hand on Joey's knee. "I said that much too bluntly. I'm really sorry. I'm just trying to get the courage to admit that we're seeing what we don't want to see." *This is tough!* "That's conclusive proof of Zoe's death."

Joey dabbed his eyes with a handkerchief. "I know it." His response was softer than a whisper.

When Morley replayed the sequence, Jude carefully scrutinized the screen. "The dot stops completely. I want it to move, but it just doesn't." He buried his face in his hands. "We're forced to face this very harsh truth."

Tilting his paper cup and tapping it to drain the last drop, Joey looked at Morley and then Jude. "In my dream, I either replayed a past moment I had with Zoe or heard him alive today. I have to decide between the two, dream of a past event or present sound." He wiped large tears from his eye.

I hate being the logical one, but future brother-in-law Joey has to come to grips with this. "Doesn't this make the choice obvious?"

"Life surely gives a guy wild mood swings—from the mountain-top on the football field last evening to this crushing valley of death! The dream gave me a glimmer of hope, but now I have nothing!"

The three men continued to look at the blank screen. Jude spoke at last. *Eliot, you were so right: mankind can only bear so much reality, but we have to accept this fact and move on.* "Here's the awful truth. Zoe is buried under a mountain of limestone in an abandoned mine corridor with a smashed computer chip on his collar. I'm sorry, but we need to face the truth."

"Here's the second part of our awful situation." Joey picked up Jude's train of thought. "If I understand you correctly, the corridor is completely filled with limestone. I'm sure they wouldn't send a search party in there to find his body so we could give him a proper burial. Why risk that for a dead dog?"

"You're probably right," Morley quickly though reluctantly agreed, "but this awful black cloud has one little bit of silver lining, though I admit it offers precious little consolation." Morley hesitated before speaking since the two men, especially Joey, continued to wipe tears from their eyes. *Maybe it's better to say nothing and end the grisly subject, but now that I've said that much, I better finish my thought.* "Zoe would have been killed instantly." *That was a stupid thing to say!* "I mean, there was no prolonged pain."

"Now there's a comforting thought that gives me joy all over," Jude immediately responded. He crinkled the paper cup in his hand and threw it in the paper basket. "Sorry, Morley, for saying that. I've got to be a man about this. Forgive my thoughtless and stupid sarcasm."

"Don't worry about it. It's obvious that you lost a beautiful and amazing pet."

Time to leave, Jude slid his chair back. "I really appreciate your doing this. Thanks for giving up your time when you should be at home with your wife Sarah and the kids on a lovely Saturday afternoon."

"My pleasure. I'm happy to do it." He looked admiringly at the football hero again. *Joey, I want to say again that you were phenomenal last night. Do you mind if I'd take your picture? Paul and Henry would be the envy of their school if they'd show their friends a photo of you.*

"I'd be happy to."

Morley took a couple pictures of Joey, albeit with red eyes, and thanked him profusely.

They shook Morley's hand and shuffled lifelessly out of his office.

Chapter 26

That Saturday evening, Pastor Gabe stopped by the Mohney farmhouse to see Pete and to congratulate Joey on his stellar performance on the football field. The family members—plus Jude, Laura, and Pastor Gabe—gathered in the den. After hearty commendations and a rehash of Joey's athletic prowess, the group eased into the big discussion of the evening, the subject of dreams.

Since the chip on Zoe's collar had stopped moving immediately at the time of the cave-in, they had proof that he was dead. Though Joey had witnessed the cessation of the moving computer chip with his own eyes, he would not let go of his dream. "I can't explain it, but somehow, the dream was not about something that happened in the past. It was happening now. Boy, if Todd and Moorhead heard me say that, they'd rip me to shreds as they did at school this morning. Laura, tell them about their ridiculous rant."

"I'd call it vicious. It was terrible!"

Sitting in the den of their western Pennsylvania antebellum farmhouse, the parlor in bygone days, Charles stopped by later in the evening. Like Pastor Wyant, he wanted to congratulate all of the Mohneys, especially Joey, on the joyous events of recent days. In a matter of months, Cory had gone from a miserable malcontent to "the happiest woman on the planet" (quoting Charles), Pete had wiggled free from the leaden weight of despondency, and Joey, in a single evening, had risen to small-town stardom.

Pretending his visit was spontaneous, Charles winked at Pete upon entering the house. *I know Jude deeply mourns the loss of his father, as well as Zoe, but it's nevertheless important to pick up the conversation I had with Pete this morning. Closure is necessary.* A short while into the conversation, Charles said, "I don't want to be the doom-and-gloom baron, but I'd be emotionally dishonest if I didn't say that Abe, through all of this happy chatter, is also on my mind."

"I completely agree," Pastor Wyant immediately responded. "Folks around here tell me that Abe was an active church member in bygone years. In fact, Old Mary once told me that he had even served as moderator for a couple terms." Glancing at Jude, the pastor paused. "I'm sorry if we're being insensitive. I realize we speak of your father."

"Your words have a calming effect, even on this difficult topic. Continue."

"My concern is spiritual since I recoil in fear when I think that the deceased may have entered a Christless eternity. I well understand that you've lost forever the dad you never had but might have gained. I'm so very sorry."

After condolences and expressions of concern for Abe Badoane, the group resumed talk on Joey's recent dream.

Warming to the subject, Charles was fascinated by their discussion and tapped his liberal knowledge base. "We moderns are pretty much removed from the science of dream interpretation though Freud, Jung, and others of the modern era have to some degree reacquainted people with that lost art."

"I hear what you're saying," Pastor Gabriel responded, "but still I look at the subject through a biblical lens. There are numerous examples in the Bible of people having dreams or visions. In Holy Writ, dreams always intimate something significant. That's why Joey's dream can't be taken lightly."

"Thanks for saying that, Pastor Gabe," Joey laughed. "It's nice to know that someone doesn't think I'm crazy!"

Pastor Gabriel delved more deeply. "Like the rest of you, I'm not sure what it means, but I do think you should pray on this and see if any of you has additional dreams. There were times in Daniel's life when dreams came in batches, a kind of grouping. Maybe the Lord will reveal Himself again through another dream." He winked in his endearing way. "I suggest you stay tuned to your local dream channel!"

After dessert, Cory's favorite crème brûlée recipe, and a word of prayer, the evening ended. But the discussion, in varying intensity, replayed in their various minds, especially Charles's. *Might there be something to Joey's dream? Does it mean that Zoe's alive? What, however, is to be made of the definite proof, the buried chip?*

In some ways, Jude was the most skeptical of all. During the conversation, he had opined, "Joey and I saw the evidence in the collar-implanted chip log. Zoe's motion came to an instantaneous halt. How can there be life?" *Nevertheless, I still wonder if any of us will have a related dream.*

After Jude and Cory sat on the porch for a while, he kissed her passionately and bade her farewell. "Goodnight, my beautiful dreamer. Parting is such sweet sorrow."

"*Romeo and Juliet!*"

"That was an easy one, but don't sit on your laurels. Your final exam, my star pupil, is coming!"

That very night Pete Mohney did indeed have a dream. He called Pastor Gabe the first thing Sunday morning to tell him, "Gabe, forgive me for calling when you're getting ready for morning worship service."

"Absolutely no problem, Pete. If my sermon's not ready by this point, I'm in trouble! What can I do for you?"

"I have good news."

"What?"

"I had a dream last night."

"That's great!"

"I'd like to talk to you about it. Can you come to the house this evening for a bite to eat before evening service?"

"Sounds good."

"And bring along your lovely wife!"

Early that Sunday evening, Pastor Gabriel, his wife, Martha, Pete, Jude and Cory, Joey and Laura gathered for Cory's light dinner—egg salad sandwiches and wedding soup. Seated on the porch after the meal, the group continued the discussion they had started during dinner.

At the request of the others, Pete related his strange dream. "My dream is so strange that I hesitate to even share it. Like Joey, I have no idea what it means. Actually, I had two dreams, and both were whacky as the dickens. In the first one, I dreamed of a huge underground cavern, a horrible place. I never thought too awful much of what hell might look like, but this was surely it. Jude and Cory used to talk about a writer who wrote of hell a lot. I don't remember the details. I can't even say his name!"

"Dante, and his masterpiece is *The Inferno*," Cory said when Pete paused.

"That rings a bell. In my dream, I was in hell and I heard screams and groans where demons and humans were chained." Pete ran his fingers through his hair and crossed his legs. "It was just plain awful, and the smell of smoke and burning odors made me sicker than a dog. I mean, in my dream, I was really sick, and everything was tinged with a red-orange glow. Like you might imagine hell to be."

"This is amazing, Pete," Pastor Gabriel interjected. "It's as though you were there!"

"It was real and it really shook me! At the entrance to this cave, I saw an even redder glow that gave off atrocious burning heat. It was the most hideous thing I'd ever seen. The hot flames shooting out of this cave scared me to death, so you see why I say I was in hell!"

The group was completely enthralled by Pete's narration. "You haven't talked this much for years!" Cory exclaimed when Pete stopped to catch his breath. "You're making this so vivid you're scaring me!"

Pete continued his narrative. "In my dream, I kept looking around and trying to figure out where I was. First thing I knew, I was swooped up and carried inside the cave. At first, I was really afraid because I didn't know where I was being taken and didn't want to be in that hideous place. I screamed and fought and tried to turn back, but then realized I was invisible and shielded from the heat. I didn't feel a thing, and the horrible creatures couldn't hurt me, even though they were monsters right out of fiction. Like the creatures Ruby and I read about in Tolkien and C. S. Lewis—demonic, hideous, scary!"

When Pete paused a moment in the narration of his dream, Jude, watching Pete catch his breath, whispered to Cory, "You're right. He's out of breath from talking so much."

"The pauses might mean something else," Cory whispered.

"What?"

"I think Dad's contemplating the horror of hell in a way he never did before."

"Good possibility."

"When I looked closely, I could see that the terrible creatures were gathered in a circle, but at first I couldn't see the center. Are you grounded? As you know, that's Jude's line! Well, this next statement is 220 volts, so you better be grounded or your brains will explode!" He laughed as he used to laugh.

Joey tapped Laura on the shoulder and quietly whispered in her ear, "That's the kind of funny thing Dad used to say. He doesn't laugh anymore."

After snickering at his own witticism, Pete resumed, "All of a sudden, my view wasn't blocked, and I could see into the middle of the circle. Plain as day, there sat Zoe surrounded by these awful creatures, but they weren't threatening to him and couldn't hurt him. Now that I think about it, it seemed they feared him or maybe showed respect. Yes, that's it. They bowed to him and even worshipped him. All eyes were definitely on our Zoe."

Joey was the first to respond. "You dreamed *that* last night? And you guys thought my dream of swimming was nuts? This takes the cake!"

"You think that was weird?" Pete proceeded with vigor. "Hang on to your britches for part two."

"You mean there's more?" Cory inquired.

"Yes, there is. This dream was in two parts."

"Please go on," Gabriel nodded.

"Here goes. In the second part of my dream, I was in a really beautiful place full of underground lakes. It was as beautiful as the first part was nasty and ugly. Very peaceful too. Like a paradise with refracting lights bright as sapphires and rubies and diamonds. They were everywhere, and they really reflected in the water. It was magnificent. In my dream, many animals were clustered around a central object. As in the other dream, I couldn't see the center at first, even though it was high and lifted up, like some sort of throne. Though my vision was temporarily blocked, I could see from the reflection in the water that he wore a pure white robe and had an object of some sort on his head."

When Pete again struggled for language to articulate such a strange dream, Charles filled the silence. "Your wonderful use of detail is helping us create a mental picture."

"That's for sure!" Cory hastily agreed. "I could put this on a canvas immediately!"

Pete was ready to resume again. "Eventually, I saw that the object was a crown, but I couldn't see who or what was wearing it. I mean, I saw the crown before the head and face. Many animals around this object were bowing down like you'd bow to a king. It was the most beautiful place I've ever seen and tranquil and holy."

"You make us want to go there!" Pastor laughed.

Pete thought for a moment and again threaded his hair with his hand. "Do you know the Edward Hicks's painting that hangs in Mama's and my bedroom?" The family knew of the painting, but the others did not. Pete directed the following comment to the Wyants and Charles. "It pictures the kingdom when Christ reigns on earth. That's when the lion lies down with the lamb and a little child leads the people. Like Elvis sings in 'Peace in the Valley.' Ruby loved listening to Elvis sing that song."

"Ruby used to speak of that painting," Martha commented. Except for her earlier statement about Cory's crème brûlée ("Every bit as good as your mama's!"), she sat quietly to this point. "Ruby talked so much about that painting that we women at quilting imagined its every detail!"

"I can just hear her!" Pete resumed. "I mention that because it was like I had entered in the world of that lovely painting. I was right there, and all the animals were so peaceful. Lions lay beside lambs and lived in peace and harmony. A bit later, when my vision wasn't obstructed, I had a full view of the throne. Guess who sat on it?"

"Zoe!" Joey yelled.

"You got it—our Zoe! But this time, he wore a robe and was crowned like a king. All the animals surrounded the throne, and they bowed and worshipped him. Can you believe it?"

"What an unbelievable dream!" Joey exclaimed.

"Whatever does it mean?" Pete looked helplessly at all of them, especially Pastor Gabriel and Charles, and then settled his eyes on Joey. "You thought your dream was crazy? Mine's nuttier than a PayDay candy bar!"

The conversation was spirited as the group commented on the two dreams and tried to make sense of them. Because reasoning minds could only can only go so far in the mystical world of dream analysis, they admitted defeat in trying to comprehend Joey's and Pete dreams.

Barely able to stifle a yawn, Pastor Gabriel ended the discussion. "We'd need a Daniel to figure out these dreams!"

Sitting opposite Pastor Gabriel, Jude nudged Cory and whispered in her ear, "Gabe is totally exhausted, and he still has an evening sermon to preach!"

"We both know what preaching takes out of him."

A short while later, the Wyants and Charles departed. Before evening church, Laura and Joey sat on the porch step, Jude and Cory in the kitchen standing at the sink. While Cory washed and Jude dried, he looked over his shoulder toward the porch. "Joey and Laura remind me of the days when we were high school sweethearts and enthralled by love's first blush."

"I never thought I'd see anyone as much in love as us, but they run a close second."

Jude peeped out just as Joey gave Laura a smooch on the cheek. "They're crazy over each other!"

"I know what you mean. I saw them kissing on the couch in the den one evening this past week when I slipped in quietly in case dad was napping. They were squeezing each other so hard I thought they'd die of suffocation!"

"Or bite their lips off!"

"That too!" Cory rinsed the remaining forks and Jude dried them. "Maybe there's a second set of lovers in the making."

"Who?"

"They tell me at work that Duke and Tina are faring very well these days."

"I've wonder about that too. I spoke with Blanche for a minute at church while you said goodbye to Gabe and Chuck. She said Duke was with Tina and Tony all day again today."

"Duke loves that boy and has taken to him like a long-lost son."

"Well, maybe he is!" Jude joshed.

Chapter 27

❦

If Jude and Cory's new life together was readily visible and applauded by all, that of mystery man Abe Badoane, father of Judah Jedidiah Hepler, was the exact opposite. He completely disappeared from the scene after the Friday evening explosion and cave-in. Had he been killed in the mine explosion and buried under the avalanche of limestone and coal? That was the prevailing sentiment though no one could present positive proof.

A neighbor, Art Tirpak, had stopped by to see Abe the Friday evening of the mine disaster. "Both the front and back doors were unlocked when I called on Abe for a chat, but when I went back the next morning, the doors were locked. How did that happen? None of us neighbors locked them. Did a mine employee hear of Abe's disappearance and probable death and stop by to shut up the house?" It remained a mystery.

The matter of Abe Badoane's whereabouts was extremely difficult for Jude. *If I'm Abe's son—and it can't be denied that I am—then I should take action, organize a search party, and settle the estate as soon as possible.* Jude planned to do that eventually, but for the time being, he needed to slow the pace. *Cory's and my injuries require healing. I need some time to think this through.* Jude spoke to an attorney and police officials in passing but progressed no further than that.

The one place where there was real change in the wake of the explosive cave-in was at the mushroom farm itself. The management team and the board of directors held an emergency meeting to chart the best course of action. Proposals ranged from the radical—ending the mine operation altogether—to the rational: thoroughly examining all mine ceilings and closely inspecting roof-bolting regulations and procedures to safeguard against future cave-ins. The installation of additional cameras throughout the mine was the immediate upshot of this thorough examination.

The managers' most serious deliberation, naturally centering on the rooms where the explosion had occurred, eventually clustered around two major questions. Should the rooms located adjacent to the cave-in room be sealed off or refitted for future use? Second, was the exposed coal seam above the mushroom mine operation a future threat? The obvious crux of the problem, this latter concern was the topic of intense debate.

The outcome was simple but intelligent, and the course of action unanimous. The mushroom mine geologist was assigned to conduct a thorough investigation to determine if the coal seam dipped down to other low and potentially hazardous points throughout the mushroom mine. Prevailing hearsay was that the explosion spot remained the single place where the coal mine shaft penetrated the limestone seam, but was the rogue seam theory accurate? Only a thorough geological study could answer the question.

By the end of the next week, the mine geologist had disseminated his findings. "Because the coal shaft is the only one that had been dug in the vicinity of the mushroom mine operation, the possibility of future coal seam-related cave-ins is virtually nonexistent." As a result of the findings, the "explosion room" was forever sealed off, whereas the other rooms in that vicinity were declared safe and ready for immediate use since, other than a few stray chunks of fallen limestone, there was no sign of danger in these adjoining rooms.

*****

This brings the Jude and Cory saga to Labor Day, three days after the epic Friday. The two sets of lovers—Jude and Cory, Joey and Laura—engaged in an outing which they had talked about for a long time. On Labor Day afternoon, they drove down Route 28 to Washington's Landing on Herrs Island where they boarded a pontoon boat which belonged to one of Jude's grad student colleagues in the English Department at IUP. Cruising down the Allegheny River, they soon passed under the historic Washington Crossing Bridge and then docked at a marina on the Allegheny River near The Point in Pittsburgh so they could attend the Labor Day festivities at Point State Park.

Because the day represented the "grand climax of the entire glorious summer" (in Jude's phrase), he wrote of it extensively in a later account.

An account of our Labor Day outing to Pittsburgh

I've stated in my journal several times this summer that one colossal event succeeded another. This happened again at the end of summer. We had no sooner experienced the drastic losses of the previous Friday evening when we came to the triumph of Labor Day Monday. In journalist fashion, I offer some favorite impressions here.

During the afternoon on Labor Day, we had picked up my friend's pontoon boat at Washington's Landing on Herrs Island, boarded it, and dined on our Miller's Hoagies as we motored downstream. Four of us were present—Joey, Laura, Cory, and me. The lovely early September day featured a blue sky, balmy temperatures, and an atmosphere of fun-loving merriment. Steelers and Pirates black and gold paraphernalia were draped everywhere on lawns, porches, mailboxes, and buildings. Joy was in all of our hearts as we motored downstream toward the great city.

Many of the grad students and IUP professors who live in or near the Pittsburgh area talk knowledgeably of its various neighborhoods, ethnic composition, multitudinous eateries, and historical highlights. A kind of outsider, I don't know my way around the city as they do, though during my graduate studies, I managed to familiarize myself with Oakland. Entering the big city evoked an incredible feeling in all of us who are more accustomed to rural settings, smaller crowds, and quaint provincialism.

During our couple-mile journey down river, Cory played some music. One of the songs was a very stirring rendition of Julia Ward Howe's "The Battle Hymn of the Republic," complete with trumpets and drums. For my benefit primarily, she then played Elvis's stirring "An American Trilogy," part of which also featured "The Battle Hymn." I recited some trivia about it as she dug in her purse for the Elvis cassette. "Did you know that Julia Ward Howe wrote this song in 1863 during the height of the Civil War at the Willard Hotel in Washington DC? It became the theme song for the Union."

I asked Cory to replay the beginning of the song again. "Listen to the language of this first verse. Trivia time: anybody know its source?" The first verse played again. "Mine eyes have seen the glory of the coming of the Lord, He is trampling out the vintage where the grapes of wrath are stored."

"Stop there. Anybody recognize the source?" I nodded toward Cory. "She with the 'inscripturated' brain will surely know!"

"That refers to Christ's reaping the harvest of souls on earth. I'm not positive, but I think that's in Revelation 14."

"Exactly! Sorry for you, guys, that this ends my riveting commentary. I see your keen disappointment!" I paused while we all laughed. "But, seriously, soul-reaping shouldn't ever be a matter of humor."

The song pounded in my ears as it always does, its catchy tune haunting my mind by the hour once I've heard it. I mention that because Cory had played this song several times over the last weeks. It plays now again as I sit here in my room and write of the catastrophic experiences of last Friday evening when all of us trod one weary step after weary step and the following joyous Labor Day.

I'm not quite sure how or why or even when the song prompted my fixation on the image of laboriously trudging feet, but it definitely did. As a result, I keep seeing images of plodding feet which battle against herculean odds: Joey's ripping up the sideline grass in his joyous touchdown sprint, Tina and Duke fighting their way to the front altar of the church, Pete dragging himself out of bed to the game, Charles trudging up Mt. Washington, Joey bulldozing a Gibraltar of human flesh into the end zone, Cory and I frantically clomping up a conveyor belt out of the canyon, and Zoe and I slogging along the mine moonscape in our hellhole escape, a fierce battle which Zoe, at my expense, lost.

When I spoke of this "weary step after weary step" recurring motif to Cory, she countered, "What of the most difficult trudge ever—Christ dragging Himself up Calvary with the Cross?"

"Absolutely right! That was the ultimate display of slogging, excruciating steps."

The whole time I wrote of this, strains of "The Battle Hymn of the Republic" played in the background. As a result, my mind is deeply embedded with its moving lyrics which now make me instantaneously flash back to last Friday evening.

It makes me think too of the constant if muted heartache during the dark years. How did I manage to slouch my broken heart forward, when, separated from the love of my life, I lived in agonizing fear that I would plod through life without her? That we had been driven apart by a combination of calculated cunning and resulting misunderstanding nearly destroyed me!

As we drifted down the Allegheny River toward Pittsburgh, I held her tightly. "Cory, I love you. You have no idea how much I idolize you!"

"You're the love of my life. There will never be another, Judah Jedidiah!"

When the mighty confluence came into view, we looked together across the expanse of water. The passage from Ezekiel, which Cory and I had read in Little Gidding just a few days before, immediately flashed in my mind.

"It shall be that every living thing that moves, wherever the rivers go, will live. There will be a very great multitude of fish because waters go there; for they will be healed, and everything will live wherever the water goes" (47:9).

After we read that passage, I noted that "Everything will live wherever the water goes." *One can't live without the water that heals. That's one thing I've certainly learned!*

"Remember how we sought the living river of life in the past?"

Staring across the watery expanse, I said nothing for a moment, lost in thought. "Yes, I do."

"A penny for your thoughts, Jude. For an English prof, that was an embarrassingly lame response."

"I'm thinking."

"About?"

"My constant thirst. Remember how I'm always thirsty, always needing water?"

"It's impossible not to notice!"

"Maybe it's the spiritual waters I've been seeking right along."

"Possibly so, and now we've found it. The blessings that accompany the healing waters will be fantastic!"

"Truly!"

"Did you know that the Ezekiel passage points to Christ's statement in Revelation, 'I will give of the fountain of the water of life freely to him who thirsts?'"

"Where is that?"

"Revelation 21, but I forget the exact verse." Checking the citation later, I learned it was verse six.

As we neared the city, I pictured in my mind the early Fort Duquesne, George Washington's presence at the confluence of the rivers during the French and Indian War, and then the bustling steel mills of a later era. To this day, Pittsburgh is hallowed ground to me, imbued with a distinct aura, an undefinable mystique. We were excited just to be there and to do this cool thing which we had wanted to do for years—ride a boat down the Allegheny, dock at the Golden Triangle, and delight in this city which had again been voted "most livable" in the nation.

So many life-changing events had happened on the previous Friday evening that our minds were still reeling. We were definitely ready for this relaxing holiday evening.

Little did we know as we docked and went ashore what awaited us!

Chapter 28

❦

Jude's account (continued)

When we ambled from the shore to Point State Park, the holiday festivities were in full swing with vendors and booths lined up in rows and numerous exhibits dotting the area. Hundreds of people milled about enjoying the lovely weather, the coming of autumn, the Pirates' late-summer surge, and the promise of another great Steelers season. Carefree and more lighthearted than we had been for days, we joined the many others who meandered from booth to booth inspecting the handmade crafts and sampling the cuisine.

How different from the scholarly world where I slaved a few short months ago—incessant reading, research writing, correcting papers, and preparing endless lectures! Best of all by far, I have this! I patted my pocket!

Pulling Cory tightly to me, I tilted my head and breathed the air, saturated with the aroma of candied apples, popcorn, grilled burgers, hotdogs, sausages, funnel cakes, and homemade fudge. I looked at Joey and Laura, walking hand in hand in front of us and totally enraptured with each other. *How much in love we two couples are! Seventy-two hours ago, we experienced unspeakable sadness and loss, yet here we are a couple days later, enchanted with life. How fast things change!*

Running hand in hand with this long-delayed trip to Pittsburgh was the little mystery that had surfaced in the last days concerning Pastor Gabe. He had requested our presence at a Labor Day concert at the Point State Park holiday celebration. At two different times, once on Saturday evening and again after church on Sunday, he checked with us to make sure we'd be present for the Monday holiday. His insistence seemed a bit odd and his tone even anxious, but maybe it was my imagination.

When we first spotted him talking with several people near the amphitheater, we weren't surprised that he was present at this holiday revelry, given his curiosity about our attendance. We were, however, more than a little curious to see him conversing with a number of important-looking people including members of a choir, probably the director, and a young man who, we learned later, was Dr. Roger Tabler, conductor of the Pittsburgh Youth Philharmonic Orchestra.

My immediate reaction was to start over right away to say hello to Pastor Gabe, but Cory cautioned me, "He looks pretty busy and tired too. Maybe we ought to talk to him when he's not so preoccupied."

"Good idea."

"He's positively exhausted, even slightly bent over. I've been worried about him lately." Cory peered with sadness at our beloved pastor. "He was so weary and care-worn when he stopped by the house for dinner last evening."

"I noticed it too. The poor guy works too hard!"

After browsing through the craft vendors, Joey, Laura, Cory, and I shared a funnel cake, each satisfied with a couple delectable bites. At the funnel stand, I watched Pastor Gabe for a moment, still engrossed and, compared to his normal composure, a tad nervous. On second thought, *anxious* is the better word. I did not think much about it at first, but when he saw me looking at him, his jittery behavior seemed to increase. "What's going on?" I said to Cory. "Pastor Gabe is as nervous as a bug in an exterminator's path. Or is my imagination working overtime again?"

"I see why you say that. He's definitely not himself."

"Wonder why?"

We walked around to inspect the talent of some of the assembled artisans, including a nearby cobbler and candlemaker who demonstrated their respective trades. About 6:45, we heard music ascending from the area of the amphitheater. *The orchestra and choir are warming up for the 7:30 concert. This should be fun!*

157

Once the orchestra commenced their playing, Gabe marched over to see us. "You'll be joining us for the combined concert and award ceremony? Dr. Tabler asked me to lead the invocation at the start of the service and assist in the conferment of the award."

Pastor Gabe, I hope it's these responsibilities that account for your anxiety. "We plan to attend."

Pastor Gabe then started to lead us in the direction of the outdoors amphitheater where he had reserved seats in the front row for us. "You'll make a…nice appearance…sitting there," he chuckled as we walked together. "Jude, your head's…bandaged, Cory's hobbling in her boot, Joey's hand is taped, and Duke's hand"—another pause—"is in a cast."

"Duke? Duke Manningham's here?" I made no effort to hide my surprise. I did not mean to interrupt Pastor's thought, but his reference to Duke shocked us since to this point, none of our group had seen him. Gabe nodded in their direction. Sure enough, we saw Duke and Tina some hundred feet away inspecting the vendors' wares.

After Pastor Gabe rejoined the others, I commented to Cory, "Did you note Gabe's faltering speech?"

"Yes, and he was unsteady on his feet too! What's with Gabe?"

"I'm beginning to think you're right about his exhaustion."

"His currents turn awry!"

"May they not lose the name of action!"

When people started to straggle into the amphitheater for the start of the concert, sharp-eyed Joey looked at the rear of the amphitheater to a makeshift cable that had been suspended from the top of a pole to a grassy area near the stage. "What's that?" By then, we had assembled at a spot between the stage and the bleachers.

"I'd also like to know." Laura gazed to the rear of the amphitheater at a large pole with a platform positioned near its top.

Pastor Gabe had a funny look on his face—"A little sheepish," I whispered to Cory—when he saw us looking at it. Cory nudged me so that I too could see the twinkle in his eye. It was one of those things one doesn't note the significance of until later. Afterward, it all made sense, but in the early part of the evening, we knew nothing about the platform and suspected less.

Just as we were getting ready to take our seats, a commotion occurred along the Allegheny River. At first, we thought nothing of it, but soon we saw an increasing number of people gather near the river's edge.

Something's going on!

Joey was the first to speak. "Let's check it out! We have time since the concert doesn't start for a while." Joey, Laura, Cory, and I started for the river, but just then, Pastor Gabe beckoned for Cory and me to join him near the stage. "I'd like to introduce you to Dr. Tabler."

Because some twenty-five people had congregated at the water's edge, we weren't able to get a good look at what attracted them, but between two bystanders in the jostling crowd, I caught a quick glimpse of an animal swimming in the river. One of the people who witnessed the activity came to the stage area to report to a friend. "A dog surfaced out of nowhere in the Allegheny River and now is swimming to shore." The friend offered no additional details.

After an introduction and brief chat with Dr. Tabler, Cory and I sauntered over to the edge of the Allegheny River to see what the excitement was all about. We squeezed into the midst of a growing crowd and, over the heads of the people, managed at last to get a fairly good look at the dog.

He was still some hundred feet from shore when Joey, ever the hawk eye, screamed, "I think it's Zoe!"

The dog admittedly favors Zoe as he swims toward shore, but that can't be possible! This dog is so covered with cuts to the head and shoulders that he's an unrecognizable mess!

A moment later, he neared the shore as we worked our way through the crowd. "It's Zoe!" Cory yelled. "It really is!"

"Look at him!" I could barely get the words out of my mouth. "He's battered and terribly scarred!"

Cory grabbed my arm. "And completely spent!"

"What's he carrying in his mouth?" Joey asked.

I thought it was a stick or some object, but then, even at that distance, I could see that he pulled a rope. "He's dragging something, but what is it?"

Joey's inquisitiveness continued. "How did he survive the cave-in?" He then turned to the nearby people who asked what was going on and hurriedly explained a few facts about Zoe's strange history. "This is our mystery dog that saved my sister, Cory, and her boyfriend up in Armstrong County." Joey nodded toward us to indicate that we were the couple. "There was a bad explosion at the mushroom mine, and this incredible dog saved them!"

Several of the people, having read about the accident in the paper, were amazed that they were seeing "the very fortunate couple" who escaped alive. To verify his statement, Cory and I quickly gestured to the injuries we had sustained in the accident, Cory to her boot cast, I self-consciously to my head bandage.

Zoe neared the steps along the shore where we awaited him. Learning of our connection with him, the people allowed the four of us to worm our way to the front so we could be there to greet him like a returning soldier from the field of victory.

Joey was so close the water he nearly fell in! "Come, Zoe!"

As we cheered Zoe on, the crowd got into the spirit and exuberantly joined us. All of us descended the steps where I knelt to my knees. "Come on, Zoe!"

As he approached the steps, I could see the deep cuts to his head. *Poor Zoe's a mess!*

"How did he get here?" various people asked.

A woman beside me shared our excitement. "Do you think he jumped out of one of those boats that are motoring around? Or did he swim here from the other side?"

Someone near the shore noted his injuries. "Your poor dog is full of sorrow and acquainted with grief. I've never seen anything like it!"

All sorts of questions ran through my mind as I tried to figure out how he got here. I made my way to the man who first spotted Zoe. "He just came to the surface out of nowhere. I'm sure about that. When I looked across the river, the water was calm, and there were no boats in the area. He just surfaced out of the blue!"

"Just like that!"

Cory, that was on the "embarrassingly lame" side too!

"Yes, all of a sudden, he was just there. He panted for air like you can't imagine when he first surfaced. That's when I shouted, 'Look at that!' I guess I said it louder than I intended because that made these people run over here to check it out."

By now, Zoe neared the stairs, climbed out of the water, and began to mount the steps. *He's hobbling just as he did in the mine! You poor dog!* Once at the top of the stairs, we had a full view of his injuries: the front paw out of joint, the wounds to his other paws, innumerable scourgelike cuts all over his body, especially his head, and by far the worst, the terrible mud-caked gash to the side.

"Zoe! Zoe!" the four of us yelled again and again.

These people think we're idiots, but they don't understand!

The one thing that encouraged me was the vigorous way Zoe tried to walk. Nevertheless, Cory wept profusely when she saw how badly he was injured. "He looks awful! He's so thin you can count all of his bones! Please say he's all right!"

"I can't tell just yet." Though I too was overcome with emotion, deep down I felt profound gratitude and joy. *Zoe's alive! His ordeal and assumed death had shaken me deeply. After all, only I had witnessed the cave-in and Zoe's heroic exploits, but just how did he survive, and just as mysterious, how in the world did he get to the confluence of the three rivers?*

"He looks as though he survived the French and Indian War battles that were fought right here," quipped an intelligent-looking man.

By now, Zoe, with our assistance, had taken a few steps away from the riverbank steps and stood still while I further examined his body. Despite the inexplicable journey that brought him here, he didn't seem as completely exhausted as we first surmised, nor did he collapse at the top of the stairs. Instead, he pillowed himself gently on the ground after greeting us and allowed us to carefully inspect his injuries. *His injuries are worse than I first thought, especially this bad wound on his side and these scourge cuts all over his head.*

I was not certain how or when he had received the injury to his side. In the mine, he had lunged at me to save my life and, while doing so, was apparently knocked straight to the ground by the large boulders, although at the time, I thought he was running beside me. Right before the avalanche of stone which buried him—at least I thought it did—Zoe had risen to his hind legs to say goodbye. At that time, I couldn't be sure if had the cut to the side, but the question of the side injury, nasty as it was, paled in comparison to the two big ones which churned in my mind relentlessly: how did Zoe survive the cave-in? And how did he get here? Though my head reeled with these questions, I joined the others who surrounded Zoe and heartily rejoiced!

"Our Zoe rose from the dead! Sorry if that sounds ridiculous or blasphemous, but this helps me see how people must have praised God when Jesus raised a child to life."

Or, Cory, when He Himself was resurrected from the dead!

We continued to greet Zoe with tears of joy and gratitude. Desperately wanting to pet him and hug him, we could not do so because his body was so badly cut and battered. I did, however, use the back of my fingers to softly stroke an uninjured spot on his snout.

I had just finished gently caressing him when he picked up the rope he had been dragging and tugged on it. Seeing that it was a strap and not a rope as I had first surmised, I pulled it up for Zoe.

My heart instantly started to race. *Unbelievable!* "It's Grandpa's satchel! Zoe rescued the novel!"

Chapter 29

—————— ✌ ——————

Jude's account (continued)

S omehow, Zoe had unearthed Grandpa's satchel back in the mine, but by what impossible set of circumstances did he get it to Pittsburgh? All of the events defied logic: his surviving the cave-in when I saw the falling rocks, his retrieval of the novel, his escape from the mine, and—the greatest mystery of all—his arriving at the confluence in Pittsburgh. *How did these miracles happen?*

My hands were shaking frantically as I drew the satchel up the steps. Fortunately, I had not disturbed the waterproof covering when I quickly looked at it in 50/10. I estimated that the water-soaked package weighed nearly ten pounds. *How was Zoe, in his weakened state, able to bear this cross such a great distance?* My hands trembled wildly as I tore it open.

There it was: Grandpa's novel completely intact and only slightly damp at the edges! A large crowd gathered when I held it up. "It's my grandpa's novel, *Kittanning*! It was lost for decades and buried in the mushroom mine up in Armstrong County!" People cheered enthusiastically. "Somehow, our dog retrieved it and brought it here!" I ended my explanation with the ultimate question: "How did angel dog get it here to Pittsburgh?"

My brief comments were reportorial, my ending question completely rhetorical as I merely offered an account to the people who were fascinated by Zoe and who looked so quizzically at him. But an intelligent-looking woman in the crowd—someone said she was employed at a leading Pittsburgh law firm—speculated that Zoe probably traversed a network of underground streams which eventually merged with Pittsburgh's mythological underground fourth river. "Your dog must have swum through a maze of subterranean streams which eventually empty into Pittsburgh's renowned fourth river. Many people believe that a fourth river converges with the other three rivers here at the famous confluence."

Several nearby people reacted simultaneously.

"Sounds good to me."

"Maybe so."

"I bet you're right."

"That's quite the theory!"

I need to examine the topographical maps of the streams, creeks, and rivers in the county as soon as possible in an effort to trace Zoe's herculean journey from the mine's 50/10 to the confluence of the three rivers. Many animals have made extraordinary journeys home, the inspirational stuff of legend, but this forty-mile journey was accomplished by a severely wounded animal, in very cold spring water, through an underground maze of Byzantine complexity, and in the pitch dark no less! The other pet-makes-it-home stories, while gripping and heartwarming, were usually fictitious. This was the stuff of hard reality!

As Cory, Joey, and Laura continued to care for Zoe, I rapidly flipped through the pages of the novel. I couldn't resist looking at this monumental work in my hands. *I'm holding Grandpa's novel, and as if that isn't enough good news for one day, our wonder dog has come back from the dead!* My heart—I should say our hearts—pounded furiously as we stood there on the shore across from Three Rivers Stadium.

"This is as great as the miracles that have happened over on that field!"

Joey's eyes are fixed on that stadium as though he views the Holy Grail! "You and your football! Is that the only thing you think of?"

"This time of year, what else is there?"

Laura pretended to pout. "Hey, tactless one! You better not say that's the only thing you think of!" We all blissfully laughed.

When Zoe rose to his feet and stood with surprising vigor, I had the chance to examine his wounds more closely. All four paws had been hurt, apparently by falling rocks. I babbled nervously, "The abrasions to the head are even more ghastly than I first realized." My attention, however, was riveted to his side. *I speculate that the wound is very deep as though he had been badly gashed. Your loss of blood must have been substantial. Zoe, how did you survive that, hypothermia, and probable kidney failure too?*

Had he rolled in the mud to stanch the flow of blood to his various injuries? While I examined his ribs, he stood rock still as though sensing the seriousness of my task. The longer I looked at the mud plaster, the more I realized it had saved Zoe. *Its work complete, the plaster should be removed since the wound could become infected now that he's no longer submerged in the purifying ice-cold water.*

Fortunately, the mud had caked together in a single large chunk of hardened plaster. Some of the sides of the mud cake were raised at the edges, so I gently placed my finger under a loose-fitting corner to see what I was dealing with. Like a patient in a doctor's exam room, Zoe stood perfectly still. I gently pried outward on the mud plaster. To my relief, the whole thing fell away like a huge scab that was ready to fall off. Several nearby people, including Cory and Laura, gasped when it fell away.

This nasty wound in the ribs corroborates my sense that something had deeply speared his side. The exact cause of the wound was another of those details, like the route of Zoe's underground journey, which I assumed we would never know for certain.

When the emcee announced over the loudspeakers that the concert would be starting momentarily, the crowd dispersed. The little excitement at the shore over, people shuffled away toward the theater, the vendors, and various exhibits, but I was aware of their buzzing among each other. *That story and Zoe's mysterious surfacing definitely aroused their interest!*

When the four of us were temporarily left alone with Zoe, Cory mentioned that we should get back to Pastor Gabe. "I'm sure he's waiting for us. He'll want to hear this tale about Zoe." Suddenly, she stopped and grabbed my arm. "You realize he'll expect us to stay." She looked again at the haggard Zoe. "He's really banking on our being here for the program."

"I agree, but don't you think Zoe's condition trumps these festivities even if Pastor Gabe is involved?"

Cory and I went over to see Pastor Gabe at the theater a couple hundred feet away while Laura and Joey continued to comfort Zoe. The amphitheater was already quite full with holiday-celebrating spectators.

"Look at all of these people," I exclaimed. "You can just feel the holiday excitement!"

Walking to the amphitheater, I continued to reflect. *Despite the loss of my dad, when have I ever been happier? I have the love of my life by my side, and now our dog's returned with Grandpa's long-lost novel to boot! "He who continually goes forth weeping, bearing seed for sowing, shall doubtless come again with rejoicing, bearing his sheaves with him" (Psalm 126:5–6). And what magnificent sheaves we've reaped!*

Chapter 30

Jude's account (continued)

Joey and Laura later shared the next part of the evening's events with Cory and me.

While Cory and I excused ourselves to chat with Pastor Gabe before the start of the concert and to tell him the remarkable events surrounding Zoe, some of the rowdies from Joey's football team appeared, the same guys who had ridiculed him in the football lobby on Saturday morning.

According to Joey, they were out for a good time and had obviously been drinking. "Laura and I could smell beer on them. I knew as soon as I saw them that they were feeling it and looking for some trouble or fun or both. They had heard us talk about 'wonder dog' at the school. That was Moorhead's name for him. Now they witnessed the dog himself in the flesh."

"Sounds like trouble."

Joey continued his story. "'Let me get this straight,' Todd, the quarterback, began. 'Super mut was buried under tons of limestone but miraculously came back to life. Then he pushes the ejection button and blasts his sweet little behind out of a solid rock tomb.' Todd paced a step or two, studiously looked down, and placed his chin on his hand—you know, a defense lawyer getting his facts straight. 'Three days later, he takes a swim in the Burgh.' A smirk on his face, he turned to the other guys. 'What do you members of the jury think? Sound rational to you?'

"It was time for the others to pile on. 'You forgot the big book and didn't say that he delivered the *message*,' Lamison needled, motioning to the manuscript.

"Moorhead then sniped, 'This dog has the powers of Superman!'"

"At this point, the gang stood in phalanx formation but, pretending to be afraid, fell backward when Zoe hobbled slightly on his paws to face them. 'Did you see that show of strength?' Moorhead mocked, 'He acts just like a king!'

"'He doesn't look so tough to me,' Todd sneered. 'Watch this!' He bent over at the waist, put his index fingers to his head like a charging bull and, encircling Zoe, pawed with his feet at the ground. Braying like bulls, the three of them cavorted around Zoe, poised for the kill.

"Lamison vigorously patted his chest as though experiencing serious arrythmia. 'I've never been so scared in my life!'"

"Their mockery appetite satisfied, the guys stopped their stupid little ridicule game and carried their boredom some other place. But as they walked away, Todd gave the satchel a savage kick and stomped the corner of it into the ground. Then he yelled over his shoulder, 'Hey, phony Mohney, if your miracle story's true, my name's Baloney. Yeah, here's what I think.' He jumped on the manuscript with both feet and stomped it into the mud. 'Start to finish, your grandpa's book is nothing but crap!'"

After recounting this incident, Joey went to get Zoe some water, then he and Laura, Zoe at their side, walked the short distance to the theater to speak with Cory and me. It was time for a campfire to make a decision—to stay or not to stay for the festivities. After a brief discussion, the four of us arrived at the same answer—negative. We elected Cory the unlucky spokesperson.

We sauntered the short distance to Pastor Gabe. "Sorry, Gabe. Much as we want to stay for the concert, our plan has been preempted." Cory touched Zoe on the snout where I had earlier and pointed to his wounds. "As you see, our miracle dog requires the immediate attention of a vet."

During our discussion, Zoe drank a great deal of water which Joey had brought to him in a large Styrofoam bowl. "Look how thirsty he is," Laura observed. "He drank every last drop!"

Cory watched as Zoe ate a fish stick and a bite of Bit-O-Honey candy. "Look at him gobble down that food! You see, he's not a ghost.

This is your flesh and blood deliverer who rescued you out of the pit!"

Pastor Gabe then performed one of those signature gestures that so typified the man's gentle behavior. He came over to Zoe, gently cupped his palm above his head, and without actually touching Zoe's bruises—Gabe was as gentle with Zoe as any of us—he expressed gratitude to God for Zoe. Picking up on Cory's comment that Zoe had saved me, Gabe alluded to him as "a kind of savior" and began to pray. "Thank You, God, for using this dog to restore Pete to life, devise the brilliant escape plan, save Jude a second time, and retrieve Jeremiah's novel. Amen." Finished with his prayer, Gabe faced us. "When someone's done all that, he can, in my book, be called a savior—a unique canine deliverer with a fascinating dual nature!"

Winking at us with that winning smile, Gabe spoke with the old vigor, but his "color was off." Cory whispered to me when Gabe, several feet away, bent over to examine Zoe's wounds. "He has an ashen color, even though he's as excited about Zoe as we are. Surely that's not a good sign!"

Gabe briskly rubbed his tired eyes. "Then I guess we separate here. I have duties at the concert, and you must get Zoe to the vet." He hung his head. "What a keen disappointment, for I really wanted you to be present at this performance! You don't think Zoe's treatment could wait while you attend the program? It's very brief."

By this time, Zoe had recovered considerably and, apart from the cuts and injured front paw, was acting quite normally. "It's a real temptation." I again noted Zoe's increased vitality. *No one is more caring and compassionate than Gabe, and if he thinks we're not being insensitive in delaying treatment, then it's probably all right to do so. How can we say no to this great man, Pastor Gabe?* But contemplating anew Zoe's sacrificial heroism and severe wounds, we still opted to depart.

Gabe looks like he's been struck with a sledge!

"Right. Then we bid our farewells here. Thank You, Jesus, for this miraculous Melchizedek!" Rubbing the back of his fingers along Zoe's snout, Pastor Gabe then started toward the theater while I picked up the manuscript of the novel and walked with our group in the opposite direction. Continuing toward the pontoon, I took the closest path to the dock so we could motor the short trip up river to retrieve our car. "Time to go, Zoe!"

To our amazement, Zoe watched us amble for a moment and then deliberately followed Gabe instead. I went back to Zoe. "We have to go home and take you to the vet immediately." He paused to look at me as if understanding perfectly, then he looked at Gabe and hobbled after him! "Will this dog just act like a dog for once in his life?"

The others also tried to coax Zoe to go with us, but he wasn't to be persuaded and vigorously followed Gabe, tail wagging as though he had not been to Hades and back in the last three days!

Despite our efforts to dissuade him, Zoe stayed with Gabe. In a short while, we were reluctantly seated in the front row, right side, in the section Gabe had reserved for us. Zoe lay on the ground in front of us, completely content and seemingly oblivious to cuts, abrasions, a speared side, and a broken foot. I whispered to Cory, "Some people adjust to adversities with grace, but this"—I nodded toward Zoe—"is flat ridiculous!"

Though I tried to focus on the concert which was about to begin, because I knew some outstanding entertainment had been planned, I could not resist staring at Zoe and eventually whispered to Cory, "Who or what is this dog?"

"What are you talking about?"

"I intend no blasphemy in saying this, but in the same way the disciples looked at Jesus after He calmed the raging waters and walked on water and blathered, 'Who is this man?' that's how I feel as I sit here looking at Zoe. What kind of a dog comprehends intelligently, thinks rationally, responds humanly, and performs impossibly?"

"You forgot 'and resurrects miraculously!'"

"Mea culpa! That most of all!"

Though trying to concentrate on the program when it finally started, I was riveted to Zoe instead of the performance. To augment my curiosity further, Zoe looked over his shoulder toward the zip line that was suspended from a tower behind the amphitheater. I didn't take particular notice the first couple times he looked, simply because, an insanely curious dog with a heightened sense of awareness, he always monitors his immediate environment. That, I realize, is a trait of most pets, but gradually, I surmised that he might be honing in on some particular object. "What could possibly interest him?" That was all I said to Cory. I was back to my normal state of mind when around Zoe—bewilderment sweetened with a pinch of mystique!

My attention at last diverted to the concert when the orchestra started softly into a stirring rendition of *Battle Hymn of the Republic*. I noted previously that this hymn had been playing in the background when I wrote my account of the recent harrowing events and had also blasted joyfully as we cruised down river. Now here at the Three Rivers—or was it Four Rivers?—I was treated to this climactic and heart-stirring interpretation by Dr. Tabler's Pittsburgh Youth Philharmonic Orchestra. What an amazing crescendo!

At the start of the song, Zoe sat up and again peered over his shoulder at the center of Point State Park where the tower stood. *Zoe, you're driving me crazy! What intrigues you so much?*

I mentioned earlier that three days prior to this—the Friday the Mohney family subsequently dubbed "the *other* good Friday"— Chuck had climbed to the top of Mt. Washington, that climactic event he had contemplated for years but had feared because of family heart history. The event, a real game-changer in his life, had dramatically increased his faith. Shortly before the start of *Battle Hymn of the Republic*, he prepared for part two of his defeat-fear-once-and-for-all initiative. I refer to his ziplining over the amphitheater to make a grand on-cue entrance during the evening program!

His doing so had roots at Grove City College several years earlier. He and several of his professor friends, including a couple internationally acclaimed authors, had been chatting outside the chapel one day after the morning worship service. The chaplain's text had been Isaiah 40:31, "They shall mount up with wings like eagles, they shall run and not be weary, they shall walk and not faint."

"Wouldn't it be nice to fly like an eagle?" Chuck had jokingly chortled to his colleagues on the steps outside the chapel after the service.

One of his professor friends, Dr. Carl Trueman, responded that he often zip lines in various locations. "You ought to try it, Charles. I know you English profs are unadulterated sissies, but beat your fear for once in your life and push the moment to its crisis." He punched Chuck in the ribs. "I can tell you love it that I cited a phrase from 'The Love Song of J. Alfred Prufrock' for your benefit! Seriously, you ought to do it sometime because nothing beats the feeling of zipping along like a soaring eagle!"

That's all it had taken. Charles zip lined quite often in the intervening years and had come to enjoy it a great deal. What that group of colleagues did not realize was that Chuck, in consultation with Pastor Gabe and the steering committee, had planned his dramatic entrance at this Three Rivers celebration in Point State Park as a kind of crescendo to the evening program. The various details had been tediously rehearsed for Chuck's "small contribution to the festive celebration," as he called it. The plan was simple but potentially climactic. His zip line descent would occur during the rousing crescendo of "The Battle Hymn of the Republic."

My first hint that something was going on occurred when Zoe, seated on his hind paws, watched Pastor Gabe signal to the flagman. My curiosity having gotten the best of me, I turned around for a quick glance and beheld Chuck mounting the zip line platform! The choir, accompanying the orchestra, was now at the stirring second verse: "I have seen Him in the watch-fires of a hundred circling camps, They have builded Him an altar in the evening dews and damps." Their loud singing sent chills up and down my spine. I glanced down at Zoe, his tail wagging with excitement. *You, most mysterious pet on the face of the earth, are you too stirred by the singing or by our friend's impending descent?*

Right when I thought this Labor Day celebration could not get crazier, it did. The choir came to the end of the second verse and stopped, though the orchestra played on. Conductor Tabler proceeded to the center of the stage and motioned for Pastor Gabe to join him. *What's going on?* I tapped Cory in the side with my elbow. "What's Gabe doing?"

"I'm as clueless as you!"

While we focused on the stage performance, Joey noted that Zoe's eyes were trained on the tower behind us. "You won't believe it!" Joey blurted a second later. "That's the professor standing on the zip line platform, and he's wearing a weirdo costume!" As discreetly as possible, the four of us diverted our attention from the stage and looked backward in utter astonishment.

By this time, the conductor and Gabe had come to the front of the stage. Dr. Tabler spoke first. "The intent of this evening is to celebrate heroism and patriotic zeal, amply evidenced in Pittsburgh's legendary history. In keeping with that illustrious tradition, it's time to introduce the individuals who have been selected this year for 'embodying those heroic ideals in an extraordinary way.'"

At first, I thought that Pastor Gabe had been singled out to introduce the evening's honoree and that this would be the extent of his involvement. I scanned the area to see if some prominent celebrity was seated in the front row or standing in the wings and ready to walk on stage. *I don't see anyone.* "I give you my good friend, Pastor Gabriel Wyant from nearby Armstrong County," Dr. Tabler announced, "to make the introduction."

Though excited, Cory spoke softly, "What a wonderful honor that Gabe was selected to introduce the recipient. People are here from all over the tristate area."

"No wonder he wanted us in the front row for such a prestigious event!"

Despite the joyous occasion, Pastor Gabe appeared feeble as Cory observed. "Did you see that? I think he limped a little as he neared the mic!"

Joey agreed. "Yeah, I saw it. What's going on with the Gabe dude?"

"He doesn't look so good." *Way to go, Hepler—your third embarrassingly lame response!*

But that didn't stop Gabe from fulfilling his mission, and what a mission it was!

Chapter 31

Jude's account (continued)

Pastor Gabe and Dr. Tabler exchanged a few comments before Gabe took the mike, during which moment I withdrew into my mind. *How splendid it all is—gorgeous early autumn evening, our family together in love, Zoe at my feet, Grandpa's novel on my lap, and the love of my life by my side.* Patting my pocket, I thought of Robert Browning's "Song from Pippa Passes:" God's in His heaven; all's right with the world.

Seated at the confluence of the majestic rivers, I took Cory's hand to my mouth and kissed it. *This defines rapture! And it's so peaceful too. What peace! A phrase comes to mind—"one white hour of peace" or something close to that. What's that from? Thinking, thinking. Got it! Sara Teasdale's "Barter:"*

> For one white singing hour of peace
> Count many a year of strife well lost,
> And for a breath of ecstasy
> Give all you have been, or could be.

This was our white singing hour of peace, our breath of ecstasy. I looked around to absorb the beautiful atmosphere—Pittsburgh's amazing skyline, the boats at the confluence, Three Rivers Stadium across the river, the joyful people. *How glorious!* Then I thought of the lines from the Edna St. Vincent Millay poem which had darted into my associative brain after my escape from the mine:

> O world, I cannot hold thee close enough.
> Long have I known a glory in it all,
> But never knew I this;
> Here such a passion is
> As stretcheth me apart.

When Pastor Gabe went to the mic to begin his comments, I was roused from my reverie. *I too want to know the award recipient. Is some well-known Pittsburgh celebrity coming to the stage?* I whispered to Joey, "Maybe one of the Steelers, Pirates, or Penguins?"

"My money's on Jack Lambert!"

I swear he beams like a boy in a Norman Rockwell painting!

Then Gabe blew us away. He had been given the honor of sitting on the selection committee for the recipient of the heroism award. "It gives me great pleasure to introduce the recipient of this year's patriotism award." He paused interminably. *You're driving us crazy, Gabe! Just say it!* "I present to you, my good friends from Armstrong County, Jude Hepler and Cory Mohney!"

We could have died, for few other statements in life sent shock waves over us like that. We couldn't believe what we heard. Cory grabbed her chest. "I'm having the big one!"

First thing we knew, Gabe launched into a brief synopsis of the extraordinary events we had endured in recent days, most of which had been given extensive coverage by the Pittsburgh media. When he finished his concise summary, he invited us to the raised platform down front, erected at center between the orchestra on the right and the choir on the left.

"Jude, I'm embarrassed out of my mind! I can't take this!"

Gabe next made a few comments about Joey's patient ascent to victory on the Kittanning football field. This account of superb athletic performance in football instantly endeared Joey to the audience. After all, this was Pittsburgh, and Three Rivers Stadium, the site of some of the most exciting moments in modern professional football, was situated across the river.

"Joey, please come to the stage since we single you out for Honorable Mention." The crowd cheered as the embarrassed Joey rose. "And bring that lovely lass beside you. We can't have her sitting alone!"

Cory and I were up front by now and had a perfect vantage point of the entire proceedings. She softly spoke in my ear, "I've never seen a redder face. You'll read Laura's obit in tomorrow's paper!"

When Joey and Laura nervously walked to the stage, a man in the crowd loudly yelled, "Sign him up!" Then another, "The Steelers can use a backup quarterback!" A wave of laughter rippled through the audience, and then I laughed very hard.

"That was a really loud laugh!"

"It's called hysteria! Some tragedies come ready-made with comic relief moments. Welcome to mine!" Though gawked at by a sea of smiling faces, we laughed like idiots!

Joey and Laura took their places on the raised platform beside Cory and me. *Joey's face is as red as Old Mary's hummingbird feeder!*

Off and on, Gabe looked up at the zip line tower during his brief comments. We instantly saw the reason: Chuck was prepping to make his dramatic flight over the crowd and land by the stage. As Gabe finished reciting the verse, "They will mount up with wings like eagles," he proclaimed. "Help me welcome these young people who have mounted up like eagles…as has eagle-man Charles Claypoole!"

Precisely on cue, Chuck zip lined right over the astonished crowd at a very low elevation and dexterously landed near the stage like a seasoned pro. The crowd cheered, yelled, and clapped at the unique event.

"I asked my good friend, Professor Charles Claypoole, to assist us in honoring our awardees, Jude and Cory, and our Honorable Mention athlete, Joey." After Chuck doffed his eagle wings and bowed with the elegance of a professional actor, he joined Pastor Gabe on the stage.

As Chuck walked toward us, Gabe explained that he had been a "confidante" during our trials. I stole a look at the professor and, beside me a moment later, whispered, "Lord, what fools these mortals be!"

Cory, hearing this aside, whispered, "*A Midsummer Night's Dream*—Act 3, scene 2!"

Glancing over my shoulder at the wings Chuck had worn, I saw the details more clearly. *They're fashioned like eagle wings.* "Chuck, you and Gabe thought of every single detail!"

"Thank you for your patience," Gabe bubbled, "but we'd be remiss if we didn't acknowledge the quiet hero of it all, the choice and master spirit who, by performing the miraculous, made all of this possible. I give you Zoe the dog. You can tell from his injuries that he's endured a great deal of pain. Please don't be alarmed, good folks. He'll be taken to the vet momentarily. Without exaggeration, we say that he laid down his life that Jude and Cory might live."

Except for the folks in the front couple rows, Zoe had been virtually out of sight; thus, most of the people in the audience, apart from the curiosity-seekers at the river, hadn't seen him. When Gabe spoke of Zoe and motioned for him to come to the front, Zoe rose to his paws and hobbled toward us on the stage. Though people had started to clap, Zoe turned back.

Joey eyed him intently. "Now what?"

Then Zoe performed one of those extraordinary things that made him the most unique creature we'd ever seen. I had left Grandpa's novel lying safely on the ground by Zoe, obviously not wanting to lug it to the stage. Zoe turned around, picked up the satchel by the strap—the same strap that he had held in his mouth as he journeyed weary mile after weary mile amid a labyrinth of underground streams—and dragged it to the front. Gabe had made several references to the novel by this time, so once Zoe came to the smaller raised stage and lifted the satchel toward me, the crowd went crazy.

"The cheering and yelling were as loud as a Steelers football game!" Joey whispered to me. "As though Bradshaw threw a touchdown pass to Stallworth!"

I thought the ceremony was now complete and that we could, thankfully at last, return to our seats and reduce this evening once again to manageable proportions.

Talk about being dead wrong!

Chapter 32

Jude's account (continued)

At the conclusion of Gabe's comments, Dr. Tabler, the conductor, came to the mic. "Now we request that our award recipients lead us in the singing of the final two verses of *Battle Hymn of the Republic*. Wouldn't you like that, audience?"

The crowd cheered enthusiastically.

"I understand there are several good singing voices in the group. Recipients of this year's Patriot Hero Award, please sing out with those patriotic voices!"

The six of us—Gabe, Charles, Joey, Laura, Cory, and I—found ourselves on the raised platform in front of a couple of mics. The crowd laughed heartily when a witty stagehand, who gave us the lyrics to the hymn, also offered a copy to Zoe. As we waited for the orchestra to commence playing, Cory quickly whispered in my ear, "There's no end to these surprises!"

"Including one dearer to my heart than all the others put together!" She was about to ask me what in the world I was talking about but couldn't as the orchestra had started playing. I merely tapped my pants pocket.

"I saw that!"

Normally, I'm embarrassed when I sing in front of a group. For the most part, I handle public speaking and classroom teaching with a minimum of anxiety, but public singing is a different matter. This evening was most unusual since my nervousness was gone at the end of the first bar as it was for the others. How we sang!

He has sounded forth the trumpet that shall never sound retreat
He is sifting out the hearts of men before the judgment seat.

Most of our group have decent singing voices—Charles a commendable bass, Gabe a very fine tenor, and I, in a desperate pinch, a (barely) passable baritone. But Cory, the excellent soprano, was the star. She was somewhat timid at the beginning, probably a little apprehensive, but soon she threw herself into it, heart and soul.

O be swift, my soul, to answer Him! Be jubilant,
my feet! Our God is marching on.

The thought ran through my mind as we sang, *Sometime angels do fly too close to the ground.* How ironic that I would think that particular thought, given the impending eventualities. Meanwhile, Cory belted out the song, as did Charles, Gabe, and the others. What really surprised me, and markedly inspired our singing, was the orchestra. When the drums, trumpets, and bagpipes came in for the last verse, the sound techs cranked up the loudspeaker volumes so high that the golfers down at Upper St. Clair Country Club could have heard us! Never in my life have I heard singing like that!

In the beauty of the lilies Christ was born across the sea,
With a glory in His bosom that transfigures you and me.
As He died to make men holy, let us die to make men free,
While God is marching on.

As the song ended, Gabe came to the mic. "To conclude our brief presentation this evening, we'd like to present this memento to our two recipients, Cory and Jude." We hesitantly walked forward, and then Pastor Gabe presented to each of us a lovely, full-stemmed, red Crimson Glory rose. The crowd again yelled and cheered.

"You can sure tell we're in Pittsburgh!" Joey nearly shouted out the corner of his mouth.

One's mind races in such nervous circumstance. At least my mind does. As I peeked down at the lovely red roses, I thought for one fleeting moment of Old Mary's dream of the roses. I have to be honest. Just for a second, Eliot's lines flashed in my too associative, too retentive brain:

> Footsteps echo in the memory
> Down the passage which we did not take
> Towards the door we never opened
> Into the rose garden

The flesh and blood counterparts of Mary's vision, we lived in reality what Eliot describes as memory and Mary experienced as dream. The nuances of the connection I did not fully ferret out until later with Cory's help, but even in that split second, I perceived one profound difference from the poem. *The speaker and guest in Eliot's poem never stroll the passage into the rose garden, nor open its door, but we actually walked the passage and opened the door too. Our life, metaphorically speaking, is that beautiful rose garden!*

Gabe then motioned to Chuck. "Now what?" Cory softly asked.

Chuck came forward to the mic. "Embodying true love as God intended it to be, Cory and Jude symbolize the sweet beauty of true love." He then showed us a braided garland of artificial but real-looking Lily of the Valley. "This is a strand of Lily of the Valley." He held it up so the crowd could see it and then presented it to Cory. "Jude and Cory, please entwine the garland around the two red roses as Pastor reads from 1 Corinthians 13."

Gabe's reading was superb:

"Love endures long and is patient and kind. It does not act unbecomingly (Cory looped the garland around the roses). Love does not insist on its own rights or its own way for it is not self-seeking (I looped it a second time). It is not touchy or fretful or resentful. It takes no account of evil done to it (Cory looped it again). Love bears up under anything, is ever ready to believe the best of every person, its hopes are fadeless under all circumstances, and it endures everything without weakening (I made the fourth loop)."

I eyeballed Cory. *Her cheeks are wet with tears, but these are tears of joy!* When we came to the crescendo ending of the passage, Pastor Gabe instructed us, "Please alternate your responses. 'Love bears all things.'" Cory spoke the words and looped the garland. "Believes all things." I reiterated the line and looped. "Endures all things." Cory's turn to speak and loop. *Her face is radiant as she speaks, for who's endured more than Cory!* "Hopes all things." I offered the last line and, simultaneously, the last loop of the Lily of the Valley-enwreathed roses. The crowd cheered as we finished and, together, held up the entwined roses.

At the end of this ceremony, inspiration struck me. When Gabe said "this illustrious group" will now end the evening's celebration with a final song and signaled to a stagehand to take his place at the control panel, I acted impulsively and gestured to Gabe that I wanted to say something before the last song. "If I may."

Holding the Lily of the Valley-entwined red roses, I decided to do right then and there what I had planned to do later that evening when Cory and I were alone on Vinlindeer. When Gabe motioned me to the mic, I started to move away from Cory who nervously gushed, "What's going on?"

I whispered in her ear, simultaneously reaching my hand in my pocket, "There are more things in heaven and earth, Horatio, than are dreamed of in your philosophy."

"*Hamlet*, Act 1!" she wittily responded.

The crowd cheered when I came forward, but I'm sure the applause wasn't for me. They enjoyed the chance to express gratitude to our group in general and, I was very certain, Zoe in particular. Nevertheless, they started yelling, "Speech, speech!"

"No speech!" Nervous out of my mind, I repetitively touched my head bandage. "But I would like to do something now that I planned to do later this evening." I turned to Cory and asked her to join me at the mic. She wiped a tear from her eye, reluctantly stepped forward, and squeezed tightly against me.

"What *are* you doing?" she asked in a not-so-quiet voice. Her face was red as Joey and Laura's had been earlier. The crowd laughed, obviously hearing her nervous question.

"Cory," I asked as I reached in my pocket, took out the small box and dropped to my knee, "will you marry me? What better moment to propose than right now?"

She was speechless and, instead of fumbling for words, gave me a huge kiss. The audience again cheered and came to their feet. "I love you, Jude Hepler...with all my heart! Yes, I will marry you. I love you!" Laura and Joey joined us at the mic and gave us big hugs.

After we stepped back to our positions on the platform, Pastor Gabe came to the mic. "Congratulations to two of my favorite people in the world. What a wonderful surprise! And how amazing is God's grace."

Gabe looks so wistful!

"Just a few days ago, this couple dodged death, and now they celebrate love!" Again, the crowd applauded. "Join us as our honorees lead in the singing of that most beloved of all hymns, 'Amazing Grace.' Technician, this is your cue, and you folks," he chuckled, indicating us, "hold on to the rail. We enjoyed watching Charles fly through the air, but we don't want a repeat!" All of us looked at each other in wonderment as the technician at the control panel prepared to push a button. *Now what's going on?*

At the sound of a click and the quiet grinding of gears, the small raised platform on which we stood started to rise. We gaped in amazement as we ascended upward, and even Zoe's ears perked up as he too, astonished, looked around. It was the first time I had ever seen a befuddled "What's happening?" look on his face. *This little event apparently lies even beyond his considerable sphere of understanding!*

When we were some fifteen feet in the air, the raised platform stopped, the crowd cheered, and the orchestra struck up a moving rendition of "Amazing Grace." Gabe invited us to lead and the audience to join. That was the most spirited singing of that song I've ever heard in my life. Cory sang with her entire being, her throat arteries bulging, her vocal cords straining, her heart bursting. Realizing in that special moment that Cory's magnificent voice deserved such attention, the rest of us spontaneously stepped back to allow her to lead.

The combined sound of the orchestra and singing was so loud that it grabbed the attention of many of the people in the park. Only about half of the crowd had come to the theater for the concert, but now pockets of people everywhere temporarily stopped their meandering. As I scanned the park from my elevated platform, I witnessed many people face the stage and robustly sing along. The full-throated singing, the orchestra, the drums, the blaring trumpets, and the bagpipes sent chills up and down my spine.

This is our one white singing hour of peace, and how beautiful it is!

Chapter 33

Jude's account (continued)

A memorable moment for me during the singing of the hymn at the Point State Park holiday celebration occurred when I picked out Duke in the audience. When our eyes connected for one brief moment, I could see that tears filled his eyes. *Duke was a hard-drinking, sex-crazed addict intent on raping Cory, but there he stands, a perfect example of the second-chance rebounder.* We winked at each other, and then, once he nudged Tina, she and I also caught each other's eye. Except for Cory, I do not recall seeing a more beaming face. My heart raced as I thought about Tina. In a matter of weeks, she had gone from a lust-driven desperately unhappy malcontent to a transformed woman with real hope and joy. *People who choose to right the wrongs of the past, like Duke and Tina, truly can become new creations in Christ, even after a life of torment!*

As we sang the last verse of John Newton's famous hymn—"When we've been there ten thousand years, bright shining as the sun"—I stole a glance at Zoe. I felt him brush against my knee as he rose to his hind paws, just as he had in the mine when he bade me goodbye. *What are you doing? Do you feel the torrent of emotion as we do? Are you also stirred by this occasion?* It was yet another variation on the old theme: what was the dividing line between his two natures, the canine and the human?

When we came to the final bars, I peered at Zoe, still raised on his hind legs. Though singing, I leaned down and stroked his snout. Many people in the audience, witnessing this simple gesture, brushed a tear from their eyes as they apparently identified with the adversity we conquered, the odds we battled, and, most likely, the dog that courageously saved us. Though I had no way of being certain, I was struck in passing by the notion that we perhaps embodied the spirit of the legendary grappling fighter from Pittsburgh—pitted against tough odds, notoriously hardworking, ever-rebounding, life-embracing, fear-conquering and, through it all, tenacious as hell.

After the program ended, life started to return to normal. We first checked out Chuck's eagle wings, though he and the others wanted to see Zoe and "have a gander" at Cory's ring. Laura was interested in the ring ("Cory, it's beautiful!"), but Joey the wings ("That is so cool!"). Chuck explained to Joey that he and the planning committee had undergone quite the rigmarole with the local authorities in having the zip line erected near the stage. "They made me demonstrate my landing!"

It's amazing the little things one recalls when looking back on such an unusual event. *The sky is the color of the vermilion sandstone which I saw in Utah, and these sounds are as festive as those I had heard after a Steelers victory over there at Three Rivers. How wonderful the jubilant laughter and the spontaneous merrymaking of happy people! The aroma of grilled hot sausage, funnel cakes, and caramel popcorn wafts through the evening air.*

I couldn't help but notes the scores of boats which cruised the rivers on this busy holiday weekend, readily visible from atop the raised platform. From that elevation, I was struck by the large number of people sporting their black and gold colors—Pirates t-shirts and ball caps, Steelers, and Penguins jerseys and sweatshirts. *Pittsburgh fans do take their sports team seriously!* The shooting spray of the large fountain at The Point had moistened the entire area, and every once in a while, the glistening spray created a misty rainbow in the evening sun. I gestured to it at one point. "See the rainbow?"

"That is so beautiful. I wish I could paint it right now!"

When the orchestra played "America the Beautiful," the patriotic fervor further overwhelmed Cory. "I ought to be writing down the ideas I'm getting for paintings."

"What else?"

"See that little boy giving his popcorn to the veteran in the wheelchair? That is an awesome picture of compassionate love—our painting ready-made as Browning's Andrea del Sarto would say."

"Exactly."

Once I let my mind settle on the utter uniqueness of the experience, I started to look with Cory's artist eye to note more fully the things that were right there in front of me, which I hadn't been seeing. Like Joey's perpetual looking over at Three Rivers Stadium (he couldn't take his eyes off the place), Duke and Tina's passionate kiss (they were really in love by now and oblivious to the fact that they made a real scene!), the women coming up to Cory and asking to see her ring ("Darling, it's lovely!"), people crowding around Zoe (hordes of folks came forward just to be near him), and the journalists jotting details in their notebooks and flashing cameras (we had no idea that the story would be given extensive coverage in Pittsburgh papers the next day).

As I reflect on the event, one detail carves itself in the marble of my mind with particular vividness—Zoe's impatience; or maybe *preoccupation* is the better word. As the festive celebration wound down, he gazed toward the shore with such intensity that I even glanced in that direction to see what he was looking at but saw nothing. *He peers at the spot where he came ashore and actually faces in that direction! Wonder why?*

"What are you seeing there, Zoebud?"

I didn't have time to think on this since we were besieged with people who wanted to congratulate us and hear more of the details on these various story strands: our miraculous escape, Zoe's sacrificial assistance, Tina and Duke's reconciliation, Charles's acquisition of special permission to zip line over the Point State Park amphitheater, and even Joey's performance in football. Though the questions and topics of conversation were endless and enjoyable, we gradually managed to free ourselves from the crowd, using the bedeviled Zoe as our excuse.

And it wasn't just an excuse. Despite his choice to follow Pastor Gabe into the theater instead of us, we knew we were delaying the inevitable. *He appears to have gathered strength through the evening, but it's nevertheless high time we get him the medical attention he des-perately needs.* Again, he gazed toward the shore, his face set like flint. *You ever strange dog! Just what is going on inside that head of yours?*

The question turned out to be more profound than I realized, the answer positively amazing.

Chapter 34

Jude's account (continued)

By this time, we had moved toward a small grove of trees near the river. While we were there, a small boy held out to Zoe a cup of his dark cherry-flavored beverage. *Sorry, young fellow! Water? Possible. Blood-red punch? Ain't no way!* Wanting to pass it by, Zoe rejected it three times but eventually delighted the boy by drinking all of it. *As if it was a cup of blessing!*

Zoe then started hobbling toward the river. At first, we didn't take particular note of his path since he headed in the general direction of the pontoon, but it soon became obvious that he was moving to the exact spot where he had come ashore. *We're only some twenty-five feet away from the river by now.* We followed, but Zoe—this is the strangest part which moves me anew to write about it—turned to face us, rose up on his hind legs, and held his left paw straight out like a board. *Having been broken during the cave-in, his right paw dangles pitifully! What a heart-wrenching sight!*

"It's as though he's telling us to stop!" Cory nearly shouted. We instantly halted, but after a moment, I continued a few paces. When Zoe again extended his paw even further, I froze in my tracks.

"He wants you to stop!" Joey yelled.

We were now huddled in a small group by ourselves, since people had departed from us, apparently sensing that we wanted to be alone and were at last seeking medical treatment for our dog. Once Zoe had stopped our movement, he came back to us. He rose up on his haunches and, though broken during the cave-in, stretched out his right paw to Pastor Gabe first and then to Chuck, each of whom extended their hands, sensing he was bidding them farewell. *He can't hold out his broken paw, but he's trying!* In turn, the men gingerly but firmly grasped the top of his leg at the chest and gently squeezed. Next, he walked to Laura and Joey, rose on his hind paws, and then hugged each of them.

"What's he doing?" Her voice low and trembling, Cory grabbed my bicep and squeezed so hard that her nails dug into my flesh.

Why do you whisper, my love? "It's as though he's saying goodbye!" *And why am I also whispering?*

Tears immediately came to Cory's eyes. "That's it! He's saying goodbye!" Cory's cheeks glistened with tears. "Zoe, honey, are you leaving us?"

Zoe by this time had hobbled to Cory who, like all of us, had hunkered down to his level. Up went Zoe to give her a big hug, and then—this touched me like nothing else—he gently placed his snout against Cory's cheek and held it there. He was completely still for a time and then backed away from Cory and looked her directly in the eye.

"It's as though you're looking into my very soul!"

Next it was my turn. *Now what's coming?* He rested his head on my shoulder and, cuddling it next to my neck, remained perfectly still. "Are you saying goodbye?" I backed away enough to gaze him in the eye. "Why can't you talk? You do everything else human!" *That really bugs me!*

When Zoe looked intently into my eyes, as he had Cory, I experienced the single-most different feeling I had ever registered in his presence. It's hard to explain, but simultaneously, I felt exposed, inadequate, even vulnerable. *It's as though he knows my thoughts, even knows me better than I know myself. Cory said it perfectly—as though he sees into our very souls!*

He held me in his gaze and licked me on the cheek. *Is this how you licked me when I lay unconscious on the mine floor after the cave-in?* He pulled away from me, picked up the satchel, and lifted it toward me. When I picked it up, he placed his paw on my hand. *This strange sequence of events gets crazier by the minute!* Sensing the gravity of the moment, all of us were silent. *Now it's we who can't talk. No wonder—there's nothing to say!*

His mission complete, his work finished, Zoe limped toward the water.

"Where are you going?" Cory was so excited she stumbled on the step.

"What are you doing?" Joey shouted with fiery fervency. "We need to know!"

Zoe, don't leave us! As he neared the water's edge, he went back up on his haunches one last time and lifted his broken paw in that same magnificent farewell gesture he had given me in the mine when he said goodbye. As it turned out, that farewell in the mine had been temporary, for even then he must have known that he would see me again a few days later.

Come to think of it, was Zoe planning his escape route when he stood near the pool of water and I furiously dug for the manuscript? Is that why he had paused and peered into the pool with such calculating intensity?

As I reflect on this point, I think back to the time when Christ had risen from the dead and walked behind the disciples on the way to Emmaus. He asked the two men what they were talking about and why they were sad, knowing full well that they despaired because their beloved Lord Jesus Christ had been crucified on a cruel Roman cross.

Did Jesus see the situation as humorous? According to one biblical scholar, Jesus knew full well that He would be revealing His identity to the Emmaus-bound men a short while later and would have anticipated, with some humor, the sheer joy that would overwhelm them when they learned that their Messiah had not only risen from the dead but, also ironically, conversed with them in person! That episode flashed to mind as I recollected Zoe's "death" in the mine. Was it somewhat comical to him that I despaired at his burial under tons of rubble when, at that very moment, he swam blissfully to freedom and carried Grandpa's precious manuscript to boot?

After Zoe hobbled the remaining couple feet down the concrete steps to the water's edge, he turned and fastened his gaze at the shooting water spout in the Point State Park fountain. Looking at the base of the water column, he slowly lifted his head in a slow deliberate upward pan. A second time, he stared at the fountain, though this time, when fixing his gaze at the base of the water column, he adopted the same bird dog stance which he had used in the mine when he peered at the conveyor belt with eyes of hope, while we peered into the canyon with eyes of despair.

Nothing you do makes rational sense, Zoe! More accurately, I should say that it made sense but on a level which we, prone to see through a glass darkly, could not grasp, again forcing us to confront his two natures: the fully canine one—comprehensible, knowable—which enraptured us endlessly; and his second nature—divine, even supernatural—which defied all logic and baffled us insanely. Little did we know how soon we would find the answer to this Oedipus riddle of the sphinx!

His mission accomplished, Zoe turned, gracefully slid into a cloud of rainbow-swirling water, and disappeared.

"He left us!" Joey shouted.

Cory wiped her tears. "Our angel dog is gone!"

Chapter 35

Jude's account (continued)

He had completely vanished! *Zoe slipped into the water and disappeared forever!*

"Where did he go?" Joey asked.

"Do you think he's going back to the fourth river?" It was Cory's turn to express befuddlement.

"If so, why?"

A barrage of questions caromed in our minds like the blasting limestone during the mine explosion. Question after question, agony after ecstasy, and the sadness of farewell after the rapture of reunion. *Our minds swirl with emotion like Lincoln at Gettysburg's cemetery! Thoughts fly in every direction!*

We gazed for a long time to see if we would spot him again. When he didn't surface in the river, we hoped we would see him on the other side and also glanced there. Even in those dark moments, I felt deep inside that he would return again in like manner. *Is this denial because I can't handle painful reality?* Our eyes went back and forth from the place where he had entered the water to the center of the confluence where, according to the bystander, he had earlier appeared out of nowhere.

Just then, the mocking football players moved in our direction. *Why don't they just go away? How I dislike these smart alecks for the way they treat Joey!* I watched them approach the young lovers who had wandered away from our group. *Did they move closer to the river to get a better view of Three Rivers Stadium or possibly to be near the spot where Zoe disappeared?* I gazed more intently at Joey. *He must be bristling on the inside, but yet he stands there with such poise! You amaze me!*

Cory and I watched from a distance as the athletes approached Joey. Swaggering up to him, Todd commenced the attack. "Your wonder dog just disappeared, just slipped back to his underworld haven? Maybe he'll come back again? Maybe Jesus will save him!"

When they mocked Jesus by pronouncing his name so derisively, I was filled with rage and thought of the righteous anger which the Bible justifies and, if not acted upon sinfully, even commands.

"Come to us, J-e-e-e-s-u-s!" Moorhead sneered. "We are exceedingly glad, for we have desired to see him for a long time!"

"Where is the promise that he'll come a second time?" Todd scoffed.

As I watched from a distance, it seemed to me that, except for Todd and Moorhead, their umbrage had lost its fire. I clutched the novel tightly to my breast. *How evil these scoffers! Our group has just been showered with congratulatory praise by a multitude of warmhearted Pittsburghers, yet these wiseass jerks, against that beautiful display of love, play out their stupid little scene simply because Joey bruised their fragile egos in a football game. What fools these mortals be!*

I was proud of Joey who turned to the guys and shrewdly exhorted, "Be careful, guys. Angry men are often humbled!"

Wow! A budding philosopher in our midst! Wordsworth's line at the end of "The Great Ode" flashed in my mind when the poet refers to "years that bring the philosophic mind." Like the philosophically wise man he is, Joey magnanimously walked away, not knowing that Cory and I had witnessed the whole disgusting scene.

After their last scan of the stadium, Joey and Laura rejoined us. What a confused cluster of hurting people we were! *Our rhapsodic joy has evaporated in an instant, and here we are, despondent out of our minds that mystery dog Zoe has disappeared forever.* I turned around, hoping to see Gabe or Charles. *Their words of wisdom always help. How we need them now!*

"I need a very big shoulder to cry on!" Cory touchingly lamented.

"Can you find two?"

Hovering in the vicinity, Chuck, thankfully, sensed our pain, came up behind us, and put his arms around our shoulders. *How comforting that feels!*

"Ripeness is all."

Cory and I in unison responded, "*King Lear.*"

"Is it all right to prefer the stage prior to full ripeness?" I jested.

"All things shall be brought to their destined end."

"Oh, *Hamlet!*" Brushing a tear from my eye, I quickly peeked at Cory. *She doesn't weep like that very often!*

Pastor Gabe then joined the conversation. *How I welcome you, wise one, into our coterie of criers!* "Chuck is exactly right. Things do come to their destined end, but we pitiful humans, constricted in the cubicle of the present, don't see these ends because of our pitifully myopic vision." He stopped for a moment and stroked his chin. "Maybe we haven't yet experienced the full ripeness of these events. The harvest isn't gleaned until the seed fully matures."

"Sir, I'm getting lost in your metaphor." *I hesitate to say this because I don't want to appear oppositional. Yet I genuinely want to know what Gabe means, since drinking from the cup of that man's wisdom is always refreshing, even invigorating. I can't afford to allow a single drop of that sacred enlightenment to fall to the ground. Still, I shouldn't have said that, for it's obvious Gabe is totally exhausted. He stands there frail and gaunt!*

"My point is simple. Zoe's life among us was extraordinary start to finish. He came out of nowhere and vanished just as mysteriously." Gabe deliberately paused.

Is he struggling to get his breath?

"During his months among us, we daily experienced what we call his dual nature. That he lived his life on two separate planes did not happen randomly. You don't see divine design in all of that?" Gabe pulled out his pocket Bible and deftly fingered the pages. "I don't know exactly what's going on here either, but I never waver in my belief that a controlling sovereignty has been demonstrably, albeit quietly, at work in our midst the entire time."

Gabe again hesitated, but this time, I knew that he was not catching his breath as much as formulating his words. *That's a relief!*

"God works out all things after the counsel of His will on both the natural and supernatural planes. In the case of the latter, God used animal life in many strange ways in the Bible. A staff turned into a snake in Exodus 7, a den of lions never stirred in Daniel 6, a dove carried an olive branch in Genesis 8, ravens fed Elijah in 1 Kings 17, God fashioned and used a worm in Jonah 4, and a donkey spoke in Numbers 22."

"I had no idea there were so many strange instances when God deployed animals for His purposes!"

"There are many other examples. The point I make is not complicated. What is so qualitatively different about a dog with human or even divine propensities in our midst? In a God-controlled world, is that, in the final analysis, so very strange?"

"Not when you put it in context like that!"

"In God's world, angelic appearances and supernatural phenomena are the norm." Gabe turned toward us with a twinkle in his eye, that beloved look we had come to love across the years. "Absolutely anything is possible in a world where a Carpenter rises from the dead!"

"How true!" Cory smiled so broadly I saw her bicuspids, both upper and lower!

"My despairing friends, you must see all of this through the lens of God's perspective—that is, through the eyes of faith. Physical eyes fry in their sockets when they attempt to behold God's supernatural work, so we must look with spirit eyes which absorb and utilize the supernatural!"

When Pastor Gabe paused, I thought he had reached the end of his ruminations, but he hadn't. "You're like Shakespeare's Gloucester: 'I stumbled when I saw.' Isn't that the line from *King Lear* which you quote on occasion?"

"It is, sir!"

He put his arm around me and concluded his reflection, "You don't want to be included in the group of blind people whom our Lord described in Matthew 13:14—those who see but do not perceive because of their dull heart."

I have the perfect response for Gabe. "You haven't read Shakespeare's *The Winter's Tale,* have you?

"No, I have not."

"What you're saying reminds me of a line in that play. The character Paulina says, 'It is required you do awake your faith.' I think that's what it comes down to—awakened faith."

"You're right. That is a powerfully relevant line. As Jesus said in Mark 9:24—'Lord, I believe; help thou mine unbelief.' Yes, awakened faith or increased belief. They're much the same."

It could have been my imagination, but it seemed that when pastor quoted this verse, his eyes deliberately stayed on Chuck. When I discreetly glanced at the professor, he bowed his head. *Is Chuck's skepticism being challenged by the events that are playing out here before our eyes? Is Gabe trying to get him to reflect on the spiritual dimension of these bizarre events? Eliot says in "The Dry Salvages," "We had the experience but missed the meaning." Is that what Gabe is doing? Making sure Chuck doesn't miss the mystifying meaning of these events?*

Cory was still very emotional because of Zoe's disappearance, so when I saw the positive effect of Gabriel's consoling words on her, I thought it best to withdraw a short distance and give them time together. When I did so, I found myself near the mocking guys who had harassed Joey earlier. I was amused to see that they had been listening to ever-wise Gabe. While they said nothing, it was obvious that of the group, only Todd and Moorhead resumed the mockery. Nodding their heads, both faked complete agreement with Gabe. Todd then commented on the pastor's earlier statement. "Of course, yes, of course. What's so strange about a talking donkey? This is a case when a talking dumbass refers to another talking dumbass!"

I was reminded of Peter's words to the Christians who were viciously persecuted during the massacre under the Caesars. Referring to them in a sermon right before July 4, Gabe said that the scoffers of the present day have died spiritually and, in the process, "lost their sense of patriotic fervor for our country." Gabe's sermon words came to mind: "The Bible indicates that 'Scoffers will come in the last days, walking according to their own lusts.'"

A tired wave of sadness swept over me as I watched Moorhead and Todd and thought of the battalions of students who, with tragic effect, assiduously cultivate the life of the mind while simultaneously neglecting, and in the process devastating, their dying souls. *If these other football players are clearly moved by Gabriel's comments—and obviously they are—then why aren't they strong enough to break away from Todd and Moorhead's evil influence and become their own men?*

As I compose this journal entry, I answer my own question: *The weak incessantly kowtow to the mighty. So now and evermore, but why? Pray tell, why?*

Chapter 36

Jude's account (continued)

T he next event on that Labor Day evening in Point State Park represents the very pinnacle of the unusual phenomenon that occurred during Zoe's months with us. As fantastic as the other experiences had been, what we were about to witness superseded all other events during his four-month stay, so much so in fact that it was as though the entire summer had been a series of rising conflicts which inexorably built toward this climax. The incredible thing is that, in seconds, it imposed sense on all the inexplicable happenings of the summer.

I realize that this is a seemingly hyperbolic thing to note. How can I dismissively say that such a monumental sequence of events—the mine cave-in and explosion, Dad's death, our narrow escape, and Zoe's miraculous reappearance—merely presaged the climactic revelation that next occurred in Pittsburgh? But I firmly believe that everything to this point had been mere prelude. How true the adage, "The past is prologue!"

For my own good, I paint the scene. After Zoe had disappeared, we huddled together by the shore, wild with flip-flopping emotions: joy over the grand evening ceremonial celebration, pulsating excitement that Cory and I were engaged—that was huge—and rapture that I held Grandpa's novel. Yet the loss of Zoe and the realization that I had a father all these years and that, at the moment of recognition, lost him forever filled us—especially me, of course—with a sadness that scarred the soul.

In the midst of those gyrating emotions, one of us looked at the fountain. I used to think it was Joey, then Cory, and sometimes I even think it was I! The point is one of us looked in that direction and gushed with excitement, "Would you look at that!"

"What?" the rest responded.

Joey shouted, "Keep watching the base of the fountain!"

We did so, and then we beheld, without exaggeration, the single-most remarkable sight of our lives to that point. Standing at the base of the fountain, an angel momentarily appeared—glorious, majestic, awesome. All of us recoiled as people in Bible days quaked in the presence of angels. Our astonished faces must have been something to behold! As several of us pointed to the fountain, Cory reflexively put her hands together as if in prayer. While people continued to meander about the Point State Park, we were frozen in our footsteps near the fountain!

"There he is again!" Laura screamed. Then he was gone but, for a second, appeared again.

"Describe what you saw," I said to the others, not trusting my own senses. Comparing our views of the angel, we noted that our reports corroborated exactly. The angel stood in the fountain, but, strangely, the water didn't gush from the bottom of the fountain but from the belly of the angel as if he was the source of the spurting jet.

Unfortunately, the football players, Todd and Moorhead, stood near us and, intently peering toward the fountain, were itching to resume their ridicule. *At least the other players have left them. That's one good thing.* One of the members of the harassing duo launched the barrage, "You really seemed to be interested in something there."

Typically, I pity these aimless souls who are cast adrift in a meaningless universe and—in their frightening world of chaos, random chance, and nothingness—are scared out of their minds. As they play out the mad folly of their lives, their options quickly dwindle: run, hide, or mock those who, in a quest for significance and purpose, attempt to work through life's ultimate questions to intelligent philosophic and spiritual meaning.

Joey informed me subsequently that it was Todd who ridiculed the most. By this time, his vitriol was aimed at all of us and not, to Joey's immense relief, just him. We had obviously used the word *angel* as our eyes locked on the fountain.

This was too much for Todd. "You see an angel there? Oh, yes, there he is! I see him too and am not *imagining* or *pretending* to see anything (he obviously saw no angel and mockingly exaggerated). There he is, right in the middle of the fountain! How very visible!"

Moorhead continued the mockery, "What am I to make of this miraculous sight? Guess I better get my arse ready for the Second Coming!"

Turning toward Todd and Moorhead, Joey spoke without a trace of malice. "Did you see him? We really did." Joey stopped for a moment, gazed again at the fountain, and then faced the men. "It would be a good thing if you had."

"No, jackass!" Todd nearly screamed. "I see nothing except two spraying jets, the fountain water, and the bullshit out of your freaking mouth. You're looking at water! This will come as a horrible shock to you, Joey Jazz. Fountains spray freaking water!"

"He's right!" Moorhead sneered. "We're at The Point, Einstein! What else is there but water? We see what is, but you and other mental midgets see only fantasy!"

"I wish you saw him."

What poise and maturation, Joey! Well done! I had not reached your level of maturity when I was a wet-behind-the-ears high school senior. Not even close! "I wish you saw him!" That was good, Joey—excellent!

We turned our attention from Todd and Moorhead and peered again, but we didn't see the angel.

"He's gone again! I can't believe we saw an angel!" Cory's voice lilted with excitement. "Talk about supernatural mind-boggling experiences: lose Zoe one minute, gain an angel the next!"

Continuing to focus our eyes on the fountain, we suddenly saw the angel again just for a moment, but this time, he was less diaphanously misty. Our eyes were riveted on the fountain, but even in that moment, I noted that Joey, because he was beside me, turned to Todd and Blake. "Did you see him that time? Right in the middle of the fountain?"

"No, moron, I didn't see an angel! Here's the deal. You maybe had a couple lucky plays on the football field, but in the world of reality, you're a walking, talking, suck fest loser!"

Moorhead piled on. "What happened to your reason? God help us if the future is entrusted to you Christian nitwits! We're freaking doomed to hell!"

All of us kept our eyes glued to the fountain. *No wonder people were overawed when they experienced angels one-on-one. Having this momentary glimpse is humbling beyond words. I couldn't imagine encountering an angel in the flesh as people did in the Bible. No wonder the Apostle John on the island of Patmos bowed in adoration after receiving the divine Revelation!*

As it turned out, the angelic visitation we experienced that evening was not over. Soon he appeared again, but this time, he was more majestic, somehow even more awesome. In the center of the fountain, we watched the angel, just for a moment, transform! It happened in an instant, but we distinctly saw it. First, one wing became a paw, then the other wing morphed, and just for a second, the head changed too. We were speechless as we tried to make out what we were seeing. Surely people thought we were crazy as we stared and pointed at the fountain. Several of us impulsively yelled, "It's Zoe! The angel is Zoe!"

"I saw it too! It is Zoe!"

"You're right!"

"Keep watching!" I screamed. *What a stupid thing to say!* I later thought to myself. What else would we do but keep eyes glued like adhesive to that fountain? It was a good thing none of us glanced away for even a second because Zoe or the angel allowed his upper torso to morph into his canine form again. I wiped away a tear to make sure I was seeing clearly. When he lowered his broken paw, his head instantly reassumed its angelic shape, and then he winked. It happened in a microsecond. I asked the others if they had seen the wink, but they didn't. *A winking angel? Surely not, but still, I know what I saw!*

Clearly visible in the center of the fountain, the angel had assumed full form by now, the water again gushing from his belly.

Do other people in the park see him? No one seems to take notice, but maybe they aren't looking in this direction. Or maybe the angel's revealing himself only to us. I don't know what to think!

If that supernatural harbinger was not visible to others, the next event definitely was. There will never be any mistaking that since it was the lead story in the Pittsburgh media. As we watched the angel, we could not help but think there was more to the event than a brief appearance in the Point Park fountain. What was the purpose of it all? To reveal Zoe's angelic identity to a handful of people? That doesn't even make sense!

More than ever, we confronted the two maddening questions. Why did Zoe come into our midst? Secondly, why had he singled us out for his visitation? We didn't have time to think much about this there in the park. After all, the appearance of the angel—from misty outline to bold appearance—occurred in a matter of seconds, but even in those fleeting moments, we knew there had to be an undergirding explanation, even if our rationally-manacled brains couldn't ascertain it. Still, we frantically attempted to impose some sense.

That's when it happened!

Chapter 37

Jude's account (continued)

The fountain angel assumed a magnificent pose, turned his head toward the highest building in Pittsburgh, the sixty-four-story UPMC tower, and imperially pointed to the top. When we turned in that direction, our little group partially bowed our heads in reverence, sensing, I suppose, that something grand was about to take place. *Something's going to happen. I don't know what, but I can just feel it!*

In that brief interval between the angel's pointing and the stunning appearance atop the tall building, the mocking athletes came near for their final shot. How they regretted it! While everybody else went merrily on with their holiday frivolity, the two mockers, having saved their final dose of venom, closed in for the kill.

Todd took the first shot. "Still seeing your angel friend with your clear rational eyes?"

"Maybe he's a voice in the wilderness. Maybe even a harbinger of Jesus!"

Moorhead again sarcastically accentuated the word, "J-e-e-e-s-u-s."

At that very moment, we heard an ear-piercing shout, "Hallelujah!" On top of the building, a huge Seraphim stood in all of his resplendent glory, his left arm stretching downward toward Point State Park, the right arm lifted upward with his fingers pointing toward heaven. Resplendent and majestic, his radiance cast a golden glow across the Pittsburgh sky.

My mind raced. *Is this the Rapture as some Christians believe? Are the faithful in Jesus Christ about to be called home to glory?* We were

Bible scholars enough to know that Christ was so dazzlingly bright that people could not look on Him. *But if that's the case, how then can this be the Christ?* The Apostle Paul had been struck blind for three days upon seeing The Holy One en route to Damascus. Accounts existed of some angels emitting a blinding light; but in this instance, the angel, veiling his glory, allowed us to behold his majesty. *In the same way one looks upon the glorious clouded enshrouded sun. But who is he, and why's he here?* He was far superior to Zoe the angel—larger, more glorious, somehow more regal. A thought crossed my mind. *Is this one of the four Seraphim who surrounds the Throne of God and beholds His majesty?*

Hearing the shout and engulfed in flooding light, all the people instantly faced the angel and gasped in awe. The magnificent Seraphim trumpeted again, "I command you to love as Jesus Christ taught you to love!" When I hastily scanned the crowd, I noted that many, awestruck, gazed at him with uncontainable joy on their faces; yet some of the people, having been slammed to the ground, screamed in fear and covered their heads with their hands. The angel thundered again, "Repent and prepare for the Lord's return!"

At that point, the Seraphim paused and lifted eyes upward. "He and only He is the way, the Truth, and the Life. This is a true testimony that God gave us eternal life. This life is only in His Son, the Lamb in the midst of the throne. There is salvation in no other name! He is the Shepherd who leads you to living fountains of healing water. The Spirit and the bride say, 'Come to the water!'"

These were his exact words, though there is little need for me to restate them here because everybody heard the holy utterances which were splashed throughout Pittsburgh and the national media and, subsequently, emblazoned on plaques and signs all over the tristate area.

Her eyes still on the angel, the befuddled Cory whispered, "Can you believe we're looking at an angel? Right here in front of us!"

Radiant and beautiful, the angel shone brightly like jewels reflecting the sparkling rays of the sun. "Hide us from the wrath of the coming Christ!" a man near me cried. Seeing him slammed to the ground in fear, I thought of the Roman guards, the elite and highly trained soldiers in the Garden of Gethsemane on the night of Christ's capture. *They helplessly fell to the ground when Jesus pronounced His name, "I am." Down went the helpless Roman garrison with the force of a sledge pulverizing granite. So much for human strength in the presence of the Lion of Judah!*

Like Zoe-turned-angel, the Seraphim stayed only for a moment, but the difference between the two supernatural angelic appearances was vast. Nobody but our group had observed Zoe, the fountain angel, whereas everybody saw the Seraphim. I was also struck by the responses of the people assembled in Point State Park—ecstatic joy or quaking fear. People had apparently either made their peace in this life with the God of gracious mercy or awaited Judgment Day when, utterly alone, they would face the wrathful God of divine justice.

I remember few other details of what was occurring around me since I was so astounded by the angel, but I do recall Pastor Gabe exclaiming, "Can you believe that this angel lives in heaven and beholds the face of the Holy God of all comfort!"

"How," I quietly asked Cory, "can we be sure that Gabe's statement is true? Is there biblical proof for it?"

"Yes, there is. Jesus Himself said, 'In heaven (children's) angels always see the face of My Father.' Imagine that!" Cory grabbed my hand and kissed it! "This angel, just moments ago, was in heaven looking on the face of God. The very thought blows me away!"

"Where's that verse in the Bible?"

"Matthew 18:10. No wonder the angel lit up the entire Pittsburgh sky!"

When the Seraphim disappeared and his revelation ended, I glanced around and saw that Todd and Moorhead, fearful as though bludgeoned, were pinned to the ground. Shaking uncontrollably, they cupped their hands over their faces to shield themselves from the majestic angel. *Such groans of horror! Their wailing is unnatural, animal-like, primordial!* After several minutes, the two men angled their heads slightly to afford a fast peek through tightly wedged fingers. Seeing that the angel was gone, they slowly struggled to their knees but involuntarily glanced over their shoulders in fear. They teetered to their feet.

The appearance of the two mocking men amazed us. They had been thrown to the ground with such force that their faces were covered with dirt. Traces of blood splattered Todd's nose and Blake's forehead, their pants and shirts were stained with grass, and contorted in primal terror, their faces were sickly white. Speechless and virtually paralyzed, they had changed in seconds from cocky youths to fearful men shaken to the very core.

They remind me of the soldier who stood at the foot of Christ's Cross on Golgotha—jeering at Jesus one moment, cowering in panicky dread the next! Hey, smart alecks, what happened to your cockiness?

Several seconds after the Seraphim disappeared, we watched the fountain to see if Zoe-turned-angel might reappear again. There he was in angelic form! For a brief moment, he metamorphosed one last time into Zoe the dog. When he saw that we were looking at him, he rose to his hind haunches—this is the part that made all of us laugh hysterically—and then winked! Yes, a winking dog! *They all saw it this time, so it wasn't my imagination earlier!* We howled with the pent-up release of nervous laughter that gushes from a giddy child.

Then, that fast, Zoe disappeared. *This time, our harbinger friend is gone forever! I just know it!*

The two oscillating emotions of the day surfaced one last time: extreme joy that we had witnessed the angels and, simultaneously, sadness too that our buddy, Zoe, was gone. Yet those human emotions were completely dwarfed by and subsumed within the worship of the majestic Christ of whom the celestial Seraphim spoke and to whom he pointed. In a sense, we were grieved to inhabit our earthly bodies, these temporary temples of clay, since like the Apostle Paul, we wanted to go to heaven but stay on earth too.

Cory wistfully gazed upward. "The Seraphim slipped through the veil and, at this very moment, flies back to heaven!"

"You're right. How real this makes our mansion over the hilltop!"

Joey's exclamation summarized our corporate feelings. "I can't begin to believe this! A Seraphim in Pittsburgh!"

Chapter 38

—— ✂ ——

Jude's account (continued)

After the departure of the majestic angel, another thought crashed into my mind. *What happened to my dad?* I whispered to Cory, "Where do you think Dad is?"

Cory's stared blankly, and then her eyes moistened with tears. "We have no way of knowing, but you fear eternal damnation." She drew close and put her arms around me.

"The thought convulses me. Look at this. My hands shake as they did after I shimmied up the rope!"

Though Pastor Gabe did not hear this last exchange, he had heard our earlier comments about longing for heaven. "We lament the crazy evil of our day, but we should focus on how the appearance of the angels has really heartened us. In God's good time, we will be taken out of this world, but for now, the battle cry is work and more work, for the night comes when all kingdom labor ceases."

"Thanks, Gabe!" *Wonder why I call you "wise one"?*

Irresistibly, we were drawn to the fountain. *Why? Because we want to be near where Zoe had been? Because we want him to return again?*

As we sauntered along, Tina, Duke, and Charles approached our group. "Can you believe it?" Chuck blurted. "We saw two angels! How fantastic!"

I marveled at the change in Chuck. His skepticism conspicuously absent, he continued to gush, "I simply can't believe it!"

Gabe was just as excited. "Talk about awesome grandeur!"

He's trying to say more but is speechless. Through that single ecstatic utterance and the subsequent speechlessness, Cory and I again noted Gabe's exhaustion.

Cory whispered, "Gabe reminds me of Daniel who had received a vision from the Archangel Gabriel."

"I don't remember that account."

"After one of his grandiose visions in Babylon, Daniel fainted and was sick for days."

"Now I know why!"

Despite Gabe's relative silence, our group commenced a frenzied discussion about the Seraphim's proclamation. What a cacophony! Having regained some strength by the fountain, Pastor Gabe eventually led us in prayer. An impromptu prayer never touched me as deeply as that one by the confluence of the rivers. *How he does pray!*

We overheard a few of the people in the vicinity of the fountain comment that they wanted to purchase a memento of the night the Seraphim appeared in Pittsburgh. As they meandered around, I noted that the vendors swarmed with people who apparently shared that idea.

Duke broke the silence in our group. His question surprised me since he had, for the most part, been quiet through the conversation, apparently too overwhelmed for speech, though I had seen him whisper to Tina. "You know what we'd like to do?" His question was directed at all of us, but he faced Pastor Gabe, so it was he who responded.

"What's that, Mr. Manningham?"

"Tina and I would like to be baptized right here in the fountain." He paused a moment to collect his words. "This water's clear as hell. Sorry! I shouldn't swear on holy ground." He laughed. "Guess I should say 'holy water' because the angel appeared in the fountain, not on the ground. Can you baptize us?"

Tina's face was radiant. "Please!"

His self-consciousness about his arm had now vanished. "Would it be all right to be baptized with one arm in the air?" He put his massive arm around Tina and drew her against him. "Sir, can you baptize a couple worthless sinners?"

"I don't see any signs that restrict stepping into the fountain."
Gabe paused for a moment and looked around to consider logistics.

"Then let's do it! You good with this, babe?"

"I want to be baptized more than anything in the world!"

A lamb to his shepherd, Duke addressed Gabe, "Can you lead
us to the fountain?"

"I can, but in a larger sense, it is 'the Lamb (Who) will shepherd
them and lead them to the living fountains of water' (Revelation
7:17). As long as we keep that profound truth in mind, I'm game.
And to answer your earlier question, I see absolutely nothing wrong
with an arm lifted like the Seraphim's." Gabe turned to Tina. "You
won't mind going back to Kittanning in wet clothes?"

"Are you kidding? It will be a good reminder of how I've been
cleansed from all the filth of my disgusting life!" Overwhelmed by
the events of the evening and the prospect of the impending baptism,
she shed joyful tears.

Cory picked up on Gabe's reference to the breeze. "When you're
walking back to your car, the cool breeze will remind you of the wind
of the Holy Spirit. Remember how Pastor Gabe said in last week's
sermon that the Holy Spirit comes upon us like a refreshing wind
at salvation?" Cory turned to the pastor. "You spoke about Christ's
conversation with Nicodemus and how the refreshing Holy Spirit is
like the wind."

"I give you Acts 3:19. 'Repent therefore and be converted, that
your sins may be blotted out, so that times of refreshing may come
from the presence of the Lord.' No refreshing equals that!"

As Cory spoke with Gabe and Tina about the Holy Spirit, I
stole a look at Chuck. *Has he ever been baptized? If we weren't tightly
clustered in a circle, I'd ask Cory. Chuck, please be baptized! You'll never
have a better occasion!*

He did not. Because he had previously been baptized? Because
he remains skeptical and isn't spiritually prepared? *I need to talk to
him about this. I have no idea what he's thinking, but standing by the
fountain, he watches the proceedings with the fascination of a transfixed
little child!*

Meanwhile, Gabe referred to Cory's point about Nicodemus. "You make a good point, Cory, for that's exactly how we see baptism, an outward symbol of the inner change that occurs when believers receive Christ." Gabe took a halting step toward the fountain. "My left leg's acting up a bit, so I'm not walking so well this evening. Duke, could you please help me into the fountain? Thank you. Baptizing you on this memorable evening will be the joy of a lifetime."

When Duke assisted Gabe, we were shocked to see him struggle to lift his left leg across the side; but once in the fountain, the buoyancy of the water aided him, and he carried on flawlessly. *How shocking to witness his near stumble!*

Positioned in the fountain, Pastor Gabriel assumed his normal authoritative comportment. "Standing here, I'm reminded of a passage I read in the Scriptures yesterday." Taking out his Bible from his breast pocket, he turned to the Psalms. "Listen to verses 8 and 9 of Psalm 36: 'They are abundantly satisfied with the fullness of Your house, and You give them drink from the river of Your pleasures. For with You is the fountain of life; In Your light we see light.' Don't those verses have a marvelous relevance to the water and light we've seen this evening here in Pittsburgh?" Gabriel looked pensively across the expanse of waters. "Surely, the book of Job refers to a sight like this when it describes 'the rivers flowing with honey and cream' (Job 20:17). This scene also makes me think of David in Psalm 65:9, 'the river of God is full of water.'" Gabe scanned the surroundings. "It certainly is full here as we see three rivers, one for each member of the Trinity!" He gestured to Duke and Tina. "Please join me here."

They stepped into the fountain. The Lord was gracious and gave us privacy for our service, all the other folks having sauntered through Point State Park to various vendors and exhibitions. Pastor Gabe movingly pronounced the ancient words, "I baptize you in the name of the Father, the Son, and the Holy Spirit." In his preferred mode of baptism, he completely dunked them in three separate immersions, one for each member of the Trinity, which he reverently pronounced.

As the ceremony proceeded, Cory and I alternated our gaze between the baptism ceremony and the base of the fountain.

"Can you believe we had an angel in our lives all those months?" I whispered.

"That is amazing. And look what else is amazing."

"What?"

"Duke and Tina are completely different from the people they've always been."

"You're right."

"Is that water coursing down Tina's face baptismal or penitential?"

"Hard to tell!"

From where I was standing by the fountain, I could not resist a fast look up to the top of the tall building. Through the dewy cloud which hung in the air like the mist above Niagara Falls, I stared at the spot where the Seraphim had appeared. Trembling again at the recollection, I bowed my head. *"God, I covenant right here and now to get serious about my spirituality. Give me strength to walk the talk and to complete the work, no matter how humble, which You have given me to do. Amen."*

As part of the brief baptism ceremony, Pastor Gabe recited a verse from Isaiah: "The Lord will guide you continually, and satisfy your soul in drought, and strengthen your bones; you shall be like a watered garden, and like a spring of water, whose waters do not fail" (58:11).

I thought of my canoe ride at Beatty's Mill last May when I had run aground in a dried tributary and was without water on that unusually hot day. *How different those stagnant waters from this gushing fountain that jets upward with such force and these mighty waters surrounding me at the confluence!* All that water made me thirsty. *Why am I always thirsty?*

"I'm always thirsty," I whispered to Cory. "I say that often."

"Because you crave water."

"Why? Maybe because I've been yearning for the water Gabe is talking about or maybe the river that flows with honey and cream. I missed Job's image."

"Job was a poet!"

"And then some! The poetry in Job is stunning."

To conclude the brief ceremony, Pastor Gabe read from Isaiah 48:18—"Oh, that you had heeded My commandments! Then your peace would have been like a river." Gabe embraced Duke and Tina. "You have indeed heeded God's commandments and will now know lasting peace like these rivers which flow as peacefully as honey and cream."

"I feel so clean!" Tina remarked, standing by the fountain's edge. "I just hope I don't stumble on my new path."

"You would do well to remember the words of Jeremiah: 'I will cause them to walk by the rivers of water,' like these still waters, 'in a straight way in which'—catch this next part—'they will not stumble' (Jeremiah 31:9). Draw strength from the comforting truth that God will walk beside you. He will keep you from stumbling."

"What great verses! Those are perfect for this holy place!" Duke passionately kissed Tina. "I know what you mean, babe. I've never felt so good! I didn't think a wretch like me could know joy like this!" Duke walked over to Cory. "Can you forgive a depraved and worthless animal?"

"You know I do, Duke. God has extended complete forgiveness to me, so the least I can do is extend that same forgiveness to you." She warmly hugged both Duke and Tina.

As we went our separate directions, I saw a tear in Duke's eye and heard him softly speak to Tina. "Jesus lives in her so completely that she even forgives me for the horrible things I did!"

"That's true love. Here's hoping we have that someday!"

Strolling to the dock, I murmured to Cory, "That is one changed guy!" I put my arm around her waist.

When we approached the pontoon, I glanced at the spot where Zoe had been sitting like a scout when we neared the city.

Zoe, you sat right there! Angel dog, where are you now? And why were you with us this beautiful summer?

Chapter 39

On the Wednesday after Labor Day, Jude, dismissed from work a bit early, drove to see Cory at her house. Still off work with her foot injury but getting around well in her boot, she enthusiastically supported Jude's idea of dashing into the Armstrong County Court House to examine the detailed physical and topographical maps of the waterways of Armstrong County. "Because Grandpa's Ordinance Survey Map and your dad's General Reference Map are of little help."

"I agree!"

On the way to the courthouse, Jude spoke excitedly about his grandpa's novel. "Good news: I've started the opening chapters."

"What's your impression so far? I'm dying to know."

"Strange to say, I'm not actually sure. I haven't read enough to form an opinion, but I'm getting a sense of where he might be headed."

"I can imagine how thrilling this is for you."

Jude struggled to formulate his thoughts. "I'm fascinated by the way Grandpa enlivens the past, especially the era of the Founding Fathers. Even in these couple chapters, I felt I was immersed in Washington's world. The great George Washington is so real in these pages."

"Until you read it, I'll back off."

"Does that include backing off me?"

"Not in this life, Judah Jedediah!"

"One serious point. I understand what Chuck meant when he said Grandpa was a kind of specialist on the topic of demons." Jude stopped to reflect on the pages he had read so far. "I actually talked to Chuck about this. His answer blew me away."

"What did he say?"

"Grandpa was so into demonology that he even asked Chuck to get him a copy of the book on that subject which England's King James I had written in 1599. That amazes me!"

"Truly."

"I'm starting to see that Grandpa was more of a scholar than I realized."

"To think that we knew so little about his novel!"

"Here's one more thing. Grandpa creates a very vivid sense of time and place, and that's an impressive accomplishment for any writer."

"Anything else?"

"The writing flows with the ease of a gliding hawk because he's such an excellent prose stylist, but if you don't mind, let me reserve further comment until I read some more."

"Good deal."

At the courthouse, Jude and Cory went to the office of a Mr. King who was excited that he was able to play a small part in the whole drama. By that time, the Labor Day event in Pittsburgh had been covered in the tristate area media. Photographs of Jude, Cory, the family, and Zoe, along with in-depth coverage, had even made it to a number of national publications. The local newspaper, the *Leader Times,* had keyed on the event and made it their lead story for both Tuesday and Wednesday.

From Mr. King's point of view, it was an honor for these local folks to show up in his office seeking his help. A man who had always been intrigued with angels, he was fascinated that Jude, Cory, and the family had spent their summer in the presence of an angel who, incredibly, had materialized in the form of a dog during those months.

"I can't believe we had an angel here in our county the whole summer! In the shape of a dog no less! That really is something when you think about it."

"No argument here!" Cory replied.

Mr. King picked up the maps in front of them. "Let's get down to business and see if we can track Zoe's underground water journey into Pittsburgh."

Carefully examining the streams that issue from the Winfield mushroom mine, the trio traced Zoe's most likely journey through an elaborate network of underground streams that eventually lead out of Armstrong County.

"I think that's the route," Mr. King theorized, pointing to the stream that exited the mushroom mine.

Jude studied the map carefully. "I agree."

"It's obvious that he started from this point, and these are the connecting waterways, so that's my best guess."

"I concur too. There appear to be no other options."

Mr. King put his elbows on the table. "I can't imagine what that three-day journey in pitch-black dark would have been like. A human could not have done that!"

From there, however, Zoe's journey south was a distinct mystery. Had Zoe resurfaced in the Allegheny River since all of Armstrong County waterways eventually empty there? At first, that seemed the tenable explanation, but Zoe had not surfaced in the Allegheny River at some point above The Point and swum downstream.

"No," Jude reiterated, "we're sure that he surfaced in the middle of the great confluence out of nowhere."

"How can you be so sure? That's the part that doesn't make sense to me."

Cory leaned forward. "We actually have proof of that. A man had been taking a movie of the three rivers in the foreground and the Duquesne Incline in the background. The movie clearly shows Zoe surfacing right in the middle of the three rivers. One second, he isn't there, and the next, he is! That's why we're so positive that Zoe didn't get to the middle of the confluence by swimming down the Allegheny."

"That's what made us wonder," Jude continued, "if he had made his way into Pittsburgh's mythological fourth river."

Mr. King carefully folded the map. "That in itself is an exciting possibility for many Pittsburghers since people have wondered across decades if the fourth river is merely the stuff of lore. A real mystery surrounds that subject. Zoe's strange appearance perhaps lends credence to its existence."

"You'll find this mysterious too," Cory added, "but our Pastor, Gabriel Wyant out at the Center Hill Church, jokingly said that Zoe was like Melchizedek in the Old Testament."

"That went right over my head. What did he mean by that?"

"Melchizedek in the Bible," Cory expounded, "had no origin and no end. He just materialized out of nowhere."

"That appears to be what your angel dog did. His final chapter was certainly very different!" Mr. King placed the map on the counter and folded his hands on it. "To think we had an angel in Armstrong County!"

Chapter 40

⁜

The meeting with Mr. King took place on Wednesday. On the next day, Morley Spencer gave Jude and Cory a telephone call and asked them to stop by his security office in the mushroom mine at their earliest convenience. Reserved by nature, Morley showed atypical excitement when he requested that the pair examine some fascinating footage from the security camera in 50/10 which he had recently come across.

"I thought at first," Morley began, "that the footage of the Friday evening cave-in was worthless. The footage taken in 50/10 was blank, but to be honest, that didn't surprise me."

Cory was immediately interested. "Why?"

"That particular camera often is often on the blink since it's an old one that was never replaced."

Jude was equally curious. "Why not?"

"Because it's an unused corridor." Morley tapped the monitor with a pen. "At any rate, when I saw the blank screen, I began to walk away, thinking that this was one of those days when the camera was AWOL."

"So the camera works occasionally?" Jude queried.

"Sometimes yes, sometimes no. On this day, the screen was completely blank. I rewound the tape to check another section just to make certain, and again, I saw nothing. Just as I had taken the last sip of coffee from my mug and got up to leave, I saw a dim flash of light on the screen."

"What was it?" Cory wondered.

"I wasn't sure. It was nothing clear, just some sort of a flickering light, but it caught my attention, so I continued to watch the screen."

The upshot of the session with Morley was one of the exciting developments in the entire Zoe-turned-angel saga. When he rewound the footage, Morley saw the corridor quite clearly.

"The screen had been blank, not because the camera was malfunctioning but because the air was so full of cave-in dust! When I was looking through that thick wall of dust, I just assumed that the camera was on the blink, but it wasn't that at all. Actually, the footage is surprisingly clear prior to the cave-in, as you'll see. And once the dust settles, it's good again."

It was fascinating for Jude to see the entire scene from this reverse angle. "I experienced the events from the other end of the corridor." He pointed to the upper part of the monitor. "After unearthing the novel, I sped clear down there in seconds. Fear, thy name is man!"

"Jude's adapting Shakespeare's 'Frailty, thy name is woman.'"

"Thanks, Cory. I've heard about Jude's poetry quotes!"

Though the camera was some seventy-five feet back from the cave-in site, it clearly showed a panorama of the whole sequence of events, including Zoe's lunge at Jude to knock him out of the way of the falling boulders.

"It's a wonder Zoe didn't snap your back! He hit you with tremendous force!"

"Tell me about it!"

"Look at how your head jerks back." Morley rewound this key footage and played it again, hitting the pause button on the recorder at the moment of impact. He tapped the screen with a pencil. "The rocks are falling as Zoe's in mid-flight. See them here at the top? He must have sensed that the loose boulders had started to slip."

"That's when he made his sacrificial lunge." Look at the size of these rocks that slammed Zoe to the ground!"

Morley extended his arm and placed his hand on Jude's shoulder. "You'll have trouble with this next sequence. Watch the trajectory of the two rocks." *Jude will hate this part!* "This slow-mo blowup shows one huge rock glancing off Zoe's back and the other landing on his front paw."

"This is really good but really moving, Morley." *It's so difficult to sit here and watch this!* "You went to a lot of work to create this. Thank you very much."

"Cory's right," Jude agreed. "It's tough to watch that ghastly moment when Zoe's front right paw was broken."

After the two boulders fell, there was a momentary delay before the actual cave-in. Jude offered his explanation. "The rocks that had fallen to the floor were wedged side by side and completely blocked the corridor. You see Zoe's dilemma. Because of his broken paw, he couldn't jump over them."

Cory slumped in her chair. "You can see that he's completely trapped!"

"Yes, but he wasn't just impeded by his physical handicap. Watch when I show this in real-time." Morley replayed the clip without the slow-motion feature. "You see how fast everything happened. There was only a slight delay between the falling of the two boulders and the cave-in."

Zoe could be seen slowly struggling to his feet, and for one brief moment, as the avalanche of rocks poured down, there is a break in the dust cloud which started to fill the corridor. On the edges of their seats, the trio watched the screen.

"Play that again!" Jude shouted all of a sudden.

Cory's head was inches from the screen. "What did you see?"

"Look in the center, up here at this cleared area in the dust." Jude pointed with a pen to an area where the dust was less dense. "There I am way down the corridor!"

"Can you blow that up?" Cory asked.

"Hang on." Morley enlarged this portion of the screen.

Cory was the first to react. "Look at the panic on your face! You are stopped dead in your tracks!"

"I am completely frozen! From this angle, you can see Zoe rising to his hind haunches."

"Now he's holding up his wounded leg!" Cory exclaimed. They continued to watch the clip. "What's he doing now? You can't tell from this rear angle, but it sure looks like a salute!"

When they watched the rocks come crashing down, Jude was confused. From his vantage point far down the corridor, it appeared as though the rocks fell directly on Zoe, but they did not.

"I was bewildered because this whole thing is an optical illusion. From where I was standing way down the corridor, it looked as though the two big boulders and the avalanche fell right on the hole—and, of course, on Zoe too—but that's not what happened. The rocks fell down the corridor on my escape side."

Cory completed the thought. "Meaning that the hole you dug didn't fill up with rocks because the cave-in never disturbed it?"

"Precisely."

Morley redirected their focus to the screen. "The sequence of events here is extraordinary. When the rocks fell, Zoe hurriedly hobbled back from the hole toward the security camera. See him go?"

Jude never batted an eye. "I see what happened. Zoe must have plopped into the water and completely disappeared from sight. Look at how the screen goes completely blank at this point because of the thick cloud of dust."

"Right. It stays that way for some time. It was this section I had first examined when I started looking at the footage. You can see why I thought the camera was dead. Not a thing is visible through the dust."

They looked at the screen for quite a while. "Is it finished?" Cory asked at last. "Is that all there is?"

"No. Eventually, the dust settles, and you'll see the water in the pool grow calm. Zoe is gone, and the corridor beyond the hole where Jude had sped is completely filled with rock."

Cory wiped a tear. "How indescribably sad!"

Jude picked up the commentary. "Except for a few isolated rocks in the area, the hole looks as it had when I finished digging. A haunting silence and tomblike stillness pervades everything." *This reminds me of Faulkner's line in* A Rose for Emily: *"A thin, acrid pall as of the tomb seemed to lie everywhere upon this room..." As of the tomb! Exactly like this tomb!*

"Nothing changes on the tape for quite a while except that the image clears as the dust settles."

The group waited and watched. Nothing happened except that the visibility improved.

"Take note of this next part. Keep watching the water."

"Why?" Cory couldn't suppress her excitement. "What's going to happen?"

Morley chose a minimalist response. *She'll go crazy!* "Just keep your eyes peeled!"

The water in the pool eventually started to ripple, gently at first, and then more vigorously. All of a sudden, Zoe surfaced!

"I get it!" Jude exploded. "The plopping sound I heard at the time of the cave-in was actually Zoe. At the time of the cave-in, I thought that a large boulder fell into the pool, but it wasn't that. It was Zoe!"

They watched the screen in silence. "This is the part that is so moving to me."

No wonder Morley felt this way. For the longest time, Zoe is visible in the water.

"Look at that!" Jude exclaimed. "His body is completely submerged except for his head and left paw. It's as though he's resting them on the limestone floor."

Morley was as fascinated as Jude and Cory. "He keeps the wounded paw submerged in the ice-cold water."

"That probably soothed his wound," Jude theorized. Their eyes were riveted to the screen.

Cory jumped back. "I'm glad this isn't in color because the pool would be red with blood. Look how his head's bleeding!"

"Now watch what happens." Morley tapped the screen. "Zoe's staring at the hole where you dug and then down at the water where he remains submerged—back and forth. Carefully look at this next sequence. I blew it up and put it into slow motion so you could see it better."

This is the part which brought tears to Jude and Cory's eyes there in Morley's office and many times later when they replayed the sequence. The footage shows Zoe, submerged in the cool water, struggling to climb out of the pool with his damaged paws.

Morley resumed his commentary. "Take note of this. See how he limps over to the hole and looks into it."

"All right, I get it. When the upright support beam slipped down into the hole, it landed directly on top of the satchel. That part's easy to figure out. When the roof crossbeam here"—Jude again pointed to the screen with his finger—"shifted downward, it increased the gap between the horizontal roof beam and the loose rocks above it. One slight disturbance to the upright pole would obviously cause the entire ceiling, crossbeam and all, to crash to the ground."

Caravaggio could have painted this! "You're right! Look how much bigger the gap is between the horizontal crossbeam and the boulders above."

Jude picked up the narrative. "I have a theory about what's going on here. Zoe, thinker that he was—and thinker with a divine nature as we learned in Pittsburgh—realized the awesome stakes."

"Stakes? What do you mean?" Morley asked.

"If he escaped down the water hole to safety, the manuscript would be gone forever. On the other hand, if he pulled the exposed strap to extract it, he knew he'd cause a catastrophic cave-in."

"I think you're right, sweetheart. It's as though he's contemplating his next move—flee to safety or risk his life to save the novel."

Zoe at this point slipped back in the cool water, reclined his head on the ledge, and stared at the hole.

"You'll be amazed at this part. Note Zoe's face."

"Perhaps he's thinking of how furiously I worked to find the novel. Maybe that's why he tried to retrieve it, but when I was digging, I was too preoccupied to note any of this."

Cory's eyes were bonded to the screen. "I think you're right. His tail was wagging madly the whole time, even though he was aware of the danger but you weren't!"

The trio continued to scrutinize the footage. After Zoe rests his head on the mine floor, his body still submerged, he again struggles out of the water, even with greater effort this time, and peers toward the hole.

Morley wiped a tear. "As he begins this pain-filled, fifteen-foot trek back to the hole, his face is set like flint."

Jude slid his chair back. "Because he's made up his mind, and there'll be no turning back. He's obviously troubled and deeply distressed."

Cory also marveled. "I call that the face of sorrow!"

They watched the resolute Zoe limp toward the hole. "He's decided to drink the sorrowful cup of woe," Jude bemoaned. "Talk about being acquainted with grief!"

"What's on his foot?" Morley asked after a moment. "I hadn't noticed that before."

"I had fashioned a boot for him to stop the bleeding and pad his paw. His foot was badly cut and left a horrible trail of blood. I worried a lot about that during our epic escape."

The footage shows Zoe again pausing at the hole. "Here's my hypothesis," Cory ventured. "He knows that the beam will kick when he tugs on the satchel. He's smart enough to know that severe injury or maybe death will result."

"Definitely," Morley concurred. They watched another moment. *They won't like this part!* "This is the ultimate act of sacrifice. Keep your tissues nearby!"

Chapter 41

The film clip shows Zoe resolutely staggering to the hole, taking the strap in his mouth, and then stepping back a couple steps to draw it taut.

"He's looking up at the ceiling one last time," Cory whispered to Jude, "calculating his chances. Look how he waits a couple seconds. It's so obvious what he's doing!"

"As though saying, 'Not my will!'"

Their eyes glued to the screen, they watched Zoe give the strap a savage tug. When he pulled it, the satchel flew completely out of the hole, but the jerking motion caused the support brace to crash to the floor along with the enormous boulders above it.

Morley's work at this point was, according to Jude, "brilliant." He had blown up this next section of tape and converted to slow motion so that the sequence was readily visible, even in the dust-filled room.

"When Zoe tugged on the satchel," Morley hypothesized, "he was apparently smart enough to stand back from the hole as far as possible, hoping of course that the beams and rocks would fall in front of him."

"That part apparently went according to plan," Cory interjected.

Looking at the footage, Jude tried to piece together the sequence of events. "For the most part, the rocks fell into the hole. However, what Zoe wasn't able to anticipate was the trajectory of the falling crossbeam. Look at the large nails projecting from the end of it. Stop the tape, Morley!"

"Why?"

"Look at the sharp spikes at the end of the top crossbeam!" When Morley paused the tape, Jude tapped the screen with his pencil to indicate the long spikes.

"I'm starting to get the picture." Cory too had a sense of what happened. "When the crossbeam detached from the support post, it smashed violently to the ground. Look in real-time how fast it occurred, but when it slammed to the floor, the crossbeam grazed Zoe's side, meaning those large spikes slashed his ribs!"

"Exactly." Note this blowup if you want absolute proof." Huddling together, the group sat on the edge of their seats and breathlessly stared at the monitor. "Look at Zoe's side." Morley blew up the sequence when the falling crossbeam gashed Zoe's ribs. The projecting nail cut into his chest so deeply that even the top of the board scraped his side. See here."

"This means that this long top spike, that one," Jude reasoned, again tapping the screen, "would have pierced deeply into Zoe's chest. The entire length of the nail slashed him right between the ribs. Watch Zoe violently jerk away from the falling beam. See that?"

"I made a blowup of the moment the large spike ripped into him. Look at this." Morley showed Jude and Cory an eight-by-ten blowup of that very moment.

Jude examined the enlarged photo. "A massive stream of blood is shooting perpendicularly from Zoe's side, a gushing torrent of hot, life-giving blood!"

Cory burst into tears. "You poor dog!" *"The life of the flesh is in the blood.... The blood sustains its life, Leviticus 17:11 and 14!" But he's losing that precious life-giving blood!*

"Just how did Zoe survive? I asked the same question. Watch Zoe drag the satchel away even as the blood gushes from his side."

Jude continued to piece together the sequence. "I think I understand. The real cave-in occurred down the corridor on the other side of the hole."

"Yes," Morley continued the explanation. "When Zoe pulled the satchel free, the crossbeam fell and gashed his side."

"Right," Jude resumed. "Then on his broken leg, he managed a deathlike crawl toward the water hole. Once in that safer vicinity, the rescued manuscript by his side, Zoe collapsed to the ground in a rapidly forming pool of blood."

"You can tell how intelligent your dog is by what he does next. Despite the horrific pain to his injuries, he squirms around like crazy to fill the wound with mud."

"To stop the bleeding!" Cory exclaimed. "That really is using your smarts!"

"This also solves the mystery of the computer chip!" Jude interrupted. "When he thrashed around to stop the blood, his collar came loose and lay on the floor! See it lying there?"

"Yes, I do. Very clearly, in fact. I didn't see that before. That explains why the chip stops and never moves again."

Dabbing her eye with a tissue, Cory watched the screen with rapt attention. "His side and head are covered with blood. The large boulders and the shower of smaller rocks pounded his poor head, and the wounds just keep spurting blood!"

"Poor Zoe! There's nothing attractive about our friend now. He's battered and marred beyond anything we've ever seen and totally unrecognizable."

"You're right, Jude. The other thing you'll notice if you go over this again is his paws. I was so intent in looking at the stream of blood issuing from his side and the avalanche of rocks on his head that I didn't take note of them. That's how I missed the obvious bandage you made. The one front paw was already broken, but watch his other paws as I rewind and play the cave-in. Look at that! All three of them are hit really hard with falling rocks. It's a wonder that he could even walk. The cold water must have healed them considerably during his three days underground. Didn't you say his paws seemed all right except for the broken one?"

"More or less," Cory answered. "The three days of cold water worked wonders, but the cuts were still evident. No denying that."

Jude sat upright in his chair. "Yet, by that third day, he was a new dog!"

"Now, look at this next moment since I think it's really important. The film clearly shows Zoe easing into the water with the strap in his mouth. The satchel plops into the water, and out of sight he goes! See that?"

"That's the beginning of Zoe's three days in the deep," Jude reflected.

"Exactly, but catch the timing. This next cave-in was so massive that it's as though an earthquake occurred. It was so bad that it shook the camera mount! Keep watching."

Cory covered her one eye with her hand. "I can't believe this!"

Morley swept his hand across the face of the screen. "Immediately after Zoe dived in the water, a huge cave-in occurred which filled the entire corridor with rocks. This last cave-in was so horrific—much bigger than the one which separated you from Zoe—that it knocked out most of the lights. Everything remains very dark from this point on."

Cory took her hand from her eye. "Talk about an eclipse of the sun at midday!"

"If the whole corridor was blocked, how did you get the camera footage?" Jude inquired.

"It was blocked over the water pool and the hole, but an emergency light near the security camera still functioned."

Like Jude, Cory was also inquisitive. "How do you know that?"

"We found that out when we entered the corridor by the camera. A bolting crew expert, Tiger Toy, went with me to retrieve the camera footage. The camera was intact, even though the lights in the corridor had blown out."

"You must have felt like a search crew retrieving the black box from an airplane crash!" Jude joked.

"I was afraid to go in there, but I'm glad I did. And I bet you are too!"

"Truly," Cory exclaimed. "More than you imagine!"

As they started to leave a moment later and thanked Morley for his characteristically good help, Jude remembered something he meant to ask him. "Oh, I nearly forgot. Did you ever follow through on your idea of taking a creative writing class at IUP?"

"Yes, I did. Actually, I'm enrolled right now in Bill Betts's class. It's excellent, and he is one awesome professor."

"Are you finding material to write about?"

"You wouldn't believe the idea I came up with."

"Lay it on me."

"Remember the jazzy little handheld tape recorder I showed you once?" Jude nodded. "Well, I surreptitiously taped several conversations with different groups of people here in the mine. I kept the recorder in my pocket, so they had no idea they were being recorded. Shhh—don't tell anyone—ha!"

"Where's the creative writing come in? Sounds like you're describing transcription of the kind we have of *The Pittsburgh Hamlet*."

"That's the cool part. I keep the dialogue pretty much intact and then add all the creative descriptions in between the speeches—expressions on faces, gestures, tone, actions and reactions of the people, even the clothes they wear, setting, background—that sort of thing. Dr. Betts enjoyed the first piece and told me to try another."

"That's an excellent idea."

"I have quite a few recorded conversations on tape. Most of them are fairly recent, but some date back to when I first bought it. A couple are real gems."

"That's a clever idea."

"I'm sure they'd fascinate you. I can't wait to write about them."

"Someday you can show me. Who knows, maybe we can use the recording idea to our advantage one day!" Jude shook his hand goodbye.

"Thanks again, Morley," Cory said, bidding farewell.

"Good luck with that course. By the way, tell Bill Betts I said hello. The guy is a prince and IUP's top prof in my humble opinion."

Chapter 42

_____ ❧ _____

O n the way home from the mine, Jude and Cory stopped at the
Center Hill Church of the Brethren. The quake from this last
large cave-in, they learned, was felt above ground and even shook area
houses and buildings. Pam, the church secretary, was in the office of
the Center Hill Church of the Brethren at the time of the cave-in.
Since the church is situated near the section of the mine where the
cave-in occurred, the tremors felt in it were some of the most violent
in the entire area.

"I was standing by the photocopy machine and was nearly
thrown off my feet!" Pam explained to Jude and Cory. "I heard a loud
sound out in the sanctuary, so I ran out to see what was going on."

"What happened?" Jude interrupted.

"The choir director's lectern was overturned, and the vase of
flowers had been knocked off the front altar table."

"I can imagine how frightened you were!" Cory empathized.

"Here's the peculiar part. The stained glass window above the
baptistry was cracked right beneath the image of the descending
dove."

"Can we take a peek?"

"Sure, Cory. No problem."

They ambled into the sanctuary from the side entrance where
Pam had greeted them.

"The truly strange thing is that the metal frame around the
stained glass fell away in that bottom center section below the dove.
We found it lying on the floor, almost as if that section of metal had
been cut out."

Cory carefully noted the stained glass. "How bizarre!"

Jude was also intrigued. "Did Pastor Gabe offer any sort of comment about this?"

"Well, we learned that so many things happened at the same time that Friday evening. Let's see if I remember. That was the evening of your miraculous escape from the mine cave-in and Zoe's retrieval of Mr. Wakefield's novel. We're still praising God for that. I can't wait to read it!"

"I've read only the first part, but I think it's a winner."

"That was the night of Joey's great performance on the football field, and wasn't that the night that Duke and Tina gave their lives to Jesus?"

Cory smiled broadly. "Yes, it was!"

"How can I forget that part? For goodness sake, I sat there in the fourth row. I don't know when anything moved me so much as when that couple went forward. Have you ever seen such changed people?"

"It's been a long time," Cory agreed. "They're the talk of the mushroom mine."

"Well, back to the baptistry window. The congregation saw in the broken window a visual reminder of all the extraordinary events of that memorable evening. Pastor Gabe said the break reminded him of how nothing blocks the work of the Holy Spirit represented by the dove. People said that comment went right over their heads. Well, it did, and I along with the others had no idea what he was talking about!"

"He thinks on a pretty deep level at times," Jude responded, "and sees into the heart of things, but his view of the world through spirit eyes is a real virtue, even if we don't always keep up to him!"

"Fortunately, Gabe explained that he was speaking symbolically. Wonder if I can remember what he said." Knitting her brow, Pam ruminated. "All right, this is a loose paraphrase. When the stained glass window was intact, the solid metal frame incasing the glass blocked the dove's descent. Do you know what he means?"

"Maybe," Cory responded. "Was he saying that the Spirit, represented by the dove, was imprisoned in his private holy world?"

"As if," Jude augmented, "the frame of the metal kept him locked up there in his stained glass abode, so He wasn't free to do His work down here?"

"That's it! That was Gabe's exact point. With the removal of the metal casement strip, He's no longer barricaded."

"Gabe makes an interesting point," Jude continued. "We now have direct access to the Holy Spirit as He has direct access to us."

"So nothing comes between us. That was Pastor Gabe's point."

Just then Charles entered the main sanctuary from the side door. "Hello folks. Don't let me interrupt your discussion."

"Not at all," Pam chuckled. "We were just talking about the broken stained glass casement above the baptistry and Gabe's explanation of it as a kind of miracle. Go ahead, Jude. You were about to say something."

"Hello, Chuck. Please join us." They warmly shook hands. "We were just saying that Gabe's interpretation of the broken casement in the baptistery stained glass is really interesting."

"Chuck, you were there," Pam recollected. "Maybe you followed Gabe's comments better than I."

"I remember this. When we told Gabe that we liked the dove freely hanging in space without the metal border, he said, 'Now he can shepherd you into truth all the better.' I didn't know exactly what he meant, so he told me to read John 16:12 which I later did. He was referring to how the Holy Spirit guides believers into all truth."

Outside on the church porch a moment later, Chuck asked Jude and Cory to join him at his home for a while. "I'd like to continue the fascinating discussion we had commenced earlier if you don't mind."

"About what?" Jude asked.

"The climbing metaphor business."

"Yes. I wanted your opinion on that."

"You gentleman enjoy your discussion, but I need to excuse myself. I told Dad I'd run some errands with him." Cory gave Jude a peck on the cheek. "Au revoir, my love. Call me when you want me to pick you up. No hurry!"

"It's a plan!"

Moments later, Jude joined Chuck on his front porch and commenced talking about the Friday evening of the cave-in. "We're talking about that epic evening when so many of the plot lines of our summer story converged," Jude said to establish context, "each piece of which was characterized by the same 'immobilized feet' metaphor."

Charles looked quizzically at Jude. "You better explain that."

"Make a mental note of these similarities. First, once Cory and I made it to the belt—which did turn out, by the way, to be just that, a conveyor belt—I had the problem of getting one foot ahead of the other. I was just like Tina and Duke when they decided to give their lives to Christ. My feet froze, as theirs had, and it took superhuman effort to get one foot ahead of the other."

"Please explain. I don't understand."

"I'm not referring to the physical exhaustion which had occurred during the grueling uphill rope climb. That durability test filled me with great fear since one false move, and we would have plummeted to our deaths. This was different because I just couldn't make my feet move. I felt just like Tina—my feet frozen solid in ice."

"Why did you have so much trouble climbing up the belt when you had already done the more challenging task of shimmying a heavy load across a deep ravine with ravaged arms and hands?"

"The answer's simple. As I climbed the conveyor belt, my mind flashed back to the day in the barn when as I carried the stool up to Grandpa. I was afraid I'd fail in the same way I did when Grandpa died."

"I see."

"A voice kept pounding in my head. 'You killed Grandpa, now you'll kill Cory. You've made it this far, but you'll not make it to the top. You'll come close as with Grandpa, then fall and die. You are the destroyer! You kill everything you love, and now you'll kill the love of your life!'" Jude began to sweat nervously as he simultaneously reflected on his climb up the conveyor belt and reexperienced the trauma of his grandpa's death. He took a sip of water. "The thoughts banging in my head were absolutely atrocious!"

"You were experiencing a wound flashback of your childhood trauma and were paralyzed with fear as you relived the awful tragedy."

"You can't imagine!"

"I understand that you feared a second failure but never realized that Jeremiah's death was that traumatic for you."

"I could never overstate the effect of his death."

"I understand that, but let's get back to Tina. She feared rejection. Living her whole life as the rejected child, she simply couldn't imagine this Christian community accepting her. Was that it? Is that what froze her feet?"

"Possibly, though I'm not sure, yet I was like Tina in another way."

"Explain."

"I too was in demonic warfare as the Center Hill folks call it."

"You're linking that warfare to the 'immobilized feet' metaphor?"

"Yes, and with Duke who struggled to get one foot in front of the other, just like Tina and like me on the conveyor belt." Jude paused to allow a couple noisy vehicles to pass. "Based on what Duke told me in Heinz Chapel after the Pittsburgh *Hamlet*, he feared he'd always be in bondage to his flesh. 'I can't resist booze and sexy women who turn me on instantly!' Gabe quoted Proverbs 11:6 for him—'The unfaithful will be caught by their lust.'"

Jude stopped to study Charles. *He's connecting with the struggling feet metaphor at a very deep level.* "Chuck, your forehead is wrinkled, and you're tapping your foot a mile a minute! I know you understand what I mean because you referred to a similar thing when you climbed Mt. Washington. I suspect you have your own twice-told tale to tell."

"Do I ever!"

"No time like the present!"

Chapter 43

Charles resumed his account of his climb up Mt. Washington. "That was the same Friday afternoon I had my cardiac appointment with Dr. Chenarides at Allegheny General Hospital. I had given you some of that background already, right?"

"Yes. You told me that Dr. Chenarides gave you a clean bill of health that very afternoon. All cardiac tests of the past weeks were negative—treadmill, EKG, echocardiogram, catheterization—so based on that clean bill of health, you did what you always vowed you'd one day do. That's where you were when we were interrupted."

"My quest was to climb the whole way to the top of Mt. Washington, but there's one more piece of the puzzle. I had purchased my own exercise heart-pacing monitor, one of those fancy gadgets people attach to their bodies to monitor electrical activity of the cardiovascular system during workouts. I did it to prove to myself that my heart could withstand even rigorous stress."

"Like climbing to the top of Mt. Washington."

"Exactly."

"What happened?"

"As I departed Dr. Chenarides' office, I told him that I was going for a walk downtown and might even climb Mt. Washington but wasn't certain if I'd keep the monitor on. Why wear it if it wasn't needed? Nevertheless, Dr. Chenarides insisted that he sync my cardiac exercise device to his equipment."

"Why did he want to do that?"

"So that I could be temporarily monitored while making the climb or walking briskly all over town. This would give me tangible incontrovertible proof that my heart could withstand such vigorous activity."

"Proceed. I like where this is going!"

"A short while later, I was at the base of Mt. Washington and ready to climb." Charles stopped talking for a moment and wiped his brow with a handkerchief. *Reliving that victorious event in my life makes me feel anew the panic of those first scary steps!* "Well, I managed to get past the first difficult paces. When Dr. Chenarides examined his monitor a bit later, he could tell that I was walking energetically, possibly climbing Mt. Washington or indulging in some sort of physical exercise, but he was not alarmed since the elevated heart rhythm fell well within the normal range. He kept the device on and went about his work."

"I picture this perfectly!"

"Now to the part that's hilarious," Charles prattled, a huge smile on his face. "At the bottom of the hill, I climbed with some difficulty. As I said, it was the same for me as it was for you, Duke and Tina. My one brother had died doing this very thing, climbing a steep hill, so I labored intensely to put one foot in front of the other for those first steps. But as I experienced no cardiac stress while climbing, I moved along with increasingly greater ease."

"Sounds as though you were ready to fly up that hill!"

"You exaggerate, but as I neared the top, I forgot that I was being monitored and that I even wore a monitor! That's how far I had removed myself from the old fears of having an episode of atrial fibrillation or maybe even a lethal heart attack like the ones that had killed my five brothers. I slowly freed myself from the fear that I was a severely debilitated 'heart patient who better take it easy in life!'"

"I had no idea our experiences were so similar."

"Sorry to take the circuitous route since brevity is the soul of wit!"

"Are you kidding? The details are great!"

"Here's the funny part. As I neared the top of Mt. Washington, I encountered two boys who were shooting their dart guns at a target which was swinging on a telephone pole. Pausing to catch my breath, I interacted briefly with the children. And during those moments, I said—just for a joke—'Here, shoot at this' and hung my monitor on the pole nail!"

"Why do that?"

"Because I decided then and there that I was going to junk it. Why keep that which emotionally constrained me and might potentially reconnect me to my old fear? I wanted rid of that sick reminder!"

"This is deliverance in a major key!"

"The boys began to blast the monitor with their dart guns! Of course, I had no idea that the device was being monitored in those very moments by one of the technicians in Dr. Chenarides' office! When the device swung wildly on the pole and was hit with darts, the technician in his office—possibly Renee—thought I was having the granddaddy of heart attacks! After all, she saw the proof right there on the monitor!" Recalling the humorous incident, Charles again laughed out loud.

"So how did this turn out?"

"Dr. Chenarides later told me that he was paged and flew down the hall to the lab. Renee showed him the EKG and said, 'Dr. Claypoole is having a major heart attack!' Holding the EKG paper in her hand, she blurted, 'Here's the proof!' Dr. Chenarides contemplated sending an ambulance up Mt. Washington in case I might be there, but of course, he had no idea of knowing my whereabouts. I could be anywhere by that point!"

"That is hilarious!"

"It's a good thing that I called down to Dr. Chenarides right away to tell him that I had triumphantly scaled Mt. Washington. Mind you, I called just to let him know of my successful climb. Little did I know that he was panicking at that moment over what he saw on the monitor. The whole thing was straightened out right away, but how we laughed about this! Dr. Chenarides told me that he'd one day show me the EKG printout of the 'massive heart attack' I had while climbing Mt. Washington."

"The larger point here is that we have another set of struggling feet as you climbed upward, step after step, that Friday evening. Your case was similar to Tina's, Duke's, and mine. It wasn't the physical challenge that made it difficult but the emotional component rooted in the family's cardiac history. Fearing the mother of all heart attacks, you subconsciously held back over the years and morphed into the proverbial couch potato. Am I getting warm?"

"Red hot! That's why my codirecting the production of *Hamlet* in Pittsburgh was a big deal. It was the first time I had done anything of significance outside the myopic bubble of my little academic world. I had even backed out of civic responsibilities to a large extent—stopped red-coating at the hospital, quit the Elks, and even missed the recent library board meetings."

"I didn't realize you lived in fear to that extent, but you placed fewer demands on yourself as a way of staving off the big one. Is that it?"

"Yes, I'm ashamed to say."

"Instead of living life in faith, as Pastor Gabe constantly admonishes, you were living in fear."

"That's it, but with every glorious step I took up Mt. Washington, I was killing off my fear. Still, those initial steps were incredibly difficult for me, and I was scared to death just to put one foot in front of the other. Truth is, I almost turned back in fear!"

"This is fascinating. All four of us—you, Tina, Duke, and I—struggled with paralyzed feet on that epic Friday evening."

"I see why you wanted to talk to me. I wasn't aware that all four dealt with the same thing at the same time."

"Yes, that's all so true, but our saga hasn't ended."

"What are you talking about?"

"What about Cory's dad? Pete's story is in some ways the most gripping of all. He had lain on the couch for weeks as he fought the throes of depression as never before."

"I didn't know it had gotten that bad."

"By playing several of Gabe's sermons over and over, he slowly squashed his fears, dragged himself off that seductive couch, and ended up at the game. What's amazing is that, in each case, things came to a head in similar ways for each of us that evening."

"What an astounding coincidence, but let's keep going. They are similar but different too. I'm especially interested in the role of fear in all of this, but you seem to want me to take the lead. Am I right?"

"Please."

"Why? You're the one who was the center of it all."

"That's true, but because this is Cory's and my story, I'm too emotionally tied to it to think as rationally as I should. I want to talk through the nuances of the fear and explore the deep psychological underpinnings. It's important to parse this out since, underneath, they vary quite a lot, and you're the man to help me trace these subtle distinctions."

I think I see what he's after. "All right, I'll give it a shot. We've traced the similarities—each of us struggled at a climactic moment in our lives when we faced a huge fear—but what are the subtle differences? We've said that Tina had to overcome her fear of rejection, but you want to go deeper than that."

"If we can."

Charles ruminated as he picked away a dead blossom from the African violet on the table. "Tina couldn't imagine God forgiving her sordid past nor could she imagine people relating to her in nonsexual ways."

"Interesting."

"Sexuality and her beautiful body have always been the basis of her interaction with others as her shapeliness, not her personality or character, was her defining characteristic. Because people's eyes automatically fixated on her voluptuous physique, she always accommodated and even encouraged the attention. In the process, however, she trapped herself in the role of the sexual wanton which she had unconsciously scripted."

"Well put. That is a fascinating insight."

"Physical attributes were for her a double-edged sword as they often are for male and females alike. On the one hand, she was affirmed since all people like to be noticed for physical attributes, improved physique, and weight loss, but it's a curse to be viewed solely as an objectified sexual entity."

"So true."

"Tina is nobody's dummy, but she never cultivated the life of the mind, never nurtured the nonphysical aspects of her being including her intelligence. Her challenge was to get past this fear and to learn that, in time, she could be appreciated for her personality and her character."

"And her brains."

"Agreed. Well, she got a glimpse of her new identity that Friday evening. How am I doing?"

"Superbly! That's a really helpful analysis." *But it's time for you to be self-reflexive, my professor friend. Are you ready for a dose of emotional honesty?* "What about your fear?"

"That's easy. My fear appeared to be physical but was actually emotional. I was afraid that a heart attack would kill me as it did my brothers. Were you aware that all five of my brothers died of heart attacks?"

Jude nodded. Charles brushed his hand through his hair and stroked his beard.

"Fear is a creeping phenomenon. It sneaks quietly, pounces quickly, and destroys totally. I wasn't aware of the extent to which fear had dominated me and influenced my decisions over the years."

"So your fear was in the emotional realm whereas Tina's was more in the psychological."

"I'd say so, but what about Pete? You're the one closest to him."

"Now, yes."

"I'm sure Pete is part of this because we all know how he just couldn't drag himself out of that den."

"Because he still mourned Ruby, he couldn't get closure, couldn't imagine going on without his beloved wife. He resigned himself to a pit of depression as vast as the canyon Cory and I shimmied across in the mine."

"That makes perfect sense."

"Pete feared that he couldn't live again, that the good years were gone forever, and that he was condemned to a death-in-life existence. His depression was exacerbated by the fact that he had become a terrible father to Cory and Joey, yet he couldn't help himself. Do you agree? You've been very close to him through the years."

"I do agree, though I remind you that I haven't been around Pete much this summer to see this first-hand." *Now your turn for emotional honesty!* "You've done well in speaking of the others, but I think you need to speak of yourself a little."

"The deal with me, Chuck, is very straightforward. In climbing the conveyor belt with Cory on my back, I was recreating—I guess *reliving* is the more accurate term—exactly what I did as a young boy when I climbed the barn beam with a stool on my back. That climb ended in disaster when I stupidly bumped grandpa's stool off the edge of the loft and fell. Although Grandpa successfully suspended himself with a rope the whole time I climbed, he let go of the rope to try to catch me. Because of his sacrificial effort, he fell to his death. You probably didn't know that he actually clasped my hand—very firmly, in fact—but couldn't hang on. I've never told anyone that sordid detail, not even Cory."

"I had no idea."

"With every step up that conveyor belt, I relived the anguish of my childhood trauma. To this day, when I think of that climb, I break into a cold sweat. At the time, my head was a spinning top on the kitchen table of life about to crash to the floor!"

"Nice metaphor! I can't believe you escaped that trap."

Jude stopped to take a drink of water, since his pulse raced as he relived the two traumatic experiences. After a brief pause, he resumed. "Here you're going to see my rage for order, Chuck, as I try to offer a thumbnail summary of these various instances."

"It's psychologically important for you to do this."

"All right, here goes. Tina feared not being forgiven. Duke feared he'd never rise about the alluring temptations of the flesh. Pete feared not being able to cope without his spouse or, painting with a broader brush, ever be able to live again. You feared a major health crisis, and I feared a repeat of a childhood trauma." Jude paused at this point. "How am I doing?"

"I'd say well."

"We can't forget Cory. She too labored to get one foot in front of another back there in early May. She'd say this so much better than I, but I do know fear was a real part of her struggle." Jude stopped speaking while a noisy truck climbed the hill. "Fear—fear that I'd never forgive her for abandoning me when Grandpa died, fear that she wouldn't be able to resist Duke's impassioned overtures, fear that she was incapable of love again, fear that I, the educated one, had somehow outclassed her and that my empire-sprawling world of academia, which included exciting international travel, dwarfed her thimble-sized closet of embarrassing obscurity."

"That's a marvelous insight, Jude. I wouldn't have known all of that was going on in Cory's mind."

"That covers a lot of it. Thanks for helping me make sense of it all." Jude got up to leave. "I've truly enjoyed talking through this." They shook hands, and Jude stood on the stairs but then turned again. "By the way you do realize that we've forgotten one additional key instance of the labored-step theme?"

"Which one? I thought we were pretty thorough."

"Joey. Don't forget his two examples. When he sat on the bench during the game that Friday evening, he just couldn't get his feet to move. Like Pete on the couch, Duke and Tina in the pew, you at the foot of Mt. Washington, and me on the conveyor belt, Joey wanted to act but couldn't, couldn't make the will strong enough to empower the feet. But he won, as he did later when he bulled the stack of football players, inch by grueling inch across the end zone for the two-point conversion."

"Step by agonizing step."

"Good day, Chuck." He glanced at the book on the end table as he departed. "Ah, William Faulkner's *Absalom, Absalom*! One of the very best American novels. Happy reading!"

Chapter 44

———— ⌘ ————

Jude and Cory's visit with Morley Spencer at the mushroom mine on Thursday turned out to be a benchmark experience for a second reason: it spawned the idea of examining the security camera footage in the room where the original explosion had taken place. Having completed his two-year teaching associate stint in the spring, Jude did not return to IUP as an instructor for the fall term, an eventuality which opened up the time to spend with Cory, compose his dissertation, and continue work in the mine. It also enabled him to be free on this Friday after Labor Day when most universities had resumed fall classes.

Enjoying her last day of sick leave, Cory planned to return to work the next Monday but for now delighted in the prospect of a free day with the love of her life. "This is going to be great. I've been really looking forward to this day!"

"That makes two of us!"

Thus, over to IUP Jude and Cory went on Friday morning with the footage of the explosion in hand. Their intent was to examine the security film footage with the more technologically advanced equipment in the com/media department. The senior technician in the office, Bill Hamilton, was one of Jude's good friends, with whom he had diligently worked across many long months to create two separate film documentaries on well-known, contemporary American poets.

Bill was happy to work again with an old friend. "Yes, I'd like to help out with the footage."

"Thank you for setting aside some valuable time. Seeing this film on your large monitor will enable us to see the obscure details."

"No problem, plus, you've heard me speak in the past of my fascination with angels. I'll enjoy collaborating with you on yet another project."

As it turned out, examining the explosion room footage was a stellar idea, since the security film vividly depicted not only the actual explosion but also the events leading up to it: the original cave-in when Cory bumped the center support post, Jude's collapse to the ground and lengthy comatose state, and Cory's dangerous entrapment under the limestone slab. That original master footage is now exhibited in the Armstrong County Museum and Historical Society on McKean Street in Kittanning.

To commence their session, Jude asked Bill, "Could you please experiment with the infrared spectrograph? That's something we're truly keen to see since after the cave-in, the room was so full of dust that little could be seen."

"You mentioned that on the phone."

"Am I right that the infrared lens functions like a spectrograph which will enable us to see through the thick dust?"

"Yes. An infrared lens typically opens up a whole new dimension."

As Bill intimated, the spectrograph revealed an entirely new world, so much so, in fact, that Cory wrote in her journal of "a supernatural magnificence to which we were totally oblivious at the time of the explosion. Without the use of spectral-imaging, Zoe is just another dog, the typically distraught pet at the side of his helpless master."

As Jude and Cory viewed the footage of the actual explosion with the aid of the lens, that hidden world was disclosed before their eyes. When Abe accidentally tripped and dropped the dynamite, Zoe immediately assumed angelic form.

"Would you look at that!" Jude shouted. "Zoe morphed into a majestic angel and hovered over the center of the cavern in mid-air!" Temporarily forgetting that he was in the IUP lab, Jude glanced around the room in embarrassment and whispered, "Sorry, I forget we're not alone!"

"But you're right!" Overwhelmed, Cory pinched Jude's arm. "He's clearly visible through the thick cloud of dust!"

"That is unbelievable!" Bill spoke with such excitement that other employees in the lab looked in their direction.

Cory's excitement continued. "What in the world was that?"

A few of the other curious workers in the lab straggled over to the monitor to look at the screen.

"The angel shot forth something like a broad band of laser light," Bill shouted, tapping the screen.

Cory grasped Jude's bicep so hard that the muscle turned white. "I'm not sure what you would call it, but that ray shoots clear to the cross where we cowered in our niche."

"The angel created a shield over us!" Jude added, placing his hand on top of Cory's.

Jude nervously picked at a loose fingernail as they watched the monitor. "Please play that again. That's amazing! The large rocks above our heads are suspended in midair!"

"Yes, right there!" one of the student workers in the lab shouted. "I see it too!"

"Look at those suspended rocks!" Jude tapped the screen." The beam stopped them cold!"

Cory held the sides of her head. "They would have smashed us like bugs if the angel hadn't intervened!"

Jude put his arm around Cory and pulled her toward him. "Amen!"

"Jude, do you remember the incense we smelled and the warmth we felt?"

"Yes, you commented on that earlier."

"We smelled a divine aroma," Cory explained to others, "when we were cuddled under his wings. Maybe that was the scent angels emanate because of their proximity to the altar in heaven!"

"Maybe so!" Jude gasped, considering the weightiness of the thought for the first time. "You mean the aroma of heaven was right there in the mine? That's amazing!"

"How marvelous!" Cory continued to watch the screen. "Have you ever seen anything so fantastic?"

"And this is just the beginning," Bill exclaimed. "To use your expression, Jude, you better be grounded because this next part will likely be 220 volts!"

"I know that's Jude's phrase," Cory laughed. "Get this—he used it on my dad!"

"He said it at least ten times in this very lab when we made the Donald Hall film!"

Jude gave Cory a peck on the cheek and turned to Bill. "But why do you say be grounded?"

"The angel's sheltering you and Cory with one laser ray, but look at his other hand. It's pointed in the opposite direction toward the other man. What's his name?"

"Abe Badoane, my long-lost dad!"

"Look there!" Cory broke in. "Bill's right. The angel shot a second laser band of light over your dad which did the same thing, stopped the falling rocks in midair right above your dad!"

"Look at him!" Jude impulsively yelled. "Kneeling stalwart and praying like a saint!"

"And laying down his life for us!" Cory put her hand on her breast. "Yet he shows no trace of fear. Can you zoom in on his face?" They waited while Bill enlarged the image.

"You're right, Cory. He was praying for us instead of saving his life!"

"How touching!" Cory again clutched Jude's arm. "His face is as wrinkled as Rembrandt's 'Portrait of Vaters!'"

"Sorry, I don't know that painting." Sitting back in his chair and fastened to the image on the screen, Jude wiped a large tear from his eye. "Instead of running to save his life, Dad stayed to pray for us!"

"What a magnanimous gesture!" Bill exclaimed. "That is one sacrificial act!"

"And look at Zoe, hanging in midair like the Angel of the Lord!" Cory paused to watch the screen. "Remember the loud noise? Each of the shooting rays was accompanied by a booming sound."

"They were horrifying! We thought we'd go deaf!"

"We didn't see the rays and, of course, we had no idea that gigantic boulders were hanging inches from our heads!"

"How he protected you!" Bill marveled.

Cory's eyes were glued to the monitor. "At the time, we thought the roaring humming sounds were part of the explosion or the cave-in, but it wasn't. It was Zoe, the angel blasting protective beams all over the place!"

"It sounded like a Jedi's lightsaber or a vibro-weapon!" Jude added.

As Jude, Cory, and Bill continued to watch the footage, they saw the angel point overhead.

"What's he doing?" Bill asked.

Jude pointed to the upper part of the screen. "Keep watching. I have a guess."

"I don't—absolutely none!"

A broad band of laser exploded from the angel's hand toward the roof and pierced through it, causing the seam of rich bituminous coal to crash to the mine floor.

After Bill played this sequence in slow motion, Cory remarked, "It's as though a mountain of coal avalanched into an abyss."

"You're right," Jude agreed. "You can see what happened. The coal floor above and the limestone roof of our room collapsed at the same time. That's what jarred the coal mine conveyor belt loose and left it dangling in space."

"Yes, I see!" Cory agreed.

A fourth longer beam shot directly downward into the pit below. "Why," Bill asked, "would Zoe send a beam down there?"

Puzzled, Cory watched intently. "I don't know nor can we see its terminus." She tapped the lower part of the monitor. "But look there! Instead of filling up with limestone and coal, the immense tonnage fell into a newly created sinkhole."

"I get it!" Jude shouted. "Zoe knocked out the floor below to create a huge canyon so that all the limestone and coal had a place to fall!"

They paused for a while and watched the shooting of the rays and the astounding effects of each. At the conclusion of the second replay of this sequence, Jude yelled out, "Hold it right there!"

"Why, darling?"

Jude peered the infrared screen and then looked at Cory. "You're absolutely right about the sink hole below, but look at what we're seeing. Remember when we watched Zoe in 50/10 and missed seeing the awful gash to his side, because our eyes focused on the larger panoramic scene instead of that crucial detail?"

"Yes," Cory agreed, explaining to Bill. "We missed seeing the stream of blood streaming from Zoe's side because we were so focused on the big picture."

"Now we're doing the exact opposite. Look at what's on the screen! Play it again, please, but this time, don't look at the separate beams in isolation as they shoot out in four separate directions." Jude used both hands and starting from the middle spread them outward. "Look at the total pattern that's formed on the screen."

When the group did so, they saw through the thick dust the perfectly distinct cross, Zoe the Angel poised at the exact center. Two equidistant radiating horizontal lasers, one pointing to Cory and Jude on the left and the other to Abe on the right, formed the transverse crossbeam. "And look here too," Jude continued. "One beam blasts up at the coal mine while the longer vertical beam fires downward into the cavern. The beams form a perfect cross with Zoe at the geometric center!"

"Amazing!" Bill exclaimed. "But please excuse me for just a moment. I'll be back in a jiffy." He ejected a flash drive from his computer and hurried over to Ken, one of the assistants in the lab.

Cory continued talking to Jude. "To think that all of this was going on at the time of the explosion, and yet we had no idea that we were in the presence of an angel!"

"Zoe protected us by thundering forth these shields of light. When I looked around for Zoe during the explosion, I thought he somehow escaped or hid. We couldn't see him, yet he was there all the time. Talk about seeing through a glass darkly!"

"As all people do," Cory comfortingly rejoined. "This gives a whole new meaning to that verse in Hebrews which says that many have unknowingly entertained angels" (Hebrews 13:2). Cory faced Bill who again sat at his desk. "Though we had an angel in our midst the whole summer, we were totally clueless!"

"There's one more thing that will likely interest you," Bill reasoned. Jude and Cory stopped talking and marveled at the images on the screen. "When you told me the story of your escape up the conveyor belt with Cory on your back, you mentioned that at one point you slipped. Remember when you said that on the phone?"

"Yes. My foot had slipped completely off the tread."

"You said you didn't fall to your death but seemed to stand on something solid in midair."

"I thought we were goners! In fact, that moment is a candidate for the single strangest moment in the whole affair."

"We need to watch that sequence through the infrared spectrographic lens," Bill resumed. "I think we'll be very surprised."

"I'm sure we will," Jude agreed.

"You guys offer the commentary."

"Here we're going up the conveyor belt." Cory spoke with a voice hushed, and her eyes bonded to the monitor as she relived the horror.

The three of them along with the technicians in the lab watched Jude and Cory's painful ascent. A closeup showed the details of their faces, Jude's etched in pain as, Atlas-like, he labored upward on the belt. "Talk about fierce concentration!" Jude joked.

"Look how my head is bowed." Cory's voice was again a muted whisper. "My eyes are tightly closed in prayer. And fear too!"

"Cory, it's a wonder Jude could breathe," Bill jested. "You're hanging on for dear life!"

"I was flashing back to that moment when I nearly fell to my death and held on for dear life to Jude's belt! By one frail, little hand!"

"What are you talking about?" Bill was incredulous.

"When I fell down his torso, I kicked sideways. For a moment, I hung in space, completely horizontal. Only my hand was attached to Jude! I was so scared!"

Bill swallowed hard. "I can't even imagine that as I have a fear of heights!"

"Watch this next part," Jude excitedly stated. "This is where I had my near-death fall."

"Look at your face! I call that the face of terror!" Bill hit pause so that they could study the details.

"I agree. Talk about a look of torment!" Jude tried to laugh. "Keep an eye on Zoe. I think we know what's coming." They intently watched the screen. "I thought so! He reassumed his angelic form and catches my foot in midair!"

"Totally unbelievable!" Cory cried." And then he repositioned your foot onto the conveyor belt!"

Jude took his pulse. "Can you believe it?"

Cory could not suppress her excitement. "The angel—I mean Zoe—is magnificent as he is poised in the air with his upstretched hand cradling your foot. Talk about the perfect subject to paint!"

"You can see why I marveled when my foot slipped."

"I recall the warmth we felt in that cold place. I remember it as much as the aroma of incense."

"No wonder! We were warmed by a hovering angel!"

"When we told Pastor Gabe about Jude's near fall," Cory explained to Bill, "he quoted a verse from the Psalms on the spot. Our pastor knows the Bible like the back of his hand!"

"What verse?" Bill asked.

"'You enlarged my path under me, so my feet did not slip.' Isn't that a marvelously applicable verse?"

"Yes, it really is. Where's it found?"

"I looked it up. Psalm 18:36."

Bill continued to stare at the screen in amazement. "If I were you, I'd make this into an enlarged photo and put that verse under it as a caption."

As Cory and Jude prepared to leave the lab a short while later, Bill stopped them. "I have a present for you. Here, I dubbed a couple cassette tapes for you. Even through the thick wall of dust, the infrared shows up beautifully. You can see Zoe morph from dog to angel and back again. The angel's clearly visible both times."

Just then, Ken approached the group. "I have them, Bill. They're in this envelope."

"Thanks, Ken. They'll really appreciate this."

A religious man himself, Bill paused a moment as they walked toward his office door. "I can't imagine experiencing that. I mean actually being in the presence of an angel the whole summer."

"It was something else," Cory agreed.

"I don't know what to say, except thanks for being so brave in getting out of that deathtrap, and thanks too for giving me the chance to work on this project. This was even more fun than making the films on famous American writers! You two really were touched by an angel, and that confirms what I've often thought."

"What's that?" Jude asked.

"Angels are always around us, but we just don't know it."

"That's what the Bible says," Cory replied. "Angels are 'ministering spirits sent forth to minister for those who will inherit salvation' (Hebrews 1:14). Our pastor helped me find that verse. An angel surely ministered to us that day!"

"Well, then, I think you'll like this reminder."

Cory looked at the envelope. "What's this?"

"Ken made blowups of Zoe at the center of the cross and at the conveyor belt ladder."

"Wow!" Cory blurted, excitedly taking the photos out of the envelope. "These are great! How beautiful!"

"Yes, they are," Jude readily agreed. "Feast your eyes on that magnificent angel. How very majestic!"

Cory's eyes beamed. "Look at the glow around the angel!"

"Yes, it emanates from him like the radiance of a brilliant, golden sunset." Jude scrutinized the photo. "Note his powerful gaze. This is unbelievable!"

"I have one question," Bill asked as Cory and Jude brushed the tears from their eyes. "If Zoe was an angel with a divine nature, and there's no denying that fact based on this evidence, then what was the real concern of his being hurt? I mean hurt in a physical sense?"

Jude was the first to respond. "That's a great question, but you have more to say. Keep going."

Bill hesitated a moment as he worked through the complexity of the thought. "I guess the point's even deeper. You showed me the camera security footage of your escape when Zoe lunged at you and pulled the manuscript from the hole. He's really beat up and fighting for his life. Here's what's bothering me. How can an angel experience physical hurt? Did he actually suffer pain during those awful moments? That's the crux of my problem. Can a supernatural being feel natural pain? That's the problem I struggle with."

"Cory talked to Pastor Gabe about that very point. Zoe, we now know, was an angel physicalized in a most unique earthy form. Not a person but a dog, and every bit as strange as a talking donkey!" (Numbers 22:30). Jude looked at Cory. "Theological intricacies are your domain, and you're the one who chatted to Gabe about this, so take it away!"

"If you insist. Like Christ on earth, Zoe was a flesh-and-blood dog that suppressed his divine nature—'laid it aside,' as Gabe said—while here on earth. Gabe said it this way. 'Zoe laid aside his divinity and enshrouded himself in earthiness.' Brilliant, wouldn't you say? All right, Jude, you take it from there."

"The bottom line, Bill, is this. Zoe experienced all the hurts, pain, and agony of any living being on earth. His scars were real, his pain intense, and his suffering unfathomable. In the clip we watched at the mine yesterday, Zoe was in a pool of water. This was before he snatched Grandpa's buried manuscript. He was deciding whether to swim to safety or risk his life by retrieving the novel. At any rate, you ought to see Zoe's face in that clip. He was filled with such fear and emotion that he looked like he was about to cry! Don't you think so, Cory?"

"Absolutely."

"Thank you. That explanation helps a lot."

Thanking Bill again for the precious gift of the cassette tapes and photographs, Jude and Cory returned to Armstrong County early Friday evening. On the way home, Cory envisioned the painting she was going to create of Zoe the Angel at the very center of the cross.

"I have it figured out. The beams of light will be shown shooting from the angel's left arm, but his right arm will gesture to the viewer, inviting him into the scene, beckoning for him to partake of the riches of the angelic presence in our daily midst. The angel's open and enlarged hand will reach toward the viewer."

"You're making it so real that I can see it."

"The prominent open hand will be the key since it pulls the reader into the scene, but the curled index finger which points upward is the other notable feature."

"How so?"

"Because it makes the viewer lift eyes to the cross and the angel. The flow of movement is upward like a Gothic cathedral, but the open hand is the gateway." She leaned into him and kissed him on the cheek. "I'm going to do it, Jude Hepler. I'm definitely going to paint this one!"

Chapter 45

———— ✑ ————

Departing the IUP campus, Jude and Cory drove home to Armstrong County and learned upon entering his grandma's house that Pastor Gabriel Wyant had been rushed to the Armstrong County Memorial Hospital. Jude explained to his grandma, "We knew he didn't speak at the Wednesday evening Bible study but didn't think his situation all that serious. Grant it, he wasn't himself in Pittsburgh, but he didn't seem sick enough to warrant hospitalization."

"He looked pretty weary during the grand ceremony," Cory added, "but we attributed that to his accumulated exhaustion and heavy responsibility during the holiday festivity."

"I give you the doctor's assessment," Rosetta replied: "'The man is an indefatigable warrior. What you're seeing are the predictable effects on his battle-scarred body!' Everyone who knows Gabe would totally agree with the doctor!"

Tests at the hospital, however, indicated that he had suffered a recent stroke, possibly even during the celebration in Pittsburgh, which affected his left side. "That would explain his difficulty in walking in the later part of the evening," Cory commented to Jude upon receiving the news. "Remember how he struggled at the fountain?"

"It was painful to watch."

The doctor theorized that he had experienced a slight stroke in Pittsburgh Monday evening and a second more major one Thursday night. As a result, he was in serious condition as he lay in the hospital, his left side severely affected. As Martha Wyant explained to Jude's grandma on the phone, "He's regained a slight bit of movement in his left arm and hand but not the leg. I hate to say it, Rosetta, but my dear Gabe's in bad shape!"

On Saturday morning, Jude and Cory dashed to the Armstrong County Memorial Hospital. Arriving at his room, they saw from the hall that Mrs. Wyant and Charles were both present at Gabe's bedside. Not wanting to intrude, they discreetly gestured to Charles. He quickly saw their intent and whispered to Martha who motioned them into the room.

Although very weak, Pastor Gabe was alert when they walked to his bedside. Partially raised on his elbow, he spoke warmly if weakly, even managing a faint smile. "So, my children, you come…to see the old war horse…as the doctor calls me!" He paused to catch his breath. "Jesus dwells in…clay vessels. Clay of my life…is old…brittle as glass!" The statements apparently taxing his energies, he fell back onto his pillow.

Like Jude, Cory watched him intently. *He moved his right leg and arm a little, but his left leg lies pitifully inert. How lifeless!*

Jude and Cory's presence in the room resuscitated Gabriel who, rallying slightly, commanded a quiet voice which he had not possessed the last couple days. Observant even in these circumstances, he saw the envelope Jude was holding. "What do…you have there?"

Jude pulled out the two eight-by-ten-inch photos of Zoe the Angel in the mine—one suspended in air at the center of the shooting beams, and the other at the conveyor belt holding Jude's foot in midair.

"I…knew it!" Gabe muttered with some excitement. "Just… knew it! Praise…God!" He then collapsed on the pillow and was quiet for a time. When he tried to open his eyes a bit later, only one eye opened, the other a mere slit. He managed a weak whisper. "Read…my last…journal…entry."

Jude watched him very carefully. *That statement took a great deal out of him. Though momentarily reinvigorated, he's growing weaker by the second!*

Pastor Gabriel then extended his right arm as if to embrace them. Each of them in turn bent over to embrace and thank him. Cory's eyes were riveted to his face as she wiped a tear from her eye. *This feels like goodbye!*

Each of them wept as they looked at their spiritual leader, and then the four of them formed a semicircle around his bed.

"You pray," Cory whispered to Jude through cupped ear.

"Thank You, God, for this warrior of the faith who has been such a powerful beacon of light in this dark day." Temporarily overcome with emotion, Jude paused. "He has been our lighthouse as we cross the stormy bay." *Emily Dickinson writes, "Futile the winds to a heart in port." Well, I haven't yet arrived at that calm port!* "We commend Gabe to You and fervently pray that You restore him to health so that he may continue Your work." Another pause. "Many lost lambs, like me, have been shown the way by his comforting light." *To be honest, many of us flounder in a tumultuous bay!* "How we need that light during this coming dark winter! Amen."

Leaning over Gabe, they took turns touching their lips to his forehead and gently squeezing his right hand. Jude and Cory then walked to the door when Pastor Gabriel, surprisingly, mustered enough strength to speak again. With his left hand lying motionless by his side, the side nearest Jude and Cory, he moved the index finger of his right hand slightly, indicating that he wanted them to return. By his side again, Cory and Jude leaned over to hear his feeble whisper.

"He's trying to speak," Jude turned and whispered to Martha. "His mouth moved a little, but no words came forth."

"Because he's so weak."

Again, the pastor tried to talk but was too debilitated to do so. Jude and Cory hovered inches from his mouth. After several moments, Gabe slowly and deliberately formed three clear but barely audible words, "Forgive Abe.... He'll—" Gabriel paused and uttered another word so quietly that they couldn't make it out.

Cory softly spoke to Jude. "I think he said 'return.' 'Forgive Abe. He'll return.' What do you think he said?"

"I thought it was 'He's learned.' 'Forgive Abe. He's learned,' but I'm not sure." *Gabe opens his eye and is looking at us with a fierce intensity. How important this thought must be which he tries so desperately to articulate! He looks like Grandpa as he lay dying on a barn floor, strug-*

gling with all his might to tell me where the novel was buried. I see that same battle in Gabe, the same cursed battle!

In the hallway outside of Gabriel's room, Jude bowed his head and whispered to Cory, "If this is the end, 'Good night, sweet prince: And flights of angels sing thee to thy rest.'"

"Lord, please save this man!"

*****

Early Sunday morning, Martha called Cory on the phone. "Good morning, Cory." A pause. "His night was decent, and he's improved a fair amount." A pause. "Thank you, Cory. You know how we appreciate the prayer."

"I'm so glad the church started a twenty-four-hour prayer vigil."

"That gives both of us enormous comfort. I'm calling about a favor."

"What? We'd do anything to help."

"Gabe is keen for you and Jude to read his journal. Could you please go to the parsonage and get it from his desk in his library? He wants you to read his last entry. That's what he was trying to say last evening. This is obviously very important to him."

"Yes, Martha. We'd be delighted to do this. Honestly, it would be a real treat."

Jude and Cory went to the parsonage after church, opened the door with the key which Martha kept under the porch geranium pot, and ambled to the desk to retrieve the journal which lay beside his Bible.

Cory reverently picked up the cherished volume and held it to her breast. "These are likely the last words Gabe wrote."

Look at Gabe's study. Jude panned the room in awe. *Shelf after shelf of books, enormous tomes, whole series, volumes of learning! What a learned scholar and what a passionate intelligence created to grapple with continents of libraries!* He softly ran his finger along a stone which Gabe had picked up near the sea of Galilee and touched the cross which he had found in the cracks between the pavement stones on the Via Dolorosa. *How Gabe treasures these Holy Land keepsakes!*

"Penny for your thoughts, Professor!"

"Look at this place. I feel the power of Gabe's presence just by being here!"

"I do too. Go ahead and sit at his desk!"

"Do you think I should?"

"He'd want you to!"

Jude eased himself into the large padded desk chair. "Grandpa Jeremiah must have felt this way when he sat in Tennyson's chair at Farringford on the Isle of Wight! His journal entry about that experience stirred me deeply." *Think, Jude, think! I ought to remember what Grandpa said about that singular event.* Jude ran the fingers of his left hand along the arm of the chair and tapped his lips with the index finger of his right hand.

Got it! Standing at Tennyson's desk, Grandpa Jeremiah said something like this: "I slid my hand across the wood grain of your desk the way a sculptor gently touches the smoothness of his sculpture to feel it tingle with that soft porcelain caress." Then he said he sat in Tennyson's chair and "nuzzled deeply into its cozy warmth and, during that sublime moment, my deeper self." Grandpa, how profound that must have been for you! I would have felt the same but lack your poetic way of saying it. You, genius, were the consummate wordsmith! Jude again ran his fingers along the side of the armchair. *I honestly feel the same thing here at Pastor's desk. Oh, that I could osmose his wisdom, just an ounce of it, for Gabe is by far the most Christlike man I know.*

"Well, that was some experience!" Cory observed as she locked the parsonage door and replaced the key under the flower pot.

"Yes, heavy stuff. We've been in that study multiple times but never to feel its power and to soak in its very ambience as we just did. What a feeling it was to be where the great one grappled so fiercely with deep matters of theology. Look at these hands. I'm trembling!"

"Well, think about it. All the brilliant sermons, the hours of wise counseling, the untold agony when he grappled on his knees in prayer—all of it occurred in that hallowed room. No wonder we're stirred!"

Jude reverently ran his fingers across the cover of Gabe's journal as they walked to their car. "Where do you think we ought to read it?" A twinkle came to Jude's eye. "We need to treat this experience with the reverence it deserves."

"How about Little Gidding? We can explore the riches of Gabe's mind there. That sanctuary is as hallowed for us as Gabe's study is for him."

"'Explore,' yes. Your use of that word makes you sound like Eliot in 'Little Gidding.'"

"I hear a quotation coming. I have no idea where you're going, but I gladly follow!"

"I give you the last lines of Eliot's 'Little Gidding:'

> We shall not cease from exploration
> And the end of all our exploring
> Will be to arrive where we started
> And know the place for the first time.

"Excellent stuff, wouldn't you say?"

"Geez, Eliot was good. That is brilliant poetry. He's saying that when we reach the end we'll be back to where we started but understand things in a whole new way—'know the place for the first time.' Is that his meaning?"

"I think so. At least, that's how I've always interpreted those lines, but a question remains." Jude looked piercingly at Cory. "Are you sure you can handle going back into the mine so soon after our little catastrophe? We were pretty traumatized the last time we were there. Should we try a less emotionally charged environment?"

"'Perfect love casts out all fear' (1 John 4:18). I can handle it, but I see a twinkle in your eye. The reason?"

"Remember when I made that phone call from Gabe's office after church?"

"I knew you went in his office for a moment but didn't know you made a phone call."

"I telephoned the Stephen Foster Memorial Library-Museum. I had read that they're having special Sunday hours today and are open this afternoon. Let's go look at the *Beautiful Dreamer* window in the library-museum. Then we can read Gabe's journal somewhere down there in Oakland—maybe in the Commons Room of the Cathedral of Learning. How's that for a winning plan?"

"Excellent! Seeing the window will be great since it played such a major part in Old Mary's recurring dream. I really like the Cathedral of Learning too. I'm referring to its architectural style. *C'est quell style?* (What style is that?)"

"*Gothique.*"

"*Qui etait l'architecte?* (Who was the architect?)"

"I'm not sure, but I think it was Charles Klauder. The style, technically, is Late Gothic Revival."

"*Quand a-t-il ete construit* (When was it constructed)?"

"Is this an exam? I don't know—maybe early 1930s?"

"Jude, this is great." Now it was Cory's turn to flash a twinkle in her eye.

"What are you thinking?"

"That if we're going to see the lovers in the *Beautiful Dreamer* window, then we have to be dressed like them as we were in Old Mary's dream. Why not?"

"If you say so! Then it's time for a fast costume change, and"—Jude sang the last line—"to Grandmother's house we go!"

Chapter 46

———— ❦ ————

As they walked from the parsonage to the car, Cory noted Jude's demeanor. *He's preoccupied about something.* "What's percolating inside that brain of yours? Fess up."

Jude looked across at the church. "I'm excited to read Gabe's journal. Don't mistake me, but can you imagine reading Dad's journal? What an experience to get inside *his* head! That's really something to say about your own father, but I'm completely serious."

"Of course you are."

"I still can't believe that he's my dad and that I was denied a normal father-son relationship. What a challenge to grow up without a parent in this world!"

"Your taste of it right before the explosion makes you long for it more than ever, right?"

"Exactly." Jude shut the car door and started the engine. "What do you think happened to him? Do you believe he's buried under tons of rubble? Be honest…as you always are!"

"The infrared lens proved that Zoe the Angel gave him temporary protection while he prayed right before the explosion."

"But did he make it? The thought obsesses me!"

"I think of him so much too." *It's a good time to change the subject!* "Speaking of journals, what of your grandpa's? That's one you'd love to read, especially his account of the days before his death."

"It might contain a clue about his conduct. Was he showing signs of dementia or undue stress? Something made him bury the manuscript."

"Wonder if we'll ever know why."

"I haven't gotten up the courage to ask Grandma about reading it. She might know."

"The whole subject would be very painful for her."

By midafternoon, they had parked their car on Bigelow Boulevard by the Cathedral of Learning and jaunted to the Stephen Foster Memorial in Oakland. They strolled through the lobby to the library-museum with a nervousness that had accumulated across months of anticipation.

"I can't believe we're getting to see the window at last!" Cory grasped Jude's arm.

"I just wish Old Mary was with us."

"Walking through this lobby flashes me back to the night of *The Pittsburgh Hamlet* when we ended up on that stage." Cory paused for a moment in the lobby to look into the theater. *We were right there!* "I still can't believe that happened!"

Cory spotted the *Beautiful Dreamer* window first. "There it is, up there! It's stunning!"

"It is! 'A thing of beauty is a joy forever.'"

"Keats, right?"

"The first lines of 'Endymion.'"

"Another literary masterpiece I need to add to my reading list." Marveling at the beauty of the window, they stood in silence for the longest time. "It's absolutely gorgeous."

"Look at the detail. It is indeed a joy forever."

"How amazing that Old Mary pictures us as these two lovers!"

"That's always been unbelievable to me too."

"Do you remember more than the first line of Keats's 'Endymion?'"

Jude intently examined the beauty of the stained glass window. "Let me see:

A thing of beauty is a joy forever:
Its loveliness increases; it will never
Pass into nothingness; but still will keep
A bower for us, and a sleep
Full of sweet dreams.

261

"That's all I remember."

"That is so beautiful and fitting too. This window will never pass into nothingness because it will always be dear to us."

"People who rush by it couldn't know that it's our private bower."

"And that it embodies our story and occasions a sleep… I forget the line. Sleep of what?"

"'A sleep full of sweet dreams.'"

"What a sweet dream Old Mary dreamed all these years!"

"That it was of us across her life never ceases to amaze me."

They stopped a passerby, an accomplished amateur photographer as it turned out who toted a large camera.

Jude approached him. "Could you please take our photo?"

"Yes, photography is my avid hobby." He held up his camera. "With this monstrosity, you can tell! Please stand there."

Jude and Cory were dressed in garments similar to the figures in the window—Cory in her long flowing blue gown, Jude in his rust-colored suit.

"I propose three separate shots," the photographer began. "One with each of you standing at the sides with the unobstructed stained glass lovers at center, a second of you together with the partially concealed image in the background, and a third—the creative one—in which you assume the poses of the beautiful dreamer and her beloved. Are you game?"

"We chose the perfect photographer!" Cory gleefully exclaimed as he adjusted the camera settings. Cory again scrutinized the stained glass window. "Imagine that Old Mary stood right here as a little girl."

"And then had the original dream of the beautiful dreamer that very night. How mysterious!"

"The biggest mystery of all is the overwhelming question—*why* did she have it?"

"And why does the dream correlate, point by point, to our lives?"

"The questions proliferate. Why did Zoe live among us all summer? To shepherd us to Grandpa's manuscript? These remain really big mysteries."

After the photographs were taken and details completed for mailing them, Jude and Cory walked over to the Commons Room in the Cathedral of Learning on the University of Pittsburgh campus.

Cory slowly swept her eyes around the four-story Gothic room. "Don't you just love the architecture?"

"I do. The arches are completely authentic. Not a bit of steel was used in their construction, and the base of each pillar weighs some five tons. I remember hearing a tour guide say that."

"This is like being in Paris's Sainte-Chapelle or one of the great cathedrals of England like York, Salisbury, or the Abbey in London."

"Or Winchester."

"Why mention that particular one?"

"Because Jane Austen and Keats lived in Winchester, and both of them loved its great cathedral."

After a brief stroll around the Commons Room, they commenced reading Pastor Gabriel's journal. Because he was a gifted writer, the prospect of reading the entire volume greatly excited them, but for the time being, they limited their perusal to the final days, per the pastor's directive. They started with two simple paragraphs.

Pastor Gabriel Wyant's Journal

I was not feeling well the entire evening of the Pittsburgh celebration. Nevertheless, all went according to plan. How I praise God for that! I feel like Simeon: kept alive long enough to see a great and culminating event—in his case, the newborn Christ; in my case, the heavenly archangel. I say with David in Psalm 41:3, "The Lord will strengthen him on his bed of illness; You will sustain him on his sickbed" and 39:4, "Lord, make me to know my end, and what is the measure of my days, that I may know how frail I am." Lord, You know how frail I am!

Another unexpected capstone of the evening, besides seeing the angel, was Jude's proposing to beautiful Cory. What a grand climax to our stellar celebration! Though my body weakens, my spirit rejoices. When I looked at them together on that platform, I thought of the weeping prophet Jeremiah: "Their souls shall be like a well-watered garden, and they shall sorrow no more at all" (31:12). Cory, your long night of suffering is behind you. How fitting that verse as I glanced across the confluence of the three mighty rivers! As if that is not enough joy for one man, I have lived to see Jeremiah's masterpiece! "The fervent effectual prayer of the righteous man avails much." Thank You, God, for answering this humble man's prayers!

"We can read all of this later, fascinating as it is. I can't believe that he had sufficient strength or time to write all of this, but note the shaky handwriting." Jude leafed through several pages of recent journal entries. "Look at this handwriting compared to the earlier entries."

"He was definitely failing when he wrote this."

"Let's turn to the last entry since Gabe wanted us to read it."

"You're right." Cory turned several pages. "The entry is dated late Thursday night after the Monday evening celebration at Point State Park in Pittsburgh."

"That means Gabe completed this entry late that evening and, after taking ill in the middle of the night, ended up in the hospital."

*****

Sleep has been elusive for me this night. I have slept fitfully and have just awakened from the most extraordinary dream. Too excited over this dream to try to sleep again, I arise to write about it. Martha, I hope I don't disturb you!

264

The dream, like Pete Mohney's, came to me in two parts. In part one, someone had driven me to the new room where Jude and Cory had endured the horrific explosion. I walked to the doorway just in time to see the most fantastic sight. In my dream, I saw a very bright light at the geometric center of a large cross. It made me think of Psalm 112:4, "Unto the upright there arises light in the darkness." This light reminded me of the morning star which according to tradition is always the brightest right before dawn. The phrase *post tenebras lux* (after darkness, light) popped into my brain. I couldn't see anything else but the blinding light in that place of foreboding darkness.

The darkness was scary black and awful. May spiritual darkness never do to me and the dear lambs of my flock what it did to Thomas Hardy as he describes it in "In Tenebris: '[D]eath will not appall / One who, past doubtings all / Waits in unhope.'"

Waiting in "unhope"—how dark! Mr. Hardy, I wish I had sat with you in your lovely, thirteenth century church at Stinsford. I would have prayed, "Send out Your light and Your truth. Let them lead me" (Psalm 43:3). I would have prayed for you to be led by God's true light! I know that Darwin's *Origin of Species* shook you to your roots. No wonder: as Proverbs 13:12 says, hope deferred makes the heart sick. You needed the sweet promise of 1 Peter 1:13, "Rest your *hope* fully upon the grace that is to be brought to you at the revelation of Jesus Christ." Or Paul's comforting reference in 1 Thessalonians 1:3 to "your patience of *hope* in our Lord Jesus Christ." Or Hebrews 10:23, "Let us hold fast the confession of our *hope* without wavering, for He who promised is faithful." You, sir, had lived too long with those who hate peace (Psalm 120:6).

I digress. As the dazzling light slowly took shape, I ascertained that it was a glorious angel. Like John at Patmos or the women at the Empty Tomb of Jesus Christ, I clutched my face in fear and gasped with joy. *I'm in the presence of an angel!* Slowly raising my eyes, I beheld a large cross, a dazzling light that shone like the jewels of the New Jerusalem—jasper, sardonyx, sapphire, ruby, and diamond—so bright that it nearly blinded me. I collapsed in awe at this wondrous sight. *Because the holy angel eradicates the darkness, we wait in hope!*

I wasn't sure of the significance of the mighty cross but was heartened to see it in that ghastly place. Jude and Cory, I reasoned in my dream, will surely be safe if they are in the vicinity of it. I tried to trace its horizontal and vertical beams. Though I was not able to see the top or bottom of the long vertical beam, I could trace the trajectory of the horizontal one. There, to my amazement, was Jude and Cory safely huddled together on one end and a man bowed in prayer at the other end of the transverse. I awoke before I identified the man, but it may have been Abraham Badoane. The angel was resplendent and shook me to the core as much as Darwin had shaken Thomas Hardy.

After a scene change, I then saw Jude and Cory struggling upward on the rope toward the conveyor belt. It was so real to me that I actually felt I witnessed the horror in real time. A verse in Job came to my mind when the author describes men mining in the bowels of the earth. God "breaks open a shaft away from people; in places forgotten by feet they hang far away from men; they swing to and fro" (Job 28:4).

I thought of God's amazing miracle of dropping the conveyor belt to them through the ceiling, their stairway to heaven, to give them a possible but extraordinarily difficult exit route. I reflected too on how Jude and Cory hung far away from people above ground and how they perilously swung back and forth on the rope high above the vast canyon. How fitting Job's description of what they endured—"in places forgotten by feet they hang far away from men; they swing to and fro"— as Jude and Cory swung high above the canyon floor! I praise God for bringing that obscure but utterly relevant verse to this distraught mind, this distracted globe, as Jude would call it!

The next part of my dream was just as unusual. When I drifted back to sleep, I dreamed again, but this time, I was at the football game the night Joey played late in the fourth quarter and won the game with his outstanding performance. I had a perfect view of his run from the near sideline of the football field. He was ahead of all the opposing players as he streaked down the field, though one player from the other team kept pace but still lagged several steps behind him. This defender would not have caught Joey because Joey, upon seeing his dad, dashed like a meteoric streak. How that lad put on a burst of speed!

As I was watching Joey run, an angel materialized out of nowhere, just suddenly appeared on the sideline facing the field! I looked carefully and couldn't believe my eyes as I watched him trip the Freeport defender who pursued Joey! I started laughing—in my dream, of course—to see such comic incongruity. As if that wasn't strange enough, the angel turned to me, put his index finger to his lips as if to say, "Shh, you must not tell anyone!" And then, plain as day, winked directly at me. Though in the immediate vicinity, no one else saw the angel. They just kept observing the exciting action on the field as if an angel wasn't standing directly beside them! That quickly, the angel disappeared!

The incident made me think of 2 Kings 6 when the band of Syrian raiders was surrounded by angels; but Elisha's servant Gehazi, overwhelmed by fear, could not see the angels. "Then the Lord opened the eyes of the young man, and he saw. And behold the mountain was full of horses and chariots of fire all around Elisha" (v. 17). I felt the same thing because the angelic protector had no doubt been there the whole time. How true the verse, "The angel of the Lord encamps all around those who fear Him" (Psalm 34:7). How he encamped beside our dear Joey that memorable Friday evening!

One final point relative to Jude and Cory's situation: Before I went to bed last night, I was going back over some of my favorite Oswald Chambers' reflections in *My Utmost for His Highest* and reread an excerpt from the June 13 entry: "The one true mark of a saint of God is the inner creativity that flows from being totally surrendered to Jesus Christ. In the life of a saint there is this amazing Well, which is a continual Source of original life. The Spirit of God is a Well of water springing up perpetually fresh."

That is so good! It reminds me of the expanse of water that surrounded us at the confluence of the three rivers and of the fountain at Point State Park, springing up, like a well, and perpetually fresh. I say to Jude and Cory that inner creativity, as Chambers ingeniously notes, is the hallmark of the surrendered saint. Now that you are fully surrendered to our Lord, tap into that inner creativity. Craft your paintings, Cory, and write those novels, Professor Jude!

P.S. Also, be sure to publish Jeremiah's novel! There was another saint of God out of whom a well of inner creativity flowed with gushing force. That man was a Niagara of power and a veritable continent of wisdom!

*****

Sitting near one of the fireplaces in the Commons Room, Jude and Cory finished reading Pastor Gabriel's journal entry which he concluded with three poetic excerpts. The first was from Shakespeare's *Richard II* when John of Gaunt gives his deathbed speech.

> More are men's ends marked than their lives before.
> The setting sun, and music at the close,
> As the last taste of sweets, is sweetest last,
> Writ in remembrance more than things long past.

—William Shakespeare, *Richard II*, 2.1.11–14

With a progressively weaker hand, Pastor Gabriel appended two brief quotations, the first from Eliot's "Little Gidding:" "The communication of the dead is tongued with fire beyond the language of the living."

"How true that is!" Jude sat upright by the fireplace. "Gabe's words, tongued with fire, are as comfy as a heated blanket and warm me to the soul!"

The last quotation was from Shakespeare's *Hamlet*—"The rest is silence."

"Is this man, after years of battle, about to gain his rest at last?"

"Think of all the wisdom that has poured from those lips across decades, all the gems that have cascaded out of that effusive brain!" Slouching backward in his chair, Jude reflected on their beloved shepherd of God. "That verse plaque which sits on Gabe's desk says it all—'The mouth of the righteous speaks wisdom' (Psalm 37:31). How true!"

Cory gazed upward to the fifty-two-feet high ceiling. "Gabe's beautiful writing reminds me of another proverb: 'A word fitly spoken is like apples of gold in settings of silver.' His profuse gems of wisdom have been like apples of gold set in silver. If he passes, we're left with apples of darkness set in black pitch!"

"To say it bluntly, the composite spiritual gene pool of Armstrong County will be cut in half!"

Chapter 47

A couple events which happened after the Pittsburgh ceremony bring the Jude-Cory saga to a close.

The first deals with an occurrence one evening in early September. Jude and Cory drove into Kittanning and parked the car on Market Street. As they ambled across the bridge, Cory took Jude's hand. "I remember something Pastor Gabe had said a couple weeks back which I keep forgetting to tell you."

"Tell me, Monet! A Gabe quote is great way to start a stroll."

"I asked him why we had to suffer so much before our love flourished. Sorry to bring up the topic of the difficult years!"

"What did the wise one say? Not being philosophically inclined, I'm totally clueless."

"As usual, he didn't hesitate and proceeded to quote part of a verse in Song of Solomon. I think it's the last part of chapter 2, verse 7, which says that we shouldn't 'stir up love nor awaken it until it pleases.' His quoting that on the spot amazed me. When I sort of played dumb and said I wasn't sure what the verse meant and how it applied to us, he said, 'If love is awakened prematurely, it doesn't blossom fully.'"

"He probably meant that waiting on God's timing is crucial and that people shouldn't push things to fruition before the right time. Maybe that's what Shakespeare meant when he said, 'ripeness is all.'"

Arriving at the center of the bridge, Jude and Cory dropped two large Crimson Glory red roses into the river. Over the eastern ridge, they watched the early evening full moon reflect its shimmering splendor in the Allegheny River. "I hoped it would be exactly like this." Cory rested her elbows on the railing. "Beautiful evening, full moon, standing here with my love, and leisurely watching our roses glide along the silvered water like a lovely Venetian gondola."

"Wow! That was one poetic line! Yes, perfect in every way. You've thought of every detail, including the positioning of the clouds. Did you arrange for the moon to peak out from behind its sequestered palace in the clouds just as we arrived at the middle of the bridge?"

"Of course, silly one!" She put her arm around his waist and cuddled her head into his shoulder. "I thought such an excellent occasion deserved one more exquisite touch." Cory rooted for her miniature cassette player in her handbag, positioned it on top, and pushed "Play." "I give you a favorite song." The strains of Patty Page's "Allegheny Moon" zephyred through the evening air.

> Allegheny moon, I need your light
> To help me find romance tonight,
> So shine, shine, shine on tonight.
> Allegheny moon, your silver beams
> Can lead the way to golden dreams
> So shine, shine, please shine.

"You know how I love that song, Cory. Thank you, darling!" They grew quiet for a moment to bask in the grandeur of the evening and watch the roses float downstream.

> High among the stars so bright above
> The magic of your lamp of love
> Can make him mine.

"Did I ever tell you why I like this song so much?"

"No, but please do."

"The first time I heard this 1956 song, I was a little boy. We were stopped in traffic on this bridge as it played on the radio. It was a summer evening just like this, and the full moon shone brightly. Ever since, I've associated "Allegheny Moon" with this bridge. My little boy brain thought it had been written for and actually described this very scene!"

"It's even more appropriate now, standing together above the Allegheny River under a full moon."

"You planned every single detail!"

> Allegheny moon, it's up to you;
> Please see what you can do
> For me and for my one and only love.

They listened to the rest of the song in silence. As Jude wrote in his journal, "We alternated our gaze between the moon, spangling a shimmering path across the silvery water plane, and the gracefully gliding roses which blithely bobbed toward the Huckleberry bend."

Jude encircled Cory's waist. *I can't help but reflect on the events of the last four months. I came to Armstrong County in early May—forlorn, messed up. Let's be honest—a walking dead man! Now it's early September, and all is excellent! Thank You, Jesus!* "We'll have each other forever, Cory. Except for Dad, everything has worked out so wonderfully. Hand in hand, we face a glorious future."

"I completely agree, but I think of one thing we should do."

"What?"

"See Old Mary. When she told me on the phone to stop by soon, she sounded so incredibly excited."

"Perfect. We can do it now. I've been really concerned about her ever since she collapsed when trying to warn us about her dream. How strange that she called you right before we left for the mushroom mine."

"Imagine how different if we'd have received her warning. That's one little event that didn't come to its ripened fulfillment!"

"Watching these roses makes me think of the miracle of the rose dream. By the way, you didn't tell me she called."

"Too much happening! Sorry, my dear."

On the way to Old Mary's apartment at Center Hill, they played one of Grandpa's old cassettes. They took the southern route so that from the Ford City bridge they could see the reflected moon in the Allegheny River over Rosston.

Cory wiped the condensation from the window and looked up river. "Soon our roses will be floating down here."

As they turned the corner at The Villa restaurant and headed up
Glade Run Road moments later, Elvis's song, "My Wish Came True,"
played on the cassette.

> My wish came true
> When I met you.

"That is certainly true!" Jude stated between the lines.

> I've searched and searched
> My whole life through.
> There's just one thing,
> Dear, before we start:
> Don't say you care,
> Then break my heart.
> When you speak of love,
> Please be sincere,
> For if you play with love,
> It can bring tears, my dear.

"We'll never play with love," Cory blurted between the lines,
"because a love this beautiful deserves our all."

> My wish came true
> To my surprise
> When you stood there
> Before my eyes.

"Remember that line," Jude quickly interjected. "I'll comment
when the song's finished."

> And when my heart
> Started beating fast,
> T'was then I knew
> I found true love at last.

As the song ended, Jude stopped the cassette. "You know that line in the song that says, 'When you stood there before my eyes?'"

"What about it?"

"That's exactly how I felt my first day of work when I was plugging in the electric cart and watched you exit the lunchroom. I was crouched behind the cart some fifteen feet away, riveted to your every move. When you paused to put your helmet on, I felt my heart pounding. So this part of Elvis's song—your standing 'there before my eyes' and 'my heart...beating fast' because 'I found true love at last'—describes that moment to a tee. And all other days too!"

"I know the feeling. My heart still flutters when you knock on the door or ring me on the phone. That, Judah Jedidiah, is how much I love you!"

"I had no idea people could love this much!"

She put her arms around him and hugged him hard. "Or that it would be this good."

In a short while, they motored up Glade Run Road toward Center Hill. How they loved this simple stretch of village homes, unchanged for decades and nestled along the winding country road. Soon they were seated with Old Mary on the porch of her house near the main intersection in the village. Bedecked with late-summer flowers, the porch was always the place she could be found on late-summer evenings. Besides the sheer joy of just being in her company, they had come to find out what she had to tell them.

"Do you think it's a missing piece in the rose dream puzzle?" Cory wondered as they climbed the slope toward her house."

"Maybe she'll piece together the entire dream."

"That would be lovely."

Old Mary had rallied from her recent health scare as she had so many times in the past and was, once again, looking quite strong. She had bumped her head the evening she fell by the phone when trying to warn Cory, but apart from that, she sustained no other injuries. Wanting to see Jude and Cory ever since the Monday evening celebration in Pittsburgh, she had clipped the stories of their heroism award and engagement from both the *Pittsburgh Post-Gazette* and the local *Leader Times*. The papers lay beside her on the porch swing.

"This is how I learned about your exciting evening." She held up the two articles. "Congratulations! May I see your ring, Cory? I can see it dazzling clear over here, but I don't think it's as bright as those shining eyes. We old-timers call that the look of love!"

Cory showed her the ring, and Old Mary gave her a warm hug. "I'm so very happy for you beautiful dreamers. Yes, I call both of you beautiful dreamers!"

The first subject, predictably, was Pastor Gabe. The three of them shared the most recent information they had, but there were few updates. "He hasn't shown much progress," Old Mary concluded. "I think the doctors are prepared for the worst. There simply isn't anything else they can do."

"I'm sure you're right," Cory pensively responded.

Old Mary sat back and solemnly drummed her fingers on the side of the porch swing. "He has burned his candle on both ends."

"It will not last the night," Cory added, remembering the old ditty. "But, ah, my foes, and oh, my friends—it gives a lovely light."

"Do you know who wrote that poem?" *I might as well join in the conversation.* The two women shook their heads. "It was written by Edna St. Vincent Millay in 1918."

"How could you possibly know that, Mr. Encyclopedia? That, my love, is ridiculously trivial!"

"I just taught a handful of Millay poems during the spring term."

When the group stopped talking, Jude lifted his eyes over the brow of the hill toward the church where Pastor Gabe faithfully ministered, the image of the burning candle still on his mind. "Shakespeare says in *The Merchant of Venice*, 'How far that little candle throws her beams! So shines a good deed in a naughty world.' If that's true, and I think we'd agree it is, then can you imagine how far the candlelight of Gabe's godly life has thrown its beams? How could one ever know the vast distance his sphere of influence has reached?"

A time of respectful silence crept upon them as they contemplated Pastor Gabriel and his current fight for life on a hospital bed a few short miles away. Like Jude and Cory, Old Mary felt the sadness of the moment, but she also sensed that, as the senior in the group, she should tack the conversation toward more tranquil waters. "Pastor Gabe would want us to delight in God's presence among us recently. That godly servant would rejoice more than all of us put together." She entwined her hands on her apron. "There's much good to discuss, so let's begin!"

In quick order, they covered some of the highlights of the recent momentous days—Joey's fast rise to prominence on the football field, Pete's wonderful turnaround, and Tina and Duke's new interest in the church. After some animated conversation and one of Old Mary's delicious donuts—nobody in Center Hill made glazed donuts like Old Mary—she came to the topic that was on her mind. "We haven't touched on one really important subject."

"What?" Cory asked. "We've covered a lot of ground."

"When's the big day?" Because Cory and Jude continued to look at each other blankly, Old Mary refined the question, her eyes gleaming. "*Your* big day. Have you set a date for your marriage?"

"Oh! We haven't set the date, but we see no reason to wait," Cory preened, clasping Jude's hand and resting her head on his shoulder. "Right, my love?"

Jude brought her hand to his mouth and kissed it. "I couldn't agree more!"

I've never been so happy for two people in my life! "You two are perfect for each other. Truly perfect!"

When Old Mary stopped swinging, Cory looked at her two little feet side by side under the swing. *I didn't realize Old Mary's feet were so very tiny!*

"Now there's one little thing I want to know about the rose ceremony during your proposal at Three Rivers. The two of you wrapped a strand of Lily of the Valley around the two roses as you held them, correct?"

Cory extended her hand to look at her ring. "Correct!"

"The one close-up picture in the *Leader Times* shows that. Did you know that the Lily of the Valley was in my dream?"

"You referred to it once," Jude retorted, "but never gave us the details."

"After you two got together again, I knew you were the roses of the vision. That part was easy to figure out, but why did the Lily of the Valley entwine the roses?"

Cory swept her hair back from her face. "To symbolize how the two roses will always be together and never separated?"

"Cory makes a good point because we need to consider the rich symbolism of this particular flower. How wonderful that it's Lily of the Valley instead of some other flower. Pastor once said in a Bible study that Lily of the Valley is one of the biblical names for Christ. Even though the biblical lily of ancient Palestine differs from today's species, the symbolism still applies."

"Now I see where you're headed," Cory nodded in agreement. "That's an interesting take. Keep going."

"The roses represent our everlasting love, whereas the Lily of the Valley symbolizes the protection of that love in Christ. Nothing can harm the love because the Lily of the Valley shields it, and nothing can separate it because the twining flower securely binds it. Cory, what do you think? You're the artist who's a pro at interpreting symbols."

"I like what you're saying, but consider this too. The love will never end because, like the Christ, it exists forever. What a lovely image!"

"I hadn't thought about symbolism and such stuff," Old Mary responded, "but this makes sense. Since the Lily of the Valley holds the roses together, nothing will part them asunder as the wedding vows say. You artists make this old brain see things it doesn't normally see!"

They then highlighted the points of coincidence between the rose dream and the events in Jude and Cory's lives—the separate down-river journeys of the roses, their near catastrophes, the snatching of the roses from the water by the gigantic wing (which turned out to be Zoe the Angel), the explosion in the mine with the fore-grounded cross-tattooed arm, and much more.

"At every point, your rose dream bears a one-to-one correspondence to our love!" Cory exclaimed.

"But why?" Inquisitive as ever, Jude faced Old Mary. "*Why* were you given the dream? I can't imagine why you'd be given a dream that sequentially encapsulates the defining moments of our love. I don't doubt it for a second, mind you. I mean, I understand the detail-by-detail correlation between the two."

"I see Jude's point. The question can be boiled down to this: why were we singled out to be the scripted players in your dream play?"

"You artists sure do have a way with words! Needless to say, I've wondered that for years. You can imagine how glad I am that the dream matches your lives. Charles says you're"—with her shaky hand, Old Mary reached for a small notebook on the swing, held it closely to her eyes, and read—"'Jude and Cory are the flesh-and-blood corollary of your recurring dream.' That's the fancy phrase the professor used when we were talking about how you fulfilled the dream. I liked it so much I wrote it down!"

Seated next to Old Mary, Cory stole a glance at the wispy thin line of her writing. *I've never seen such handwriting. It's dainty as a fragile hair root and absolutely beautiful!*

"Well, you know Charles and his professor words. I understand about half of what that man says! And that goes for you too, Mr. Jude!" Old Mary gave her hearty eye-twinkling laugh.

"I have a question." Cory wiped the crumbs of Mary's delicious donut from her mouth. "What happened in your dream after you saw the roses wreathed with Lily of the Valley?" Unaware she did so, Cory crept to the edge of her chair. "Is that the end of the rose story? I'd like to know if that's where *our* story ends."

"I've wondered about that too. For years I've thought of that, but I was always more interested in the 'who' or the 'what' than the 'why.' I wanted to know who or what the roses stood for." Old Mary fixed her gaze on Cory. "I knew way back that you were the one rose, so right along, I thought you'd be together with your true love one day and that he'd be the other rose, but of course, I could never be certain."

"How very fascinating!" Cory interjected.

"But it wasn't just that. Remember the day when I tried to call you and fell in the kitchen?"

"How could we forget?"

"That day, the idea hit me for the first time that beautiful dreamer was not sleeping but dead."

After all the years of puzzling over this key point, what made her so sure? "Why did you come to that conclusion?" Jude knit his brow. *How was she suddenly certain?*

"Because beautiful dreamer had crossed to the other side of the Jordan River and was no longer on earth!"

I hate to be dumb about this, but I have to know her meaning. "What do you mean that beautiful dreamer had crossed over the Jordan?" Cory breathed faster. "You mean she crossed over into the afterlife and was now dead?" *I hate to keep pushing, but I need to know!* "Is that what made you certain?"

"Look at the stained glass window. The beautiful dreamer has crossed the river and is now on the other side!"

"And in the afterlife!" Jude added, at last catching Old Mary's meaning.

"Exactly! You see why I was so afraid that Cory would die in the explosion? That was the first time I realized she had crossed over Jordan!"

Cory nervously rubbed her ring. "No wonder you were frantic!"

"I was right since you were nearly killed that day!"

Jude clasped Cory's hand. "Right for a while, but wrong in the long run!"

"So true. Beautiful dreamer merely sleeps and is alive as you two!"

"Thankfully!" Cory laughed.

"You see how I acted on faith when I told you across the years not be discouraged. That was a leap of faith on my part since I felt in my heart that you'd be united with your true love, but I had no way of being certain."

Cory squeezed Jude's hand. "Old Mary kept her strong faith."

"What was my line through all those years?"

"How could I forget? 'The final chapter hasn't yet been written!'"

"That's it!" Old Mary clasped her wrinkled hands together in her lap. "Pastor Gauntz said that a lot, and so it's been with me for years. You remember him, Jude?"

"Very well. He made a big impression on this little boy."

"Well, I always thought that sentence applied to you, Cory. I hoped you'd find your lover and live as happily as I did with my husband." She stopped to reflect. "That good and dear man! He was taken from me at forty-seven. Now I worry that Gabe will be taken."

"So that's the who or what of the vision," Cory responded contemplatively, refocusing the conversation, "but that offers no clue about the why of it. *Why* were you given this dream that so precisely foreshadowed—I guess I should say mirrored—the major events in our lives point by point?"

Jude scratched his head. "I'm puzzled too since it's crazy that your recurring dream of a stained glass window in Pittsburgh perfectly corresponds to our lives."

"Maybe you'll find significance in an additional detail of the vision that came to me the other night. This had been part of the original vision, but I completely forgot about it over the years. This is the real reason I called you over. In fact, it's the main thing."

"What?" Cory exclaimed. "What is it?"

"The final piece of the puzzle! I know you'll just love it!"

Chapter 48

⧜

Old Mary paused and took a sip of tea to moisten her throat. "Once I knew for sure that you two were the roses, snatches of the original dream started coming to me again, especially the end part. Ever since I read of your rose ceremony in Pittsburgh, I've had the rose dream almost every night. To tell the truth, I've been able to think of little else!"

"That makes three of us!" Jude broke in.

"Well, last night, or I guess it was the night before, a new part of the dream came to me. This is what I'm calling the last piece." Old Mary paused.

"We're dying to know!" *Maybe my exclamation will hasten her narrative speed. Is she noting how Cory and I clutch the ends of our chairs in feverish anticipation?*

Old Mary launched into her description, "Remember the T. S. Eliot lines from 'Burnt Norton?' 'Footsteps echo in the memory?'" She stopped there. "I can't quote them, but you'd think I could after all these years." She quickly glanced at Jude. "Can you recite them?"

"Yes:

> Footsteps echo in the memory
> Down the path which we did not take
> Toward the door we never opened
> Into the rose garden.

"I think that's right."

"Thank you, Jude. Well, at the very moment when I heard those words, I saw two people standing still at the head of a path.

I'm talking about the new part of my dream. The lovers had walked to that point and stopped but soon started strolling down the path toward a rose garden. Behind it was an impressive old English home, Burnt Norton, the manor house in the lovely English Cotswolds. I adjusted my glasses to see better and realized it was the two of you walking the path toward that beautiful rose garden." A broad smile on her lips, Old Mary stopped swinging. "How lovely it was!"

Old Mary picked up her copy of the poem, held it to her face, and located the pertinent lines, the left eye squinted shut as she read. "'Footsteps echo in the memory down the path which we did not take.' The poet says that they didn't walk the path, nor did they open the door nor stand in the garden. They were just near to these places, but you actually experienced them. In my dream—this is the new part—you walked into the rose garden which was full of those stunning Crimson Glory roses. The air was so thick with the scent that I actually smelled them! You stood directly beside the rose garden where Jude embraced his beautiful dreamer."

"Is that the end of the vision?" Cory asked when Old Mary again paused.

"Be patient, child!" Old Mary grinned. "In my dream, I looked again and saw your faces as you stood together in the rose garden. I love this part which I keep replaying in my mind because you were overflowing with love. All of a sudden, I was distracted from seeing you or even the manor house because I was temporarily blinded by a bright and shining light from above. I looked up and, sake's alive, an angel descended right between you!"

"You too saw an angel!" Cory exclaimed.

"Yes, I certainly did." Old Mary paused and scratched her head. "I just thought of something. I wonder if he was Zoe. Anyhow, he put a book in your hand. I mean the angel. The angel put a big book in your hand, Jude, and exclaimed, 'Write!'"

"You're kidding!"

"Every word is true!"

"I wonder if the book is Grandpa's novel. Do you think so?"

"I have no idea."

"Is that where the dream ends?" Cory drummed her fingers. "Right there in the rose garden? Sorry to be so impatient, but I keep seeing these pictures I want to paint. I especially want to capture the final climactic scene in oils because I envision it as a kind of crescendo."

"Patience, beautiful dreamer, patience! We're close to the end but not there just yet. Arm in arm, you ambled along the path away from the rose garden with the manuscript between you. The angel was above you and the fountain pool in front of you."

"You dreamed all of this?" To keep them still, Jude folded his hands. "What an amazing final scene!"

"I dreamed it all but with one difference. The pool was no longer empty as it was when you stood beside it. Remember the way Mr. Eliot describes it?"

"Yes, I do recall. Eliot adds several details about the drained pool, the dry concrete, the brown edges, and more."

"But this time," Old Mary resumed, "the pool was full of water and had a spouting fountain at its center like the fountain at Pittsburgh's Point State Park. It was a smaller version of The Point fountain, you might say."

Old Mary sat back on the swing, spent from recounting her vivid dream. "That's the end, but how beautiful is that final scene in my mind!"

"Can you think of other details so I can paint it more exactly?"

"Let me think. Well, the two of you meandered hand in hand toward the pool. The fountain was shooting upward between you, and the pool reflected the pink glow of the setting sun. The angel was above you, Jude, as you held the manuscript in your hand." Old Mary crossed her tiny feet and smiled broadly. "Now, beautiful dreamer, we've come to the end of the dream. I think it's just wonderful!"

"That's exactly what happened at Pittsburgh!" Cory nearly whooped. "Together we strolled toward the large fountain, but there was something different about that walk toward the fountain."

"What?" Old Mary leaned forward.

"I sported a shiny new ring on my finger!"

Old Mary clapped her gnarled hands. "How wonderful!"

As they sat on her porch, Jude noted the details surrounding them. *The azure blue of the evening sky gradually merges with those tinges of saffron yellow and orchid pink. At the bottom a misty band of autumn orange cozily laps the horizon. Old Mary's hummingbirds still feed, but the breeze has stopped.*

Intently watching the hummingbirds, Old Mary whispered, "It usually gets very calm this time of the evening." All of a sudden, a look of sadness came over. *I cannot taint this present joy! Solomon says, "The time of singing has come" and "the turtledove is heard" (Song of Solomon, 2:12), but I hear hummingbirds instead of turtledoves."* She took a tissue from her apron pocket. *Mary, focus on joyful things, not sad!* "They usually feed this time of the evening."

Cory discreetly studied Old Mary's facial expression. *Her voice is weaker than it was earlier, almost quavering, but I don't think her weakened tonal modulation owes just to exhaustion.* Thinking of no smooth transition, she bluntly asked, "Old Mary, forgive my forwardness, but I have the feeling that something else weighs heavily on your mind." She peered deeply into Old Mary's eyes. *Did I say something I shouldn't?* "If I'm right and if it touches Jude and me, I'd like to know about it. I do apologize if I'm overly bold in saying that."

That's all it took, this one simple reference to the subject that preyed on Old Mary daily. "Lands sake, girl, I swear you're the most astute child I ever did see! Just how did you know that? You remind me of your mama!"

"In what way?"

As Old Mary's eyes swept across the upper lawn toward the lilac bushes, she reflected on Ruby Mohney. "Your mother was always a perceptive sensitive soul, just like you. You're one bright girl, Cory. I always knew that."

"Thank you, but let's speak of Mother. You say she was sensitive?"

Old Mary looked at Jude. "Beautiful dreamer is the sensitive one! I've seen her cry over the beauty of a rainbow or a sunset or a bunny with an injured foot. This time, she's being astute too. Something else has been on my mind, almost constantly since the cave-in."

"What?" Jude asked.

"You must know what it is since it touches you so directly."

It touches me directly? You're kidding! I'm not a mind-reader! I'm dying to know what you're thinking, but as I sit here, I'm fully aware of Old Mary's weakness and frailty since her hospital stay. I wish I knew where she's headed, yet I realize that, given her exhaustion, we should terminate this conversation soon so as not to tire her further. I was on the verge of proposing a delay for the second part of our discussion when, out of the blue, she brings up this matter which she says touches me directly! How to reply to a comment like that? Old Mary, how probingly you look at me! I've heard of your cordial attitude toward my dad in the past, and I've actually even witnessed it a time or two. Is that what this is all about? "Does this have something to do with Abe? You want to know about my dad?"

Old Mary rolled her upper lip over the lower one, the slightest of gestures, and then nodded slightly. *He's another brain, so I figured he'd guess what I was talking about!* "Very much so."

Knowledgeable as he was about body language, Jude caught it. *I hit the target. Large tears form in her eyes and ripple across the papery creases of her cheeks. Her tears, slowly winding downward, remind me of a valley rivulet as it jounces over jagged flinty shale.* "You want to know if my dad survived the explosion, correct?"

"Very much so!"

It was Cory's turn to show her love for this wise and beloved woman. Sitting beside her on the swing, she put her right arm around Old Mary to comfort her. "No need to be sad."

Jude was pleased to see Cory comfort Old Mary because there was no good way to soften his words. "We still have no word about what happened to my dad, not a single word." Jude turned his head and, as if seeking courage to continue, marveled at the magnificent sunset. "As you can imagine, he's never out of my mind either."

"I feared that."

Indulging another displacement gesture, Jude lifted his gaze upward over Old Mary's head at the faraway cemetery. *That place where all wayfarers end. At this point, silence perhaps is best until Old Mary settles herself. As I glimpse at the cemetery, I can't help but think of Thomas Gray's "Elegy Written in a Country Churchyard." Everything ends there, all of life's enterprises, all the plans and years of busy labor await the inevitable hour. "The paths of glory lead but to the grave." I think I've quoted Gray's immortal poem properly but am not sure. I also reflect on Marc Antony as he beheld the butchered Julius Caesar in the Roman Forum and contemplated the little six feet of soil into which that legendary leader would be ignominiously crammed: 'O mighty Caesar, Dost thou lie so low? Are all thy conquests, glories, triumphs, spoils, Shrunk to this little measure?" Dad, where is your little measure? Are you shrunk to your six feet limestone coffin?*

"Through the excitement of seeing angels and proposing to a beautiful woman and planning this marriage made in heaven—through it all, my dad has never been out of mind. I'm sorry to say this so brusquely, but you deserve total honesty."

"It's all right. I knew as much myself, but seeing you talk and act just like Abe makes me think of him so very much. Do you realize that you're the spitting image of that brilliant man?"

Now it was Jude's time to come up short for words. He looked passed Cory and again lifted his eyes over the knoll toward the church. *Four months ago, I walked with beautiful dreamer out the side door of that church, perfectly visible from here, into the old cemetery. We stood by an old grave marker on the top of the hill.*

"You're deep in thought, Jude," Cory finally uttered as she sat on the swing by Old Mary. "A penny for what's going on inside that kaleidoscopic brain of yours."

"Did you know that Keats was born in that year and that Washington had just started his second term as president?"

"What are you saying, ever crazy one?" Cory laughed. "My love, what does that have to do with anything?" *But at least he diverted the subject! You're smart, Jude!*

"I was thinking of the first night I saw you at evening Bible study last May. It's been four months already, four months almost to the day! We had walked out that side door." Jude gestured toward the church. "We stood in the cemetery, and I was shaking like Old Mary's lilac tree during a storm! We stood by David Bowser's grave. I noted that he had been born in 1795 and the other David Bowser, his relative, in 1788. In my nervousness, I started blabbing about things that happened in 1795. Remember now?"

"I do! How could I forget that wonderful evening?" She looked at Jude and smiled and then explained to Old Mary, "The music of my life had died. If anyone knows that, it's you. Well, that evening, I began to hear enraptured life-restoring music!"

A tear came to Cory's eye as she thought back on the dark years. Old Mary put her hand on Cory's knee to console her. "Those dark days are behind you forever!" Patting Cory's knee, she gazed at Jude. "You, sir, write that book. You realize that I'm not too old to turn you over my knee if you don't!" She laughed robustly.

In turn, they warmly hugged Old Mary, kissed her on the cheek, and bade her farewell.

Chapter 49

— ∾ —

As they sauntered down the knoll from Old Mary's apartment, Cory was the first to comment on the western sky. "Look at the color striations in that beautiful sunset. A wisp of blue ribbons the rosy palette of the evening sky and, underneath it, melts into yellow mingled with orange. Van Gogh would go out of his mind!"

"The whole of it set in an ocean of savoy azure blue."

"Aren't we the descriptive poets? Seriously, the blues and yellows are like Van Gogh's *Starry Night*."

"Does the autumn orange which hugs the horizon make you think of any famous paintings?"

"Maybe Van Gogh's *Landscape with Couple Walking* or Claude Monet's *Sunset in Venice*. That's the exact shade in Monet's painting. Almost all the colors of the rainbow are in that sunset, and you know what rainbows symbolize!"

"God's promise and our rainbow future. Am I getting warm, Monet?"

"Red hot! We need to keep an eye on that sunset. It will be more lovely if it deepens into vermilion."

Jude tapped the steering wheel, a simple but decisive gesture. "I have some place I'd like to go."

"Where?"

"It's time to beat my fear by coming full circle."

"Which fear?"

"Climbing the large beam in the barn which I mounted the day Grandpa fell. I've always shied away from doing that. You won't forget that I ran like a coward from the beam in the Younkins' barn at the church picnic."

"That was nothing. So what?"

"Let's go to the upper loft after we say hi to Grandma. You haven't seen her for a couple days. Like my little plan?"

"You bet I do, darling. I ditched my lifetime fear once and for all on a Pittsburgh stage. It's high time you did the same, and seeing Grandma Rosetta is the perfect warm-up act."

The kitchen of Grandma's home was permeated with the aroma of a freshly baked peach cobbler. "I don't need to tell you that I just took it out of the oven."

"The kitchen smells like a bakery, Grandma! What perfect timing!"

"I think you'll enjoy these Chambersburg peaches."

"The scent knocks me over!" Cory tilted her head and whiffed the sweet aroma. "That really smells good. Mom especially liked Loring and Sun High peaches for her cobblers. What kind of peaches are these?"

"I think either Redhaven or Sun High. Jude's grandpa always liked the Sun High peaches. He said it made 'the best peach cobbler on earth,' but far as that goes, he'd say that about any peach as long as it came from Chambersburg, Pennsylvania!"

Rosetta Wakefield carried the cobbler to the table and brought plates and forks. "I know you're headed somewhere, probably up to Vinlindeer, but can you take a minute to eat this while it's piping hot?"

"Definitely!" Jude laughed. "We always try to maintain proper priorities!"

While Cory and Jude devoured the cobbler, Grandma summoned the courage to speak of Jeremiah's manuscript. "You know I was never crazy about his writing that last novel since I always linked it to his death." *This is a difficult subject for Jude, so I'll step cautiously, but it's best to ease into it while Cory's present.* "Guess I've mellowed over the years and don't feel that way anymore, so I'd like your opinion. Did you start it yet?"

"Only the beginning." Jude wiped his mouth with a napkin. "To be honest, it's difficult for me to be objective since it's Grandpa's novel. It engages my emotions to the point that I can't read with a scholar's necessary critical detachment. I hope you understand that." *I'll say this since Grandpa was a fine writer.* "His sentences flow like a minstrel's melodious lay."

"Nice alliteration, love!"

Jude poured more milk on his cobbler while he formulated his response. *Grandma wants me to go deeper.* "Grandpa knew the Founding Fathers extremely well. Even in these opening pages, Washington was so real that I felt I was reading his private journal." Jude took another bite. "His descriptions of Washington's struggle against demonic evil are also spellbinding."

"You commented on that recently," Cory offered to give Jude time to think.

I probably should tell Cory about the twins he imagines us having, but I can't be a spoiler! Jude stole a quick look at Cory. *Did you know that Grandpa imagined us parenting twins? I even know their names! But I won't mention that delightful subject though it warms the soul!* "I'm reading a section where General Washington has an incredible dream, which was as real to him as Old Mary's dream was to her." Jude squeezed Cory's hand. "I can't wait to read the rest of the novel. It's truly good."

Rosetta looked at Jude as if she wanted further reaction. "Please tell me more. I know you've read only a small part, but you whet my appetite!"

"I enjoy all the references to Kittanning. Grandpa does such a great job of creating a sense of place and time."

"What's that mean?"

"He plops you right into the center of the county as though you're actually there." When Jude stopped, Rosetta gave a circling motion with her hand as if she wanted additional details. "His fun facts about the county and its rich history are also captivating. Who knows all this history?"

"Can you give an example?" *I'm trying to help Jude go deeper, though I know he prefers to wait till he's read all of it.*

"Did you know that Charles Dickens rode through the Freeport Canal in 1842 and that the Reynolds House in Kittanning was so famous that it ranked with the best of European and USA hotels?"

"You're kidding!" Rosetta exclaimed.

"No, I am not. And how about this priceless gem? In his novel, *Work of Art*, Sinclair Lewis of *Main Street, Elmer Gantry,* and *Babbitt* fame, lists Harry Reynolds as one of the foremost innkeepers in the world. Imagine that being said of the Reynolds House in little ole Kittanning by a genius who won the Nobel Prize for literature! I'll stop at that, but you can see how the novel's tidbit gems really do fascinate."

"I didn't know that nor did I know that Lewis won the Nobel Prize."

"Yes, Cory, he did. In 1930, I think. If memory serves correctly, he was the first American ever to win it."

Jude walked over to Rosetta and gave her a hug. "That was delicious, Grandma. Yummy in my tummy as Joey drooled over Cory's chicken parmigiana last evening." He and Cory drifted toward the door. "We changed our minds and are going to the barn instead. By the way, if you ever change *your* mind, I'd like to read Grandpa's journal. That would be the mother lode of all journals!"

"Thank you, Mrs. Wakefield. That was scrumptious. I'd love to have that recipe."

"You're so kind. I'll be sure to give you a copy!"

Chapter 50

"Don't you just love to watch the various colors of a brilliant sunset?" the enraptured Cory exclaimed as they dawdled on the porch.

"Yes, I do, but pretty soon, it will be 'The twilight of such day as after sunset fadeth in the west.'"

"Of course, you're quoting Shakespeare. I'm guessing *Sonnet 73*?"

"You got it!"

The barn was dark when they entered as dusk had already neatly tucked its mantle into the edges of the cooling day. Jude flipped the light switch. "You go first." He watched Cory sprightly climb the ladder. At the top, she skipped into the hayloft.

It's time for me to do that too! Step by step, Jude ascended, flashing back, remembering his fall—the flying ladder, the awkward tumbling of Grandpa through space, the excruciatingly hard thud, the book in his pocket. The imagery had seared the screen of his brain, but this time, it did not bother Jude. He peeked at Cory. "My heart isn't even racing. In fact, after climbing the conveyor belt with you on my back, this is a piece of cake!"

"Excuse me, tactless one! You're using this occasion to say I was a burdensome weight?"

"I bungle a lot, but not this time! Seriously, the weight of the world has been lifted from these scarred shoulders."

"I can only imagine your relief."

They walked to the upper window, sat in the haymow, and watched the sky's shimmering strata of autumn orange darken to vermilion.

Jude carefully observed the waning light. "The sunset darkens to the shade of Sangria wine, 'Which by and by black night doth take away, Death's second self, that seals up all in rest.'"

"I'm not surprised you've memorized Shakespeare's sonnet, but the reference to the darkened sunset morphing to death is morbid. Why mention death in a love poem?"

"Remember the hopeful context. The sonnet ends with the speaker saying we love people more intensely as they grow older and approach their end."

Cory placed her head on Jude's chest. "No two people have been happier in love than we, and unlike our senior friends, we don't approach our end!" *What's a good line of poetry?* "Here's a line for you. We've 'loved with a love that was more than love.'"

"I know that one. Edgar Allen Poe's 'Annabel Lee!' I couldn't agree more." He kissed her passionately. "I wish we were married right now so I could show you the more-than-love. You know of what I incessantly fantasize!"

"It won't be long. We should set the big day immediately."

"No argument here!"

They grew quiet and scanned the lush vale with its rolling fields of sun-ripened corn. At the bottom of the vale across the river, they saw a faraway speck. Seeing deer and even coyotes in the evening fields of Armstrong County was common, so at first glance, they surmised that an animal grazed along the tree line or came to the river for water. Concerned about their passionate embrace, they gave the object the slightest attention.

Jude studied Cory's face as she peered across the vale. A bronze ray of sunlight, its galactic journey complete, enveloped her right cheek in a golden halo. The barn light from below, as if perfect symmetry had been divinely ordered, feather-brushed her left cheek.

"Let's set the date right away."

How enchantingly beautiful! Completely absorbed in her magnificent beauty, Jude didn't respond.

"We merely have to check the calendar." Cory again scanned the field.

"I'm more interested in this beautiful face in front of me and the exquisite interplay of light and dark on it than an animal down there. Are the shadows and light on your face an example of chiaroscuro? Is that the new artsy word you taught me?"

"Very good! Chiaroscuro is the interplay of light and shade or the arrangement of dark and light. That's what you see in this face of breathtaking sculptured Venus beauty?"

"Joke if you want. I'm not!" Jude ran the back of his hand along the side of her face. "I call you 'Head by Scopas' or 'Athena' as sculpted by Praxiteles."

"Might you be a tad biased? Just a speck?"

"Impossible!"

In the evening serenity, they lifted their eyes to the mite on the far side of the river.

"I think it's a coyote," Jude offhandedly observed, "but I can't be sure." *That doesn't interest me, but this essence of beauty in front of me does!* After kissing her passionately, he glimpsed at the faraway field. "It's hard to tell since it's dark along the undergrowth."

"What's that behind him?" Cory inquired a moment later. "Is that a man coming out of the woods behind the animal? Those large branches block the view. If it is, then the animal wouldn't be a coyote."

Jude paused for a moment and, for the first time, looked intently. "The animal's turning and gazing backward as though waiting for something or someone to catch up. I wonder what it is. Maybe you can tell if you look through these binoculars." He reached for an old set of binoculars that hung in the upper loft by the window. "Grandpa kept these here because he used to spot deer in the evening." He wiggled more closely to her, leaned his head against the side of Cory's face, and then shut his eyes to bask in her warmth and imbibe the scent of her Parisian perfume. "Head by Scopas wrecks my focus. No hocus-pocus: love has woke us."

"You get sillier by the day!"

Cory carefully looked at the animal. "It's definitely a dog." She leaned forward to eagle-eye it. "The weeds block his front, but the setting sun on his exposed back makes him shine like the bright and morning star." She continued to gaze through the binoculars. "Remember the picture of us on horseback, the one where we're backlit and silhouetted by the morning sun? You always said you liked that one."

"It might be my very favorite photo."

"That's what we're seeing, a backlit silhouette on the far side of the sparkling river." They stared at the tree line, and the sunset reflected in the shimmering water.

"If Shelley viewed that magnificent sight, he'd offer a lyric like this: 'The river glistens like fire, a faraway ribbon of gleaming gold, gliding serenely along the vale.' More prosaically, I simply say, there is a river which flows like honey and cream."

"That's beautiful, Shelley and Jude! Praise God we found that river!"

Just then, Rosetta Wakefield entered the barn and, in a tremulous voice, called up to Jude and Cory, "Are you lovebirds up there in your nest?"

Crossing to the vertical beam, Jude stood on the precise spot where Jeremiah Wakefield had clung to the rope before falling to his death. Rosetta trudged toward the ladder.

She's really been weeping! "What's wrong, Grandma?"

"I just had a phone call from Martha Wyant." In the dusk, her voice trembling, Rosetta paused and clutched the step of the beam. "Old Mary was rushed to the hospital in an ambulance…and died on the way! I knew you'd want…to know right away."

"I can't believe it! We were with her just a short while ago!"

Cory rushed to Jude's side. "That is so sad!"

"I know!" Looking down at the barn floor near the base of the ladder, Rosetta said nothing. Very slowly, she turned her eyes toward the side and peeked at the spot where Jeremiah fell to his death all those years ago. She snapped her head back and dabbed her cheeks. *So true, Job: "Man who is born of woman is of few days and full of trouble!"*

Rosetta started to walk toward the door. Pausing in the entrance, she pivoted again to glance at the barn floor. *Did Jeremiah's head cause that depression in the floorboards, that little dip? Did his head hit there?*

Jude watched his grandma exit the barn. *She can hardly get one foot in front of the other!*

Cory stood beside Jude and put her arm around him. "Your poor grandma!"

"She's flashing back to Grandpa's death."

Hand in hand, they plodded back to the window. "How fitting is that verse, 'Precious in the sight of the Lord is the death of His saints' (Psalm 116:15). Who's more precious than saintly Old Mary? And we were her last visitors before she passed!"

Jude hugged her tightly. "Old Mary and her rose dream have been the very nerve center of our love." He shook his head in disbelief. "What titans of faith she and Pastor Gabe have always been!"

"We probably should call Charles to see if there's anything we can do."

"What a blow to the Center Hill community to lose a saint like that!"

"And Pastor Gabe does poorly too."

They bowed their heads and said nothing. *Cory's right. How sad that Pastor Gabe endures such a devastating illness and that Old Mary had been quite sickly in her final weeks.* "I hope I wasn't right about what I said it at the hospital when we visited Pastor Gabe."

"Right about what?"

"When I said, 'Good night, sweet prince, and flights of angels sing thee to thy rest.'"

"May his rest come later. Years from now! We definitely don't want to lose these two spiritual giants back-to-back. I cannot believe that Old Mary has passed over Jordan!"

"Like Foster's *Beautiful Dreamer.*"

"She seemed so good when we were just with her."

Jude poured a cup of cold water from his thermos. "Remember when Gabe said that he who gives a cold cup of water in the name of a disciple receives a reward" (Matthew 10:42)?

"I do."

"He also said that out of the believer's heart will flow rivers of water. Of late, I've felt the stirring of those sacred waters."

"Music to my ears, my love! In fact, I hear a symphony!"

Jude lifted the cup to his lips. "I drink this in honor of Gabe for whose recovery we fervently pray, and in memory of Old Mary whose legacy we celebrate." He took a sip of water, passed the cup to Cory, and then nestled tightly against her. "That was a refreshing drink!"

"Whoever drinks of the water that I shall give him will never thirst. But the water that I shall give him will become in him a fountain of water springing up into everlasting life" (John 4:14).

"That's beautiful!"

"You've found that water, and out of your heart will flow rivers of flowing water! Remember what Gabe said in his journal?"

"What's that?"

"The true mark of the Christian saint is the inner creativity that flows from his surrendered self. In your case, the fountain of water is the creativity that will gush out of you when you start writing!"

"That thought humbles me beyond words."

"It certainly offsets our heavy gloom—a lost father, a lost manuscript, and now a lost saint! How sad to think Old Mary's gone! No wonder my emotions gyrate like Kennywood's Steel Curtain roller coaster!"

I want to divert Cory away from her grief. "I really like that verse, the one about flowing rivers of water. Where's it found?"

Cory reflected for a moment. "I think John 7:38."

"I prefer a flowing river over a dry and parched mouth!"

Through the binoculars, Cory peered at the two forms now standing on this side of the river and bathed in golden light. She tightly clasped Jude's arm. "Look! I can't believe it!"

With the binoculars, Jude hurriedly peered across the field and then dashed down the stairs. "It really is! Right by the river."

Dashing behind him, Cory breathlessly yelled, "'Eye has not seen, nor ear heard, nor have entered into the heart of man the things which God has prepared for those who love Him'" (1 Corinthians 2:9)!

"And what a glorious thing God has prepared for us!"

Plot Summary

***

The Rose and the Serpent
(Novel 1 in the Saga)

After a painful five-year separation, Jude Hepler and Cory Mohney joyfully reconcile but are again pitted against the brilliant and evil Abe Badoane. More intelligent and savvy than Hannibal Lecter, Badoane schemes to destroy the lovers as he had five years earlier. Beleaguered by their own emotional devastation and reeling from past traumas, the lovers battle both Abe's evil plotting and the carnal stooges like macho strongman Duke Manningham, whom Abe uses to do his dirty work.

Two subplots inform the fast-paced storyline. First, the events in Jude and Cory's lives mirror the uncanny and recurring rose vision, which wise Old Mary has dreamed across many decades. Second, the characters and even the storyline events correlate to the great Shakespearean tragedy, *Hamlet*. That correspondence, hinted at in *The Rose and the Serpent*, becomes a full-blown intermeshing by the novel's sequel, *The Pittsburgh Hamlet*.

At the end of *The Rose and the Serpent*, Jude and Cory stumble upon the highly guarded secrets—two wrenching traumas—which had occurred earlier in Abe's life. Feeling exposed and vulnerable, he vows revenge. No one stands a chance against Hannibal Lecture, but never has his equal, the wily Abe Badoane, faced spirit-filled lovers like Jude and Cory who possess such fire-tested faith. Despite failings and horror-filled adversity, they cling to each other in this dramatic, suspense-filled story of love. Who will win this epic clash of good versus evil?

The Pittsburgh Hamlet
(Novel 2 in the Saga)

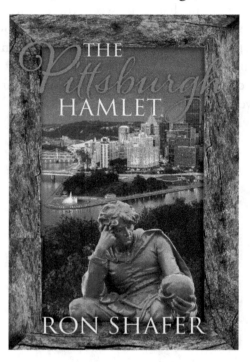

After Jude Hepler and his girlfriend, Cory Mohney, unwittingly stumble onto the zealously guarded secrets of the highly intelligent Abe Badoane (as narrated in the prequel, *The Rose and the Serpent*), the enraged Abe vows revenge. To advance his scheme, he dupes fellow mine employee Duke Manningham into an attempted heart-stopping rape of the beautiful Cory and ultimately enlists Duke's aid to rid the mushroom mine of Jude forever. To frame Jude, Abe lulls a stooge into sabotaging Duke's gem '57 Chevy.

Upon seeing Jude's fingerprints on his car, Duke errantly deduces that Jude is guilty and, to regain Cory's favor, agrees to join Abe at a live production of *Hamlet* in Pittsburgh. Brilliant and cunning as Hannibal Lecter, Abe Badoane smugly sits in the theater with the incriminating fingerprint evidence, but unbeknown to him, Jude and Cory have plotted a dangerous play-within-a-play scheme to trap him.

Who will win the battle between these towering intellects, wherein the compelling Cory and Jude story of love, faith, and gripping heroism runs parallel to—and actually intermeshes with—Shakespeare's masterpiece, *Hamlet*? Do Jude and Cory actually think they can take down the ingenious Abe Badoane during this double-plotted, live performance of the famous tragedy? Who will survive this epic white-knuckle clash?

Beautiful Dreamer
(Novel 3 in the Saga)

His treacherous machinations exposed during the live performance of Hamlet, the brilliant and cunning Abe Badoane seeks revenge on the innocent lovers, Jude Hepler and Cory Mohney. While the infuriated Abe inches his horrific plot forward, Jude and

Cory desperately try to decode Cory's medication-induced riddle which bears an uncanny parallel to Old Mary's haunting vision of the rose. Her vision, in turn, correlates to the major events of Cory and Jude's lives, including their impending fate.

Spiritually convicted, the lovers try to help the psychologically tormented Abe by magnanimously devising a plan to rescue him. But Abe simultaneously has settled on his diabolical scheme, a catastrophic cave-in, which will destroy the lovers forever. During a dream, frail Old Mary comes to the shocking realization that the beautiful dreamer in the Stephen Foster Memorial Window is not sleeping but dead. Because her dreams bear a one-to-one correspondence to Cory's life, Old Mary knows that Cory is in imminent danger and frantically tries to warn her. But when Old Mary collapses, Jude and Cory, still not warned, blithely head to the mine and their horrific fate.

The resulting cave-in pummels the unsuspecting couple and throws Jude into a stream-of-conscious dream reverie. "Events swirled in my mind as I floated in a twilight zone between consciousness and unconsciousness." Are his sad ruminations of a post-life Cory real or imagined? Does their beautiful love meet its tragic doom?

About the Author

Dr. Ronald G. Shafer was a professor for over forty years at Indiana University of Pennsylvania (IUP) where he holds a lifetime distinguished University Chair. His accolades include a Senior Fulbright Visiting Professorship to Egypt; Silver Medalist Professor of the Year Award in the Carnegie Foundation/CASE's national top-professor search; citation by *Change Magazine* for outstanding professorial leadership; Exemplary Teaching Excellence Award from the American Association of Higher Education; IUP's top award, the President's Medal of Distinction; and a flagship grant by the National Endowment for the Humanities.

He has traveled to some fifty countries for teaching-abroad stints and invited guest lectures. Shafer has authored numerous scholarly articles, edited two volumes of essays, and presided over The Pennsylvania College English Association. Founder of the Friends of Milton's Cottage, he was executive head of this organization, which restored the home where John Milton completed *Paradise Lost* and which initiated the first two International Milton Symposia.

At Milton's Cottage, Chalfont St. Giles, United Kingdom, Shafer enjoyed an audience with Her Majesty, Queen Elizabeth. The three film documentaries he has coproduced and codirected on Poets Laureate Robert Pinsky and Donald Hall and renowned author John Updike have garnered national and international acclaim.

His first novel, *The Rose and the Serpent*, was published by WestBow Press. The second and third installments in this compelling saga, *The Pittsburgh Hamlet* and *Beautiful Dreamer*, were published by Christian Faith Publishing. He continues to enjoy extensive world travel, novel-writing, and the love of his life: his five granddaughters.

CPSIA information can be obtained
at www.ICGtesting.com
Printed in the USA
BVHW081322041121
620762BV00002B/2